Lassickie

Lassickie, set in Aberdeenshire and Shetland in the late 19th century, is Lindsay Inkster's first novel and the first of The Charlotte Series.

Also by Lindsay Inkster,

Writing as Lindsay Reid

Scottish Midwives: Twentieth Century Voices

Midwifery: Freedom to Practise?

Midwifery in Scotland: A History

Lindsay lives in Fife, Scotland, is married and has three sons, one daughter and five grandchildren.

'Are you all right Miss?'

'Yes, I'm fine thank you. I woke up and thought I'd come up here for a while.'

'That's fine, people often come up on a fine morning to watch the dawn.' The stewardess added, 'Here, I'll show you a good spot out of the breeze. And how about a mug of cocoa?'

'That sounds like a really good idea. Thank you.' Charlotte allowed herself to be led to the sheltered neuk. From here she could still see the dawn, the sky now spreading golden pink round the horizon. The stewardess was back in minutes armed in one hand with a cup of hot cocoa. On her other arm she carried a blanket.

'Here,' she said. 'Get this round you. You don't want to catch cold.' She bustled off to sort out the early tea trays for her other passengers.

Charlotte snuggled into the folds of the blanket and sipped the cocoa. She looked out at the sea and sky. How many people have sat here before me, she wondered, and questioned what on earth they were doing? How did she come to be, at the tender age of not-yet-twenty, sitting by herself in the early morning, on the deck of a Northbound ship, and heading for a group of islands which she knew about in theory from learning and then teaching Scottish geography but still required a map to pinpoint its whereabouts and even then finished up in a wee box to the side of the map?

Chapter 1

En route to Shetland
AUGUST
1894

Charlotte sat up in the dark. Her bed moved, back and forth with an occasional side-to-side tremble. She put out her hand and felt an unfamiliar wall on her left. The bed moved again. Then she remembered. The St Clair, the passenger ship taking her all the way from Aberdeen to Lerwick.

She leaned back against the cabin wall. All was quiet and she could hear the ship's sinews straining as it ploughed on through the August night. The dark cabin felt slightly claustrophobic. She could hear her cabin companion breathing quietly and regularly. Deeply asleep. Charlotte quietly pushed back the heavy ship's blanket and wriggled her feet up and over the side of her bunk. She felt on the floor for her slippers and groped at the end of the bunk for her warm woollen ankle-length wrapper. Quietly she put it on, feet into slippers and felt her way to the cabin door.

Once out into the passage, it was a little lighter and she could see better. The thrum of the engines was louder. She made her way slowly to the end of the passageway and found the steps of the companionway which led to the main deck and the outside. Here it was light enough for her to check the time. Four o'clock. She looked about her. The deck was deserted. When she looked up towards the bridge she could see lights and the occasional movement. As she watched, she saw a sailor climb nimbly up the steps to the bridge with two steaming mugs in his hand. Probably cocoa she thought. That would be nice.

She moved to the rail and looked out over the sea. It was not flat calm but certainly not rough – just enough to give the St Clair the movement which she had felt below. In the north-east she could see where the sky was lightening rapidly with the new dawn.

'Excuse me Miss.' A voice spoke at her elbow.

Charlotte jumped. 'Sorry Miss, I didn't mean to give you a fright,' the voice said. It was the stewardess, well built, rosy-cheeked, standing astride, riding the movement of the ship. She was used to the St Clair in all weathers.

Acknowledgements

Lassickie has been a long time coming. I should like to take a little more time to thank all those who have helped, advised and encouraged along the way. They include:

June Wishart, from *The Shetland Times,* and her colleagues, for initial reading, helpful advice and encouragement.

Alan and Ruby Inkster, Whiteness, Shetland. They were partners to brainstorming, historical research and much else. I'm sorry Alan isn't here to see *Lassickie* but his research keeps popping up.

My family and friends for listening and support over the years.

Gareth Christie, digital artist, for his expertise and patience in designing the covers.

Veronica Hansmann, for her much-needed wise counsel on time-management and many other matters.

And David – if I needed a book of customs to trawl, he supplied it; if I needed some research done, he did it; if I needed a shoulder to sigh (or cry) on, he was there.

Thank you to you all.

Author's note

From north-east Scotland to Shetland, Charlotte Gordon's life from wee girl to adult is one of transition and new customs. Not least of these are her language difficulties when she goes to school for the first time.

Charlotte's first language is Scots. However, she must conform to the unbending rules of the 1872 Education (Scotland) Act and speak English when at school.

This book is, in the main, written in English. However, the language of many folk, and the fairm-toun of Milton of Glenbuchat where Charlotte spent her early days and where her roots remain, is Scots. So, you will find some of the dialogue, especially that which centres round the fairm-toun and the village of Towie is in Scots. There are also Scots words here and there throughout the book, included where, for me, they would naturally land.

To help with meanings of words, there is a Glossary situated at the end of the book.

I have written *Lassickie* as Charlotte's story of her life until she is a young woman. There are times within the story where Charlotte's own voice needs to be heard. These sections are headed with her name.

Lindsay Inkster
2013

For CLS

First Published 2013

by Black Devon Books,
Dunfermline,
Scotland

Reprinted 2013 November

Cover design by www.garethchristie.com

Reprint by Airdrie Print Services

Lassickie

*Aberdeenshire to Shetland – Charlotte's
New Horizons*

by

Lindsay Inkster

BLACK DEVON BOOKS

Dunfermline

Chapter 2

Trancie House, Towie
APRIL 1874

Dr Andrew Grant was at peace with the world, at one with this fine, quiet evening. He had no idea that the news he was about to hear would affect his whole life.

That evening's confinement had not been easy. The young mother had screamed and cried her way through labour, terrified no doubt of what was happening to her. Annie, the midwife or howdie had been her usual stalwart self, done her best to keep the girl going but in the end it had taken two of them to get the baby born. She sent for Andrew's help two hours before the birth and between them they delivered a live baby.

Andrew nodded his thanks to Jock, his horseman since his arrival in Towie as GP twenty years previously.

'Sorry to keep you so late Jock.'

'Ach, that's aa richt, Doctor. A'm jist glad the lassie and her bairn are weel.'

'Aye, they'll be fine now. Now, away home. See you tomorrow.'

He jumped down from the gig, raised his hand in salute and made for the front door. As he climbed the steps, the door opened and Margaret stood there.

'Is it all right?'

'Oh aye, Jean and the baby are fine, now. Annie would have managed fine herself if the lassie had not been so frightened. But, you know what it's like.'

Margaret knew what it was like. The Grants had seven children in their twenty five year marriage, the last three of whom were Towie-born bairns. It might have been the Towie lüft that did it. Whatever it was, after Mary's birth in 1857, Margaret at 34 said, 'enough' and there had been no more Grant babies. She probably would have liked more. But seven mouths to tend to, wash, clothe and feed were quite enough. And yet, after Mary grew more independent, she often felt as if she should have a baby to carry about like other women. It was a funny sensation feeling the monthly broodiness, and knowing she was deliberately not becoming pregnant. She knew Andrew agreed with her about no more babies, but she felt that he too missed the spontaneity of sexual intercourse without thinking whether it was safe or not first.

3

Other women, too, troubled her. It didn't matter now. She was well past that stage. But years before, when the children were wee, she felt folk were looking and watching and gossiping and asking when she was going to have another. One day she actually heard she was pregnant. Oh, in a roundabout way of course. She had changed her way of dressing into a looser, more comfortable style. A few weeks later her housekeeper and cook, Katie, who was an old and trusted friend as well as anything else, came to her.

'Mam, hiv ye heard fit they're sayin?'

'No Katie, what would that be?'

Katie hesitated: 'Well, it's gaan roon that, well ye're hae'in anither.'

'What?' Margaret looked at Katie. 'Do you think this?'

'No, I dinna think it. Ye've aye had yer monthlies and, and....'

'And what, Katie?'

'Well, I think ye'd have telt me?'

'You're right. Katie. You would have been the first to know.' Well nearly the first. Margaret thought a minute. 'I'll tell you what. Come and let's have a look.'

The next day, Margaret dressed carefully, went out with her basket, walked into the village, stopped and chatted to women going about their business, noted their looks of surprise, laughed to herself and returned to Trancie House. 'Katie', she called. 'I'm back. Can you come and get me out of this abominably tight frock and stays. I think they've done the trick.'

She pulled herself back to the present.

'Come on in. You must be exhausted.'

They entered the parlour, soft light, fire on, comfortable, a drinks trolley there with glasses, whisky and water for which Andrew headed.

This was her favourite room. Twenty years before, they needed a house in Towie, where they could all fit in, the two of them, four children and another expected, as well as Katie and a lassie to help. Trancie House seemed to fit the bill. It had lain empty for a year or two at Nether Towie in the lee of Trancie Hill which reared up at the back and helped protect the house from the sharp winter nor'easterlies. They liked the house immediately, facing south west, good solid stone, plenty of space. But Margaret liked best the parlour; she did not want to call it a drawing- or withdrawing room. She wanted it to be an open friendly room. She did not want to withdraw whatever the etiquette said. So that room had set the scene for many occasions, confidences and discussions, good and bad, happy and sad.

It was like the rest of the house. Gradually, over the years, Margaret and Andrew had made it into their house with their own character and innovations. Like the new range in the kitchen which Katie liked so much. And, in addition, Trancie House now had a bathroom and water-closet. When they first arrived in Towie the nearest thing they had to a water-closet was a shed in the garden (known as the 'wee hoosie') with a seat in it next to the midden, a dry-closet rather than a water-closet. The bath was a zinc tub taken out ceremoniously on bath-night and placed in front of the fire in the kitchen and laboriously filled with hot water. Margaret longed for a proper bathroom

4

and a bath and a proper flushing lavatory. Now just two years ago they had taken the plunge and fitted a bathroom into an unused room on the mezzanine floor at the back of the house. They had thought of installing one of the latest spray-baths but decided on a bath-tub instead. Beside this wonderful room was a small room which contained the much desired real water-closet complete with flush which let down three gallons of water every time the chain was pulled. It took quite a while for that novelty to wear off. Margaret smiled at the memory then her face grew serious as she remembered the news she had to tell. She put another log on the parlour fire.

'All well?' Andrew concentrated on pouring his whisky.

'Well', Margaret hesitated, 'well, I....' He turned, glass in hand.

'What is it, Margaret?' He walked across the room to her as she sank into a chair looking at him. 'What's the matter?'

'It's Mary. I think she's pregnant.'

'What?' he looked at her blankly. 'How?'

'The usual way of course.' Margaret's voice was sharp.

'But who? When?' This was his youngest, his baby. He had dandled her as a wee baby, helped her first staggering steps, to read, to count. Later, as she had grown, he showed her his medical bag, where he kept his equipment. She had been interested. He knew she had. She had even thought of taking up medicine as a career. He knew it would be a hard row for a lassie to sow but he was sure Mary had the determination if she really wanted to. And now it would be all thrown away. Pregnant. At seventeen. And to – to whom? He looked at Margaret. 'Who's the father?'

'John Gordon of Milton of Glenbuchat. You know, his parents are over at Bellabeg. He's one of the loons at the Milton – been there since last Martinmas. They've been slipping off seeing each other for weeks.' Margaret looked at him. 'She's seventeen. I can't watch her every minute of the day.'

'How did you find out?'

'Katie really', Margaret said. 'You know she watches over us all and she came to me and said she had heard Mary being sick in the old wee hoosie early one morning last week. And the next, and the next. So I asked her how she was feeling and out it all came. She didn't recognise the first missed period for what it was but then she began to feel terrible and....'She faltered... 'Oh Andrew, our wee lassie.... What can we do?'

'What does she want to do?'

'She doesn't know. John Gordon has offered to marry her, He says he loves her. She's not sure. But it's April now. I think she must be about three months, nearly. Makes the baby due in October. She could have it adopted. She could go away to Aberdeen for the summer and then come back after it's all over. Then she'd be able to carry on with her studies.'

He buried his face in his hands. 'I was going to contact the university to see how the land lay regarding women students. That will all be gone for nothing if she gets married.'

5

'Andrew.' Margaret took his hands and held them tightly. 'We can't let her give up her baby for adoption. This is our own flesh and blood however begotten. We must help her some other way.'

'Yes, yes, you're right.' He raised his head and she could see the tears. 'My wee lassie. Let's see if she'll speak to us.'

'I'll go and see if she's awake.'

Upstairs, she tapped gently on the door of the room where Mary had slept by herself, since Jessie her elder sister had gone off to be a nurse two years before.

'Mary, are you awake.'

'Yes, Mother. Come in.'

Margaret looked at her youngest child with a strange mixture of compassion, anger and sorrow. How easy it was to become carried away on a sea of emotion and she of all people knew how difficult it was to prevent conception in these nineteenth century days. She also knew of the coping with others and their gossip and idle chatter when one of a group was seen to have transgressed. The people of Towie and the neighbouring parishes would certainly view Mary in this light. John was different, of course; he was a man. Women bore the brunt.

'Does, Father know?' Mary's eyes were anxious.

'Yes, Mary.'

'Is, is he very angry with me?'

'He wants to talk to you with me, together, to try and think about the best thing to do. Could you come down? Now? Here, put on your wrapper over your goonie.'

Downstairs, Andrew threw another log on the fire. Katie entered quietly with their night time drinks. Three mugs on the tray, Andrew noted wryly. Not much escaped Katie's sharp eyes and ears.

'Thanks Katie.'

She looked at him. 'Nae problem Doctor. Jist see fit ye can dee fur the lassie. She's nae a bad lassie ye ken.'

He sighed. 'I ken, I ken. It's just what to do for the best. And think of the spik in Towie.'

'Dinna you worry aboot that,' she said. 'I'll sort them. Jist you think first o yer lassie.'

He smiled as she went out. My lassie. Aye. But I'm going to have to let her go. And too soon. In fact he thought, she's gone already. And I mustn't forget it. Because of this, she's a woman now, even though she is only seventeen. He turned as the door clicked and mother and daughter came in.

'Here Mary, sit down by the fire and keep warm. Here's your drink.' She sat, tentatively at first but relaxing to the warming fire, the hot drink, and, probably at the knowledge that he was not shouting in anger at her. She had heard of this. One of her friends had been banished from the house as soon as her pregnancy became known. Another friend's father had taken a strap to her and called her a limmer and a hooer. She shivered.

6

'Father, Father, I'm sorry.' She looked at him. 'What am I going to do?' The tears fell now as she gazed up at them. She had let them down she knew, but when she was with John all sense and plans for the future flew out of the window. She took a deep breath and said, 'I'll marry him. We'll get married.'

'But Mary,' her father said, 'What about your plans, your studies, university.'

'Well what else can I do?' Her voice was sharp. 'I'm not having the baby adopted if that's what you're thinking. Anyway, I, I love John, and he loves me. We've talked about it. He can get a cottage up at Glenbuchat, at the Milton where he's working. We can get married and live there.'

'What on?' Her mother chipped in. 'John's wages as a farmhand are hardly riches.'

'We'll manage.' Mary was adamant. 'I'm not having my baby adopted. I know Mima Smith went to Aberdeen and came back months later with no baby. Have you seen her? Have you spoken to her? She's in a daze. She might as well not be here at all. I won't do it to my baby.'

'It's all right.' Her mother put her arm round her shoulders and shushed her. 'Nobody's making you do that. But marriage to John in a farm cottage is not an easy option. And yet I can't see what else you can do. And think of the claik either way.'

'Never mind the claik.' Her father interrupted. He laughed slightly grimly. 'Katie says she'll sort them.'

'She would too.' Margaret gave a half-smile. 'We'll all help. There's going to be tittle-tattle whatever you do. Let's do what's best for you and the baby.'

'Well, best for me and the baby is to marry John,' insisted Mary. 'John wants it and so do I. He's in the loons' bothy up at the Milton just now but there's an empty cottage that I think we could have and we'll be fine there. But please', she hesitated, 'Don't be too far away from me. Let me still be your quinie.'

Mother and father looked at each other over the head of their daughter who sat waiting. Their eyes held each other for a moment of complete understanding and togetherness before, as one, they stretched out their arms around her.

'We are here for you,' Andrew said. 'This was not in the plan. However plans change and we must go with the change.' He sighed inwardly. This was not an easy path to choose, for any of them. Doctors' daughters were not supposed to become pregnant out of wedlock. But at least Glenbuchat was only about six miles from Towie and he was often in Glenbuchat seeing folk, healing the sick, giving first aid and comforting the dying as well as helping the babies to be born. He could keep an eye on the little family at the Milton. Maybe even yet, all would be well.

Margaret's mind was turning on more practical woman-like thoughts like pots and pans and kettles and the like. 'We'll need to get you and John some furniture she said. Tomorrow we'll go up into the attic and see what we can find.'

'But tomorrow I'll have to see John and tell him yes, I'll marry him.' Mary started crying again. 'We can't make arrangements without him.'

'Well look, tomorrow I have to see some folk in Glenbuchat. I'll go in by the Milton and see if he can come down. After he finishes work he can come across and we can talk the whole thing out. How's that?' She nodded, sniffing.

7

'Thanks father. I think he's quite worried about what to do.'

'Right, now away to bed. Wait a wee minute,' he added. 'When do you think you're due?' The father was also the doctor and he needed to know.

'October, Father,' Mary said, 'I think.'

'We'll sort all the details out soon. It's too late tonight. But are you feeling all right. Not too sick?'

'We-ell,' she admitted. 'A bit sick but I'm all right, really. It passes.'

' Right, keep eating and maybe a wee cup of tea in bed in the morning might help.'

'Thanks Father.' Mary held him closely. 'And Mother,' reaching out a hand to her mother. 'I don't know what I'd do without you.' She went away then, with a heart lighter than it had been for weeks.

Lying in bed a wee while later she went over in her mind what was happening. The realisation of her pregnancy had brought with it not the happiness of creation of a new life, but fear, fear of the situation she found herself in. Here she was, not married, expecting a baby, unable to tell anyone up until now, with the prospect of recriminations from all. Even John had put his head in his hands when she told him what she thought. He did not overtly say anything that implied that she might be a fault. But, 'Oh no,' he had said. 'Oh, no. You can't be.' They had quarrelled after that. It was as if the baby had come between them. Which, in a way it had.

So the fear was for her and John too. Could their love stand up to this? Were they strong enough? It was great fun in the hay-shed and out on the moors but now this was the real, responsible world and she was only seventeen. She had been frightened of what her parents would say and do. Sometimes they had appeared strict in their upbringing. But underneath it all was a slower, non-judgemental kindness which when it came to trouble, took over and they came together and worked together to find an appropriate solution. And, Mary knew, they would stand up for her. For standing up would be needed, she knew. Village gossip could be very unkind and judgemental. Folk who went to the Kirk on a Sunday, said their prayers, believed in a loving God and yet seemed quite prepared to grind a wrong-doer into the dust. Or that was the way Mary saw it. She was not sure but she felt her parents had similar feelings. She felt the apprehension in her mother's voice as she said 'think about the claik'. But there was Katie. Dear Katie who she had known all her life. She would sort them. And she would just have to hold her head up. After all she wasn't the first girl who was expecting and not married and she wouldn't be the last.

But now she had another fear to face: the minister. Up till now Mary had not taken this feeling of apprehension out and looked at it properly. She had always mentally pushed aside what she would do when it came to the point of acknowledging that she and John would get married and what they would have to do to bring this about. In Towie all the marriages were done by the minister. It was just a fact. A few folk were married without benefit of the minister. But this meant going to the Registrar in Alford and Mary did not know of anyone from Towie who had done this. And anyway, her parents would not be so willing to help her with that. And then there was the old Scottish way of 'consent makes marriage'. This was appealing, Mary thought. To go away with John and nobody else and just agree with each other to be married. That would be it. It seemed so sensible. Yet Mary knew her parents would not be too keen to go along with this idea either, however tempting it seemed. And as for the folk in Towie, it would be an even greater opportunity for spik, and tittle-tattle. No, Mary thought, her parents would want them to put their heads up and face the music – and the minister. She sighed inwardly. The minister.

The Reverend Archie Shand had been the Towie minister for nearly three decades, ever since the last minister had died. He was all right of course. Mary had known him since she was a baby. He had come to Trancie House when she was very small and baptised her. She sat and listened to his preaching on a Sunday; he went to Towie Primary School to see the children and tell them about Jesus. Mary almost wished she were back in the primary school. Looking back, it all seemed so safe. Mr Shand talking to the children about God and being good and doing the right thing. He also sometimes came and had a dram with her father and sometimes they met up together in a house where someone was very ill. They had watched together on numerous occasions. She knew her father and mother thought well of him. But now she was on the receiving end. What would he say? He would know what she and John had done. After all being pregnant meant you had been together. And that was supposed to be a sin, wasn't it? Mary turned over on her side. How could something so happy and exciting be a sin? How could a new baby, accidental or not, be a sin? New babies did not know about sin.

So why blame them? I won't blame my baby, she thought sleepily. I'll love her and feed her and take care of her always. She fell asleep comforted by the thought of a warm baby cuddled into her.

Chapter 3

The next morning reality faced Mary once again. It all started badly. Katie brought her a cup of tea as requested by her mother. Mary tried to drink it but felt so sick that she had to run to the lavatory. At least now her secret was out she did not have to creep to the old wee hoosie.

Her mother came rapping at the door. 'Mary are you all right?'

'Yes, Mother. Just give me a wee minute. I'm fine, really.' Mary wiped her face and unlocked the door.

'Come on.' Her mother took one look at her face and said, 'Back to bed with you, my girl.' Disregarding Mary's protests she pushed her back up the stairs and tucked her in again.

'Now stay there and I'll bring you fresh tea. And a piece of toast. Then we'll see how you are.' Mary sank back on the pillows. It was quite a relief in a way to be ordered about – just for once.

Her mother returned with a tray.

'Now, eat,' she commanded. 'Just, slowly. This will pass soon, after the first three months are over.' Mary ate, gingerly at first, then with more enthusiasm as she felt herself less nauseated.

'That's better.' Her mother came back into the room. 'The colour's come back to your face. Father's going up the glen after he's done his morning surgery and he'll go and find John. We all need to talk about this. And', she said firmly, 'we'll need to speak to Mr Shand.'

'Aye, mother, I was thinking about the minister last night. What will he be like, do you think?' Mary's mouth drooped a little. She knew the minister and her father got on fine but for her, he was a faraway presence, in the pulpit, visiting the school, not a close person with whom she could freely discuss being pregnant.

'He'll be all right,' her mother insisted. 'I'm not saying he'll approve, mind you. He's quite a stickler for good behaviour. And, I know father told him about your maybe going for medicine and he'll be sorry to see that having to be shelved. However, he and father are good friends. They work together a lot. I think once he knows he'll help all he can. And, that includes marrying you and John.'

'Will it be in the Manse?'

'Yes. Nearly everybody is married in the Manse. It's not just when you are pregnant. Remember your Aunt Frances and Uncle Peter. Remember the folk in the minister's parlour. There was hardly room for anybody. I've been to a few Manse weddings. And now we'll need to sort out yours.'

Mary's eyes filled. 'Oh Mother', she cried. 'I wish it could have been different.'

'I know.' Her mother's face softened as she looked at her youngest child. 'I know, but what's done is done and we just have to get on with it. Now, are you feeling a bit better?'

'Aye, I'm fine now.' Mary swung her legs out over the bed. 'I'll get dressed and come down the back way. I can hear the folk coming into the surgery.'

At 12.45 pm precisely, Margaret heard the gig pulling up outside the house. A few murmured voices and Andrew walked in the back door carrying his black medical bag. He put it carefully on a chair before turning to her.

'I saw John,' he said. 'I went up the glen to see old Mrs Leith and then went in past the Milton to see him. He was working in the byre – cleaning it out I think. There was another lad there so we went and walked a wee bit oot-by.'

'What was he like? I mean, you know what he looks like because you've seen him before in passing, but how did he seem to you?'

'Well', the doctor considered carefully. 'He looked very anxious. I saw him before he saw me and even then he looked worried and not happy. When he noticed me coming through the byre-door he went really pale. I felt quite sorry for the lad. Anyway, I went up to him and reminded him who I was although he knew, and I asked him if we could have five minutes together. The other lad he was working with seemed to be a wee bit older than John as he said, "Aa richt John , five minutes", and then we went for a quick walk past the first gate. He knew why I was there of course.'

'So what happened?'

'Well, he now knows that we know about the baby. He's coming down tonight and we'll sort it out then. He seems a nice enough lad. Tall, strong, dark hair – but of course you know that. And, he seemed ready to co-operate. Thank goodness. I was a wee bit worried we might have trouble. I mean I wondered if he might not want to get married, but I get the feeling he's very fond of our Mary and wouldn't leave her in the lurch like some others I could mention.'

Andrew and the midwife had delivered a few bairns in the last twenty years to girls whose so-called lovers had gone off once they heard of their impending fatherhood. The negation of responsibility made Andrew angry: angry at the carelessness; angry for the girls' and babies' sakes; and, angry at these irresponsible men having their fun and fleeing from the consequences.

Margaret knew him well and knew what he was thinking. 'Come on Andrew.' She pulled out his chair. 'Here's your soup. When's he coming.'

'Oh about seven o'clock. He says he'll have his tea and clean up first. Then he'll come. Ah, Mary –' he raised his head from his soup as Mary came in. 'How are you today?'

'Fine, father.' She sat down to her soup opposite him.

12

'I saw John up at the glen this morning.' He went on. 'He'll be down tonight. I think he's going to borrow someone's bike.'

'Thanks father.' She looked at him straight. 'I'm really grateful. Not every father would do what you are doing.'

'Ach away', he took another spoonful of soup. 'We just want things right for you. I hope this is it.'

That evening John Gordon arrived at Trancie House as arranged and probably with some trepidation. After all he was a fairm loon and his lass was the doctor's daughter. He thought about the situation he was in as he rode on the old bone-shaker of a bike kept on the farm for the loons to use now and then. The coorse road between the Milton of Glenbuchat and Towie did not help the bike's fortunes. The road past the Milton was not made-up and was covered with loose stones and full of pot-holes for the unwary horse and cyclist.

At the Bridge of Buchat the road met the main Strathdon road. Even this one was in a state and badly neglected. John bumped and rattled the six backside-weary miles, falling off sideways a couple of times for lack of attention. Well, who could attend totally to the state of the road when going to meet destiny in the shape of the doctor, his wife and their beautiful and much cherished youngest child? And how was he to handle this situation? True, he had seen the doctor that morning and no word in anger was said. But that was a rushed meeting, a pre-meeting meeting. What would he be like now?

John turned off the main road at Glenkindie on to the lesser road leading to Towie. More rubble and potholes. He crossed the River Don at the bridge, through the village and then left up the track which would take him to Nether Towie and Trancie House. By this time he had skidded on the road, nearly landed in the ditch and was about to get off and walk when he saw the gates of Trancie House in front of him. Come on then he thought, this is it. They can't kill you. And, he was dying to see Mary again. He loved her so much. What would it be like seeing her all the time. He was so busy thinking of this idyllic situation that he was at the door before he knew it and came skidding to a halt with a clatter of brakes and tackety boots.

They were waiting in the parlour, Andrew and Margaret with outward composure and dignity as befitted parents of a much-loved daughter who had, it had to be said, blotted her copy-book. Mary was very nervous. It was a few days since she and John had seen each other. They had parted, if not exactly in anger, but with a feeling of insecurity with their situation and what to do next. They all heard John's skidding stop at the door. Mary leapt to her feet.

'Mother, Father, I'll go, please let me go first. I'll bring him in.' Strictly speaking this procedure was not *de rigeur* for the late nineteenth century. But the Grants were not conventional parents for the time. They bowed to their daughter's pleading cries and she hurried to the door.

She opened the door and paused on the top step. Below her, John was holding the bone-shaker with one hand and attempting to dust down his trousers with the other. Stour flew around him.

'John', she breathed. He looked up and his eyes lit up. He let the bike drop to the ground and stepped forward, arms outstretched. She flew down the steps to him.

'Oh John, oh John.' He held her tightly.

'Are you all right?'

'Yes, yes, and I'm so glad to see you. But we have to go in and talk now. They're waiting.' He picked up the bike and set it carefully against the step, propped up by a pedal. She held out her hand. 'Come on. They're in there. We must face them together, but they're doing their best.'

They walked together up the steps, through the porch and the hall and into the parlour which had heard so many other conversations and confidences. Mary held her head high.

'Father, Mother, this is John....' Her voice faltered. 'Father, I know you met this morning. John, this is my Mother.' John stepped forward and held out his hand to Margaret.

'Mrs Grant,' he started, 'I'm glad to meet you.' But then he could go no further. He let it out in a rush. 'I love your daughter. I love her. I want to marry her.' His outburst subsided into silence, broken only by the hissing of a damp log on the fire, a door banging far away, his own fast, anxious breathing.

Margaret shook his hand then stood, considering. She was strong but not without compassion – already shown to her daughter. Now she had to show it to this young man who, some would say, had done her daughter ill, and, through her daughter therefore her family. They were all affected by what had happened. But Margaret could not think like that. She considered Mary was just as much responsible for her actions as John. This had been no coerced joining. It was quite obvious that Mary and John had been happy together, no will had imposed on the other. But now they needed help to cope with the results.

'John,' she said, 'sit down. It's good to meet you, although,' she smiled faintly, 'I could imagine less dramatic circumstances.'

Sitting down was better, thought Mary. It's less confrontational. Although she knew by now that there was not going to be a confrontation as such (in the strongest sense of the word) there was still that feeling that sitting together was gentler, and in a kind of way, a step forward.

Her father too, sat down. He leaned forward in his chair and scrutinised the couple sitting together on the sofa.

'Right, you two, there's no use pussy-footing around this issue. Let's make some decisions about what you're to do. 'John', he addressed him directly. 'What have you to say.'

'Well', John had recovered his composure a wee bit by this time. 'I love Mary. She says she loves me. I know the news about the baby was a shock to begin with. I know I was angry. But I've had time to think now and,' he looked sideways to Mary, 'so has Mary. We really do want to get married. Aye we're young but we'll work together and there's a cottage up at the Milton we could have…'

'Have you spoken to anyone else about this?'

'No.' He met Andrew's eyes. 'It didn't seem right to go discussing it with other folk until we had sorted it out with you. But I think the wee hoose would be all right. And it's not too far for Mary to be away from you. I'll put in to stay with the Milton well afore the next feein market. I think it'll be all right. I get on fine with Mr Stewart.'

'Mmphm. I know him fine. How's that gash on his leg?' The doctor had been up at the Milton a few times recently to attend to the farmer's leg. 'A nasty accident that.'

'Ay,' agreed John. 'But he's fine now. His dressings are off and he's nae hirplin.'

'Right, well – 'Andrew took his mind from Mr Stewarts leg and back to the current problem. 'So you think he'll take you on again?'

'Oh ay, I think so. And I think he'll be happy to have the cottage in use. It's better that nor empty.'

'Good point. Right. You sort that out tomorrow. Now,' he turned to them both. 'Ye both say you want to get married?'

'Oh yes, Father.' Mary's hand crept into Johns and they held tightly. Andrew looked across at Margaret. She nodded slightly but left him to speak.

'All right. Mind you,' he cut in as they smiled at each other, 'I'm not best pleased. I'm only agreeing to this because of the bairn. Mary, you're giving up a lot and you'll just have to accept this. There's nothing else for it.'

Mary nodded. 'I know Father.' She hesitated, then slightly wistfully, 'I really wanted to be a doctor.' Then she shook herself. 'But as we said yesterday plans change and there it is. And, thanks for saying yes and not getting all uppity with us.' She disengaged her hand and went over and hugged her father.

'I know I'm an awful nuisance to you,' she murmured, 'but thanks. I love you.' She went over to her Mother. 'Mother I know you've been there for me in all this. Thanks.'

Margaret held her tightly. She could feel the tears pricking behind her eyelids. She knew if she said a word she would cry. Her hand crept up her sleeve for her hanky.

'Right.' Andrew took control of what was fast becoming an emotional situation. 'What's next? The minister.'

The minister. Mary and John looked at each other. This was reality.

'Now come on you two. We've got to this point. The next jump is the getting married. You can't do that without the minister. Don't look so worried. I ken Archie Shand fine. He'll be all disapproving to begin with. Just accept it and in five minutes he'll be doing anything he can to help you.'

15

Chapter 4

The Reverend Archie Shand walked peacefully in his garden in what would have been the cool of the day if the day had been a little warmer in the first place. However being April, there was still snow on the distant hills, a nip in the air, the wind not yet from the south and the West Aberdeenshire cool of the day remained decidedly chilly.

Mr Shand was looking at his garden and making plans for the summer. He loved his garden. The cares of the day and other people's problems did not exactly fade – they could never do that. But somehow he felt more able to cope with them after a spell in his garden. His beloved wife Phemie was sitting in the window doing her needlepoint. This was her relaxation. Usually if not darning his socks she was knitting for him and other folk, or baking to take baskets out to folk in Towie and further afield, or doing her own round of visiting and comforting. And then there was her work for the Ladies' Missionary Association based in Edinburgh. At last women were going out into the mission fields not as mere appendages of the men to whom they belonged, but as missionaries in their own right. They still had men to conduct their meetings but slowly, slowly it was becoming accepted that women were able to work independently and, given time and goodwill, even to speak in public. Phemie was an ardent follower of the doings of the Ladies' Missionary Association and made sure that the women of Towie were aware of all the latest news from Edinburgh and the work of Scottish women missionaries in India, Africa, China and the Holy Land. He really admired the way she had put her back into this new venture. He caught her eye as he walked past the window and gave her a wave.

The minister reached the section of his garden where the spring bulbs grew in profusion before giving way to later summer flowers. He always wondered at the rotation and spent a lot of time in the summer evenings weeding, coaxing and encouraging. Of course he had help with the heavier work. Jimmy Smith was aye there when he needed an extra hand. Archie Shand was not a young man now. Approaching seventy summers he was still fit, a little stooped but active, white haired but red-cheeked with his times in his garden and walks to his parishioners. His parish stretched the length and breadth of Towie. Sometimes he took his gig but somehow he felt better walking. He could stop and speak to folk he might not otherwise see. What the folk thought is unrecorded but he felt himself to be reasonably well accepted. He hoped so anyway. It is always difficult entering into a small rural community from another place and it had not been easy to begin with. But more than twenty years had passed since then and folk and their attitudes to him as an outsider had mellowed, and, he supposed, he hoped, he had mellowed too. He bent down to retrieve a stray weed from amongst the flowers.

As he straightened up he noticed the young couple coming towards him. They were still a wee bit off, walking along the road, heads deep in conversation. Now what are they wanting, the minister wondered to himself. I do believe it's Mary Grant from Trancie House. Who's that with her and why are they heading this way at this time of night? Logic told him what he did not want to know. This young couple were coming to him for a specific purpose, for something which as far as they were concerned, only he could provide: marriage. Aye, he thought to himself that'll be it, and it's one I don't want to do, but I'll have to. I wonder what her father and mother are saying to it.

By this time Mary and John had reached the Manse gate. The stopped and looked at the Rev Archie Shand.

'Well,' he said. 'Fine night. I'm just taking a look at my flowers here.'

'Em, Mr Shand,' Mary hesitated. 'Could we have a word with you please.'

'Oh, oh aye, come in.' The minister swung the gate back a bit for them to enter. 'In you come. It's a fine night. Would you like to be outside. Come over to this wee seat we sometimes use.'

'Now,' he said when they were all settled. 'What is it that I can do for you.' He looked them both up and down with his sharp blue eyes.

'Well, it's like this....'

'Mr Shand,' John interrupted. 'I don't think we've met before. I'm John Gordon and I work up at the Milton. I've been there since Martinmas.' He held out his hand.

'It's good to meet you.' The minister shook his hand gravely. 'I think I might have seen you in the Kirk.'

'Aye, if we have the work done in time we sometimes come along to the service.'

'So what is it that brings you here this evening?'

John hesitated. He was just about to open his mouth when Mary spoke up.

'Mr Shand, we need your help please. You see, I'm, I'm going to have a baby. We know we shouldn't have done this but now it has happened. Please will you help us by marrying us.' It was out. She stole a look at John who had gone very pale. However he straightened his shoulders and held her hand firmly.

'Yes,' he said. 'We love each other. I'll be a good husband to Mary. We can have the cottage up at the Milton I think. But please can you help?'

'What about your parents?' The old minister looked at Mary. His heart grieved for his friend Andrew Grant and his wife. How many times had they waited and watched together and Andrew had confessed his hopes and dreams for his bright happy daughter. He had been prepared to sacrifice much to get her started going to classes at university even though at this time women still could not graduate. But times were changing and who knew, perhaps in a few years she could have followed in her father's footsteps and been a doctor. Now that was gone. He clenched his fists in sudden anger. What a waste. This was what Phemie kept going on about: the need for women to go further, join the professions, widen their horizons.

Mary and John saw the tightening of the minister's hands and waited for the censure and recrimination. which they felt was coming. But he shook his head.

'Oh lassie, lassie. The pair of you have set something going now that'll be hard to control. Love in a cottage on a farm-loon's wage is very difficult.' He looked at them.

'Oh aye, I'll marry you, here in the Manse. But don't think I'm happy about it. What are you parents saying?' he asked again.

'Well, they're not that happy,' Mary said. 'But they're prepared to help where they can and they said we should come to you.'

'Aye aye,' the old minister could not hide his vexation. 'We'll sort it out. But…what a waste. And you, Mr Gordon,' turning to John, 'you should have known better than to get a lassie into trouble like this.'

John could only mutter, 'I'm sorry but', more bravely, 'we do love each other and we will be happy, if we're just given the chance.'

'Oh Mr Shand,' pleaded Mary. 'What do we have to do next?'

'Well,' Mr Shand considered slowly, thinking things through. 'Strictly speaking, you should appear before the Kirk Session and be censured for your sins. And then if you are to be married we need to be Proclaiming the Banns. And they should be proclaimed three times, but,' he paused, 'when were you wanting to get married?' They looked at each other.

'Two weeks?' suggested Mary.

'Aye,' agreed John, 'two weeks would be fine.'

'Hmmm,' the minister thought about this. 'But two weeks hardly gives me three proclamations of the Banns. But,' he said, as their faces fell, 'seeing as how I know you so well, Mary, and, he turned to John, I have seen you in the Kirk sometimes, and I can get a note of your character and confirmation of how long you have been in Glenbuchat from Mr Stewart, I think I can have the authority to call the Banns on two Sundays only, and so two weeks from now for a wedding would be all right.'

'Now,' he said sternly, waving away their thanks, 'The other thing is the Kirk Session. According to the Kirk rules, you should be censured before the Session in public at a Sunday Service. However,' He stopped and looked kindly at Mary as she gasped in horror. 'I have never been too keen on this procedure myself. I always felt that it was unnecessarily harsh, to put two people who are going through a very upsetting time of their lives, through such further distress. So,' he looked at them both, 'what I propose to do, is to talk to the Session Clerk, Mr Coutts who you know well Mary, and you two can come back here one evening next week and see us both in a Disciplinary Committee as representatives of the Kirk Session.'

Mary did indeed know Mr Colin Coutts. He was her old much respected and revered teacher, the dominie of Towie School, Session Clerk and Senior Elder of the Kirk. A man not to be trifled with, but fair and just in his dealings. He only used the pointer on children's fingers when he was very exasperated and most schooldays his tawse was kept out of sight.

John was looking at her. He was extremely unsure of himself and all these procedures he suddenly found himself involved with.

19

'What do you think Mary?'

'We must do it,' she said urgently. 'We have no option, no choice at all. And this way is better than standing up in the Kirk.' The minister nodded.

'She's right. Let's just get organised. I need to take a few notes. Shall we go in and I can wash my hands and find a pen.'

Two weeks later on a sunny spring afternoon, the small wedding party walked up from Trancie House to the Manse: Mary and John, Andrew and Margaret Grant and John's parents who had come over from Bellabeg. There in the Manse parlour, all censure past, the Reverend Archie Shand married Mary Grant and John Gordon, with Mary's parents as official witnesses.

Chapter 5

Milton of Glenbuchat

Mary was restless, out of sorts. John was out working. She could not sit still, kept prowling about the farmworker's tiny cottage where she and John had lived since April, putting things away, taking them out again. She knew her time was near, but how near? She walked outside and up the rough grass a little way, the wind in her face, blowing her hair out of her eyes. Clouds skimmed across, carrying rain she didn't doubt. No sunshine today. She shivered, pulling her shawl more tightly about her.

Suddenly she felt it. Not a sharp pain but a sort of double creeping sensation, starting in the middle of her back below her waist and spreading out to both sides, reaching steadily round before meeting at the front and then dying away. She stopped and looked down at herself. Is this it? I've never felt that before. The baby moved within. She put a hand over it in protection, 'It won't be long now'.

She walked calmly back to the cottage and took out the waiting tiny baby clothes, blankets and the shawl that Katie had knitted with such love. Katie who remembered her so well when she was a baby and who now was helping to prepare for the next generation. And her mother. What a lot of sewing and knitting and work had gone into these long embroidered baby dresses, winceyette barry-coats (sleeveless and all tapes, and you could open it to change the baby's nappy), bootees and jackets which now waited for the baby.

Mary's eye fell on the wooden rocking cradle with its hood which would keep the draughts away as well as any lurking evil spirits. It had been hers when she was a baby. Now it was her baby's turn. She gave the rocker a little push with her foot; the cradle shifted slightly. Soon there'll be a baby in there she mused, soon, soon.... She gave a little gasp as the creeping sensation came again stronger this time. This is the day she thought. I must get John down from the field to warn Annie, and Father and Mother. This is something I can't stop. Here it comes again. They came again, and again, a little stronger, a little longer, more closely together. Mary threw her shawl about her shoulders again. She grabbed their pre-arranged signal – a large white towel – and went out into the wind.

Up in the field John was lifting tatties. It was a good crop but back-breaking work. He was anxious about Mary. He knew she must be near her time. Mr Stewart had warned him that when the time came he could stop work immediately and go and get help. He was grateful for the man's consideration. Many bosses would have told him to make other arrangements. He just wished it was all over with. Things took so long. He stood up and straightened his back, looked back towards the farm buildings and saw their signal. The white flag fluttered in the wind.

'Mary,' he shouted to Sandy, the other farm loon. 'She's signaling. I'll have to go.'

'On ye go. Good luck.' Sandy gave him a wave and bent to the tatties again.

John ran over the field to where Mary stood.

'What's happened? Are you aa richt?'

'Aye aye, John, but I think it's started. I think you'd better go and get Annie and Father and Mother.'

'Of course, but here, let's get you back doon ti the hoose first.' He put his arm round her and led her back down to the cottage. Oh jings, I dinna like leavin ye. Are ye shair ye'll be aa richt?'

'Aye, aye, John. Just go on.' She bit her lip as she felt another contraction. They were surely getting stronger.

He rushed to the old boneshaker, standing there ready.

'Go inside and keep warm. I'll be as quick as I can. I'll go in past Annie first and then on to your parents.'

'That's fine.' Mary stood at the door and watched him go. He had a good bit to cycle. First to Towie where Annie who had been midwife and nurse to Towie and Glenbuchat and the surrounding area for many years. Then on up to Nether Towie and Trancie House to fetch her parents. Mary hoped her father had not been called out elsewhere. He knew she would need him but if anyone else needed him first and called him out he would go.

She went into the tiny kitchen, filled the kettle and put it over the fire. Come on fire, she rattled up the glowing coals and put on a few more bits. The coals jumped, sparked and crackled. Now, she thought. What's next? I must warm the things for the baby. Another contraction caught her as she was bending over the cradle and she gasped at the sharpness of it. That was a good one. I'm sure that's what Annie would say. I'm not sure what I think though.

She sat down and dreamed over the baby's things as she waited for the kettle to boil. Are you a boy or a girl, I wonder? Who do you look like? Another contraction gripped her and she stood up and leant on the table. That's better.

The kettle boiled. She took it to the waiting stone pig, slowly filled it with hot water and then wrapped the baby clothes and shawl round it before putting the bundled pig into the cradle and covering it with a blanket. Then she made herself a cup of tea and sat down beside the fire. She felt very alone.

Come on somebody, she thought. I need company, and help.

Annie was in her house peeling tatties for her tea when she heard she was needed. She had been out earlier at her other patients, some old folk in the village who required daily visits, bathing and care, a young lad who had a huge boil on his back which needed dressing and then her mothers and babies, what she called her postnatals. These babies she had delivered either personally or with Dr Andrew Grant (they made a good team) and then for the first week or two after the birth she visited mother and baby every day, to attend to both.

This involved meticulous care of mother and baby in the way of cleanliness, prevention of infection and establishment of breastfeeding. All Annie's babies breastfed and indeed, all the mothers in Towie and the area seemed happy to do so. Annie loved her babies. Of course she loved the mothers too but the babies: she loved the smell of them, the softness of their skin, their little hands. Then she could watch them grow and develop under her careful eye and mature into adults themselves. She had reached the stage that she knew all the children and young adults in Towie and on a few occasions was on to her second generation of babies.

So it was with Mary. Annie had helped Margaret Grant give birth to Mary in Trancie House seventeen years before. Now she awaited word from Mary. Her bag was ready; she felt it wouldn't be too long. She had seen Mary during her pregnancy, often in passing and a couple of times on official 'midwife business' when she had checked Mary over carefully. She also discussed the situation with Mary's father and both agreed there was no reason why Mary should not give birth successfully although being a first it might take a little time. First babies often did, although, she thought hopefully, there were always exceptions. However, she was disappointed for the sake of the whole family that Mary had become pregnant at seventeen. Silly girl, she tutted into her tattie peelings, but it's happened now. We just must get on with it.

A loud knock at the door interrupted her musings.

'Who's that?' She wiped her wet hands on her apron and turned to the door just as John opened it.

'Annie,' he could hardly get the words out. 'Come, now, it's Mary.... the baby.'

'All right, John.' Mary whipped off her apron. 'Help me put the pony into the trap. He's in the shed ready.' John flew outside.

'Now,' she said to herself, 'my bag.' She grabbed her delivery bag, threw her shawl round her shoulders and ran out. John was coming out of the shed, leading the pony who looked not a little disgruntled at having his afternoon hay interrupted.

'Thanks John.' Together they manoeuvred the reluctant pony between the shafts and put the harness together.

'I'll go over for the doctor and Mary's mother,' he said.

'That's right. You go on for them. Don't worry. I'll go right now to Mary.' The midwife looked at his anxious face. 'She'll be all right. Now go.'

He leapt on to the old boneshaker and cycled off down the Nether Towie road as hard as he could. Annie stepped up into the trap, clicked her tongue at the pony and headed up the road to the bridge crossing the Don, then left at Glenkindie and then on to the old Glenbuchat road at Bridge of Buchat.

Nearly an hour later, with the pony doing his best to avoid the stones and the potholes she drew to a halt outside the cottage. She tied the reins to the gatepost and ran in. Mary stood leaning on the kitchen table, coping with the relentless contractions, a far cry from the creeping sensations of earlier. She turned.

'Oh Annie,' she said, 'I'm so glad to see you.'

'Come on then quinie.' Annie soothed the hair off her hot, flushed, sweating face. You'll be fine now.'

John reached Trancie House, came to another shuddering stop and ran up the steps. Margaret met him in the doorway.

'Mrs Grant, it's Mary. She needs you, and the Doctor.'

'Right, John.' Margaret, very calm, put her hand on his shoulder. 'Tell me.'

'The baby's coming. I've told Annie. She's on her way to the Milton.'

'That's fine, John. Now we have a wee problem here. The Doctor is out on an emergency – no, wait, I think I can see him coming.' In the distance, they could see the gig coming up the road, Jock at the reins. Andrew could see them waiting for him and knew by the maternity bag by Margaret's side that he was needed, this time by his own daughter. Jock turned the gig and with no time wasted, they were off again.

Up at the Milton Mary and Annie had become a team: Annie had calmed Mary down, helped her breathe through the contractions, assisted her into as comfortable and practical a position as possible. Everything was ready. Now they needed a baby.

The Trancie House gig driven by Jock the horseman and carrying Mary's mother, father and husband came to a halt.

'Wait now,' said Andrew. 'We don't want to upset things. If everything's fine and they're well on we shouldn't interrupt. It may be too late for us to go in.' They stopped outside as they heard Annie's voice. 'Come on now lassie, one last push and you're there…. That's great, now pant, pant, breathe it out. There's the head. Have a wee rest. You're doing this real well.'

Another contraction. Another push.

'It's a girl.' Annie cleaned the girl-baby's mouth and nose and together they listened to her first loud cry and watched the pink flush over her skin. Mary held her breath.

'Oh, she's bonny. Let me hold her.' She reached out her arms for her daughter.

'Charlotte,' she said. 'Charlotte Margaret Gordon.'

Charlotte Margaret Gordon opened her eyes and looked into her mother's face with the wise eyes of the newly born. She opened her mouth and gave a tiny pink yawn. Mary said, 'Hello, Charlotte,' and snuggled the baby in towards her. Annie, watching, smiled quietly as she got on with her midwife's business.

The door opened quietly. John came in with her father and mother. Mary looked up, her face full of pride and joy.

'Come in. Come in and meet Charlotte.'

Chapter 6

1881

Charlotte had never imagined a life without Mam and Dad. She never gave it a thought. They were there. They were part of her life and that was it. Then one day Mam came to her and said, 'We must pack up your clothes today. You see, you are going away to stay with Granny and Granpa.' Six year old Charlotte looked up, wide-eyed.

'Fit?' she said.

Granny and Granpa lived in Towie, a nearby parish about six miles away. But six miles in 1881 was a long way from the farm cottage at the Milton of Glenbuchat. It might as well have been the other side of the country. The roads were potholed and stony and anyway the Gordons, impecunious and with six children in just short of seven years did not have the wherewithal to possess a horse let alone a gig or trap for it to pull. On the other hand Grandpa was the local doctor with a gig, a horse and a horseman. Granny was his wife.

Mam was their daughter, their youngest child, Mary. She was married to Dad and they lived with Charlotte and her brothers and sisters in a tiny cottage at the Milton of Glenbuchat. Mam and Dad always seemed to be worried about something. Mam was always tired, Dad worked very hard on the farm but they never seemed to have enough money. Sometimes, Charlotte noticed that her mother did not have much on her plate. The children always had enough of what was very basic fare, and when she offered her mother some of hers she just smiled, patted her hand and said she was not very hungry.

Granny and Granpa tried to help. Granpa was always dropping in when he was on his rounds to say 'hello' and he always had something interesting in his hand like a piece of salmon from the River Don that someone had given him or a rabbit or something else for the pot. Granny too, would come up in an afternoon with a batch of scones or a Victoria sponge with home-made jam in it.

But pride precluded the Gordon parents' acceptance of what they saw as 'charity'. Small gifts maybe – and they were grateful for them. But anything more substantial, or money,was out of the question. Until now.

The week before, Andrew and Margaret Grant had sat down relishing the prospect of an evening by the fireside. Outside was the February snow. Inside was the parlour, chairs drawn up to the fire and barring unforeseen circumstances like babies arriving or accidents occurring, a peaceful evening. Inevitably, the conversation turned to the struggles of the family at the Milton.

'I'm getting worried about Charlotte.' Margaret stopped her darning in the poor light and turning her gaze to her husband. 'She's over six now and there is no sign of her going to school. I tried to ask Mary about it but she just said, "Mother leave it for the moment. There's plenty time." She's so tired she can hardly think.'

'She's a bright lassie too,' Andrew said. 'I had her out in the gig the other day and she really was interested. But she needs to learn to read. But *we* can't be up there all the time. And they can't come down here. Anyway I have my work. I do what I can taking her out when I'm on my rounds.'

'I know,' Margaret soothed. 'The school in Glenbuchat is quite good too – if they could just get her started.'

'I don't think Mary is able to get organised enough to get her out in the morning.'

'But Andrew, she'll have to go soon. School's compulsory now. In fact I'm surprised the truant officer has not been round to them already. It's a shame. I heard that all the children at Glanbuchat school learn to read and write really well. She would too if she could only get there.'

'The Towie school is good too. Colin Coutts is first class. Remember how keen he was with Mary's education. He's got a few there now making good progress and hoping to get into university if they can make it. He spends ages with them.'

'Andrew,' Margaret hesitated.

'Mhmm?' He looked at her. 'What is it?'

'What about us having Charlotte? I don't mean just for a holiday, but taking her on, helping her, educating her, bringing her up.' She warmed to her subject. 'She's very bright. Anyone can see that. It's a shame she's not getting the chance. And, after all, lots of children finish up with relatives for one reason or another. And being with us wouldn't be like boarding-out where the child goes to a different part of the country and knows nobody.'

'Aye, but how do you think she would take it? I see what you're getting at but she might be very homesick.'

'Yes, she would be to begin with but think of the chance she would get. Even if she goes to school at Glenbuchat she won't get peace at home. We could help her, and take a bit of the burden off Mary and John at the same time. You know how difficult it is to get them to accept help.'

He knew that but was this the right way to go about it? The minister was right when he said to Mary nearly seven years ago that she and John had set something going that would be hard to control. One baby, or two, in a farmworker's cottage and on such a low wage, you could cope with, but six bairns in seven years, all healthy he had to admit, was a crowd. He knew each time another pregnancy was announced his heart had sunk a little lower and he grieved for the struggles of the family at the Milton.

How long would they remain healthy at this rate? Mary, his bonny lassie, was now tired, thin and pale. She had been delighted with Charlotte and then Lizzie the following year. But now there were six. John's wage at 10/- a week and the rent-free two-roomed cottage with its vegetable-garden did not get them far, even with the farmer's perquisites of oatmeal, a little coal and peat, milk to drink and the right to grow potatoes in his field. Andrew and Margaret did their best to help and gave what they could. A bit of salmon or the occasional piece of venison from the laird's shooting parties were always appreciated and shared.

But still they worried that the children were going hungry or deficient in some way. As far as behaviour was concerned, they were left to their own devices. Mary was far too tired and thrang getting through the day to try and correct the children much, although Charlotte could be quite bossy with her siblings when she had a fit of being the big sister. Mostly, the children played and fought under Mary's feet. She felt too dispirited to sit down with them and teach them to play games, read them a story or learn to count to ten.

Andrew's thoughts ran on. If Charlotte came to them surely all would benefit. She would be well fed, be able to go to school and see her family when she wanted. They would work hard to make her happy. There would be one less mouth to feed at the cottage at the Milton. Mary would not be so tired (although he had to admit that Charlotte was a good wee helper to her mother. But that was because she was not at school and *that* was a necessity).

On the other hand, they would be taking a child from a family. That was a very big step. Andrew in his capacity as a General Practitioner with occasional attendance at official meetings in Aberdeen when he could get there, had heard all the arguments about boarded out children in Scotland. Boarding out was a very common practice at the time. Some children lived in poverty-ridden appalling circumstances. Nevertheless well-meaning childcare services had been the cause of much unhappiness and damage by suddenly uplifting these children from their homes and introducing them into conditions that were supposed to be better. Sometimes these places were homes and orphanages. Sometimes they were other families, but in totally different areas.

For instance you might have a city child being sent to a family in the Outer Hebrides. It sounded idyllic, but not if you were longing for a single-end in a tenement. In addition while many families were kind to the children they took on, some were not, and, mis-spending the money they were given, treated the children very badly. But, this would not happen to their Charlotte, Andrew thought. They were proposing she would come to them – her loving grandparents. It was quite different. He hoped Charlotte would see it in that light too. He turned to Margaret.

'Let's do it,' he said. 'It won't be straightforward, but we've got to try. You're quite right'.

At last they could see the cottage in the distance. They stepped down, Andrew carrying the usual basket of scones and braddies from Trancie House. Jock took the horse and gig round to the shed. It was dinnertime. They were all there, even John in from the field, busy spooning away at home-made broth, all except Wee Alicky the baby, asleep in his cradle by the fireside.

William waved his hands in delight when he saw them, 'What's in the basket Granny?' He got up and ran to her and lifted the cloth.

'Ooh, braddies. Oh, can we have one now?' Lizzie, quieter, joined him.

'Please,' she said.

'You shouldn't ask for braddies like that,' Charlotte said. 'You should wait for Granny to say.'

Margaret looked at Mary. 'Can they?'

'Och yes, let them, Thanks Mother.'

'Braddies, braddies,' the children crowded round.

John finished his soup and pushed back his chair. 'I must get on,' he said. 'See you later'. He made for the door but Andrew said,' John, wait a minute, we've come because we want to talk to you, you and Mary. Please could we? Without the children?'

John and Mary looked at each other.

'They could go next door for a minute.' Mary ran to next cottage where Sandy the older farmhand and his new wife Ina lived. Within minutes she was back with Ina.

'Come on bairns, come and play in my hoosie for a wee while. Get your shawlies and your boots.'

'Come on everybody.' Charlotte was running about, fussing them all into their boots. 'I know something,' she said, hurrying them. 'There are new kittlins next door.'

'Kittlins,' they shouted and ran off with Ina, braddies in hand.

Peace fell. The clock ticked. Wee Alicky slept. The young couple looked enquiringly at their elders. Mary spoke.

'What is it, Father... Mother...?'

Andrew cleared his throat. This was the most difficult thing he had ever had to do.

'Well,' he began, 'It's like this. We, we know things are difficult for you all up here. We, that is, your Mother and I, would like to help you somehow. We've thought and thought about this. We know you want to be independent, and admire you both for it. But there comes a point when something wider needs to be done.' Mary leant forward.

'What are you saying, Father?'

'Well, for a start, Charlotte needs to go to school. She's a bright lassie, but if she doesn't go soon she'll be all behind with her reading and so on and everything else that a school can give.'

'But Father, Mother and I have already mentioned school. There's time yet.' She wiped her forehead wearily. 'It's just so difficult in the mornings with them all. Getting them all up, and the breakfast and feeding the bairn and everything.'

28

'Mary,' her Mother said, 'I know that. Believe me I know. I remember what it was like when you all were small – and I had help. That's why we now want to help you.'

'But what…?' Mary looked bewildered. John sat with his head in his hands.

'Look,' Andrew said. 'What we're offering and it is because we love you all and want to help, is to have Charlotte to stay with us. She would be happy in Towie, she could go to the school there and come up and see you every now and again. What do you say?'

'What,' Mary and John looked at each other. 'But Charlotte is *our* daughter. We should have her here.'

'Yes, I know.' Andrew was patient and kind. 'That would be the ideal. But the reality is that six bairns under seven is a lot to cope with, and Charlotte is missing out. She's here all day helping you when she could be at school doing the things other children do. And getting the opportunity to read and develop. She could go far, that one.'

'But,' Mary's voice shook, 'they all need to learn and read and so on.'

'Aye I know. They all deserve a good chance, but don't you see, at the moment, Charlotte is not getting her chance. She's six and a half. She needs to be allowed to shine. We love her and can help her do this. I know she'll miss you and you'll miss her but we're not so very far away.'

John and Mary looked at each other.

'What do you think?' John's voice was filled with doubt as he looked at Mary. Andrew felt heart-sorry for him. He imagined how he would feel if the circumstances were reversed.

'Could we try it for a wee whilie?' Mary wondered. 'Just to help us get out of the bit. Not for ever….' Her voice trembled. 'I can't bear the thought….'

'Mary,' Margaret went over to her and held her closely. 'Let's just do a step at a time.'

'John?' Mary turned to him. 'John, could she go to Towie for a wee while?' Eyes brimming, she got up and went over to where he was standing, head bowed. They held each other tightly.

'She's the bairn of the moors and fields,' he whispered, 'the wee lassickie. But she has to move on too. We must give her her chance.' He turned to Charlotte's grandparents.

'All right. This is a very big decision for us. We'll never really know if it is the right thing to do, but we'll do it because we believe it must be right for Charlotte to have this chance. But please,' his voice broke, 'please bring her back often so that she doesn't forget us and the bairns. And in the fine weather the others can come and visit her.'

'Of course,' said Margaret. 'We'll do everything we can.'

Silence fell, each with their own thoughts: the father remorseful that he was not able to provide enough, however hard he worked. From such a hopeful start, how had they come to this point? The mother, having to pass on her firstborn to be cared for by others even though they were her own beloved parents. The grandparents, trying to help in the only way they could see.

Margaret was the first to break the quiet. 'How do you want to do this?' she asked. 'We could take her today but that would be very sudden for her. What about tomorrow?'

'Jock could come up and get her,' Andrew said. 'Wait a minute and I'll consult about the weather. If there's more snow he won't get up the hill tomorrow.' He went outside and they heard murmured voices. He came back in, stamping his snowy feet on the step.

'That's all right. Jock says it's going to be fresh tomorrow, the wind's going round. So he can come up again with the gig and bring Charlotte down to Towie with her things. What do you think?'

Mary and John nodded, their faces giving away what they were feeling.

'Right,' said Margaret briskly, 'We'll be on our way and Jock will be up just after dinner tomorrow. You tell her. Tell her we're looking forward to having her. We'll see her tomorrow.'

Chapter 7

Charlotte

Mam told me about what they planned early the following morning: that I would be going today to stay with Granny and Granpa in Towie and that I would be going to Towie school.

'Will it be lik a holiday?' I asked.

'No'.

'Then fit? For a few wiks?'

Mam looked uncomfortable. She also looked tired, drawn and pale. Even I at six years old could see that. She was always so busy with me and my younger brothers and sisters. There was always a new baby, or it seemed that way. Now wee Alicky had arrived a few months ago.

It was heavy going. Six children in a two-roomed farmworker's cottage, father on minimum wages and mother struggling to make ends meet, feed the new one and sort out the rest not easy. Yet we did not seem unhappy. But here now was Mam telling me something about going away.

'Mair nor a few wiks, Charlotte. They're gaan ti tak you in.'

'Mam, Mam, A dinna wint ti be takken in. A wint ti bide here wi ye.'

She sighed, touched me briefly on the head, and looked at me with her dark grey eyes which I had inherited.

'See, here, Charlotte, we canna g'on lik is. Ye're the aalest. Ye're a bricht lassie, Ye need ti gang ti squeel. Ye'll be fine wi Granpa and Granny. They'll larn ye fit's richt. Ye'll larn things, better nor here. Ye'll ay be ma quinie, bit this is the wy its got ti be.'

I couldn't believe it. But it was true. We went through to the ben room where I slept along with my brothers and sisters, head and tail in two beds. Of the six of us, I was the eldest and I was six. Lizzie came next – she was five; then Willie four, Jean three, John the old baby, a toddling bundle of energetic birr with the stickiest fingers you have ever seen, and now wee Alicky. Wee Alicky slept along with Mam and Dad in the box bed in the kitchen. At least he didn't sleep in the box bed; he had the cradle which was sometimes by the bed, sometimes by the fireside, sometimes even outside on a fine day.

Anyway on this day Mam had a box ready for my things. I started to cry. I couldn't help it but I sensed the feeling of something big in my life and that things would never be the same again. Mam paid no attention to my noise. Probably she was hurting inside but she just set her mouth in the same way as she sometimes did when my Dad came in smelling of beer, and got on with putting my clothes in the box.

Clothes – what did I have in the way of clothes? A few skimpy items: shrunken semmits, an old cut-down skirt made out of one of my mothers, a knitted jersey handed in from somewhere else, things like that. Nothing really pretty. My stockings had holes in them and my boots were through the sole and let in the water.

In the summer it was easier, it was warm enough not to worry so much and we usually went barefoot. Last summer Granny had given us a whole lot of new stockings that she and Katie had knitted – they knitted constantly. But Mam let us wear them too soon, before winter set in. We took them off when we got too hot and left them up the hill. We couldn't find them after that.

The one special thing I had was my doll, Beanie. Dad made her for me before my last birthday in October out of a piece of wood, with swinging arms and legs and a head that went round and round. Mam had made some clothes for her which I could take off and on. I loved her. Beanie came to bed with me, she comforted me when I was sad, was company for me in my frequent lonely walks up in the hills behind the cottage. I whispered secrets to her knowing that she would tell no one. I held on tightly to her in case Mam would not let me take her away.

By this time, the others came breenging in.

'Mam, fit's gaan on?' asked Lizzie.

'Aye, Mam,' Willie was tugging at her skirt.

'Me too, me too,' Jean never wanted to be left out. John began to bawl adding to my weeping with his own din.

Mam shouted, 'Be quiet the lot of you. A canna hear masel think.' We were shocked into silence. Mam took a deep breath.

'Now,' she said firmly in English, highlighting the importance of the occasion. 'Charlotte is going to stay with Granny and Granpa in Towie. She'll still be your sister but she'll be there with them. You'll see her sometimes but she's going to go to school in Towie and live with them for just now.' Having delivered this shocking statement she turned to me and said, 'Come on noo, Charlotte. Dry yer een, tak Beanie and be a big lassie.'

She picked up the box with my possessions and went through to the kitchen. I followed slowly and sat at the table.

Mam looked round from the stove. I could see her eyes were wet. She was feeling it too but I was angry. Why me? Had I not always done everything I could to help her. It was not my fault that the babies kept coming. I had even sensed the despair in Mam and Dad when more mouths arrived to be filled. And the winters were bad, the lambs died, the summers were poor and the reluctantly ripening harvests were laid flat underneath the equinoxial rains and gales.

And I was the scapegoat. I was too young to understand that although it looked like that, I was getting an opportunity of education, of fulfilling needs as yet undreamed of. All I could think of was what seemed to me the withdrawing of the basic need: the love of my parents. How could they love me if they were sending me away?

Later that day Granpa's gig came for me. Even Dad came in from his work in the field to say good bye. They all came out and Dad lifted me up beside old Jock, Granpa's horseman and helper. I couldn't say a word. Mam hugged me and said to be a good quinie. Dad patted my head and whispered, 'See ye soon, Lassickie.' That did not comfort me either. 'Lassickie' was his own special word for me. Would he pass it on to Lizzie when I wasn't there?

The others were silent except for John the big baby, who as if sensing without understanding that something important was happening, cried and cried. Dad picked him up.

'See, wave your handie ti Charlotte.' But John buried his head in Dad's shoulder and would not look up.

Old Jock was a kind man. We proceeded down the track and out on to the road. To begin with, apart from quiet murmurings of encouragement to the horse like 'hud awa' or 'giddy up' or 'woah now,' he said nothing. I sat beside him and sniffled into my scarf, holding Beanie closer to me. Then when we were clear of the sight of home Jock spoke. His voice came rumbling up from somewhere inside. It was deep, gruff, not sharp, but firm. Not a voice to be frightened of but, one to be respected. One that could comfort.

'Ye manna greet,' the voice said. 'It'll be aa richt. A ken its nae fine for ye bit jist ee wait an see. Yer Granny an Grandpa are fine folk and they're lookin forrit ti havin ye. Bit they ken it's nae easy fur ye. Here, here's ma hunky – hae a blaa an mak the best o't.' With that, a not very clean hanky was pushed into my hand. I blew obediently into it and wiped my eyes.

'At's better. Noo, hae a sweetie. Granny's sooker.'

From the depths of his trouser pocket came two pandrops one of which Jock put in his own mouth and birled around against his falsers. The other he gave to me. We only usually got pandrops on a Sunday for the kirk and I felt a bit guilty about indulging in this way on any other day. However, I thought it must be all right if Jock had one too so I surreptitiously slunk it into my cheek.

We drove along for a few minutes, sucking in silence. Then he said, 'A've been wi your grandpa for a lang time. Ever since he came to Towie. Noo, let me see, he came in 1854. Yer mam wisna born at the time. I mind that day fine as weel, a bonny bairnie. So, it's 1881 noo. Foo mony years wit aat be, dae ye think, that A've workit for yer Grandpa?'

'A dinna ken,' I whispered.

'Weel noo, lets see, 1854 to 1864 is ten years, 1864 to 1874 is anither ten, at maks twenty year....'

'That's the year I was born,' I butted in, forgetting my trouble in the calculations.

'Aye that's richt, so ye ken that dae ye? Weel, 1874 till noo is, 75, 76, 77, 78, 79, 80, 81, it'll be seeven years. So that maks 27 years a thegither. Fit a lang time. The thing A wis gaan ti say is I've been wi him aa that time and I've nivver heard him raise his voice til onybiddy. He's an afa fine man an ye'll get on great wi him. An there's aye me. Ye can aye come oot tae the steadin and gie me a hand.' I began to feel a wee bit better. But it wasn't just Grandpa.

'But what about Granny?' I said. She seemed all right. She was good at bringing baking and things but *living* with her was a different story.

'Weel,' Jock considered this question seriously. 'She's a great wumman. Dae as yer telt, and you'll be fine. The same with Katie and Jessie. Ye ken them.'

'Aye,' I said, 'but, tell me again. Fa are they?'

'Oh, Katie's the hoosekeeper and cook and Jessie does aa'thin else.'

'Ye mean they work in the hoose?'

'Aye,' he said. 'Div ye nae ken aboot at?'

I had never really thought about it before. When we visited Granny and Granpa they were there and I think I just took their presence for granted. I had never heard about women working in the house for another woman before except for in the big farm hoose where the farmer's wife had folk to help her, lassies who had reached the age when they could go into service, or wifies like the grieve's wife who was very important and sometimes acted as housekeeper or manager to the farmer's wife when she was very busy. Occasionally you saw the wife of a farm worker helping too, but they were usually hodden doon with bairns. Like my Mam was.

My Mam did everything herself, cooking, washing, scrubbing, milking, butter-making, hens, eggs and of course looking after us. And all the other mams that I knew around the farm did the same. There were times when they all helped each other, like when somebody was ill or having a baby.

That was a funny thing, when babies came all the wifies came in and the men and other bairns were put out. Then when you came back in again, the baby was there cooried in beside the mam in the bed. I saw it myself when wee Alicky was born. I don't know where he came from but there he was in the bed. And all the women around chattering and laughing and the howdie of course. Maybe the howdie brought the baby. She seemed to get everywhere. Everybody knew her.

Anyway did this mean that Trancie House where Granny and Grandpa lived was a really big hoose? Surely it was if they needed Katie and Jessie. And what were Katie and Jessie really like? More new folk to get used to. My heart went down a bit and I held Beanie closer. As if he felt my disquiet, Jock began to hum a tune. A low growly hum. Not a low growly tune though.

Soon I joined in, my childish treble joining with the deep bass:

'There's mony a bonny lass in the Howe o Auchterless,
There's mony a bonny lass in the Garioch o,
There's mony a bonny jean in the toon o Aiberdeen,
But the floo'r o them aa is in Fyvie o.

'Come doon the stair pretty Peggy my dear,
Come doon the stair pretty Peggy o,
Come doon the stair, bind up yer yella hair,
Tak a last fareweel o yer daddy o.

'There wis a troop o Irish Dragoons
Cam mairchin doon through Fyvie, o,
The Captain's name wis Ned,
And he died for a maid,
He died for the bonny lass o Fyvie, o.'

Soon my mood had quite recovered and we jogged along in fine style, singing together about Ned of the Irish Dragoons… Life looked good, the catkins were just coming out, no lambs but plenty of waiting sheep in the fields, birds chirping and Jock conducting the singing with his free hand. We sang and sang and covered the distance from Glenbuchat to Towie in no time at all.

It was when we turned into Towie that I remembered again. Here I was aged six and a bit, removed from my home without notice, with my parents' consent, leaving them and my brothers and sisters, and going to my grandparents whom I at the time did not consider to be close family, with a very different lifestyle from mine, with people called Katie and Jessie in the house, not family, but who worked there.

And, Mam had mentioned the word 'school'. Now, to me, experience of school was an unknown thing. I had heard about it of course. I knew some children who went to school. In fact ever since the Education Act in Scotland of 1872 going to school was compulsory for children aged from five to thirteen although children who had a certificate in reading, writing and arithmetic were exempt if they wished. And here I was at six years old past October and I had not entered the school gate. Neither did I wish to.

I had no conception of the benefits of school. Of how my mind would open and grow once I learned to read. Of how books and reading and writing and the magic of numbers and eventually teaching these core skills would grasp and hold my attention for the rest of my life. That day, jogging into Towie up on the gig beside old Jock, the very thought of school filled me with a dread that hung over me and added to the misery of being sent away from home to live with near strangers.

The gig clattered through Towie and turned left up the Nether Towie road. There seemed to be even more stones and potholes on this one but it was not for long. Suddenly we were there, the gig drew up at the side of the house and Jock jumped down.

'Come on noo quinie. It'll be aa richt,' he whispered. 'Here's yer Granny waitin.'

I looked and there she was at the front door. She was smiling and holding out her hand.

'Hello Charlotte. It's good to see you.' She bent down and kissed my cheek. I hung my head. I felt very small, very shy and very alone. She took my hand.

'Come in,' she said. 'Jock will you please take Charlotte's box up to her room.'

'Aye, aye, richt awa'. John was up the steps behind us carrying my box containing all my possessions, except for, of course, Beanie. She, I kept clutched firmly to me.

'Who's this?' Granny asked.

'Beanie,' I whispered.

'She's really nice,' said Granny. 'Did your Dad make her for you?'

'Aye,' I said, and then in a rush of confidence, 'and Mam made her claes.'

'They're really very well made.' Granny was looking with interest. 'And, I can recognise some of the materials. I remember that'. She pointed to Beanie's frock. 'That was an old frock of your mother's.'

'Aye, that's richt,' I said, forgetting my shyness. 'She made it last year too, for my birthday.' I stopped, reminded of the day when Dad and Mam had wished me a Happy Birthday and given me Beanie. I think Dad spent ages hiding in the shed making her and Mam had done all the clothes from old things which had been turned so many times they were fit only to be cut up into smaller items like dolls' clothes. I could feel the tears coming again and sniffed miserably.

'Come on,' said Granny. 'Let's go and see if Katie has anything for tea.'

Katie. Although I had met her, I did not really know this Katie. I knew that she had been with Granny and Granpa for years. Mam had called her 'Granny's right hand woman' whatever that meant. Now she was to be part of my life too. I was not sure. What would she be like?

Granny walked me firmly through to the kitchen.

'Katie, are you there?'

'Aye, Mam, I'm here.' Katie, raised a flushed face from the range oven from which she was removing a tray of what looked like the fluffiest scones I had ever seen.

'Katie, this is Charlotte. You remember meeting her last time she visited, last summer.'

'Oh aye.' Katie held out a floury hand which I took carefully. She grasped my little hand and shook it firmly.

'Well now Charlotte, it's fine ti see ye here. Ye'll be a rare bit of company for me. We can have some right claiks.'

Just then the front door banged and a voice called, 'Hello-o, I'm back'.

'That's Granpa,' said Granny. 'Lets go and say "hello" and then we can get ready for tea. Are you ready for us, Katie?'

"Aye Mam It's aa ready, keeping warm for when ye're ready.'

Granpa was quite tall, grey hair, slightly stooped as he wasn't getting any younger. When I shyly held out my hand to shake as Mam had reminded me to do, he drew me to him and hugged me instead. I didn't often get hugs like that but I quite liked it. It made me feel a wee bit better inside.

'Oh it's grand for us to have you here,' he said. 'What's for tea, Granny? 'I'm starving.'

'Mince and potatoes,' Granny said, 'and Katie has made scones and there's some cake and German biscuits.'

'My favourite. What do you think Charlotte? Are you a mince and tattie quine?' I had to laugh. I didn't really feel like laughing but he was so cheery and smiling at me so kindly that it was infectious. I let a small giggle escape.

'Aha,' he said, 'I knew it. I knew there was a laugh in there somewhere. Come on, tea time, I hope.'

'Yes, yes,' said Granny, 'just give me a minute to help Katie serve it up.' She bustled off.

'Tell you what,' said Granpa, 'We'll go and wash our hands first. We must do that. Come up to the bathroom.'

'The bathroom?' I said. 'Div ye hae a bathroom?'

'Oh have you not seen it? This is your Granny's pride and joy.' By this time we were half way up the stairs and he flung open a door. There in truth was a bathroom. I had never seen one before.

'A hale room jist for a bath?'

'Aye,' he said, 'and a basin with water, look.' He went in and I followed slowly, looking around. There stood a most imposing basin with two taps. The bath also had two taps.

'Fit wye dae ye need twa taps?' I asked.

'Hot and cold,' Granpa explained. 'See.' He turned on the basin taps. 'If you look, the hot tap has an 'H' on the top for Hot and the cold has a 'C' for Cold. Then you know exactly which one you need to use.'

'You mean,' I asked, 'haet watter comes oot o the tap wi 'H'?'

'Yes,' he said. 'Have you not seen this before – mind you,' he added, not without a little pride, 'it is the only bathroom in Towie.' Mercy, I thought, what next? And more was to follow.

'And,' he said triumphantly, 'next door we have a water-closet.'

'A fit?'

'A water-closet. Come.' He couldn't wait to show me. There, in the wee room next to the bathroom, was in all its glory, a water-closet.

'You see,' he explained, 'you won't need to go outside to the dry-closet any more. You just come in here. And, when you're finished, you just pull this,' he indicated the flush, 'and three gallons of water will come down from that tank and run it all away.'

To demonstrate he pulled hard on the chain, the water came tumbling down from the tank up above with such a roar that I clapped my hands over my ears and ran out on to the landing. Granny was just coming up the stairs.

'What on earth is going on?'

'Fit a noise that thing maks,' I said.

'Andrew, you've shown her,' Granny said. 'I was going to show her at bath-time.'

'Bath-time,' I said, completely diverted, 'but it's nae Saturday.'

'Well I think tonight you can have a lovely bath and hair-wash as a special treat. Now come on down. Your tea's on the table.'

I didn't know what to think. A bathroom with a bath in it, a bath on a not-Saturday and tea on a table with a white cloth in a different room from the kitchen. Granny called it the dining room. The mince and tatties were fine though, just like Mam's. I suddenly realised I was very hungry and despite my misgivings about what might happen next, I ate everything put in front of me.

'Katie makes a grand plate o mince,' I announced.

'Would you like a scone,' Granpa asked. So I ate until I was full. And then made to leave the table.

'Charlotte,' Granny said, 'Would you like to get down from the table.'

'Aye.'

'Then say "Please may I get down from the table"'.

'Fit?' I was genuinely puzzled.

'If you want to leave the table when others are still sitting, then please say, "Please may I get down from the table" '.

I had never heard of this before but just looked at her and Granpa (who, inexplicably had his hand up in front of his mouth as though he were trying not to laugh) and said, 'Please may I get down from the table'.

'Yes of course Charlotte. Where are you off to?'

I hesitated. I had not thought this far ahead.

'Well, I could go to the kitchen and see Katie.'

'Yes you could. I'll tell you what. Ask her to show you your bedroom. I don't think you've seen it yet have you?'

I found my way back to the kitchen and found Katie at her ease in a chair in front of the range.

'Well, did you enjoy your tea?'

'Yes, thank you Katie. Granny said to ask you to show me my bedroom.'

'Oh aye.' She levered herself out of her chair. 'Mechty me, A'm getting stiff in ma aal age. Aye aye. Come on and see.'

Upstairs again. Into the bonniest wee room I have ever seen. White walls and the rest sunshiney yellow. And a bed with yellow pillows and sheets on it. I was speechless.

'Like it?' Katie looked at me.

'It's lovely. But fa else sleeps here?'

'Jist you.'

'Jist me?' Another unheard of thing. 'But will A nae be afa lonely by masel?'

'Na, na, Granny and Granpa are jist next door and A'm jist abeen.'

'And,' a thought struck me, 'I have Beanie.'

'So that's aa richt then.'

The next big thing was the bath. At home bathnight was on a Saturday evening. Pans and kettles of water were put on to boil and the zinc tub was taken out, and put in front of the fire in the kitchen. We took turns to be bathed, all in the same water, the smallest and hopefully the cleanest first and then so on. As I was the eldest (and, in my opinion, probably the cleanest of the lot), by the time it came to my turn the water was often scummy and chilly. Mam would sometimes top it up but I had never in my memory been first in the bath. I suppose it must have happened when I was a baby and there was nobody else.

Then there was the nit-hunt. This was always done on a Saturday night too. Mam kept a special nit-comb with very fine teeth which came out and one by one we were put through its tortures. It was worse for the girls as we had long hair and we had to suffer in silence as Mam would say triumphantly, 'there they are.' And she would comb away and gather the nits and lice up on the comb and wipe it on a piece of old cloth for burning on the fire. My hair was long and dark and curly, always in a tangle and a perfect nit-haven. It took ages to do.

Sometimes we even had to have a flea hunt. We played a great deal with the cats and their kittlins. When they went after the rabbits especially the baby ones in spring they got rabbit-fleas which they passed on to us. Mam knew they were there by the way we scratched at ourselves and by the tell-tale bites. Then she went into the attack. Not a flea was left alive if she could help it. 'That's een. A've got it,' she would say as she searched our clothes and bodies and cracked the nit between her thumb-nails.

That first night at Trancie House, I was escorted to the bathroom by Granny and Katie. I looked again at the bath with its 'H' and 'C' taps. The bath itself looked huge, very high sides and four clawed feet. I felt really apprehensive.

'Come on noo,' said Katie. 'A'll put in the watter.'

'And I'll help you with your clothes,' offered Granny. I stood there mutely. Granny very kindly but firmly (she stood no nonsense) got me out of all my clothes and Katie said, 'Right in you get then,' and before I had time to be frightened of the big bath, I was in, sitting down with warm water nearly up to my oxters. They looked and nodded at each other in satisfaction. I think they thought I might have made a fuss but they did not give me time to say anything. They just put me in. I gasped and then relaxed.

I put my hands below the water and it was clean. I could see them. There was no scum or murk. And the soap. Usually at home we had a piece of soap cut off a bar. Here, it was still called a bar but that was where the resemblance ended. This bar of soap was pink, lathered into lots of bubbles and smelt of roses. I loved it. (Later I heard Granny calling it a *tablet* of soap which really put it into the realms of exclusivity).

I was not so keen on the next procedure: the nits. I thought Granny, not being used to little girls might forget but Katie went into the cupboard and brought out the all too familiar nit comb.

'Ooh no-o.'

'Ooh aye. Come on noo, Charlotte let's get it done and we can wash yer hair and mak it aa bonny. And fa kens, mebbe the nits'll gang awa fur ever.'

When it was all over and I was clean, dried and dressed in a white nightie which had miraculously appeared, and combed and brushed and smelling of roses Granny and Katie sat back and looked at me with pleasure.

'That's better. How do you feel.'

I suddenly felt rather shy again.

'Nice, I think. I like the smell.'

They laughed.

'That's good. Now,' added Granny, 'come and see Granpa before you go to bed.'

'And,' said Katie, 'Just this once I'll clean oot the bath. Efter the nicht ye clean out yer bath yersel.'

'Yes, Katie,' I said. 'Thank you very much.'

Granpa sat in his chair by the fireside. After all bathing children was women's work. I went timidly and stood in front of him. It seemed a long time before he lowered his paper and looked at me.

'Now then, who is this?' he asked. 'I don't know this girl at all.'

'Granpa,' I said. 'It's me, Charlotte.'

'Oh, *Charlotte*'. He was teasing me. 'Of course. What about the *pediculus capitis*? Are they all gone?'

'The fit?'

'*Pediculus capitis*. The nits. Aha,' as I touched my dark shiny hair. 'I know you had the nit comb out.'

'Aye, but Katie hopes now they will never come back,' I said.

'That's good. And even if they do, we can just get rid of them again.' He looked at me again. 'You look lovely. Now, what about a story?'

A story? This I seldom had. 'Ooh yes, please.'

'Right.' He went over to the bookshelf and took out a big green book.

'Look,' he said. 'It's called Andersen's Fairy Tales and it was written by a Danish gentleman called Mr Hans Christian Andersen. He lived in Denmark and wrote lots of stories about Denmark and some of them are in this book. When you are able to read you can come and read this book any time you want to. It will always be here for you to use. In the meantime until you can read, I'll read the stories one by one for you.'

He showed me the book and its pictures, and the Contents page and how I would be able to choose any story I liked from this page, look up the page number and find the story. I was fascinated and could not wait to get started.

'Well, what about starting with one story tonight and we'll go on from there?' he suggested. 'How about the *Ugly Duckling*? It has a happy ending.'

'All right,' I said, although I did not see how a story about an ugly duckling could have a happy ending. I was soon to find out.

'And,' Granpa said, pulling something out from its hiding place down the side of his chair. 'Here's something else'. He handed over a piece of soft red leather about an inch and a half wide and six or seven inches long.

'See,'he explained, 'It's a bookmark.'

'Fit's a bookmark?'

40

'Well, when you have finished reading for the time being, you put your bookmark into the place where you stopped and then you know where to start next time. And, this one has your name on it. Look.'

'Oh, thank you, Granpa.' Now that I looked properly I could see the letters 'C h a r l o t t e' going along the leather. 'That's afa bonny. Let's put it in the book. I've never had a bookmark afore.'

That initial story with Granpa was to become the first of many as our bed-time ritual developed into a nightly tradition of time together. Sometimes Granny joined us, sometimes she did other things. Always Granpa was there for me at that time. To begin with he read the story. Then as my reading skills began to grow and expand we took turns at the reading. And, as the years went on and my tastes grew more eclectic we still read, but we also discussed what we read, together or apart, and came to talk about what was going on round about us and in the wider world.

All this, however, was ahead of me that first night at Trancie House. Then, I was content to sit on his knee, 'help' him find the page in the book that he wanted and listen to his voice reading the story. He was right to choose a story with a happy ending. Anything sad – and Hans Christian Anderson's stories sometimes had sad endings – would not have done on that first night of emotional friability.

True, I appeared quite happy on the surface. But my inner self was a turmoil of mixed emotions both good and bad. I had just been removed from everybody and everything that I knew. My new lifestyle was to be totally different – eating in a dining room, asking to 'get down from the table', bathing in a bathroom, and sleeping alone. These changes had to be classed as negative at the time although some developed through time into positive assets. On the other hand, a positive feature right from the first day, was my special time with Granpa. Granny, with Katie to help her, attended to all my physical needs: feeding, washing, nit combing, dressing and of course, not so physical but considered very important, behaviour. Perhaps I consciously did not see those as assets on my first evening but they were there and came to be as natural as breathing. And although I did not recognise them as positive features that first evening they added with Granpa's 'time' to create a feeling of comfort which I was able to take with me to bed in my yellow and white room.

And of course there was Beanie, my consolation, my link with things and people I knew. All this time since my arrival, Beanie accompanied me, either sitting or lying on the floor beside me, or cuddled in my oxter or sitting in the bathroom, watching with her painted eyes and shoddy clothes, my transformation from scruffy little girl with dishevelled mane, to white-nightie and shiny hair. It did not seem fair and indeed Katie promised that Beanie also should have something new to wear. But that night Beanie came to bed with me in her old clothes. I held her closely to me and when I woke in the night and looked for my siblings Beanie was there for me, unchanged and ever ready to listen and respond in her own way to my loneliness.

Chapter 8

Charlotte woke in the morning light and wondered where she was. The sun streamed in through the yellow curtains bathing the little room with light. She found the faithful Beanie on the pillow beside her and said, 'Far are we Beanie?' before she remembered. She sat up and stretched and swung her legs out over the bed. The door opened quietly and Granny's head looked round.

'Oh you're awake are you? I've been peeping in this last while to see what stage you were at and you were sound asleep. How are you today?'

'Fine, thank you. Can I rise noo?'

'Yes, of course. See put on this wee warm shawlie for just now and come and have some porridge.' Charlotte noticed then that a small soft woolly shawl lay at the foot of the bed.

'Fa's is't?'

'It's for you if you'd like it. To keep you cosy before you get dressed. See, I'll help you.' She picked up the shawl and arranged it round Charlotte's shoulders. It fell down past her middle in folds.

'Now, downstairs.'

Breakfast was in the kitchen. Nobody else was there.

'Far's aa'biddy ?'

'Well, Jessie's hanging up washing, Granpa's in the surgery before he goes out on his rounds, Jock's in the stable with the horse, Katie's gone down to Towie for some things and you and me are here.'

'Fit time is it.'

'Half past nine.'

'Mercy, A'm afa late the day.'

Granny smiled and said it didn't matter for her first morning. She doled out a bowl of porridge and set it down in front of Charlotte with a smaller bowl of cream beside it.

'Do you like oatmeal on the top?'

'Yes please, that's the wye we ay hae it at hame.'

Granny sat at the other end of the table thinking about clothes. She needed to be careful. She didn't want to make out that Charlotte's entire wardrobe required a complete makeover but at the same time the child couldn't go about, let alone to church or school in the clothes she had arrived with. She chose her words carefully.

'Katie and I were thinking. How would you feel if we were to get you some new clothes. You seemed pleased with your nightie last night. How about some more new things?'

'Fit like?' Katie ate her porridge at great speed and dropped her spoon in the bowl with a clatter. 'Is there ony mair.'

'Please,' said Granny.

'Please,' repeated Charlotte.

'Yes, here you are.' As she was pouring the porridge Granny tried again. 'Well what do you think – about clothes? Something bonny.'

'Bonny?' Charlotte's eyes lit up, attention caught. 'Ye mean really bonny? With, maybe, frilly bits.'

'I don't see why not,' said Granny.

Charlotte jumped down, ran round the table and stood in front of Granny.

'Div ye mean that? A can hiv bonny things? Aa fur masel?'

'Yes Charlotte.' Granny's brain was whirling at the ease with which the idea of new clothes had been accepted.

'A've nivver hid bonny things,' Charlotte shouted. Suddenly tears streamed down her face. 'A've nivver hid bonny things,' she sobbed. 'A've aye winted bonny things. Can A really hiv them.'

Granny held her closely. 'Of course you can have them. We'll start today. But stop crying now.'

'A dinna ken fit wye A'm greetin. Did ye say the day? Fit wye can ye manage that? My Mam aye says "sometime soon" and then it disna haippen.'

'Well it will happen here.'

'Bit far are they?'

'Well, for a start, Katie and I've been working away for a day or two to make you a few things you can wear right away. Here's Katie now. I can hear her feet at the back door. Hello Katie,' to the laden figure who appeared.

'Aye, aye, Mam.' Katie was rosy and windswept from her walk. 'Mercy, fit a gale o wind. Good morning Charlotte. Did you sleep well?'

'Yes thank you Katie,' Charlotte said and then mindful of her manners said,

'Good morning to you too.'

'Have you been greetin?' Katie looked at Charlotte's tear-stained face.

Granny interrupted smoothly. 'Charlotte and I were just talking about clothes. We thought we might have a look at what we've got ready.'

'Aye, aye, A'll jist get ma coat aff.'

Charlotte danced about in the white nightie, the shawlie slipping down her back.

'A'm gettin bonny things, bonny things, bonny things…'

Katie looked at Granny in amazement. 'Fit wye did ye manage this?'

'Well, I just mentioned the word "bonny" and there we were.'

'Let's look in the kist then.'

Charlotte hopped to where the kist sat ready to reveal what was hiding inside.

Katie opened the lid and Granma began to take out the clothes.

44

'Remember Charlotte, this is just to get you dressed for the next wee whilie. Once we have more time we'll get more material and make up more frocks. As she was speaking she was taking clothes out of the kist.

'Now,' she said, 'to begin with we need semmits to keep your chest warm.' She showed Charlotte two soft hand knitted woollen vests, one white and one pink. At the neck and armholes were wee holies that Katie had cleverly made. Through the wee holies was threaded pink ribbon which could be pulled to the right size and tied with a bow.

'Oh Granny,' said Charlotte, 'I like the pink ribbons and the bows. I nivver hid onythin lik at afore.'

'Katie knitted them,' said Granny.

'Oh, thank you Katie. I like them afa weel. But fit are these bits for?' She pointed to four tapes hanging down from the bottom of the vests. Each tape had a buttonhole in the end. What could they be for?

'Well,' said Katie. 'Ye'll need to wear stockins. So I've made them for you – here you are' – she pulled a pair of black knitted stockings out of the kist and showed Charlotte. 'At the top of each stockin is twa mair wee bitties o tape wi buttons to match the buttonhole on the semmit tape. That'll keep them up.'

'That's afa clivver. I nivver heard o that idea. My Mam jist uses garters.'

'Well,' said Granny, 'garters would keep your stockings up but we think buttons and tapes are better for growing legs. Now let's look at the other things. Have a look at the bloomers.'

The bloomers were a sight to behold. Wide, baggy and down to the knees they might have been but at the knees there was more pink ribbon and an edging of broderie anglaise. At the sight of this Charlotte clapped her hands over her mouth with joy.

'Like them?' Granny smiled at the child. Well did she remember her first pretty things. She had spent ages in the half-light sewing on the broderie anglaise and it was gratifying to see Charlotte's reaction.

'Oh yes,' breathed Charlotte. 'They're afa bonny.'

'Now let's get on. We've got two wincey frocks here for everyday wear, petticoats for underneath, chemises for extra warmth, and combinations to go under everything.' Charlotte's face fell when she saw the combies as they all called them.

'But they mak your legs afa sair up at the top.'

'Yes, but these are really quite soft,' explained Granny, 'and you need to wear them. All the children do. And we'll keep them really carefully so that they don't get hard and sore. And think of all the other bonny things. We could even sew some ribbon on the combies if you like. Come on now,' she went on. 'We haven't finished yet.' She took the rest of the clothes out of the kist. Charlotte looked in amazement. There was the Sunday frock: dark blue velvet, with a collar and cuffs on the long sleeves, long gathered skirt, sash round the middle and oh, joy of joys, more frills on the collar. Charlotte was speechless.

'Are you all right?' said Granny.

'A'm greetin again,' sobbed Charlotte. And indeed she was. It was a great deal for a six year old to take in at one time and Granny saw the need for a diversion.

'Come on, let's get you dressed,' she said, 'and we'll feel a wee bit more organised.'

It took a little while to get dressed as there was so much to put on and to make sure it was all in the right order. The buttons and tapes caused gales of mirth and Charlotte's cup was full when she found she was expected to wear frilly aprons or peenies over her dresses and a special one to go over the Sunday frock. When all was complete she stood in front of Granny and Katie for inspection.

'That's jist fine,' opined Katie, 'except for ae thing.'

'Fit's that?'

'Ye've nae beets on.'

'Neither I have. Oh Granny fit'll A dee?'

'Now Katie stop teasing her. Here Charlotte see what I've got here. One of my friends was going to Alford yesterday and I got her to bring us back two pairs of boots on appro.'

'What's "on appro"?'

'It's short for "on approval". And that means, a chance to look at something to see if it is all right before we buy it. So I have two pairs of boots here and we'll see which pair fits you.' She undid the parcel and revealed two pairs of brown boots with buttons up the sides.

'Now which pair is right for you?'

Charlotte had never tried on new boots before. They were admittedly a bit stiff but once she got her feet into the pair that fitted her and (with Katie's help) did up the buttons, she felt her outfit was complete.

But more was to come.

'I've got something else on appro from Alford,' said Granny. 'You need a coat.' Charlotte put on the button up coat which suddenly appeared and with it a tammy with a huge toorie on the top.

'Oh thank you. Thank you. Where's Granpa? I must show him.'

'Show me what?' said Granpa's voice. 'Mercy me, who's this fine lady?' He hugged her. 'You look grand. Now I must fly. Jock's been waiting for me for a while and I need to go. I'll be back at lunchtime. I'll leave you women to it.' He rushed out at a great rate. They heard him call to Jock and they were gone.

'Now,' said Granny. 'We'll just carry the extra things upstairs to your room and I'll show you where to hang your coat. Oh,' she remembered, 'one last thing for the moment' Here's your button hook.' She handed it to Charlotte. 'Now you're in charge of it and mustn't lose it as you'll need it every day when you put on your boots. You need to think of a place where you always keep it. You'll also need to learn to use it properly as they can be real tweaky things if you nip your leg with it.'

She turned, 'Katie, after all that my mouth is as dry as a bone. How about a wee fly-cup?'

'Richt awa. The kettle's on.'

46

Monday brought Charlotte's first day at school. The night before as if to emphasise the importance of the occasion she had yet another bath before her story with Granpa. In addition, Granny helped her lay out her clothes for the morning so that they would be ready for her. She had two frocks to choose from. Not the velvet of course, that was kept for Sundays, but two serviceable wincey ones, one a dark piney green and the other soft grey. After much deliberation, Charlotte chose the green for her first day. With it went a white peeny with gathered frills over the shoulder, black stockings buttoned with tapes to her semmit and the boots. And of course, all the undergarments.

The crack of dawn brought Charlotte leaping out of bed and dressing. This time she tried herself but Granny came in after a while and helped her with the last bits and the boots. Breakfast came and went. Granpa gave her a good luck hug and Katie solemnly handed over a very small tin box.

'Fit's this for?'

'Open it an see.' Inside was a small piece of sponge. Charlotte looked at it and then up at Katie. 'It's for cleanin your slate. Aa the bairns'll have een. Ye weet it and clean aff your writin.'

'Oh, thank you Katie. I didna ken aboot this.'

'And,' said Granny, 'You'll need a piece for dinner time.'

Katie picked up a small bag and showed her. Inside were bread, butter and jam sandwiches and an apple.

'That'll keep you going until half past three when you get home again. Now one more thing – a school bag. This was your mother's school bag and Granpa got it out of the attic and polished it up for you. What do you think?'

The bag was brown leather with carrying straps at the back. It was a shiny nutty brown – Granpa had worked hard on it.

'Wis this really Mam's?' Charlotte stroked the shiny leather. Knowing this was a comfort. Mam had been through this too.

'Yes, it really was. So anything you get at school like a book or anything else you can carry it in your bag and it won't get wet in the rain. Now,' Granny was watching the clock and wanted to get moving. 'Let's go. I'll walk you down the road to Towie.'

Chapter 9

Charlotte

I felt quite apprehensive that day as Granny and I walked from Trancie House to Towie where the school was. It was only a mile, if that, but there was still a lot of snow about and we had to watch where we were putting our feet. Granpa had offered us the gig with Jock to drive us but Granny said 'no, thank you'. For one thing, she didn't want to create more of a stir than was necessary. Everybody walked to school. For another, I had to get used to walking to school by myself and she needed to be sure that I knew the way. Fortunately we were by now well into February, St Bride's Day and Candlemas were well past, the days were becoming longer and I could see where I was going. What happened in the darkness of the back end of the year, I could find out next winter.

I was anxious though, about going into yet another new situation. I now accepted that I had to go to school but that didn't stop me wondering what it would be like, who would be there, would I make a friend, why was it all so important? With Granpa there to help before bed-time, I really felt that I could learn to read at Trancie House but evidently there was more to school than reading.

There was another thing bothering me. Granny and Granpa had not said anything to me about the way I spoke. I had been brought up to speak the language of the 'fairmtoun', the Scots my parents and all those round about me spoke. It was my first language and until the week before school when I went to Trancie House, I didn't think about it. However on the Saturday before school I was out visiting Jock in the stable where he was grooming his horses.

'Aye, aye, bairn.'

"Dinna ca me 'bairn' ony mair. A'm gaan tae the squeel on Monday.' Jock gave me a look.

'Aye, A ken that. Bit,' he thought a bit before he spoke. 'Ye'll need tae watch the wey ye're spikken.'

'Fit dae ye mean, Jock? Fit's wrang wi ma spikken?'

'Weel, A dinna richtly ken, bit A think ye hiv tae spik a bittie mair proper-like at the squeel.'

'Bit Jock, A canna spik proper. Fit is at onywey?'

I hadn't thought of this and although the conversation at the time moved on I remembered and wondered about it later.

At story-time Granpa said , 'What's the matter? You're looking like one of Mr Andersen's ducklings.'

'Granpa,' I said, 'Fit's wrang wi ma spikken? Jock says A'll hae tae spik proper. A dinna ken foo tae dae that.'

Granpa gave me a big comforting hug and said, 'Now, don't you worry about that. You'll manage fine.' And then we went on with the story. But the problem still lurked at the back of my mind.

The other thing that worried me was my age. I was six and a half. That was not old by anybody's standards but it was older than five, the standard age for entering school. Here I was the oldest in my family where I was someone, and starting school knowing nothing and where I was no one. I would be in with the babies. Maybe they would laugh at me for not being able to read.

So, here was Monday morning and along with all the other children we approached the school gate. I knew the building as I had passed it a few times but had never bothered to look properly. Now I looked. It was very grey. The walls were of grey stone which I later found out was granite. I also found out that little bits of it glinted in the sun – but on that February day there was no glinting. The roof was of grey slate. Attached to the school and built of the same stone was the schoolhouse where lived Mr Colin Coutts. He was known as the Dominie and was a very important man in Towie. He had been there for a long time as I remember my mother saying he had taught her. He must be very old, I thought, even older than Granpa. There was a garden at the schoolhouse but around the outside of the school end of the building was ground which was divided by a wall into two areas separated by a high wall. Judging by the occupants of these areas boys and girls were kept apart at playtime. There were also two doors for the school entering from the playgrounds. Carved into the granite lintel above each door were the words, 'BOYS' and 'GIRLS'. The doors themselves were big, heavy, imposing and painted dark brown.

As we drew nearer Granny said, 'Oh there's Miss MacHardie. She'll be your teacher I think.'

We approached the lady who was standing at the school gate. 'Good morning Mrs Grant,' she said, coming forward and holding out her hand. 'And this is Charlotte?'

'Yes, this is Charlotte.' Granny gave my arm a wee nudge. 'Charlotte this is Miss MacHardie.' We shook hands.

'Well then, Charlotte. It's good to see you. Now, who can I find to look after you. You must feel a bit strange on your first day.' She looked around. 'Ah, there's Mima. She'll see you right. Mima,' she called. A girl of about my own age came running up.

'Yes, Miss MacHardie?'

'Mima, this is Charlotte. It is her first day and I would like you to look after her please and show her how we do things in Towie School. Will you do that for me?'

'Yes Miss MacHardie.' Mima held out her hand to me as if to lead me away. I wasn't sure what I was meant to do. Granny came to my rescue. 'Go on Charlotte. It will be fine. I'll be back here at half past three. That's the time you stop for the day isn't it?' She looked at Miss MacHardie.

'Yes, that's right.' She turned towards us, 'Now off you go girls.'

I looked at Granny who smiled at me encouragingly. 'Have a happy day.' I suddenly felt all tearful again and bit my lips tightly together. I gave her a little wave and was led away into the playground with the school door marked GIRLS.

A few minutes later a bell began to ring loudly. I jumped and said, 'Fit is't ? Is there a fire?'

'Na na, that's the bell for makkin up the lines. See aa the quines are linin up here and aa the loons are linin up ower ere.' I looked and sure enough two long straggly lines were forming outside each door.

'Come on.' Mima grabbed my hand again. 'We must be there as weel.' We ran to the girls' lines and stood in twos. Both sets of doors opened simultaneously and at the top of each set of steps for girls and boys respectively stood Miss MacHardie and a man whom I could only guess was Mr Colin Coutts the Dominie. Miss MacHardie looked reasonably normal in her long dark dress with its high neck and pulled in waist. However Mr Coutts was wearing a long black gown and hood down his back as befitted his academic status. The only other people I had seen dressed in this way were the ministers of Glenbuchat and Towie. So, this was another thing to ponder. The Dominie was not wearing a clerical collar so obviously he was not a minister too but he did look very important. And why did Miss MacHardie not have a black gown too?

Mima pulled my arm. 'Stand up stracht,' she whispered. 'And mak the lines stracht. They shout if ye dinna.' Sure enough I could hear Mr Coutts shouting at the boys to straighten up, no talking in the lines, and get their shoulders back. Miss MacHardie looked down over our lines.

'All right,' she said. 'March in.'

The lines began to move as I moved with them I found myself over the door step and inside Towie Public School.

The first place we encountered was a porch with pegs for coats and hats. That seemed simple enough. I took off my things like everybody else and hung them up. From there we entered a passage from which opened the two classrooms. One, which had nothing to do with me at that time was for the bigger pupils and was the domain of the dominie. The other classroom was for the younger pupils who were taught by Miss MacHardie. It was here that I was to spend the next few years of my school life.

My first and over-riding impression was not what I saw, but the smell. I, who was used to the wide open spaces of the hills and fields of Glenbuchat, was initially almost overwhelmed by a mixture of aromas which combined to create one distinctive odour. This I never forgot and which became known in my mind as the 'school smell'. Other schools had it as well to a greater or lesser degree and even when I was older and a teacher myself I could not entirely eliminate it.

Firstly, the school smell encompassed an overall stuffiness. No gasp of fresh air was allowed to billow through those classrooms. The stuffiness was compounded by a fine layer of white chalky stour or dust which I noticed swirled up when Miss

MacHardie beat her chalk-duster on the blackboard. Chalk lay everywhere and pervaded everything and its smell got up our noses and hung there. When I looked for windows, they were there, but high up and firmly closed – even, it turned out in the summer. Then there was the smell of unwashed growing-children's bodies. At Glenbuchat we were used to a Saturday night bath but there was no real body-washing between Saturdays, maybe hands and face but that was all. No wonder the bath water was scummy and dirty. And if we looked on the weekly bath as the norm for us, there were many families around who did not even have that. Not only that, some wore the same pair of combies all winter.

Another item which added to the overall smell was the open fire, one in each classroom. I think Miss MacHardie looked after the fire in her room herself. Certainly she seemed to know all about it and occasionally when I arrived at school early, I found her chopping kindling and carrying in smaller sticks to get the fire started for the day. In addition to this, each child carried a peat to school every day and after my first day I remembered this rule and put my peat into the bunker sitting beside the fire. (It was said in delicious school gossip that some boys occasionally stole a peat from Mr Coutts' peat stack but nobody ever told. It was a very risky thing to do though. Definitely worth a thrashing with the tawse). Probably by itself the fire-smell would have been fine – peat-reek from a chimney on a cold night smells quite unique. However, added to the other smells it helped to clog up the atmosphere without adding a significant amount of heat to the draughty classroom.

And then there were other smells which joined in with the general oom: a sour smell which turned out to be milk. This was long before the days of official school milk. However, just occasionally for a big treat and if someone brought some milk in, we were given cocoa. Milk invariably got spilt and not properly cleaned up as it ran down the cracks in the floorboards and was left to sour.

The smell of stale food also was around. What became known as 'penny dinners' had just started in Towie in the 1880s. In our case this consisted of a pot of soup which a local Towie housewife made and carried into the school at mid-day. We each paid a penny for a small bowl of this soup: usually broth on Monday and Tuesday, potato on Wednesday and Thursday and pea on Friday. There was no statutory rule laid down at this time for feeding children at school. However the idea caught on and many schools were supplying soup for dinner by the end of the decade. That first day I did not have a penny with me but Miss MacHardie said I could have some soup and bring an extra penny the next day. The downside of the wonderful soup was the invariable mess and the subsequent addition to the school smell.

Just occasionally, someone would vomit in the class-room. The routine for this was well known. In a corner sat a bucket of sawdust and a shovel. Whoever was nearest the bucket ran to get it and quickly sprinkled the vomit with sawdust. This was supposed to eliminate the smell and make it easier to clean up. The whole thing was compounded, although I did not understand this at the time, by a lack of overall cleaning. The only time the floor was washed properly was after an occasional social function when the public hired out the school. The chalk dust was in such quantities that any attempt at dusting merely succeeded in keeping the dust in a sort of perpetual circulation.

As I hesitated at the classroom entrance, taking in the school smell, I felt a tug at my sleeve. I did not realise I had stopped.

'Go on,' said Mima. 'You're holding up the queue.'

I stepped inside and looked around. The walls were a fyachie green. I have since noticed that many school walls were this same sickly shade. Perhaps too much of this paint was around and needed to be used up; or possibly this particular shade was meant to be kind to the eyes. Covering some of the green were large shiny maps of different countries hanging from a picture rail running round the room. There was an extra large one called *'The World'*. It was dominated by countries coloured pink. I had no idea why there should be so much pink around until Mima informed me in a very important voice belittling my ignorance, that pink was for the Empire. What is the Empire? I thought, but, fearful of appearing still more uninformed, I did not ask aloud.

In rows to the back of the classroom were seats and desks for the children, about thirty in all. If we only knew it, we were lucky. To have two classrooms in a wee country school was a luxury not afforded to all. Some schools were built to accommodate a hundred children in one large room. The seats in Towie were set in pairs, clamped to cast iron supports and teamed in front with a narrow desk-like shelf for writing. On the order of the teacher this desk could be swung up into a vertical position and a book propped up on it. Under the desk was a space not unlike an unlidded wooden box, for storing reading book, slate and eventually, when one reached that stage, a jotter. On the top of the desk at the right-hand side (everyone was supposed to be right handed) was a hole for an ink-well.

But I had no thoughts of jotters and inkwells on that first day. Miss MacHardie told me to sit beside Mima for the day and gave me a slate and slate-pencil. I had no idea what to do next so I waited to see what would happen. Miss MacHardie moved to behind her big table-desk (with easy access to her drawer in which she kept essential items like her tawse), with her back to the fire and facing the children, who were by this time all standing shuffling at their places. She waited for silence. When the last boy had stopped rubbing his right shoe up and down his left calf she said, 'Good morning, everyone.'

'Good *Morn*ing, Miss Mac-Hardie,' chorused the class. What a funny way to say 'Good morning' I thought. It only took two days and I was saying it the same way.

'We will begin with Religious Education.' What is that, I wondered. Mima nudged me. 'Bible,' she mouthed.

'I to the hills,' Miss MacHardie moved to the piano and played the opening bars of the Tune, 'French'. The class sang:

'I to the hill swill lift my nies

From whence doth come my naid.'

I had heard this psalm in church so was glad to be able to recognise something although it did not make much sense to me. What, for instance did swill have to do with God? The singing ended and Miss MacHardie said, 'Sit'. The class sat.

'Now,' she said, 'the Bible. Let us begin at the beginning. Starting with you Alec, please, and then moving round.' Alec sat at the back of the class on the right hand side, a position indicating that he was top of the class for the moment. Seats were moved according to individual performance every week on a Friday afternoon ready for the following Monday.

Alec, stood up very straight and put his hands behind his back.

'In the beginning, God created the heavens and the earth.'

'Next.'

'And the earth was without form and void.'

'Next'.

'And darkness was upon the face of the deep.'

'Next.' The next girl could not say 'r'.

'And the Spiwit of God moved upon the face of the waters.'

'Next.'

'And God said, let there be light.'

'Next.'

'And there was light.'

'Next.'

And so it went on right round the class. They came to a stumbling halt at, 'The evening and the morning were the fourth day.' The very little children were not included in this exercise and I, too, because of my newness, was missed out. However it brought home to me the kind of thing that was in front of me. Apart from the reading and writing, I was going to learn with all the rest, large portions of *The Bible* which, even when I was an old woman would return to my mind time and again. Christmas Bible readings were very popular. Every December we all learned and repeated in the same way, St Luke's passage beginning 'And there were in the same country shepherds abiding the field, keeping watch over their flocks by night.' In between times there were the psalms to be learnt – the easier metrical for singing and the prose version for round the class. And woe betide anyone who stumbled or got it wrong.

After the Bible verses came instruction on *The Shorter Catechism*. Each child had a copy of the wee blue book 'prepared for the use of Schools' and as the new girl, I was given a copy as well. At the time I had no idea what it was or what it meant. However, I eventually found that it contained in all, 107 questions, each with its answer, explanatory comment and Biblical proof of its truth. Some questions contained 'revising questions' just to make sure the learner had retained what they were supposed to. Again Alec had the honour of starting and when Miss MacHaffie said to him, 'Alec, what is the chief end of man?' he snapped back smartly, 'Man's chief end is to glorify God and to enjoy him forever.'

'Good.'

And it went on. Every day we did a bit of the Catechism in the same way. I do not remember ever getting to the end of it in class although the older children were given questions to take home to read, learn the answer and write down what they felt it meant using Biblical references.

The rest of the day passed in a blur of different new experiences. My fears that I might be laughed at because I could not read, seemed unfounded. Because Miss MacHardie taught the first four years of the Elementary school together my lack of reading ability was not so noticeable. She handed me a reading book with words like 'cat' and 'mat' in it. I also had to learn very quickly how to identify the letters of the alphabet. They were set up on the wall and I spent much time in my early days at school learning the letters by rote and recognition. Some of the time she grouped the beginner-readers together in a standing semi-circle around her desk. We all liked it there as we were much nearer the fire and any extra warmth on a cold February day was welcome. There we read aloud in unison, trying to sound out the letters. Very occasionally Miss MacHardie called us out to read individually to her. This seemed at random at first until I observed that if she noticed anyone in the group stumbling over their words she called her out later to read alone to make sure all was well. She was very quick to notice things like that.

So, the mornings were full of sober subjects like Bible as everyone called it, reading, arithmetic and writing. Here the slate came into its own. I sat for what seemed ages with my slate and slate-pencil making rows of 'pot-hooks' until my squiggles were deemed good enough to make into a whole letter. Then there were rows of the letter and then after much practice I was allowed to write a whole word. In the end the whole lot was cleaned off with my sponge, wet, in theory with a little water. In practice, saliva proved to be an instant, if unhygienic way of wetting the sponge.

Afternoons seemed to be slightly more relaxed than the serious work of the mornings and probably by this time Miss MacHardie realised that something different was required. She would take down one of the big maps with a long hooked pointer and hang it on the easel so that we could see it more clearly. Then we would 'do' Geography which involved eventually a great deal of learning off by heart, facts about rivers, mountains, towns, islands and lochs. She also told us stories about events and battles of long ago which she called History. Sometimes we had singing. Not just songs, but learning how to read the tonic sol-fah, doh to high doh and back down, from the modulator which she kept rolled up in between lessons. I loved it. Singing was one of the best bits of school.

On that first afternoon, Miss MacHardie settled the older children in the class with some silent reading and called all the younger girls including me, out to form a group round her desk.

'Now,' she said, 'I think it is time you did some sewing and so I have prepared something for you.' She handed out to each a small piece of hessian material about two inches wide and eight inches in length. Each piece had been carefully prepared with its hem turned back and stitched so that we would not at this stage have to bother about the edges. I thought I knew what it was.

'What is it, Miss?' asked one very small girl.

'Do any of you know what I have given you?' Miss MacHardie looked round the group. 'Yes Charlotte?' She looked at me. I think she saw my spark of recognition.

'Please Miss,' I stammered.

'Yes, Charlotte, what do you think it is?'

'Please Miss, I think it's a bookmark.'

'Well done. Right everyone, this is a bookmark for holding your place in a book you are reading. Starting today you can sew your names on to your own bookmarks and, if you like, the date.'

I was so happy. Another bookmark and I could put the date of my first day at school on it, *and* I got the question right. All the other uncertainties faded into the background for a wee while and when half past three came I skipped skipped out with the rest to meet Granny as the late sun was setting over the hills.

But the biggest initial problem for Charlotte in school had not yet been addressed. She was entering school as a natural Scots speaker: Scots or 'Scotch' was her first language. School was an environment where Scots language was frowned upon and, indeed, to slip up and lapse into the vernacular was a punishable offence. This stamping out of the Scottish tongue was a part of a growing trend in Scotland and eventually was to change the way Scottish people lived, thought and spoke.

Of course Charlotte was not alone. However as she started school in the middle of the school term she felt at the time that she was the only child with this problem. Other children, possibly only at school for a short time, had quickly learnt by painful experience, the rule of English in school. To Charlotte they seemed a long way on from her and she became quite anxious about it.

Miss MacHardie was very aware of her problem. She had seen it many times as each child came into school and had to conform with the rule resulting from the 1872 Education (Scotland) Act. With the long-term purpose of equipping children for life outside their home areas, the Act laid down compulsory schooling, government inspection, and a uniform curriculum and examination system. In addition, the schools through their teachers were expected to give children appropriate linguistic skills to cope away from their own district. In the Highlands this policy contributed to the partial removal of Scottish Gaelic as a first language for many. In the north-east of Scotland the policy involved a crushing of the local tongue known to some as Doric and to others as Scots. Both Gaelic and Scots were replaced by English for teaching and eventually for many as the preferred language of ordinary communication.

Charlotte's first day at school passed peacefully enough. She spoke very little beyond her initial hesitant steps at reading, and the triumphant matter of getting the bookmark question right. At dinner-time she sat and ate her soup with Mima and the others and all was well.

However, as time went on her troubles began. The reading was no real problem. The words were printed out and she had to sound them with, if necessary Miss MacHardie's prompting. She came to grief when she was told to make up part of a group at the front and to answer questions about the subject at hand. Time and time again she gave the answer in Scots and had to be corrected. She lost confidence, hung her head and stopped trying.

Another huge problem for her was the *way* the children spoke English. They all came into school as Scots speakers and were therefore learning English as a second language as they went along. To make sure of making as few mistakes as possible their body-language when addressing the teacher included drawing themselves up to full height, very straight and tense with their mouths prepared for the English- speaking by working their mouths into affected pursed pouts. Charlotte had noted on her first morning the strange exaggerated way the children said 'Good *Morn*ing, Miss MacHardie'. It did not take long for her to notice that all English spoken to the teacher in the first class was articulated in this way, each word by itself with a gap in between. This was particularly noticeable in the younger group; as time passed the children became more used to the new way of speaking. But to begin with Charlotte listened and thought, Fit wey are they spikkin wi bools in their mooths?

Miss MacHardie understood the dilemma. She was a Scots speaker herself but under present circumstances would not have let any child hear a Scots word pass her lips. And, because of the rule, she could not let the children away with it either. So when Charlotte responded to a question with an 'Aye,' Miss MacHardie said, 'Don't say "Aye" Charlotte. Say "Yes"'. Or, when learning about the rivers of Scotland on the map one time, Charlotte said, 'Fit wye dis the river gang intil that sea and nae the ither sea'. This intelligent question had to be set aside while Miss MacHardie sorted out Charlotte's language. By the time that was achieved, the initial question was forgotten.

Charlotte was not totally alone. However hard they tried some children fell into the trap. They probably forgot themselves with the enthusiasm of telling the story, giving the correct answer. Like one wee boy who was relating the story of Adam and Eve. He had reached the point of Adam's temptation.

'Very good, Jimmy,' said Miss MacHardie, 'Go on. What happened next?'

'Please Miss,' Jimmy hesitated.

'Yes, Jimmy?'

'Eve said – she said, "Hey Adam, could ye go an aipple"?'

The whole class erupted with laughter. Miss MacHardie herself had to go into her walk-in cupboard until she had removed the involuntary smile from her face and Jimmy was covered in confusion.

Charlotte's language problems continued. She just could not grasp the English in school and her progress was made slower because of the constant stopping and correcting, not the answer, but the way it was made. Her friend Mima could not understand her. She aye spoke English for the teacher. It kept Miss MacHardie happy and Mima out of trouble. What could be simpler than that? And, you could always speak the way you wanted to in the playground. After all you had to learn to speak proper in this world, and she could not see why Charlotte would not co-operate.

After two weeks of not getting very far Miss MacHardie met Granny in Towie outside the shop one Saturday morning.

'Mrs Grant, I was hoping to have a word with you. Can you spare a minute?'

'Yes, of course. No trouble I hope. Is Charlotte behaving?'

'Oh, she's a dear little girl, but there is one little thing I'd like to discuss with you.' The two ladies strolled off, heads together in close conversation.

That afternoon, Granny sat down in the quiet of the kitchen. Both Katie and Jessie were out doing their Saturday afternoon visiting.

'Sit down beside me, Charlotte,' Granny said. 'There is something I need to talk to you about.'

'Aa richt Granny.' Charlotte plumped herself down beside her.

'Well,' Granny said, 'It's about the way you speak. You are here now and Granpa and I would like you to speak the way we do. I know in school you are not allowed to speak Scots and I would like you to try very hard to speak English. That's the way they speak in school and to make it easier for yourself you should try and speak it here too.' 'But, but, I am Scots amn't I ?

'Well, yes,' admitted Granny.

'And you're Scots, and Granpa?'

'Yes.'

'So why can't we speak Scots?'

'Charlotte,' said Granny, 'it's not as simple as that. Everybody speaks English.'

Charlotte found this very difficult. She knew Granny spoke English but, not of course with an English voice. Come to think of it, she had never at the time heard an English voice except for the laird and his family when they clattered through the Milton on their horses. The laird's daughter's horse had cast a shoe and she needed a bit of help. Although they knew what they were saying Charlotte and her sister Lizzie had spent the rest of the day talking to each other in pseudo 'Haw haw, Yaw yaw' in exaggerated imitation. So, that to them was an English voice.

Granny's English was much gentler, and scattered with Scottish words, Granpa's even more so. But as for everybody speaking English, well she felt that couldn't be correct. After all Mam spoke Scots. And yet, as she thought of Mam, she remembered only a couple of days before she left the Milton when Mam was telling the children that Charlotte was going to Towie, she spoke English to them. When she had an important message to get across like that, she said it in English. But she could speak both. She had gone to Towie school and must therefore (according to what Granny was telling her) have spoken English there. But now she spoke Scots up at the Milton. Did that mean you could speak English in one situation and Scots in another? Another thought struck her.

'But Granny,' she said, 'Katie speaks Scots.'

'That's quite different.'

'But why?'

'Just because,' was the maddening rejoinder which told her nothing.

'Anyway Charlotte,' carried on Granny, 'Please try and speak the way we speak here, will you?' She looked at her.

'Aye, aye,' Charlotte sighed. Then she collected herself. She hurriedly said 'Yes, Granny, I'll try, just to please you.'

From that point Charlotte made a noticeable effort. However she had already observed that her mother could and did speak both tongues, that the children quite happily communicated in Scots in the playground or other situations where no teacher was around, that Jock spoke Scots out in the stable and that Katie spoke Scots in the house (even to Granny who strangely enough did not seem to object). Thus, she was able, however unconsciously, to reinforce her earlier deduction that each language could be used for different situations and individuals. With this compromise achieved, Charlotte became happier and more settled. Her schoolwork became more confident, and day-to-day life at Trancie House carried on as though she had always lived there.

Chapter 10

By the time the summer holidays of 1888 arrived at the end of June, Charlotte was nearly fourteen years old. The last seven years had seen huge changes in her, not only in physical stature and looks but also in personality. We'll never know what she would have been like if she had been left up at the Milton as the eldest of six children in very poor circumstances. But in the gentler atmosphere of Trancie House Charlotte flourished and without recognising what she was doing, grasped the chances she was offered with both hands. Although the initial transition to Trancie House was a difficult one for her to make, it was probably done at the right time. She was young but young enough to accept the change. At the same time she was old enough to have things explained to her, to be reasoned with and to accept the chances that her grandparents and school and the combinations of these assets could bring to her life.

So, by this time Charlotte was physically quite small, just over five feet, slim, small hands and feet, long dark hair, tied back at the nape of her neck in the fashion of the day. Mentally she was ahead of most of her age-group even though she had started school later than most. This was in no small way thanks to the encouragement and help of Granny and Granpa who helped her every step of the way and Miss MacHardie and Mr Coutts who were well aware of her background.

Emotionally, Charlotte's strength of character had helped her through the first difficult days and weeks of transition. Perhaps part of the problem was that her character enabled her to hide her feelings too well. True, there were outbursts of emotional weeping like the time when she suddenly found herself about to be the owner of bonny clothes. But on many occasions Charlotte kept her emotions outwardly calm although she betrayed her inner insecurity by employing coping strategies like whenever possible having Beanie her doll near her, occasional nail-biting, although Granny gave her a manicure set of her own to help encourage pride in her nails rather than Katie's rough and ready cure – the application of bitter aloes – Katie said nothing else worked. Charlotte was always to be thankful to Granny for not allowing her to have to go through that.

Another sign of anxiety which small Charlotte displayed was to suck a lock of hair. Katie said she would grow a hairball in her stomach. Granny put the hair out of the way and said it was not good for her and anyway it did not look good for a young lady to be sucking her hair. They both worked hard in their own way to teach her as easily and practically as possible the ways of life in Trancie House. This included as well as their customs and mores and mealtimes and manners, simple housewifery, baking and cooking and other kitchen work so that whatever Charlotte might accomplish in the future she possessed a grounding in all the arts of home-making. Granpa too was there for her. He was, in a different way from Granny, confidante and mentor, teacher and friend.

Slowly Charlotte's developing confidence helped her eliminate the outward signs of insecurity. Her success at school meant she could hold her head up there and she quickly gained a reputation for hard work, speedy application and mental agility. You might think that this would not endear her to her class-mates. However, this was not so. Mima, Charlotte's first-day guide, remained her firm friend. Others in school quickly came to respect her for her ability and her modesty in dealing with the way she caught up and passed her peers.

The subject she liked best, particularly in the beginning of her school-life was reading. Charlotte took to reading like a duck to water. Once she got past the cat and mat stage, and learned the alphabet, she quickly learned the technique of sounding out words and then phrases. Soon she was flying through the reading books and if she could have got away with it would have read all the time at home. She quickly reached the stage where she would tackle most things. Her friend Mr Hans Christian Andersen remained a firm favourite with Granpa's evening reading time.

But Granny also turned up trumps. One day after Charlotte had established her lifetime passion for the printed word Granny took her upstairs to the attic of Trancie House and showed her what was kept there. Amongst all the old boxes and trunks filled with Goodness knows what all, there was an elderly bookcase filled with books.

'Whose are these, Granny?'

'They were your mother's when she was a girl,' said Granny, 'so, I suppose they are still hers, waiting for whoever wants to read them next.'

'Oh, Granny. Can I – can I take one out?' She could hardly keep her hands off the shelves of old books.

'Of course,' said Granny, 'Let's see what we've got here.' She started pulling out some of the books. 'Oh, I'd forgotten this was here, this used to be mine,' She held out a very battered volume. 'And here's another. Mary must have kept them all. Now it's your turn.'

Mam's books from the attic proved to be a godsend, probably for both Charlotte and her grandparents. She was just reaching the stage of always wanting more to read when Granny took her up to look at the books. From that point, Charlotte had a bookshelf in her bedroom and the books were transferred one wet Saturday afternoon.

Granny and Granpa helped her choose which would be best to read in order of difficulty and suitability. In this way she became early friends of Lousia M Alcott's 'March girls' as portrayed in *Little Women* and its sequels. And at around the same time, *What Katy Did*, and the other *Katy* books by Susan Coolidge were read and re-read. Charlotte was not a once-only reader. Once she had read and enjoyed a book she was very likely to take it off the shelf a few weeks or months later and read it again. It was amazing what she picked up second time around.

But Katy and the March girls were not alone. Another favourite was *Black Beauty* which Anna Sewell wrote as a protest against maltreatment of horses. Charlotte's blood boiled at the way Black Beauty and his horse friends were treated by 'masters' of all social classes. She went marching out to Jock in the stable to see if he knew about how some horses were treated.

'Weel lassie, fit's got intil ye the day?' Jock looked at Charlotte's firm mouth and flashing eyes.

'Jock, do you know how awful some people are to horses?'

'Fit wye div ye mean?'

'Well look, I've just been reading *Black Beauty* and the way some owners treat the horses, overworking them, and hitting them and making their harness too tight to pull their heads up – it's just dreadful. Do you know anyone who does that?'

'Well,' Jock considered. 'I dinna ken onybiddy *here* fit dis that. Ye see aabiddy kens aathin that goes on around here and they widna get awa wi it. But I suppose in the cities it'll haippen. The thing is, there's an afa lot going on in the toons and ye canna keep up wi aabiddy.'

'Isn't cruelty to animals against the law?'

'Weel, A'm thinkin they're trying tae mak it against the law. But A ken the book ye've been reading. A read it masel a whilie back and wis fair mad at the fowk in the book fit wis haird on the horses. Bit ye see, that's fit wye the wifie wrote the book. Tae mak ither fowk see fit wis gyaan on. And we're the ither fowk, ye see. And noo we ken aboot it and it aa moves the situation, and the 'be better tae horses' and aa animals as weel, a bit mair furrit. Div ye see fit A'm saying. We're helpin jist by spikkin aboot it. Noo we'll notice mair and mebbe we'll dee somethin tae help as weel. It's the same wi onythin. If you read aboot it or are telt aboot it then ye can dae mair aboot it.'

This, from Jock was a very long speech. Charlotte nodded taking in what he had to say. She looked over to the horses standing so patiently in their stalls waiting for their grooming to be over.

'Thanks Jock, I'll remember that. I suppose that applies to cruelty to anything.'

'Exactly. Even the insects deserve respect.'

That evening, during her time with Granpa , Charlotte reported her conversation with Jock.

'Jock's quite right,' he commented. 'What do *you* think?' He was always trying to push Charlotte further, make her think.

'Yes he is, but that must include children too,' said Charlotte. Her grandfather's face clouded.

'Yes,' he said. 'Cruelty to children is one of the worst sins we can commit.'

'Have you ever seen it, Granpa?'

'What?' he said. 'Where someone has been cruel to a child?'

'Yes,' she nodded.

63

'Aye I have. Cruelty done by parents and cruelty done by the State under a pretence of goodness. Even cruelty done by teachers in schools. Now,' changing the subject, 'What will we read tonight? Seeing we're on the subject, let's read a chapter of *Black Beauty*. Let's do the first one about his early days. The two of them settled together with Black Beauty in the field with his mother.

Charlotte at that time was eight years old. As the months and years went on her reading moved quickly to other popular Victorian authors. She early took to Charlotte Brontë's *Jane Eyre* and her dark hero Rochester although Granny shook her head and said she doubted it was suitable and did she not want something lighter instead. She went on to Jane Austen's *Pride and Prejudice* and *Northanger Abbey* and enjoyed the widening influence of George Eliot's *The Mill on the Floss*.

Her grandparents were glad that she should read so well and so widely. They did not want her to grow up into the restricted idea of Victorian womanhood where the automatic and only appropriate future for a young woman was marriage. This concurred with the current thinking that a loosening of the current bonds of the feminine role was necessary. It was very restrictive and in addition, it was in conflict with the reality faced by many middle class girls and women.

In the years between childhood and marriage only an affluent family could support its daughters as 'daughters at home'. Some women would never marry and either had to support themselves or take on a life of domesticity, housekeeping for male siblings or elderly parents or living with relatives as a maiden aunt. The Education Acts of the 1870s made education compulsory for all children, girls as well as boys. In addition further changes made education more formal. This helped the reform along and girls became better prepared for a working life after school.

Changes in education went hand in hand with changes in opportunities for female employment. 'Respectable' early Victorian occupations of governess, companion or needle-worker expanded as women in the last third of the century began to demand occupations which required not only school education but also further education in the form of training. So women learned to type, they acquired clerical and sales jobs (although their pay was naturally and conveniently less than that of their male counterparts) and gradually the professions of nursing, midwifery and teaching began to develop. This ethos also fitted in with the earlier ambitions of Phemie Shand of Towie Manse that women should be able to work independently and, eventually to speak in public. Even medicine, Granpa's dream for Mary, became a possibility for women after a long struggle.

So Charlotte's wide reading fitted in with the thinking of the time and, with. that of her forward looking grandparents. It was not all *Jane Eyre* and Rochester or Maggie Tullit's troubles in *The Mill on the Floss* although these books influenced her thinking greatly. Alcott and Coolidge's books gave a fairly conventional view of what girls of the day were expected to do although the rebellious streak in key characters Katy, and Jo March, indicates the direction of the current trend. Thus their authors appeared to be showing that women didn't have to settle for what was regarded as conventional womanhood.

Charlotte found another book on the attic shelves published earlier in the century in 1856: *The Daisy Chain* by Charlotte Yonge. This was again an example of 'girls' fiction'. It revolved around family life: a female, whether mother or daughter, was the axis around which the family's spiritual and moral survival revolved; boys but not girls went to school; and, the life of a woman was one of self-sacrifice. Granny knew the book well (it had been hers before it reached Mary's bookshelves) and was careful to point out to Charlotte that this book, although interesting and well written, was out of date with the wider thinking of the late 1800s. At the same time she and Granpa continued to stir Charlotte's social conscience by encouraging her to read Dickens.

In addition there appeared a new kind of publication in the shape of the girls' magazine. Earlier in the century philanthropists had produced religious tracts and periodicals with dreary long-winded preaching and moralising. The new *Boys'Own Paper* first published in 1879 and its sister paper the *Girls' Own Paper* 1880 were also published by the Religious Tract Society. However these magazines particularly the GOP turned out to be very successful. The GOP was not the only one of its kind. However it in particular seemed to reflect the mood of the time and the change and continuity in experience of young women and girls during the thirty years of its existence.

Charlotte had never seen it before Granpa brought her a copy from one of his committee visits to Aberdeen. Although this penny weekly originally targeted young women in their late teens, girls often a few years younger embraced its content with enthusiasm. It offered a variety of different aspects including fiction, articles about female education and women's work, fashion tips, ideas about home decorating and even an 'Answers to Correspondents' column. It was all packaged in a lively readable style together both entertaining and informative. Although its fiction still reflected the Victorian feminine ideal of filial and wifely duty and sweet femininity whatever the father or husband might be like, its non-fiction tried hard to put across that women could advance themselves in life through means other than that of marriage or home duties. Charlotte loved it and persuaded Granpa to order it for her on a regular basis. All the girls at school took turns to read it and even Miss MacHardie had been seen having a look at it.

But Charlotte's activities were not restricted to reading. Her grandparents and Miss MacHardie and, later, Mr Coutts saw to that. At school she tackled her other subjects with enthusiasm; she spent hours perfecting her handwriting; the early slate pothooks so laboriously inscribed with a squeaky slate-pencil graduated into words and sentences printed first and then written in joined-up writing on special jotters in real pencil and then pen and ink. This meant that she had to have ink in the inkwell on her desk, carefully filled by the ink-monitor of the week who was entrusted with the heavy glass bottle of 'Stephens' Blue Black Writing Fluid'. The label of this imposing bottle was also decorated with a Crown signifying its importance of use for the Public Service in Government departments and authorities. Charlotte was very impressed.

Having an inkwell meant that she required another small piece of equipment. On the day of her first ink-filling, Charlotte ran all the way home and burst into the kitchen where Katie was as usual busy at the range.

'Katie,' she cried, 'Can I hae a wee bittie o cloot fur the tap o ma inkwell.'

'Fit?'

Charlotte tried again and remembered how she was supposed to be speaking.

'Katie,' she said, 'I have ink in my inkwell now. But everyone has a wee bit of cloth to cover it to keep the dust out and I don't and if the dust gets in, my ink will get all stoury and then it will go on my pen and then my writing will get all spoilt.' She paused for breath. 'Please.'

'Aye, aye,' Katie stepped back from the range. 'Dinna fash yersel. Let's hae a look in the rag-bag.' The ragbag hung on a hook at the back of a pantry door. It contained all sorts of interesting bits of cloth saved from old clothes, cuttings from dressmaking and so on. Katie understood well that what the school 'inkwell-cloot' was made of and its colour was something of a status symbol especially amongst the girls. She let Charlotte rummage about in the ragbag until she came up with what she wanted – a piece of ruby-red velvet which had been part of an old dress of Granny's.

'Oh this is afa bonny,' she said. 'It'll dae fine.'

'Richt.' Katie was there with the scissors. 'Foo mony bitties are you wintin. Een and a spare? Will that dae the noo? Ye can aye get mair.'

So Charlotte moved into the status of being a 'writer with ink' – small beer to those grown-ups who did it every day, but an important step for a wee girl.

She also had a special copybook for practising writing in. This traditionally had four guide-lines in the writing space; the bulk of the letter went between the two middle lines; the outer two were to guide where the top edges of the letters had to go.

The style of writing used was known as copperplate, based on that used on copperplate engravings. So, for instance, capital letters reached the top of the outer guideline and if, appropriate, the bottom outer guideline as in the written capital 'G'.

Lower case letters had differing lines and levels to reach. Thus, 'a' had to be exactly between the two middle lines; also, for example, 'c,' 'e,' 'o'; but letters with loopy tops, like 'l' and 'b' had varying destinations for the loops; 'l' came nearly to the top line, but 'b' and similarly, 'd' had to stop at a lower level; on the bottom loops, 'g' reached nearly to the bottom line but not quite, while 'f' had loops which had to reach halfway to the top and bottom lines. In addition all letters had to start and finish correctly with appropriate starter up-strokes and finishing tails, and crossing-over points of loops had to be on the appropriate line. It all took a lot of practice and a great deal of time. Charlotte spent ages on it, both at home and at school. Punishment for not reaching, or going over the lines could be a telling off, correction marks on the book and, of course, more practice. In addition the pupils were marked on their accuracy, style, tidiness and cleanliness. (Miss MacHardie told all the children to wash their hands before taking their copybooks out at home. Judging by the fingermarks, dirt, crumbs and curled page corners it is probable that few did). Writing marks were reflected in the termly report. It was a very serious matter.

And there was arithmetic. At the time, all other subjects were dependent on the three 'R's: reading, writing and arithmetic. Early arithmetic consisted of adding and subtracting, before proceeding to multiplying and dividing. They all began with work on single numbers before proceeding to tens, hundreds and thousands. Each sum was taught in a prescribed way and no deviation from the method was allowed (even if one's parents argued that theirs was a 'better' way).

But the crux of all arithmetic was 'the tables'. These were, of course, the multiplication tables without which no arithmetical calculation could take place. Away beyond the multiplication tables were tables of, for instance, weight, length, volume and money (no decimalisation in Charlotte's day). Table learning was achieved by copying down, chanting in unison, learning again at home and round the class quick-fire answers (or not, if you were unfortunate) and, it has to be admitted, an element of fear of getting the answer wrong. Miss MacHardie was very loath to give the strap for getting it wrong. She was very aware that fear can turn the mind to a blank and had seen many a child's face frozen with big eyes like a rabbit's in the middle of the road when a gig's lamps bore down on it in the dark, because he couldn't get the answer out in time. For this reason she tried to exercise patience, took the class in groups to learn by rote, helped them copy the tables over and over, and even questioned some children individually to help them.

The same theories of learning by rote applied to spelling. The words were taken out of a graded spelling book. Miss MacHardie wrote them on the blackboard; the children wrote them down. They chanted: 'ess ee ee spells 'see'' and other words of like difficulty before taking the words home to learn. The next day they had to write the words down unseen and were marked accordingly. Spelling went on, on a daily basis, up through the school until the top class where they had to learn words which did not fit any particular pattern like 'accommodate' (two 'c's and two 'm's), and 'recommend' (one 'c' and two 'm's).

The three 'R's' created the base for other subjects. Charlotte enjoyed it all: the geography and history, English grammar, parsing of words and analysis of sentences. When Miss MacHardie took the class out for a nature walk she and Mima walked together, looking for special leaves, birds' nests with or without eggs or gorblins (surely the Powers that be could not object to a lovely Scots word like 'gorblin') wild flowers, identifying insects and birds, and having exercise at the same time. When they returned to school with their spoils, they had to record what they had seen, and often drew what they had brought back. Nature walks and drawing led to the study of basic botany later in Mr Coutts' class.

Exercise in school at the time was basic, military in style and probably not given the importance it deserved. These country children walked to and from school and many covered a lot of ground to get there. They played outside at playtime and they had their occasional nature walks when it was fine and when time permitted. Apart from that the children were drilled into straight lines before entering school and required to march in step into school. Miss MacHardie sometimes played a brisk march on the piano and the children marched around the class in time to the music. Very occasionally she would play different styles of music such as loud, soft, fast, slow, dreamy, stormy, and encouraged the children to interpret the music by their movements. But apart from this there was little in the way of gymnastics at the time. It was only later that sport and team-games were first permitted and later encouraged for older pupils with football, rugby and cricket for boys and netball and hockey for girls. With the backing of the gymnastic specialists of the early twentieth century the 'encouragement' soon became an authoritarian tradition.

Charlotte liked Miss MacHardie's piano-playing very much. She enjoyed the moving to different moods of music, she liked the singing, she even liked the challenge of the modulator. She wished she could play the piano but pianos were things that other people played – people like teachers, organists, grown-ups in entertainment groups.

A few children at Glenbuchat had lessons but piano-playing was not for the likes of the children at the Milton. There would not have been space nor peace to practise anyway. There was one in the best room at the farmhouse but Charlotte had never heard of anyone playing it.

This apparent lack of knowledge of instrumental music at the Milton was in contrast to the huge interest at the time in Glenbuchat, Towie, Strathdon and the surrounding parishes. Many of the folk could play an instrument particularly the violin and in the long dark winter evenings they frequently got together in each other's houses for musical evenings or, more formally in the village halls but, at village hall status, they were called concerts. Strathspeys, reels, singing – all were included and all could enjoy.

Charlotte had only once been to a concert before moving to Trancie House. It had been a late autumn evening and a concert was planned for the Glenbuchat Hall. Mam, who loved music, could not often go out in the evening. She always had too much to do, was too tired or, was nursing the latest baby. However this time she thought, why not? John came home in time to be with the little ones and she took Charlotte and Lizzie (who by this time were in a state of high excitement at the unexpected treat) and they set off on foot for the hall. The place was a-buzz.

'Aye aye Mary, fa hiv ye got here then?' The man at the door looked kindly at the two wee girls.

'Aye, Pete. This is Charlotte and Lizzie. It's their first concert.' Mary dug in her purse for the money.

'Its afa fine to see you twa quinies here. We need to get the little eens at the concerts. I'll tell e fit.' He bent over to Mary. 'Jist ee pey fur yersel. They winna tak up much space.'

'Oh Pete, are ye shair?'

'Aye, aye , think nae mair o't.'

'Thanks Pete.' Mary handed over money for herself and he gravely handed over their entry tickets.

Charlotte never forgot that evening. The hall was packed with laughing happy folk enjoying a well-earned break from the daily darg. That in itself was exciting. But when the artistes (that was what she was told to call them) came on Charlotte's happiness knew no bounds.

Charlotte

When the band came on at the beginning I just had never heard anything like it. I could only listen and wonder at the men and women with their fiddles, accordions, double bass and holding the lot together, the piano. It was wonderful. They played reels, strathspeys, slow marches, fast marches, jigs and waltzes. I did not know these names then but I could hear and feel the changes in tunes and timings. I could feel a tremendous excitement inside myself and, I wanted to be able to play something as well. But how could I? This was not something to which I could aspire.

After the band had done its turn there were others. A choir sang Scottish songs with the audience joining in the choruses. A young man marched on-stage solemnly carrying two real swords which he laid with a flourish at right angles on the floor. Then, a piper struck up the tune, *ghillie callum* and the young man executed what to me was an amazing dance over the swords. He did not touch the swords once. This was no mean feat as the stage floor was quite bouncy and we could see the swords shoogling with the vibration. The fourth fast step was so exciting that I held my breath until it was over before joining in the rapturous applause. The folk at the back were shouting, 'Mair, mair, come on, gie's anither,' and indeed, after he got his breath back the lad came on again and did the highland fling as what Mam explained to me was an encore. The choir sang again, a lassie sang with a lovely piano accompaniment, a man played the accordion which he swung dizzyingly back and forth as the tune swooped up and down, a fiddler did musical acrobatics (or so it seemed) and again, the wonderful band.

At the interval, folk got up and moved about. Some came down and spoke to Mam and even spoke to Lizzie and me. They asked if we were enjoying the concert but we were so overcome with our unusual situation that we hung our heads and couldn't answer. Then Lizzie, of course, said she wanted to pee. Mam sighed and said, 'Charlotte, would you be a very big girl and stay here and keep these seats for us while we go out for a minute.' I nodded my head. I had never been entrusted with such an important task before and I was determined to guard these seats against all comers. In the event nobody came except one old woman with no teeth who came up to me and cackled as I spread out my hands in defence of our places, 'It's aa richt quinie, A hiv a

69

seat o ma ain. Hae a Granny's sooker.' With that she thrust a poke of rather dubious-looking pandrops into my lap and went on her way.

Mam and Lizzie came rushing back just as the music was about to begin again. (Apparently there had been some difficulty with Lizzie's combies and a patch of nettles which her bare bottom was trying to avoid). I showed Mam the pandrops but when she heard where they had come from, she turned round, nodded thanks to the donor and then put the poke into her pocket for later disposal.

'But Mam....' I began.

'Wheesht,' she said, 'ye're nae eatin these. A ken that aal wifie and while she's afa kin', you dinna eat sweeties fae her. Ye dinna ken far they've been. Noo, settle doon. Here's the concert mannie again.'

And the compère (for such was his official title) appeared again to announce the first act of the second half of the concert. It was all over too soon for me and I never forgot that happy evening, so full of surprises and one which awoke a feeling in me which never left – I too wanted to 'play' and make music.

Chapter 11

At that time Charlotte was just five years old and this new ambition although it remained there in the background, was impossible at least for one so young and in her situation at the Milton. But there was one thing she could do and probably she made the connection at that concert: playing the piano was music and so was singing.

She had always been able to sing from an early age – all the children learned by ear from their mothers and fathers and on the farms from the bothy loons. So she had picked up quite a few bothy ballads from the loons at Glenbuchat. Bothy ballads were fun to sing and could be quite topical, political, historical and disrespectful by turn, sometimes very amusing and occasionally, very sad. They belonged to an old tradition in Scotland of home or farm entertainment to which children were exposed at an early age.

When she went to school she was exposed to more formal singing for the first time. This included not just singing in tune, but also attention to diction and breathing and, as she grew older, singing descant or taking part in other harmonies. Her earlier connection between singing and music making developed and so did her musical ear.

Charlotte knew she could sing. Not only that, she was able to listen to others and tell if they were singing in tune or not. One day she and Granny were in the kitchen baking scones and a sponge cake to take up to the Milton the following day. They were singing Charlotte's latest song from school which Granny had also learnt when she was a girl, *The Rowan tree*, when Charlotte stopped and asked, 'Granny, why are you not in the church choir? I really like your singing. And anyway Miss MacHardie likes it too. She said so.'

'Did she now?' Granny sounded amused. 'When were you talking about this?'

'Well, we were singing and she started us off with the piano and then she kept us singing and came up and down the class and listened to each one of us. She said I had a good voice and was in tune. She said I was like you, Granny, and that you are a good singer. So, if the choir is for good singers, why aren't you in the choir?'

'Well, Charlotte,' Granny considered her answer. 'It's all to do with what church choirs are for.'

'What do you mean, Granny?'

'Well, some say choirs are to lead the congregation when the congregation is singing. Some say the choir is to sing on behalf of the congregation, and certainly in big churches with big choral traditions and big trained choirs, I think they may have a point. And some people say that there is a place for the best and strongest singers to take their place within the body of the congregation to give encouragement to the rest of the people to sing but without drawing attention to themselves. And, I think this last opinion is the one that I go along with. So does that answer your question, Charlotte?'

'Yes, I think so. But why should it be important for the congregation to sing?'

'Well you see, singing was introduced after the Reformation in Scotland for the congregations because the congregations had no real part in church activity before this. Everything was done on their behalf. But when congregational singing began, they had something to do. See?'

'What was the Ref...Reformation?' Charlotte sounded out the new word slowly. 'I don't know about that.'

'Well, you won't have done it in history yet, probably, but it was when some people in the Church said they didn't want the Roman Catholic Church to be the main church in Scotland any more and they changed it. They stopped having priests and had ministers instead. But the way they had the church services changed too and the music changed as well.'

'Oh,' Charlotte said, 'so is that why you stay in the ordinary seats.'

Granny laughed. 'Yes, I suppose so. I just feel I should be there. Anyway,' she said, 'Talking of singing, do you like the singing at school?'

'Oh yes,' said Charlotte, her eyes sparkling, 'apart from reading I think it's my favourite thing. And, when Miss MacHardie plays the piano.'

'Hmm.' Granny thought for a minute. 'What about the piano? Would you like to learn to play?'

'What, me?' Charlotte's eyes widened.

'Yes, you,' Granny, stood up and wiped her hands carefully. 'Let's go through and look at the piano, (the baking will be fine for the moment) and see what you think. Wash your hands first. That's the first rule.'

She went through to the sitting-room and opened the lid of the piano. She sat down and ran her hands up and down the key-board. Charlotte came through with clean hands and stood watching.

'Granny,' she said, 'I never knew you could do that.'

Granny smiled. 'I don't play as often as I should. Come on, let's get some music out.'

Charlotte looked at the piano music but could not make head nor tail of it. The lines and black notes and strange symbols looked like magic to her untutored eyes. How could anyone make sense out of this?

'Here's *The Rowan tree*, said Granny, 'Let's sing again.' She played the opening bars and they launched into the song again, this time with full piano accompaniment.

'Oh Granny,' breathed Charlotte, 'that was great.'

'Right,' said Granny. 'Would you like to have piano lessons? The piano's here, you're here, Mrs Smith is just up the road looking for another pupil, Granpa and I would like you to do it. What's the answer? Yes or no?'

'Yes please.' Charlotte was overcome with excitement, jiggling around and hugging herself and she went over to Granny with tears shining in her eyes, and flung her arms around her. 'Thank you, thank you.'

'The best way you can thank me,' said Granny, speaking crisply to hide her own emotion, 'is to practise every day and do your best.'

'Oh I will.'

Granny, stopped, and sniffed. 'Mercy me, the baking.' They both made a dash for the kitchen and the forgotten scones.

'Are they all right?' Charlotte hovered anxiously.

'Well, they'll do. They're a bit hard-fired but I've no doubt the Milton folk won't complain.' Granny lifted the very hot, slightly over-browned scones from the tray on to the cooling tray. 'Let's have one now.'

Charlotte's piano-playing career started that week. Mrs Smith, already primed by Granny, supplied her with a starter's piano book and Charlotte carried a piano notebook with her to lessons in which Mrs Smith noted down things to remember, to do and how to do it, for the following week.

She was quite strict. She was a stickler for daily piano practice, and drilled her pupils on five-finger exercises starting to begin with, on middle 'C,' left hand, right hand, both hands together starting with thumbs and then both hands together in parallel movement. Other keys and scales followed, broken chords and, much later, arpeggios. And, in the beginning, a few very simple tunes like 'Baa, baa, black sheep' and 'Twinkle, twinkle little star' (with both hands) just to reassure the pupil that she really was progressing to playing real music.

Charlotte found that as her lesson time was at half past four Mrs Smith was usually taking tea at the same time. This involved an elaborate tray with tray cloth, bone china cup, saucer, silver teaspoon and knife, plate, napkin, milk jug, sugar bowl and of course the tea in a little pot and scones, and tiny sandwiches or pancakes, all prepared and borne into the music-room by Mrs Smith's little maid, a fourteen year old Towie girl called Gwen (quite an unusual name for Towie but the story went that Gwen's father had come from Wales and when Gwen was born he insisted on calling her that, as he said the name reminded him of his beloved hills and valleys of Wales). Gwen had not long left school and Mrs Smith was training her in the art of being a housemaid. The tea tray was invariably incomplete and Mrs Smith would stand and check its contents before saying, 'Well, what do you think you've forgotten today, Gwen?'

'A dinna ken.' And Gwen would gaze at the tray and think and think while Charlotte, her piano playing interrupted by this intrusion, would glance at the tray and try and catch Gwen's eye, and mouth 'the teaspoon' or 'the milk' without Mrs Smith's noticing. When all was satisfactory and Mrs Smith started on her tea, Gwen would retire to the fastness of the kitchen and Charlotte continued with her piano-playing. Invariably Mrs Smith stopped her for something. It might be a wrong note, imprecise positioning of her hands and wrists which had to be exactly correct at all times, a note played by the wrong finger, incorrect timing. And when Mrs Smith stopped her she had a tendency to speak with her mouth full of scone. One of Charlotte's abiding memories of her music lessons was the unavoidable spray of scone crumbs which came when Mrs Smith spoke over her with her mouth full.

To be fair, apart from such little foibles, Mrs Smith was a very good piano teacher. She was a Licentiate of the Royal Academy of Music, she loved what she did and she loved her children, and, they loved her. True, she kept a ruler handy for smacking undisciplined fingers, but this was rarely used. Charlotte looked forward to Wednesday which was piano day, practised diligently at home and made good progress which speeded up as her confidence grew and she could learn more musical 'pieces' as well as the five finger exercises and scales. Within the first year or two of starting, she, like some of her contemporaries, started sitting Music Board examinations which were graded from 1-8. It was all part of her development and very like the home-life of a child of educated professional people of the times.

But, a far cry from the fairm-toun life at the Milton of Glenbuchat.

Contact between Charlotte and Mam and Dad and her brothers and sisters at the Milton was, not a problem, but an issue which required attention from the start of Charlotte's life at Trancie House. It was important that Charlotte should not lose touch with her roots. It was also important that the rest of her family should respond to her need and in doing so continue to keep in contact for the sake of the family as a whole. At the same time, Granny and Granpa were keen to give Charlotte a settling down period to begin with.

So, a month at Towie had elapsed before Granny suggested a visit to the Milton. She and Granpa had visited, he when on his rounds, and Granny had gone up two or three times with some baking with Jock when the gig was free and whilst Charlotte was at school. One Saturday near the end of March dawned sunny and clear, most of the snow gone, except for the hills.

Charlotte and Granny were sitting in the kitchen enjoying a relaxed Saturday morning breakfast. Granpa was doing his Saturday morning surgery and Katie was in her room tidying her bed, herself, her room and anything else she could lay her hands on (she was a great tidier).

Out of the blue, Granny, said, 'How would you like to go and visit your Mam and Dad and Lizzie and the rest today? We could take some baking from Katie.' Charlotte, stopped eating and looked at her, thinking, hesitating. She knew this day had to come. She desperately wanted to see them all again. What was the matter with her?

'Would you like to go?' Granny's voice was gentle.

'Yes, but....' Charlotte hesitated. She looked up at Granny, the six year old face full of doubt. 'I feel funny about it'. Her eyes filled. 'I really want to see them, but, I'm frightened'.

Granny said, 'Look, you've been through a lot. Granpa and I think you've done really well, this past month. It's very difficult to go back to where you have come from but it's important for all your sakes that you do this. Believe me, the first time will be the most difficult and then it will slowly become easier for you. Your Mam and Dad

74

love you and have been asking how you are and asking when you were coming. We just wanted to give you a wee bit of settling in time here. But I think you should try now.'

Charlotte gulped and sniffed. 'Do you think they'll still like me?'

'Who?'

'Lizzie and Willie and the rest.'

'Do *you* think you'll still like them?'

'Yes, of course.'

'Well then, of course they'll still like you. They're dying to see you.'

'I thought they might stop liking me if I wasn't there.'

'Nonsense,' said Granny, 'you don't stop liking someone just because you don't see her every day.' Charlotte breathed a huge sigh.

' Could we go in the gig?'

'Yes. Granpa says we can have it.'

'Can I take Beanie?'

'Of course, I'm sure she'll enjoy the outing. And you can show off the frock Katie made for her.'

'Charlotte jumped up and ran over to Granny.'

'Yes,' she said, 'Oh yes. When will we go?'

'Right, let's get ourselves sorted. We can have the gig this morning and I'm sure Jock will be glad to drive us up.'

Later in the gig, Charlotte fell silent. It was a whole month since she had seen her parents and all her brothers and sisters. She was now at school, learning to read and doing lots of other school activities. Much had happened in that short time. She was aware, although perhaps only vaguely at the time, of changes taking place in herself. There was also the Scots and English speaking question which she was only beginning to accept. As she felt shy a month ago on entering Trancie House, she now felt shy and a little confused at the thought of this first visit back to the Milton. She almost asked if they could turn round and go back to Trancie House again.

Charlotte

There I was sitting in the gig with Granny, and I was afraid. As we trundled along I looked out at the familiar hills round about. Only a little snow now on the tops. I looked back and imagined Towie in the distance getting further and further away. And, in front, the Milton, where I had once felt so safe and now which I viewed with trepidation. Would they all still like me? I looked down at myself and saw the new me with clean shiny hair, new coat, boots and frock. Would they understand that underneath was still the real me? I held my hands tightly. Then I felt my clenched hands being warmly covered. Granny was there, understanding, giving me strength.

As if at a signal, I could hear the old bass voice rumbling away from the front of the gig: 'There's many a bonny lass in the toon o Auchterless / There's many a bonny lass in the Garioch o'…' Granny picked up the song and after a few moments' I joined in: 'There's mony a bonny jean in the toon o Aiberdeen, / But the flooer o them aa is in Fyvie o.'

Jock turned round on his seat. 'Better?' he asked. I nodded. 'Hae a Granny's sooker then.' He passed the pandrops back.

Before very long we were rumbling up the stony road to the Milton. Up past Easter Buchat, the road to Blackhillock entering the very glen itself where the Water of Buchat tumbled down to the Mill, we arrived at the Milton and its fairm-toun and in particular my family cottage. The gig clattered to a halt. The ensuing silence did not help my anxiety.

Suddenly round the corner of the cottage ran Lizzie, my biggest little sister, hair streaming, arms wide as she saw me, shouting, 'Charlotte, Charlotte, fit are ye deein sittin there. Come awa and play wi the kittlins.'

Everything fell into place. I looked at Granny, and said, 'Is that all right?'

'Of course,' she said. And, giving me one of her little shoves, 'go on then.'

I jumped down from the gig and Lizzie and I fell into each other's arms and hugged and hugged. We squealed and danced for joy. We stood and looked at each other. Lizzie held out a tentative hand, 'Afa bonny coat,' she said. 'And yer hair, fit wey did ye get it lik that?' I suddenly realised that she was as anxious as I was. She needed me to help her. I took her hand.

'Come on Lizzie, lets go and say hello to Mam and Dad and then we can gang an play wi the kittlins.'

We ran into the house where they were in the kitchen. All looked the same: the kettle over the range, Wee Alicky in his cradle – a bit bigger but otherwise the same cuddly bundle, the clothes off the line airing on the horse. And, Mam and Dad. I stopped, hopped on one foot, looking. Then, as they held out their arms to me, I ran to them and we were a trio of hugging, laughing happiness.

'Oh Lassickie,' whispered Dad, 'A've missed ye.' My heart gave a great bound. Lassickie. He called me Lassickie. He hadn't given my special name to Lizzie then. I was still his Lassickie. Mam just stood there stroking my head and looking over to Granny with tears in her eyes.

'Are you all right?' said Granny quietly.

'Aye,' said Mam, 'just a wee bit, you know....'Her voice tailed off.

'Yes, I know.' Granny put her hand round Mam's shoulders and squeezed them gently. 'It's difficult, but it will get easier now she's been back for the first time.'

Mam looked me up and down. 'Ye're looking afa weel. Div ye lik the squeel.'

'Aye, Mam, and, A'm learnin ti read noo. Ma teacher is cried Miss MacHardie and she's an afa fine wifie.'

'Weel, weel.' Dad sounded impressed. 'An A suppose ye winna be wintin ti spik wi us noo ye're at the squeel.'

'Dad,' I said, 'It's nae lik at ava.'

He laughed, 'A ken, A ken. A'm jist haein ye on.'

'Let's see yer frock,' said Mam. 'My, that's afa bonny,' as I opened my coat. 'Mind and dinna get glaur on't oot there in the byre.'

'Aye Mam, A winna.'

'A wouldna bet on't,' said Mam. 'Pit an aald peeny on the tap.'

'Come on Charlotte,' interrupted Lizzie, who now had a thumb-sucking snottery nosed, dumbstruck John, (the big baby) by the hand. 'Mam can we hae a piece please.'

'Here you are.' Granny was ready with her basket. 'And,' she said sternly, 'more stockings from Katie. And please don't leave them on the hill this time.'

'No Granny,' said Lizzie. 'Thank you very much.' And with that, we were on our way. I took off my coat, put on the old peeny and we all rushed off, pieces in hand, to the byre where the boys and the kittlins were waiting and left the grown-ups to their deliberations over tea and scones.

1888

That visit was the first of many returns to the Milton. Relationships were easy and friendly, Dad still thought of Charlotte as his Lassickie, Mam still sometimes wistfully stroked her hair, Charlotte still took Beanie to bed with her as company and comfort. But they all came to accept the situation and over a few months, on the surface anyway, it was as if this way had always been.

Over the years Charlotte changed, not in her feelings towards her family, but she developed from a little girl who started school late and unsure of herself to a young woman in no doubt of her ability. One fine Saturday in the early summer of 1888 when she was sitting at lunch with Granny and Granpa, Charlotte took a deep breath.

'I wanted to talk to you both about something.' She looked up and down the table at her grandparents.

'Aye,' Granpa said, 'and what would that be?'

'I'm really serious, Granpa,' Charlotte said. 'I was speaking to Mr Coutts yesterday and I think I would like to go on and be a teacher. He seemed to think it was a good idea. I've been in the little ones' class a few times recently helping Miss MacHardie, just to see what it was like and I really enjoyed it. And the wee ones liked me being there, I think.'

'Are you prepared for all the work involved?' asked Granny.

'Yes, I spoke to him about that too. If I don't stay on at school, I could leave school this summer. But if I wanted to be a teacher, I would have to stay on as a pupil for another two years. I'd have to do more Latin, Greek, Science, English and Drawing and carry on with my Music, and start on Algebra and Geometry. If I pass, Mr Coutts says he could probably take me on then as a pupil teacher working at school and studying after school. And *then*,' Charlotte paused, 'If I passed the pupil teachers' examination I could go to Teacher Training College in Aberdeen for two years. And then, if I pass that, I get to be a probationer teacher for two years, and *then*, I would at last be eligible for what they call the parchment certificate.' She stopped and looked at them. 'What do you think?'

'Well,' observed Granpa. 'You seem to have gone into it all very thoroughly.'

'Mr Coutts and I had a long talk about it. And Miss MacHardie too. They seem very keen that I should do it.'

'And what about you, Charlotte? Are you keen too?' Granny wanted to be sure that her girl was doing the right thing. As they watched Charlotte growing up, she and Granpa had talked about this (and indeed Mr Coutts had broached the subject to them) but they needed to hear Charlotte herself outline her plans and hopes and dreams. They needed to be sure that this was what she wanted to do.

'Oh, yes,' Charlotte's eyes shone. 'It's just wonderful working with the wee ones. And when they suddenly understand something, it's just great to see.'

Granpa laughed. 'There speaks a born teacher.'

'The only thing is,' Charlotte hesitated, 'it all costs money. If I stay on at school, for another two years, I won't be earning anything. And then If I am accepted as a pupil teacher the pay is not much, and then in Aberdeen I'd have to go into lodgings and there would be food and fees and so on. Maybe it's all too expensive.' She looked at them.

'Charlotte,' said Granpa. 'Don't be ridiculous. We don't want you to leave school now if you can go on and do something that you really want to do. We've thought this sort of eventuality all through. Don't worry about the money.'

'How can I ever repay you?'

'By working hard and making a good teacher and enjoying it at the same time.'

'Charlotte,' Granny said, 'is this what you really want to do?'

'Yes, it is.'

'Then go and do it. Granpa and I will get great joy from seeing you fulfil your ambition.'

'Thanks Granny. And Granpa.' Charlotte got up and walked round the table and gave each of them a hug. 'I don't know what I would have done without you.'

'Oh, you'd have managed somehow.' Granpa's remark hid his feelings. He looked across the table at Granny, his wife, partner and friend of so many years. They caught and held each other's eyes and smiled. Their last unexpected little one was on her way.

Chapter 12

En route for Shetland
1892

Charlotte relaxed with her cocoa in the warmth of the stewardess's blanket and let her mind wander. She thought about the big milestones or, she smiled to herself, the bookmarks in her life.

The first had been the move from Glenbuchat to Towie. How angry she had been and then how quickly Granpa and Granny had taken her and held her and given her the confidence to face the new life. True, it had taken a while: for the sense of hurt to go; the feeling of rejection; the pangs of jealousy of her brothers and sisters who were left at home.

To begin with, she also missed the freedom of the hills around Glenbuchat. A doctor's household was inevitably more formal, meals at set times to conform to Granpa's going out and coming in, and, in the dining room; baths in the bathroom (not forgetting the flushing watercloset); manners to be learnt; bed at an organised time. On the other hand, at Glenbuchat she was expected to help with each baby as it came along so her time was not really her own. Even when she was very small Charlotte remembered being told to rock the cradle to get the baby to sleep.

As she had grown bigger and the babies had kept coming, she thought, her baby-watching duties along with helping Mam with housework became greater. School seemed to be a place where other children went to, but not her. Until she went to Trancie House and Granpa marked the day with a first special bookmark on the first of their reading sessions. And, going to school represented another memorable bookmark in Charlotte's personal timeline and for her, was represented by that day's embroidered bookmark.

She remembered her first day. The people: Granny at the gate, giving her a wee confidence push on her way; Mima, her first school friend and with whom she had remained friends all these years; Miss MacHardie and her kindness; Mr Coutts in his long black academic gown; the giggling girls; the awkward boys. She remembered the pale green walls; the wall-maps with Empire pink patches; the desks; the peat fire; the ever-present school smell; the soup for lunch; the occasional mug of school cocoa when there was milk and sugar to spare. At this thought Charlotte took an appreciative sip of her current St Clair cocoa. The taste was just the same.

She also remembered the reading and writing, how reading had come to be her number one occupation, so much so that Granny threatened to ration reading time to make her go out to play. But reading became such a big thing in her life that even in the playground Charlotte sometimes sat with a book rather than play with the other children. She knew that Granny spoke to Miss MacHardie about it but Miss MacHardie just said, 'It's all right. She has catching up to do, and she's very determined to do it.'

There were so many important happenings. Her first piano lessons – she still kept all her notebooks written neatly by Mrs Smith, with the occasional crumb stuck in the pages from Mrs Smith's tea-times. And her first copybooks – Charlotte had saved them all. The inkwell covers were important too. Charlotte smiled when she remembered Mima's desire to have a bit of the red velvet from the Trancie House ragbag for her inkwell too. That was a real status symbol.

Another important day (she didn't have a tangible bookmark for it but she felt as though she did, she remembered it so well) was her first return to the Milton. How scared she was and what a happy time they had. Because of that day all her other returns to the Milton were happy and she liked to think that perhaps she had been influential in getting Lizzie and then the others when their time came, off to school. Certainly Lizzie started at Glenbuchat School not long after that first visit.

In what seemed no time at all she was nearly fourteen and it was the last day of the school year. Many of the children left school at this point. But Charlotte's ambition to be a teacher which had been growing steadily over the years meant that she did not leave school then although, as she thought back that last day of term was indeed another bookmark day with another real bookmark to record the day. As Dux of the elementary part of the school she received on prize-giving day, a book-prize and inside a bookmark inscribed with the date and her name.

She smiled in her sheltered corner of the St Clair as she remembered that day. Granpa and Granny were there smiling and proud (fortunately no-one was in labour although Annie the midwife called for him in the afternoon.). Very importantly too, Mam and Dad made the journey from the Milton, accompanied by Lizzie in what looked like a new hat. Charlotte was not sure if they were coming or not and her heart leapt as she saw them arrive at the school gate.

'Dad, Mam, Lizzie, you came.' Her lips trembled and she pressed them tightly together.

'Aye, aye, Lassickie, we couldna miss this: ma dochter the squeel Dux. Man, A canna get ma caip on the day, A'm that fair awa wi masel.'

Mam found it difficult to speak, just held her closely in a warm hug. Lizzie, growing tall now, stood straight and serious, well aware of the importance of the occasion. She smiled at Charlotte.

' Weel deen, big sister; dinna get ower far awa fae me noo.'

' Lizzie, as if I would. We'll aye be best friends. Let's wish for that.'

The two sisters stood together, linked fingers and intoned together:

'Pinkie ti pinkie, thumb ti thumb,

Wish a wish, it'll surely come'.

The daftness of the wishing rhyme broke the emotional atmosphere and they all laughed.

'Bairns to the end,' said Granpa. 'Come on, let's go in.'

There were days in the following two years when Charlotte wondered what she had taken on. The extra subjects were a big struggle especially Algebra and Geometry. Charlotte, not a born mathematician, turned to Granpa in despair. He, in turn, delighted in returning to the old equations, theorems, diagrams and calculations. Examination days came and went and Charlotte passed in the summer of 1890. That August she became officially a pupil-teacher.

Charlotte thought back to that other first day. Although she was going to her own school, this was in a different capacity. Now, she was almost a member of staff. Not quite staff-room status, but Miss MacHardie found her a wee cubby-hole of a room with a tiny window to hold her own things. Charlotte loved her space here and soon its shelves were covered with books, notes to herself, notes on teaching methods, teaching plans which Miss MacHardie showed her how to do, different grades of reading books, children's copybooks (marked and unmarked), ink, pens, pencils, spare slates and slate-pencils, chalk, dusters and all the rest of a primary teacher's paraphernalia.

She worked all day in school (undertaking to teach from three to six hours per day). Her contract which was signed between the Towie School Board and her grandfather as surety, allowed her in return for her teaching time, £16 in her first year and £20 in the second. In addition, she received five hours a week instruction in teaching after school hours. This was a laid-down requirement by the 'Scotch' Education Department but one which Miss MacHardie gave gladly. Having known Charlotte from the beginning of her difficult start at school she now looked on her as her protégé and did all she could to help.

Charlotte did most of her teaching as a pupil teacher with Miss MacHardie. This was partly because of her youth. After all she had only recently been a contemporary of many of the children in Mr Coutts' class. The little children looked up to her even then and this made the transition from helper to official pupil teacher in the wee ones' class much easier. Another reason for Charlotte's main place of work being with Miss MacHardie was written in the conditions of service:

Candidates had to be of the same sex as the teacher they served, though in a mixed school girls were allowed to work with a master so long as some respectable woman, approved by the managers, be invariably present during the whole time that such instruction is being given.

(Scotland J, 1969 *The History of Scottish Education* Vol 2 Edinburgh, 105.)

How Granpa had laughed when he read that bit. However the narrow minded rule was there and had to be obeyed, to begin with at any rate, until Mr Coutts found a way

81

round the problem. By the time Charlotte was looking for experience with the older children in Mr Coutts's class she was in her second year. Her reputation for reliability and good teaching was well established amongst the pupils, the teachers, and, with the members of Towie School Board. Mr Coutts reminded the Board how well Charlotte was doing but that she required teaching experience with older children and this would need to be in his classroom. To comply with the rule of having a 'respectable woman' present he suggested that the doors to the classrooms be left open so that Miss MacHardie could be aware, from her classroom of what was happening in Mr Coutts's domain.

The Board, after some deliberation agreed. 'After all,' said one elderly member, 'we do not want to be seen to be flouting the 'Scotch' Education Department's rules do we'.

'No,' said another, 'but Miss Gordon has only recently come from Mr Coutts's class as a school pupil. I don't remember any fancy rules about male teachers and girl pupils then, or now for that matter. I think we should let them get on with it.'

'Aye, aye,' rumbled the rest of the group. And so it was that Charlotte Gordon and Mr Colin Coutts worked together for much of Charlotte's last year as a pupil teacher – with the doors open.

The pupil teacher's exams came and went. Charlotte was sure she had failed. She still found Algebra very difficult and knowledge of characters such as Xenophon and Livy along with the ability to translate pieces of Latin prose took up much time as well as learning how to teach basic subjects. She knew her on-going reports were very good but what about the examination marks? Her grandparents and mentors just smiled and said, 'Wait and see. It will be all right.'

And in June 1892 Charlotte received through the post the all-important brown envelope containing the Pupil Teacher's Certificate. This imposing document set out a record of her entire course over the previous two years and was signed by the Chairman of the School Board, the Convenor of the Pupil Teachers' Committee, the Clerk to the Board and the Headmaster of Towie School, Mr Colin Coutts.

Charlotte watched the dawn from the St Clair and remembered that day. How pleased everyone had been for her. Katie made her favourite pudding, Jock gave her a delighted smile when she waved her certificate at him in the stable (he would have hugged her but decorum precluded such closeness), Granpa and Granny could not keep the smiles off their faces and the folk at the Milton – well Mam cried for joy and Dad whispered, 'Weel deen, my Lassickie' as he hugged her.

And then it was off to Aberdeen and more 'well dones' came two years later when Charlotte qualified as a teacher from the Free Church Training College in Aberdeen. This had been quite an ordeal. The College was fine. It was one of two Teacher Training Colleges in Aberdeen: the other one was run under the auspices of the Church of Scotland. It was fully booked by the time Charlotte made application for entry and she was glad to get a place at the equally well known Free Church College.

Charlotte enjoyed her College days. She was well-prepared after her two years as a pupil teacher at Towie and was well ahead of the class. She quickly realised what high standards Mr Coutts and Miss MacHardie had set her as a pupil teacher and was glad with hindsight that they had made her work so hard. It paid off when she reached Aberdeen.

The drawback was that she had to live in lodgings in Aberdeen during the term. All students' lodgings were recommended and vetted by the College. Mrs Ainslie's house situated near the College seemed ideal. Mrs Ainslie, a widow, had been letting rooms to students since her husband's death five years before. At full capacity, she took six students, all women, two to each of her three bedrooms to let. It sounded fine.

When she arrived at Aberdeen Joint Station on the train from Alford Charlotte collected her luggage from the guard's van and headed for the row of small carriages outside the station.

'Aye, that'll be anither new een,' when she told the driver where she wanted to be taken. She gave a smile. He was quite friendly but seemed to know everything. He claiked all the way along the road about the College, students he had transported and lodgings he had found out about. He asked the name of Charlotte's new landlady.

'Mrs Ainslie.'

'Oh her,' he said. 'A ken her fine. Afa gweed at the bakin bit watch oot fur her tongue. It wid cut onythin.'

Charlotte's heart sank. 'Here we are noo.' The carriage whirled round a corner and pulled up smartly in front of a terraced house with gleaming brass plate on the door inside a small front garden. The door stood open. At the sound of the carriage, a busy figure came forward bearing an official looking paper.

'Good afternoon. I'm Mrs Ainslie. And you are Miss…?'

'Gordon,' supplied Charlotte. 'I'm Charlotte Gordon.' She held out her hand 'How do you do?' Her hand received a brief acknowledging shake.

'Now,' said Mrs Ainslie. 'Driver, please bring the luggage in.'

'Aye aye, Mam.' The driver gave Charlotte a look of complicity behind Mrs Ainslie's back and dragged Charlotte's case from the carriage.

'Oh let me help.' She moved to give him a lift with the case.

'Na, na, lassie, tak the wee bag yersel, an we'll be fine.'

He dumped the case inside the hall and accepted his fee with a hearty, 'That's fine noo, aa the best. Cheery bye.' With that he was gone.

'Now, Miss Gordon,' Mrs Ainslie stood with her paper. 'You are in room number three with Miss MacDonald. She has not arrived yet. She's coming from further up north. I'll show you where to go.' She marched off up the stairs leaving Charlotte to grapple with her cases. Mrs Ainslie watched her from the top of the stairs.

'Right,' she said. 'Is that it? Now here is your room.' It was reasonably sized with two single beds, looked out over the street and furnished enough. Not luxurious by any means thought Charlotte wryly thinking of her bedroom at Trancie House but it'll do. I'll soon get a picture on the walls and my things will make it homey. Barely had the thought come into her head when Mrs Ainslie said, 'And I do not like too many fripperies around. You are here to work, not to waste time and while I am here I'll give you a list of the House Rules. She handed over another paper headed by 'House Rules'.

'Thank you.' Charlotte ran her eyes over the list. Breakfast at eight am seemed all right but then she noticed that if you were more than five minutes late you did not get any. High tea was at six pm; again there was no excuse for lateness. Baths were on a strict rota – to be arranged by Mrs Ainslie. And, everyone had to be in by nine pm, even at weekends. No food was allowed in the bedrooms. And so on.

Charlotte was unpacking her clothes and books when she heard voices on the stairs. Mrs Ainslie's voice laying down the law and a lighter, brighter one. As the bedroom door opened Charlotte heard Mrs Ainslie say... 'and, I do not like people answering me back.' The door opened wide and a girl of about twenty, tall, slim with curly red hair and a big smile came in.

'Hello,' she addressed Charlotte. 'I'm Kirsty MacDonald. I'm told I'm in here with you.'

'Miss Gordon,' said Mrs Ainslie, 'this is Miss MacDonald. Miss MacDonald, Miss Gordon.' The two girls shook hands gravely. 'Now,' continued Mrs Ainslie, 'high tea is at six. Please do not be late. The bathroom is down the corridor. Please leave it as you would like to find it. And, please do not make a noise. We all have to live together and that is why...' she looked meaningfully at Kirsty, 'we have Rules.' She went out, closing the door behind her with a click. The girls looked at each other.

'What was all that about?' said Charlotte.

'Well,' said Kirsty, 'She just handed me the House Rules and I made a few comments about them and the old bat didn't like what I said. Oh well, that'll be me in the black books for ever.'

'Well never mind now,' Charlotte said. 'Look I've chosen this bed. Are you happy with the other?'

'Yes, no problem.' Kirsty looked around. 'This place needs brightening up. Pictures and so forth. But,' she consulted the Paper, 'ah, Rules I suppose. What, only seven items on the dressing-table? That's daft. Do you mean she comes up and counts them?'

'I expect so. Come on. Let's finish unpacking before tea.'

Tea, as long as you got there on time was mercifully, well-cooked good food. The taxi-driver was right about Mrs Ainslie's baking. Charlotte found during her whole two years in Mrs Ainslie's house that the food was invariably good, wholesome and well-cooked. Being Aberdeen they consumed a lot of fish; also some meat, vegetables from the garden, puddings and home baking of the highest quality. But Mrs Ainslie herself was unbending, rule-bound and clock-watching.

It was only in the last few weeks of Charlotte and Kirsty's final term when they could see a few cracks appear in the hitherto stony surface. It was May and the girls were working late in their room for their final examinations which were to take place the following week. A light tap came to the door. They looked at each other. Surely Mrs Ainslie was not going to tell them off again for working late. But this time, the head came round the door and, 'Girls,' Mrs Ainslie said, 'you must be very tired, would you like some cocoa?'

'Well, thank you.' Kirsty was the first to respond.

'I'll make some.'

'Thank you,' said Charlotte. 'But Mrs Ainslie…'

'Yes?'

'Why don't you have some too and have it up here with us. We could do with a break.'

Mrs Ainslie's face broke at last into a genuine smile. 'All right, she said. I'll be back in a minute.'

The girls looked at each other. 'What's going on?' whispered Kirsty. 'I've never seen her like this before.'

'Don't know. Let's see what happens.'

A few minutes later the landlady was back with three mugs of cocoa. They sat sipping.

Charlotte broke the silence. 'This is really nice. Thank you. We were ready for it.'

'Yes,' said Kirsty. 'We're just at the last set of revisions, I hope. You came in just at the right time Mrs Ainslie.'

'You know,' said Mrs Ainslie, 'I wish I'd got to know you two better before now. Yes, I know,' she said as Charlotte made to speak. 'I know you've been here nearly two years but I have held you all at arm's length for so long. I'm sorry, I didn't mean it.' Her eyes filled. 'It's just, well I missed my husband so much when he died , the only way I could cope was to fill it with work and rules and keep my defence up. And then you two came along and instead of being rude like some of the others you've just gone along with things. And I just wanted to say thank you before it's too late and you go away.'

'Mrs Ainslie,' Charlotte put out her hand. 'I'm so sorry. We had no idea you were so sad inside. I'm glad you have told us. What can we do to help?'

'Just carry on being yourselves. I really have wanted to be friendlier with you all but, well, maybe it will be easier now.' She heaved a sigh. 'It's been nearly seven years now, since he died, I mean. Maybe now I can move on a wee bit myself.'

'I hope so,' said Kirsty.'

'Yes,' Charlotte said, 'and thank you for taking us into your confidence.' Mrs Ainslie smiled at them both. 'You're good, both of you. You'll do well.'

The exams came and went. The students went about for an anxious month wondering what they would do and how they would break the news to their families if they failed. At the same time they had to think of the future. The end of one school year heralded the beginning of the next after the summer holidays. Custom decreed that the lists of final year students' names were put on the main Notice Board. Against each name were the names of two schools which had been registered with the Education Department as requiring a new teacher. As the lists went up the students crowded round to see their fate. Charlotte looked.

'Lawrencekirk,' she said, 'or Jarlshavn.'

'Where are they?' asked Kirsty looking at her own choices – Midmar and Brora.

'Lawrencekirk is in Kincardineshire, down the coast from Stonehaven, but Jarlshavn, it's in Shetland. I'd have to go on the boat.'

'So?'

'Well, it's a long way.'

'Think of the adventure, the exploration into somewhere you have never been before. I think you're really fortunate getting that chance to go somewhere different.'

'What will you do?' asked Charlotte.

'Well, I think I'll go for Brora. It's further north than my home on the Black Isle but I haven't been there before and they say it is lovely. Go on you should try Jarlshavn. Here let's have a look on the big map.' For once Shetland was in its proper place – well to the north.

'Overnight on a boat for you,' said Kirsty cheerfully.

'We-el...'

'Oh come on, you'll love it. And they'll love you. Let's go and sign up now.'

So, here she was, overnight on the boat. Charlotte stretched her cramped limbs. The sun was fully up now. The stewardess came bustling round her again.

'All right, are you?'

'Yes, thank you. And, thanks for the cocoa.'

'That's all right. Now you see we are just going past Sumburgh Head. That's the southernmost point of Shetland. When we see that, we're nearly there, or, at least not that far away. Do you want some breakfast.'

Charlotte realised she was very hungry. She ran down the companionway, back to her cabin and dressed properly, nodding 'good morning' to her sleepy cabin companion on the way. Ship's porridge and milk went down well with floury baps and tea. And then it was up on deck to watch Lerwick harbour growing nearer as the St Clair slipped into the Sound of Bressay.

Suddenly she felt nervous again. What was she doing? How was she to get to Jarlshavn? Would there be anyone there to meet her?

The St Clair drew nearer the harbour. Men put out fenders and a gentle bump told her that they were alongside. A flurry of activity next: rattling of anchors; gangways in place; luggage being carried ashore; animals being hoisted from ship to shore; passengers disembarking.

Charlotte carrying her overnight bag stepped carefully down the gangway. She looked down at the small crowd which had gathered on the pier. Would someone be there for her? She reached the ground and looked about her. People were meeting and greeting. She stood, uncertain, hesitant. Suddenly, a figure pushed through the crowd.

'Are you Miss Gordon?' A strong Shetland voice, different from what she was used to, not unpleasant, just different.

Charlotte turned to meet the voice. A male figure, not tall, striking blue eyes, a bit older than her, wearing what Charlotte was to learn later was a harbourmaster's hat. He lifted it courteously.

'Yes,' she said. 'I'm Charlotte Gordon.'

'That's grand. I'm glad I found you so easily. Sometimes it's easy to miss someone in a crowd. I'm Alexander Sinclair. I've come to meet you and to welcome you to Shetland. I live in Jarlshavn and am on the Jarlshavn School Board. This is my son, Magnus.' He introduced with some pride the boy standing beside him.

'How do you do.' Charlotte shook hands with both of them. 'Thank you very much for coming to meet me.'

'No problem. Our pleasure.' Alexander Sinclair cast his eyes around. 'Now where's your box?' All the luggage was on one corner of the pier. The pile was diminishing rapidly as owners claimed their boxes.

'There's mine,' said Charlotte. 'The brown box with the blue markings on it.'

'Right, come on Magnus.'

She quickly found herself sitting in the back of the gig with the Sinclairs up front. Not much was said, Magnus threw her a friendly smile every now and again but that was all. Charlotte began to wish for Jock and his granny's sookers. But the six miles to Jarlshavn were soon over and they drew up in front of a middle-sized house on the foreshore of the village of Jarlshavn.

'Here we are – this is where we live. Welcome to Harbour House. We thought you might like to meet my wife and have some lunch before going to see your schoolhouse.'

'Well, thank you very much.' Charlotte had not expected this. One bit of her was really looking forward to seeing her new home. On the other hand she was interested in meeting the people of this new place that she had come to. She was going to be the teacher; they were going to have to work together. Also at that moment she knew nobody. Meeting the Sinclair family was a good start. And, of course, they wanted to get to know her.

'There's Margery waiting at the door.' At the door holding the hand of a very small girl stood Alexander's wife. Charlotte's first impression was of someone who looked so frail that a gust of wind would blow her down. She got down from the gig and stepped forward.

'How do you do. I'm Charlotte.'

The hand she held was thin but the face although also thin and pale had a welcoming friendly smile.

'Hello, Charlotte. Can I call you Charlotte?'

'Of course.'

'And I'm Margery. Just call me that. Let's not be formal.'

As if to add weight to her words, Magnus leapt off the gig and picked up the wee girl to whirl her through the air.

'And this,' he said, 'is Christina, my sister and best friend.'

'Hurray-y Magnie,' shouted the small girl. She looked up at Charlotte. 'Who are you?'

'This,' said her mother, 'is Miss Gordon.' She looked at Charlotte. 'She must call you that. You'll be teaching her when she gets to school.'

Charlotte, bent down and took Christina's hand.

'Hello, Christina. How are you?'

'Fine, thank you. See my doll?' She held out her doll for inspection.

'She's lovely,' commented Charlotte gravely. 'I like her clothes too. I have my doll in my box. I'll show you soon if you like.'

'Come in,' said Alexander. 'Don't stand on the door step. 'We'll leave your box there for the moment and I'll take you up to the schoolhouse afterwards.'

'Thanks very much. I really appreciate this.' Charlotte stepped into the house with him.

'Lunch is ready,' said Margery. 'You must be hungry.'

Suddenly Charlotte found that she was, even after the St Clair porridge.

'It must be the Shetland air,' she said. 'I am.'

So it was that Charlotte arrived in Shetland and made her first Shetland friends. At the time none of them had any idea how closely their lives were to be entwined. They only knew that they liked the look of each other. The teacher: and the father and school board member; the mother, soon to be her close friend and confidante; the son who came to care for her so deeply; the daughter who came to rely upon her so much.

Chapter 13

Jarlshavn
1894

Charlotte arrived in Jarlshavn on 16 August 1894. That afternoon after lunch Alexander Sinclair in his official capacity as a member of Jarlshavn Public School Board escorted her accompanied by Magnus and Christina (who insisted in going too) to her Schoolhouse (known in the village as Da Peerie Skulehoose as it was the house provided by the Board for the second or junior teacher).

As they walked up the front path between well-tended flower borders to the front door Charlotte felt she was walking into a dream. Could this really be for her? This little house with its harling so clean and whitewashed, sitting in the sunshine?

'Just you wait,' said Alexander, 'It's fine now but just enjoy it while it's here.'

They approached the door; it opened at once. A young girl stood there.

'Now then Edie,' Alexander said. 'Is everything ready?'

'Yes sir.' Edie turned to Charlotte.

'This is Miss Gordon.'

'Very pleased to meet you.' Edie bobbed a curtsey at Charlotte.

'How do you do Edie?' Charlotte smiled at the nervous-looking girl. I wonder what she was expecting Charlotte thought.

'Edie will be your maid,' said Alexander. 'No,' as Charlotte made to demur. 'The Board has discussed this and would like you to have someone and Edie has been in post for a week. She lives quite near and so comes to work in the morning and goes home at night. What time do you start?' he asked Edie.

'Seven, Sir.'

'Is that all right, Miss Gordon?' asked Alexander.

'Yes, that's fine thanks, but I wasn't expecting a maid. I could manage on my own.'

'No, no, but will you be all right by yourself at night?' he asked.

'Oh yes, that's no problem . And thank you for arranging for Edie to be here. I'm sure we'll get on fine, won't we Edie.'

'Yes Miss. Would you like to come in now?'

'Yes, that's a good idea.' Alexander was keen to get things organised.

'Magnus, Christina, we're going in now,' he called.

'Come on Christina,' Magnus grabbed the toddler and lifted her in his arms.

'Want to walk,' shouted Christina, wriggling.

'Come on then. Hold my hand.' They rushed up the path to catch up.

'Now Edie,' Alexander instructed, 'you know this house better than us all now. Can you show us round, please.'

'Yes, sir.' Edie stood up straight and smoothed her apron with her fingers.

'Well, this – well – this is the hall. In here is the best room.' She indicated a door to the left. They walked in and looked around a smallish room, with a fire laid ready to light against a cooler evening, a couple of armchairs, bookshelves, a table in the window with dining chairs and a bowl of roses.

'They are beautiful,' said Charlotte. Edie looked at her feet.

'My Mam sent them,' she said. 'She said they would brighten the place up.'

'They are lovely,' said Charlotte. 'I'll need to find your mother so that I can thank her. And,' she added, 'you've arranged them beautifully.' Edie glowed with the praise.

'Right,' she said, 'you should look at the rest.'

'So we should, indeed,' agreed Alexander.

It did not take long to go over the rest of the little schoolhouse. The kitchen, on the other side of the front door from the 'best room' took up most of the rest of the ground floor. Both of these rooms ran the depth of the house from front to back and each had a window in the front and back walls. Charlotte noted this immediately and with pleasure: the view from the front was the sea and from the back were hills with sheep and small, slightly shaggy, grazing ponies. Charlotte was to learn that both the sheep and ponies were the distinctively small Shetland breeds. As well as the view, the extra windows would give added light to the rooms especially in the long dark Shetland winters. Fortunately both windows had thick velour curtains to protect from the winter gales.

Upstairs were two bedrooms, both of which were furnished. The slightly larger room had been made ready for its new occupant.

'Miss,' said Edie.

'Yes, Edie,' Charlotte smiled in encouragement at the hesitating Edie.

'Miss, I made up this room for you because it is slightly bigger and has a lovely view, but if you don't like it, I'll do the other one for you.'

'Edie, this is very nice thank you. I'm sure I'll be very comfortable here. It's the one I would have chosen myself. And,' Charlotte added as she noticed the tell-tale lump in the middle of the bed, 'I think you've even put a pig in the bed for me. That's really kind.' Edie shot a scandalised glance at Alexander. Fancy even mentioning the pig in the bed in front of Mr Sinclair.

'Oh, I hope you don't mind Miss. I just wanted to air the bed. I'll warm it up again later.'

'I have a pig in my bed,' volunteered Magnus. 'Best thing for warming your feet on.'

'Want a pig in bed,' said Christina.

'You're too wee,' said her brother. 'When you're bigger.'

All the talk of beds and pigs therein was embarrassing Edie who was going very pink. Alexander was looking out of the window pretending not to listen. Charlotte said, taking control, 'The house is grand. Thank you very much Edie for all your hard work and Mr Sinclair (she gave him his proper title) for organising everything.' They clattered down the stairs and stood in the hall.

'Magnus,' said his father, 'come and we'll bring the box in. Where would you like it, Miss Gordon?'

'Oh just in the sitting room would be fine, thanks,' she said. 'Then I can sort my things out from there.'

'Sure?' and, as she nodded, 'come on then Magnus.' The two of them went out and Edie, Charlotte and Christina went into the kitchen to explore the mysteries of the range which Edie had lit some hours before. In a few moments, they heard the box being carried in and dumped on the sitting room floor.

Alexander came through. 'That's it then. I think we should leave you to get settled in now.'

'Well, thanks again for everything. And you too Magnus, and Christina.' The little girl came to her and gave her legs a hug.

'Me see you again?'

'Yes of course. I hope we'll see each other lots.' Charlotte returned the hug. 'But go with Magnus and your father now.'

Once the Sinclairs were gone, Edie took it upon herself to show Charlotte what she called the 'back premises' which she obviously felt she could not mention in front of members of the opposite sex. At the back of the schoolhouse in a lean-to was a very small bathroom with running water, a basin and a bath. Edie showed this off with some pride as not many homes had this facility and it was only through the school board's hard work that Da Peerie Skulehoose had acquired it. But no watercloset as at Trancie House. Out at the back, and fortunately not too far away stood the 'wee hoosie' with a dry closet. Edie took Charlotte out to inspect. It was painted pristine white outside and in and scrubbed to the last degree.

'I cleaned it specially for you, Miss,' said Edie anxiously. 'I hope it's all right. I know it's not a real watercloset but ...'

'Edie, it's fine,' said Charlotte, 'and so clean, Thank you very much.'

'And it's not too far for you to go out,' added Edie.

'Of course not. It is all so nice. I can't thank you enough for all your hard work. Now,' changing the subject, 'What about you putting on the kettle and making us a nice cup of tea while I open my box and make a start on unpacking.'

Charlotte

Dear Granny and Granpa,

This is the evening of my first day in Jarlshavn. I must just pen a few lines to you both and Mam and Dad before I lie down, to tell you that I have arrived safely and am well and happy.

The journey north was, in the main, quite enjoyable. I went up on deck early in the morning and sat in a wee corner and watched the sun rise. The Stewardess very kindly brought me a mug of cocoa and a blanket against the early air and I was quite happy.

Mr Sinclair and his son Magnus met me at the boat and transported me to their house in Jarlshavn in his gig for lunch. There I met Mrs Sinclair who has already invited me to call her Margery. She looks very thin and pale. I think there must be something wrong with her but am not sure yet what it is. I also met their youngest child Christina who is between two and three I think. She is a very amenable child.

I am now into my 'Peerie Skulehoose'. It's an attractive wee house, two rooms upstairs and two down with offices at the back.

I will stop now. Do not worry. I will settle here very well, I have no doubt.

From your affectionate grand-daughter,
Charlotte.

Da Peerie Skulehoose,
Jarlshavn,
Shetland.
16 August, 1894

Dear Mam and Dad,
This is just to let you know that I have arrived safely and all is well. I have a nice little house with a lovely view of the sea and I am sure I shall be happy here.

The sea-voyage north was no problem to me. It was not rough as we had feared and the Stewardess was very kind.

Mr Sinclair of the School Board met me and transported me and my box to Jarlshavn. He and his wife and family seem very hospitable.

I will write again in a few days but think I will go to bed now as it is getting late. Please give my love to the children.
Your loving daughter,
Charlotte.

After I had written my letters I put them out for the morning for advice on posting from Edie and went to bed. I didn't realise until I lay down how very tired I was. The bed was warm and comfortable and as I stretched out and put my feet on Edie's warm stone pig I could feel the sleep coming over me in waves.

Many hours later I heard a scuffling sound followed by a tapping. Someone was at the door. I opened my eyes and realised that it was broad daylight.

'Hello,' I called. The door opened. Edie stood there bearing a breakfast tray.

'Good morning Miss.'

'Oh Edie, thank you but you shouldn't have brought me breakfast. How very kind.'

'Well Miss I just thought you might need to have your sleep so I just let you sleep. But then I thought you might want a wee bit of breakfast so here it is.' Edie advanced to the bed bearing her tray and as Charlotte struggled into a sitting position, parked it tray on her lap.

'This is wonderful. Thank you. But only today mind. What time is it?' Charlotte asked.

'Nine o'clock,' said Edie, drawing back the curtains.

'Nine? I must have slept for hours.'

'Yes, Miss,' agreed Edie. 'But then you did have a very long journey. Eat your egg, Miss, before it gets cold. I hope it's all right.'

'It's lovely Edie, thank you.' Edie disappeared and left me to eat my boiled egg and toast and tea.

The next few days were busy ones. School was due to start for the autumn term on 23 August. On that first morning, fortunately after I was up and dressed, the Senior teacher, Mrs Manson, arrived to visit me. She lived in the main Schoolhouse which joined on to Jarlshavn School, about half a mile from my wee house. I saw the figure heading towards the house and went out to meet her.

'Good morning. I'm Mrs Manson, the head mistress. You'll be Miss Gordon?' She looked at me appraisingly. 'How are you, after all your travelling?'

'I'm fine thanks,' I said, as we shook hands. 'I had a wonderful night's sleep and I'm just about to get on with my unpacking. But come in, would you like a cup of tea.'

'That sounds good,' she said.

'Edie,' I called. 'Do you think we could have some tea please?'

Edie came hurrying through. 'Good morning Mrs Manson.' She wiped her hands on her apron. 'Tea, was it, Miss.'

'Yes please,' I said, 'and Edie, have we any more of these delicious scones?'

'Oh yes Miss, I have some on the girdle right now.'

She dashed off. Mrs Manson smiled.

'How is she getting on.'

'She's fine,' I said. 'But I never expected help in the house.'

'Oh yes,' said Mrs Manson, 'the Board insisted, and I agree, that when you're working all day it's not fair to start on housework at night especially when you have marking and so on to do, not to speak of preparation for the next day. Now tell me a little about yourself,' she asked as Edie came in with the tea and scones.

'Well,' I said, as Edie flew back to the kitchen, and we settled to our tea. 'I have just qualified as you will probably know. I was a pupil-teacher at my own school in Towie, Aberdeenshire for two years before going to the Free Church Training College in Aberdeen.'

'That's a well-known one,' nodded Mrs Manson. 'It has a very good reputation. So you taught during your pupil teacher years at Towie and then you would have had more teaching experience on placement from College?'

'Yes, that's right. It's not a lot I know but…'

'Not at all.' Mrs Manson spoke robustly. 'We've all got to start somewhere and your old dominie, Mr Coutts is it? speaks very well of you. And I got a wee note from your other teacher, Miss MacHardie. I don't think she wanted to lose you.'

I smiled. How good of them both to write on my behalf. 'Thank you for telling me. It's nice to know.'

'Praise where praise is due. Now,' she said briskly. 'We have a few days in hand before the term begins What I'd like us to do once you have settled in, is to meet up at the school, maybe tomorrow, and I'll show you everything, your classroom and storage and private working space. You can bring up work that you have ready, like lesson plans of what you have already taught and we can go over them. I'll tell you about the island children although I imagine children are children the world over, but they all have different little habits, ways of working, games they like to play and so on. How does that sound?'

'That's fine,' I said. What time would you like me to come to the school tomorrow?'

'Oh, say ten-ish. I think that would be time enough. Well, I must be off.' She straightened her skirt. 'I'm really glad you're here. It's been quite a time the last few weeks of term without a teacher and I think we'll get on really well.'

'I'm sure we shall,' I said. 'I'm glad to be here too. It's much better being in the new situation than worrying about what it's going to be like.'

'I know,' she agreed. 'Well, see you tomorrow. Thanks for the tea, Edie,' she called. Then she was off, no nonsense, practical, firm but always helpful.

Thus it was that the following morning I walked up the road to the School to meet again with Mrs Manson and see round my new place of work. The playground was of course deserted of children but I met a few on my way up the road. From each, my 'Good morning' drew a shy response. I felt awkward in a way. They all seemed to know who I was but I did not know any of the names yet. I was sure it wouldn't take long. Edie was already supplying me with stories and histories of children in the village she knew – it seemed to be everybody. Once she got over her initial shyness and realised that I was not going to bite her she became a mine of information. Where to get supplies, which fish to buy, which church was which and who went to them and how to get the coach to Lerwick and back.

Edie herself was Jarlshavn born and bred had only just left Jarlshavn school herself at the age of thirteen, had been there since she was six years old, could read, write and do basic arithmetic. I think she was apprehensive that I might try and test her arithmetical tables but I was more than content with her ability to add up the prices on the shopping list. And, her talents in the kitchen were never in doubt. Taught to cook and bake at home by her mother, she transferred these skills to the range and oven of Da Peerie Skulehoose. She arrived on the dot of seven in the morning, went home around lunchtime, returned for the afternoon and had my tea ready for me at six o'clock before she went away.

The last days of the holidays before the beginning of term passed in a haze of unpacking, sorting school work and getting to know a few people. The unpacking itself did not take long. It was a joy to take out my things and arrange them in my 'own' house.

I still had my old friend Beanie, now a little worn but very important. I told myself that I needed her as a visual aid for teaching and that was why I had brought her, but in my heart of hearts, I just could not bear to leave her behind. Well, we all need a little self-indulgence and perhaps Beanie was mine. She was part of my childhood, my past. Edie was very intrigued by her and if she thought it was strange for a 'grown teacher' to have a doll with her, she never said but handled her as carefully as she did all my other things.

School papers, books and lesson plans I kept initially in the parlour. This was, I think my favourite room in the house. Indeed, Edie called it the best room in the traditional style. However I adhered to the word 'parlour' as Granny did with the parlour in Trancie House. A room for talking in, and hopefully being at home in. I kept my books and papers and homework here and with frequent use and firing with the Shetland peats which came from the School's very own peat-bank a few miles outside

Jarlshavn the 'best room' atmosphere gave way to a room with a lived in, often-used feel which I, and I think others who came to visit, enjoyed being in.

However, some school things had to stay in the school. The day after Mrs Manson's visit, I gathered up what I thought was necessary and made my way to the school for the first time. In the fashion of the time the playground was divided into two to separate the boys and girls at playtime. This time though there was only one main door but, as I was to find out, boys and girls formed two lines to enter, and the lines were kept three feet apart. The door stood open for me that day and as I entered, Mrs Manson came out of her classroom and ushered me in.

My own classroom for the youngest children was nearby. A pleasant if austere room, the usual fire, fuelled by peats stood ready at one end of the class. I was glad to see a stout fireguard around it. I was also glad to see the absence of the sickly green paint so constantly used in Towie. The Shetland schools of the day seemed to go in for cream as that was the only colour I ever saw on a school wall there. Still, it was better than green and did not reflect so unhealthily on the faces of the children.

We spent a pleasant and busy morning going over the customs of the school, my duties as second teacher, work I had already prepared and taught and new lessons Mrs Manson wanted me to think about. The overall curriculum was very similar to the rest of the elementary schools in Scotland although each area including Shetland had its own little idiosyncracies. Therefore local history, geography and customs were included where possible in the curriculum.

One custom in particular about which I knew little was the Festival of Up Helly Aa. This huge burning of the galley festival is now a firm Shetland tradition which Mrs Manson mentioned on that August day as one of the highlights of the calendar. She was in her fifties and told me she could remember when Up Helly Aa was very different. That was before the 'City Fathers' of Lerwick took a hand to moderate the excesses of the old festival.

'Traditionally,' she said, 'Up Helly Aa marked the end of the Yule festivities. It really is of pagan origin and in theory is celebrated on the twenty-fourth day of Yule in the old calendar, which is 30 January. To keep things tidy they settled on the last Tuesday in January.'

'So, what happened?' I asked. 'Why did the 'City Fathers' change things?'

'Oh, it was becoming very rowdy and disorganised,' she said. 'It was so primitive and boisterous and probably dangerous too. Crowds of youths dragged clanking chains of sledges carrying up to ten barrels of blazing tar and wood shavings through the streets and blasted their horns all the time. I think there was a lot of alcohol about. Not that I'm against alcohol in moderation,' she added hastily, 'but this was totally in excess of what decent people could put up with. And, every year it was getting worse. And, there was fighting between squads of youths from different areas of the town. It was getting worse and worse. So, in 1874 the Council took a stand and banned tar-barrelling.'

'What happened next?'

'Well, there was a bit of a gap for a few years. A few further attempts at tar-barrelling were squashed by the authorities once it was banned. You see, it is a very old festival and you can't blame the people for wanting to keep it going. I think it's a shame for old traditions to die out. At the same time I don't like seeing their being ruined by people who don't know when to stop. Finally in 1882 a committee was formed to sort the thing out. That was only twelve years ago. I can hardly believe it. It feels as though the new way has been going on for ever.' She paused, remembering. I waited to hear the rest.

'Well,' she continued, 'The committee was headed by a ceremonial chief of the celebrations called a 'Worthy Chief Guiser'. Two years later, in 1884, I remember it very clearly, they started a torchlight procession of guisers in different squads for Up Helly Aa and soon after that they built the first full sized Norse galley. The galley led the procession singing *The Up Helly Aa Song* through the streets to the Burning Site. This is at the pier head but I hear whispers that they might change it to a public park. It happens every year. When they get to the Burning Site, the guisers, still in their squads, form a flaming circle round the galley. They sing '*The Galley Song*' and give three cheers: for Up Helly Aa, for the builders of the galley and, for the Worthy Chief Guiser. Then, on the command of a bugle call, all the blazing torches are thrown into the galley.' Mrs Manson's voice dropped. 'In a moment she is a sea of fire and as she burns, the guisers sing their final song, *The Norseman's Home*. Then she is gone, all save embers and ashes.'

'So you can see,' she said in her normal voice, 'how important this is for the children. Everyone seems to be involved preparing for what feels like months ahead. In January the children learn the songs, and they are allowed as a special favour to go to the burning site to watch the procession arrive and see the galley burning. They get very excited about it. The other interesting thing is it all goes like clockwork. It is so well organised. Changed days.'

The rest of the morning was spent in organising the first few days of the term. I would have the small children in classes 1-3 and Mrs Manson was going to take the rest.

One change which was coming in slowly was the introduction of Secondary schools in Scotland. One, the Anderson Educational Institute had only recently been established in Lerwick. This meant that although the minimum age for a child to leave school was still set at thirteen years of age, children whose parents wanted them to take their school education further could go to a secondary school if they wished. This meant that Elementary schools like Jarlshavn had fewer pupils of twelve and over and therefore brought the school roll down to manageable proportions. It was said that there was accommodation in the school for one hundred children. This was a great many for two teachers to handle although many schools in Scotland did cope with similar numbers. However, by the time I reached Jarlshavn I was glad that the anticipated roll stood at around sixty children reasonably equally divided between the two classrooms.

I spent some time thinking about 'the school day'. The timing seemed to be similar to what I'd been used to. Into school at 9am, Register first, then Catechism and Bible, then the three 'R's. Even the way it was done seemed to be in the same pattern as Towie and schools in Aberdeen where I had done teaching practice. Harder more academic subjects in the morning , while so-called easier things were kept for the afternoon. This included drawing, nature walks when the weather was fine, singing and movement to music. Depending on timing, subjects which were not directly reading and writing but which depended on them, like Geography and History could be tackled morning or afternoon. However, with my younger children the concept of history particularly was started with stories about history, and geography was begun with stories about people from other countries, accompanied of course by the wall map of *The World* which appeared to hang in every classroom in Scotland.

There was one thing which I was to find was very different between the children of Towie, inland and country bred , and Jarlshavn, island-bred, living by the sea and often frequently going on the sea on fishing trips or from island to island. This was the concept of space and 'others' and other places.

Many of the fathers or uncles of the Jarlshavn children were sea-faring men and went all over the world and were often away for months at a time. Through the stories and things that they brought back, the children had some concept of where they were going and what they were doing. Also, that there were people who lived in those far off lands who spoke differently, looked different sometimes, wore different clothes, made different things and had different customs. So, teaching geography to the Jarlshavn children turned out to be a big change from teaching the same subject to the children of West Aberdeenshire.

I found the folk friendly and willing to welcome the 'new teacher'. In the few days between my arrival and the start of school, folk kept coming to my door with little welcoming presents: half a dozen eggs, a baking of scones, a few flowers from a garden, some peats one day and even some drift-wood for my fire. Their generosity was unmistakeable. If I went down to the shops, they stopped to say hello, introduce their children and generally put themselves about to make me feel welcome.

Chapter 14

Charlotte

On Saturday, at the end of my first week in Shetland, I was working in my parlour, setting out what I required for school the next week. I heard footsteps and went to greet the visitor. It turned out to be Margery with little Christina by the hand.

'Hello Margery. How nice of you to come. And good morning Christina.' I shook her hand too. 'How are you today?'

'Fine, thank you.' Christina was straining at her mother's hand to get into the house.

'Please come in. I'm dying for an excuse for a cup of tea.'

Margery laughed. 'Well, for a wee while then. But what we really came up to ask you was: will you come to us at Harbour House for lunch on Sunday – tomorrow? We'd be very happy if you would.'

'Thank you very much. I'd like to do that very much.' I heard the rattle of the tray. 'Here's Edie with some tea. She must have heard you. Her kettle's always on the boil.'

'Here you are.' Edie put the tray on the table. 'Would you like me to look after Christina for a wee while Mrs Sinclair?' She looked at Margery. 'She could help me in the kitchen and you ladies would get five minutes peace.'

'I couldn't have put it better myself,' said Margery. She looked at me. 'Is that all right with you?'

'Yes of course,' I said. 'Christina would you like to go and help Edie in the kitchen? I know she has a biscuit there for you.'

'Yes,' shouted Christina. 'Me help Edie.' She grabbed Edie's hand and rushed her off.

In the following silence, I poured the tea and handed Margery her cup. 'Here, sit down and have a rest. Toddlers are hard work, I think.'

'Oh, she's very good really, and I have Meg at home who helps greatly. But it's nice to have a break.'

There was a silence.

'And Magnus, is he well?'

'Yes, he's fine. He's looking forward to going back to school.'

'That's in Lerwick?'

'Yes, he started there last year and enjoys it. The only thing is, he has to stay there through the week in lodgings. It's a pity but it's the only way. As it is, most Sunday evenings he walks over the hill to Lerwick and walks back on a Friday night. Not this coming week though. Term starts on Tuesday 23rd and because of his box of luggage, Alexander will take him over in the gig. Then he'll walk back on Friday.'

'You must miss him when he's away.'

'Yes I do, but it's so good to have the Secondary school now. It has widened their scope so much. They do have to work very hard though. Christina misses him too. She dotes on him.' She paused. 'Sometimes I think it's good for him to get away as she wants to be with him all the time and there is such an age gap.'

I looked at her.

'I don't suppose you know,' she said. 'There was not supposed to be such a gap. We lost three children in between Magnus and Christina.'

I put my hands up to my mouth. 'Oh I'm so sorry. I didn't know.'

'Why should you?' She smiled sadly. 'After Magnus was born in 1881 we had little Ingrid in 1882 so at the time we had two babies really. It was hard work but they were so lovely together. Then almost right away we had Frances in 1883. So, then there were three. We really felt our family was complete. We were so happy. We were busy but happy with our three lovely children. Then wee Frances took very ill in the winter and died. Winter's awful for babies. She got a bad cold; it went into her chest. I can hear her struggling to breathe yet. We tried everything but it was no use. It was pneumonia and she just was too small to cope with it. She died in my arms one wild night.' She put her hands over her face. 'Oh if only I had her now. She would be a little girl of eleven. Imagine. Running about and playing.'

I went to her and sat on the floor at her feet holding her hands. I knew now there was more to come. She coughed, took a deep breath and continued.

'We carried on,' she said, 'and were happy, or tried to be. Magnus is lovely – so much the big brother. He missed Frances very much. He was not much more than a baby himself when she died, but do you know, he used to go around the house looking for her after she had gone. He couldn't understand what had happened to her.'

'Oh Margery.' I was unable to stop my own tears. 'Poor little boy. How did you cope?'

'Well, we just got on with it. You have to, you know, for the sake of the ones who are left. And poor little Ingrid was too small even to miss Frances. So we kept going for the sake of Magnus and Ingrid and on the face of it we were a happy family. But I never forgot her even though she was just a baby. People said that you know – they said, "well she was a just a baby. You're young, you can have another". But it's not like that. You can't just go and have another, like replacing something you have lost. It doesn't work like that.' She coughed again, into her hanky. It seemed that speaking a lot brought it on. She recovered and continued.

'Then Ingrid died two years later. She's buried out at the kirkyard with Frances. I couldn't believe that God could be so cruel as to take her too. Magnus and Ingrid both had whooping cough at the same time. A lot of the children had it. There was a real epidemic of it in Shetland at the time. And a lot of the children didn't get better. The really strong ones did, like Magnus. But Ingrid just coughed and coughed and vomited and we tried everything. She became weaker in front of our eyes. We just saw her fading away.'

I sat by her saying nothing. I didn't know what to say. This was beyond my experience. Then I asked, 'How was Magnus then?'

'I think he understood a bit better that she had died,' said Margery, 'as he was older by this time. He had also been ill himself and needed a lot of attention. I remember him walking about after he was able to be up and asking, "Where's my sister? Where's Ingrid? I want to play with Ingrid". One day we sat down with him and told him that Jesus wanted Ingrid in Heaven with him so she had gone. I have to say he was very angry. He shouted at God. It's funny,' she sighed. 'He was really saying what I wanted to say, but when you are a grown-up you have to be so, well, grown up, don't you?'

'How were you and Alexander, I mean Mr Sinclair?'

'Well, I think we found it more difficult to speak about it after Ingrid died. It was as if a barrier came up and we didn't know what to do to get it down. Then soon after that I found I was pregnant again. Even though I felt that nothing would ever replace the children I had lost, one bit of me was so happy that I was having another chance to have a baby.

'There was another bit of me that was filled with a – a sort of foreboding. I had this terrible feeling that something else was going to go wrong. It was a difficult pregnancy. I wasn't so much sick but just didn't feel well. I didn't look right either. The baby seemed to be small and didn't move around much and my ankles swelled. So did my fingers. I had to take off my wedding ring because it got too tight.

'Well, I went into labour a month early and wee Kenneth was such a peerie baby. Beautiful but very small. The midwife and doctor were both there that time as they were worried about me. Neither held out much hope for him. He was just too wee and not strong enough. We fed him off a little spoon as he could not take the breast. But a few days later he died too. Alexander took him in his tiny coffin all the way to the kirkyard in the gig and the minister buried him there beside Frances and Ingrid.'

I groped for my handkerchief again. 'Oh, Margery,' I said, 'how can you bear it?'

'Well,' she said. 'You just do. I can't talk about it out and about too much. People don't know how to handle those who are grieving. They either avoid you or, they make the most inappropriate remarks like, as I said, "you can always have another one", or, "you'll be getting over it now". As if,' she said, indignantly, 'you grieve by the clock or by the date. I'll never get over it, but I'll learn to live with it. But thank you for listening.' She heaved a sigh. 'Whether you know it or not, it's good to be able to talk about it now and again.'

'I'm glad you felt you could do that.' I was deeply saddened by the story. I knew that the death rate amongst infants and children was very high because I had heard of it from Granpa but I had never come across it first hand before. Now a very new friend had taken me into her confidence as never before.

She smiled. 'I suppose I should tell you the happy bit now?' And as I nodded, she said, 'and then there was Christina. My bright little girl who has brought the sparkle back into her father's eyes and her brother's and of course mine. Magnus was very wary when she was born. It was as if he couldn't trust her not to die too, as the others had done. But she has been fit and healthy since she was born. You can hear her.'

And certainly as she spoke, we could hear feet running down the stairs and high excited giggling as Edie chased Christina along to the parlour door.

Margery held out her hand and touched mine. 'Thanks for listening. It means a lot.' I held her hand tightly.

'If I can ever be of any help…'

'I know. I'll come.'

The door burst open as we knew it would and Christina ran in with Edie close behind.

'Oh Mama, I'se had fun with Edie.' The little girl was pink faced and dishevelled, the bow slipping off her hair.

They took their leave of me then after first reminding me about Sunday lunch. I waved goodbye and turned back to the house to mull over the things I had been told.

'Miss,' Edie was at my elbow as I moved back to the parlour. 'Miss, would you like more tea, or anything else? You look – sad.' She obviously knew the story and knew by my face that I too now was aware of the sadness of Harbour House.

'Edie that would help, I think. Thank you.' I could not gossip with Edie about the Sinclairs but it helped to know that she knew and understood my sombre mood.

The rest of the day was quiet. The School Board had agreed Edie should have a day off on Sunday but that Saturday I let her away after lunch.

It was good to have the house to myself and I wrote my letters home, finished preparing for Tuesday's start of school and took out a book I had been meaning to read for ages.

Chapter 15

Whatever else, Sunday meant Church. In Towie, there was little choice of establishment. The church in Towie was Church of Scotland, the Kirk. If you happened to be of another persuasion, like Roman Catholic, you got yourself somehow (but mostly on foot) to the nearest Roman Catholic Church. Most of the local folk went to the Kirk although it was a different story over the hill from Glenbuchat, in Glenlivet, where many of the families were Roman Catholic. There used to be a seminary around the Braes of Glenlivet where priests were trained and it is said the priests used to write to Paris and Rome dramatising their isolated position. However, the real locals of Donside or Glenlivet never thought of themselves as isolated. It was everybody else who was remote.

So, on her first Sunday in Jarlshavn, Charlotte decided in the interests of continuity, personal feelings of security and probably family loyalty, to go to the morning service in the Kirk. She knew from Edie that the Sinclairs would be heading for the Congregational Church as Alexander was a life-long Congregationalist like his parents before him. He was also a highly respected Deacon.

The morning dawned cloudy with a brisk westerly blowing in from the sea promising rain later. All was quiet in the Peerie Skule-hoose. Charlotte awakened for the first time to real quietness, no bustle of Edie downstairs and no feet going past outside. She lay for a moment, thinking.

This was the first time she had been really alone for a long time. On the one hand, it was very peaceful. On the other, well, she had a wee pang at the thought of Granny singing around the house and the knowledge that Granpa would be there relishing the thought of one of those infrequent but hoped-for whole day off. There was always someone who needed him and his bag was always packed ready for any emergency. Most Sundays he managed to get to the Kirk and at least anyone looking for him knew where to go to find him. Charlotte smiled as she remembered the occasions when he had been called out of Kirk. Everyone else became all excited and distracted at the thought of the doctor being called for 'in the Kirk of all places' and 'who could it be for?' and 'fit wis wrang?' and 'fa wis ready ti hae their bairn next?' All good gossip material. She felt sorry for the minister trying to re-claim their attention after such a disturbance. For his part, Granpa took it all in his stride as he was so used to such interruptions.

Charlotte set aside her reminiscing and jumped out of bed. She looked out of the window, made a face at the weather and prepared a breakfast tray which she carried into her parlour.

When, later, she left the house for the Kirk, the rain was beginning to blow in the wind with a sharp taste of salt in the air. She licked her lips in appreciation and held her hat on firmly. There were others out too, all heading for the 11 o'clock service in the Kirk which stood very near the sea and was frequently battered by wind and tide. A stout wall stood around it, built up especially strongly on the sea-ward side where strong winds and high tides threatened erosion. A few brave maritime plants and flowers braved the elements among the rocks. Charlotte noticed a path running up the side of the wall and leading up and round and out of sight and promised herself an exploratory walk one day. In the meantime she headed like many others towards the Kirk.

Sunday faces were firmly in place. People who had leant up against her gate talking to her a couple of days before, and brought her eggs and peats, acknowledged her Sunday presence with a formal, 'Good morning, Miss Gordon' , or, 'no so fine the day'. Smiles were more hesitant, chat not forthcoming.

Charlotte gripped tightly her hat and her bag containing her Bible, her purse with her collection, a handkerchief and the traditional pandrop hiding at the bottom. She didn't know if she would dare to eat it. Perhaps it would be too much for the residents of Jarlshavn to see the new teacher slipping a Granny's sooker into her mouth in preparation for the sermon. She had a momentary mental flash of Jock up in front of his gig passing his granny's sookers to her from the depths of his ancient pockets, and smiled involuntarily. How pleased Jock had been to see her 'get on'. He always seemed to be there ready to listen to her, whether it was failures or successes or sudden hobby-horses that she felt like going and sounding him out about.

But here she was at the door now. The elders stood there, soberly dressed, unnaturally shiny Sunday shoes, black suits smelling slightly of mothballs from the kists where the suits had been all week. Collars were white and board-hard, jackets buttoned up usually it seemed, with difficulty as though too many tatties with butter had been consumed the previous week. Nevertheless, the elders greeted her courteously, soberly, reverently. They handed her a hymn book 'For the use of Visitors'. She supposed that she still was officially a visitor and anyway they could not see that she had her Bible (with the metrical psalms and paraphrases at the back, a useful invention of the Church of Scotland) in her bag.

She slipped into a pew about halfway down the Kirk on the left hand side. She always, if she could, sat on that side. Partly from habit, but also, people tended to sit where they felt most comfortable. She had read somewhere that there was some psychological reason behind where people chose to sit in public places and conveyances, whether left or right hand, front or back. She could not remember – something else to look up sometime.

She sat, hands folded in front of her. Should I pray, she thought? One usually did. But she felt so new, different, self-conscious. Prayer seemed impossible. She looked in front of her. One or two faces she recognised from the past week. Edie, she suddenly saw, was sitting further over and slightly in front of her with whom Charlotte supposed were her parents. Edie was dressed in very Sunday best: longer coat than usual, big sleeves, nipped in waist, light navy. She half turned round to acknowledge Charlotte's presence then returned to face the front of the Kirk as the beadle entered and walked sonorously up the pulpit steps with the big Bible. This he laid on the pulpit with a slight dunt which raised a small puff of stour. Charlotte wondered how many women would like to take that pulpit cushion out and give it a good beating . The choir was in by this time too, about a dozen all told. They processed to their seats and awaited the presence of the minister.

All this time the bell was ringing, tolling its 'come to kirk' message. As the last clang was heard, the door opened and the beadle came in followed by the black-gowned minister wearing the purple and ermine academic hood of Edinburgh University. He strode with authority behind the beadle, and, as was the custom of the day up the pulpit steps and into the pulpit. Again Charlotte thought back to Towie Kirk – the procedure was indeed very similar. The minister from the pulpit acknowledged the waiting beadle who retired to his nearby seat.

So the service began: in total, five singings, one metrical psalm, three hymns and one Scottish paraphrase. This happened to be one of Charlotte's favourites, number 2, O God of Bethel sung to the tune Salzburg. So, for her the service which could have been a lonely experience, ended on a comforting note as she realised that places may change but some customs remain the same. The fillers to the hymn-sandwich were the prayers, the readings, one Old Testament and one New, the sermon and a very brief children's address which, as its name suggests was designed for the children but to which the grownups listened intently.

Afterwards, the minister swished down the aisle in his gowns and stood at the door to greet his congregation individually.

'Ah, Miss Gordon.' He shook Charlotte's hand. 'I heard you had arrived. Settling in all right, I hope.'

'Yes thank you, Minister, everything's fine. The house too, was beautifully prepared.' Charlotte liked the look of the man, youngish, in his thirties, sincere but with a twinkle in his eye and a ready smile even though it was Sunday.

'That's good. Nice to see you. I'll come up and visit, if I may.'

'Yes, please do.'

She left the church and walked down the road to Harbour House. Already in the distance she could see its chimneys; a small plume of smoke came from them even though it was only August. The rain fell steadily and she could feel the wind tugging at her skirts as she walked quickly along.

Inside, all was bright and bustlingly friendly. Margery said, 'Oh, Charlotte, you're soaked. Let's get your coat and hat off and we'll hang them up.'

'Thanks.' Charlotte looked down at herself. 'I suppose I am a bit wet. I'm all right underneath. It's only my coat.'

Margery chatted on, hanging things up. 'How was church? We go up to the Congregational – but I think you know that. I see the Kirk has a fairly new minister – is he all right?'

'Yes, he was fine. And the hymns were all ones I knew. It was all fine. Very like what I'm used to really.'

'Come to the Cong.' Alexander's voice preceded him as he came out of the parlour to welcome her. 'You'll get a really good sermon there – strong meat.'

'Oh, Alexander.' Margery ushered Charlotte into the room. 'Maybe Charlotte doesn't want strong meat.'

'Of course she does.' He turned towards Charlotte. 'Good afternoon Charlotte. You don't mind my addressing you as Charlotte, do you. I know one should be formal but in the house surely we may drop the ceremonials of the public place.'

'Of course. I agree entirely.' They shook hands.

'Good. And you must call me Alexander. Leave the Mister bit for elsewhere. Tell me,' he continued. 'How are you settling down? Is the Peerie Skule-hoose all right or is it just too peerie?'

'No, no. I like it very much. It's just right for me and I've settled in well. Edie is such a help and seems happy.'

'That's good. And school starts on Tuesday? Have you met with Mrs Manson.'

'Yes, we've had some productive times together and we're all ready, I think.'

'Are you having the wee ones?' Alexander was the School Board member and making sure all was in order.

'Yes, that's what we've agreed. I'm looking forward to it.'

'Are you two talking shop? That should be illegal on a Sunday.' Margery came through from the kitchen. 'Lunch is ready. I'll call the children.' She went to the bottom of the stairs, 'Magnus, Christina, lunch time.'

Magnus came to the top of the stairs. 'Come on, Christina. She's been under her bed, playing hiding,' he explained. A very ruffled Christina appeared beside him.

'Me hiding under the bed.' She held up her hands. 'Dirty hands,' she said.

'Well, let's go and wash them.' Her mother was very patient.

'Me want Miss – you know – her,' she pointed at Charlotte, 'to wash them.' 'Come up,' she ordered. Charlotte looked at Margery.

'Oh well, if you don't mind,' said Margery. She's taken a notion to you.'

'Little monkey.' Alexander scowled. 'She shouldn't get everything her own way. But a lot of the time she does.'

Charlotte went up to Christina. 'Come on Christina, lunch is ready but we'll wash your hands first. Where is the bathroom?'

'Here.' Christina led her by the dirty hand into the bathroom. 'See, taps with water.' Charlotte supervised the washing operation joined by Magnus whose hands which had not been under the bed were still very grubby.

'Right, all done.' Finally they settled at the table.

'Hands together, eyes closed.' Alexander said Grace and at last they could start.

Halfway through the Shetland lamb, mint sauce, roast potatoes and peas, Margery began to cough. She put her napkin up to her mouth and held her head away from the table. When the coughing did not stop immediately, she looked up at Alexander, who said to Charlotte, 'Will you supervise Christina please?' He got up, went round to his wife's seat, lifted her gently by the elbow and escorted her from the room.

'Where's Mummy going?'

'Just to have a drink of water and stop her cough.' Charlotte hoped it was as simple as that but did not like to see the pale face and the thin body bending with the coughing. 'Come on, eat up your nice lunch. Do you want me to help you?'

'No, I'se can manage.' Christina grabbed her fork and started eating quickly. 'See how soon I can see the mouse,' referring to the picture of the mouse on the bottom of her plate. Magnus, above such infantilisms, finished his lamb and put his knife and fork together. He leant forward, very much in the role of host.

'How do you think you are going to enjoy Shetland, Miss Gordon?'

'I think I'm going to be very happy here. I've started well with the Sinclair family's help.' She smiled at him. 'I'm sure I'll be fine. You don't go to the Jarlshavn school any more?'

'No,' he said. 'The Anderson in Lerwick takes people from all over Shetland now, you know, if you want to go on at school, and Father and Mother decided that I would be better there and get a broader education.'

'I think they're right.' Charlotte agreed. 'I had to stay at the elementary school and although I was quite happy to stay, I think it broadens your outlook to move into a Secondary school. You get different teachers for different subjects, different points of view and so on.'

'Yes, I can see that.' Magnus looked at her. 'The big disadvantage here is having to stay in lodgings. I'd really rather be at home. Apart from anything else,' he hesitated and looked at Christina to check that she was not listening. 'Apart from anything else, I think there's something wrong with my mother. Something that they're not telling me.'

Charlotte's heart filled with dread. She had been wondering about this since the day last week when they all met. Margery so thin and pale, yet sometimes with a bright pink flush high on her cheeks, her sudden bouts of coughing.

'Look at today,' Magnus said. 'She couldn't stop coughing. And I'll tell you something else,' he added. 'Mother has stopped kissing us properly, you know at bed-time and so on. She always has a hanky in her hand and she always manages to not kiss us when she's kissing us. She thinks we don't notice, and I don't suppose Christina does, but I do notice and I wish she would tell me what is wrong.' His eyes filled with tears. 'I don't really want to go away to Lerwick just now. I'm frightened something happens to her.' He looked across the table at Charlotte. 'What do you think?'

Charlotte looked steadily back at him. 'I don't know what to think,' she said. 'I'm not going to say I haven't noticed anything, because of course, I have, but at the moment, I don't know what, if anything is wrong.'

A tear trickled down the boy's cheek. He brushed it away angrily. 'I just wish they would treat me as a grown-up. I just want to know so that I can help.'

'I know. If I can help you in any way, I will. Would you like me to ask your father to talk to you. He might be ready to do that after today.'

'Yes, all right.' Magnus sighed. 'I suppose that would help, thanks. Look at Christina,' he changed the subject as he looked at his sister. 'She's finished.'

'Well done, Christina.' Charlotte looked at the mouse on the bottom of Christina's plate. 'What does the mouse say?'

'Eeek,' said Christina.

The door opened and in came Meg, the Sinclair's housemaid, to clear the table.

'I'll just clear up these dishes now,' she said, 'and bring in the pudding.'

'Is Mother all right?' said Magnus.

'She's in the parlour,' Meg gathered the plates together quickly. 'Your father will be back in a minute.' She went out and returned with pudding, wonderful, fruity summer pudding with fresh cream.

'Fortunately this is cold and won't mind waiting.' She put it on the table beside Charlotte. 'I think they'll be through in a minute.' She went out.

Charlotte heard voices in the hall and Alexander and Margery came in, his arm protectively around her waist as he helped her tenderly to her seat.

'Thanks,' she murmured. 'Sorry about that everyone, that cough is just a nuisance. Now where's the pudding. Charlotte, I see it's landed beside you. Could you dish it out please?'

'Of course.' Charlotte seized the serving spoon, glad to be doing anything at all to help. 'Christina will I start with you?'

'Ye-es,' shrilled Christina, who obviously felt that she had waited long enough. 'Pudding please.'

Lunch continued without further incident. Afterwards, Meg bore Christina off for her usual afternoon nap and as the rain was off, Magnus went out for a Sunday afternoon walk with his friends although that day his heart was not into the customary beach-combing and driftwood collecting. Alexander, Margery and Charlotte went back to the parlour for a cup of tea and chatted quietly about school, the children, the folk of Jarlshavn, Charlotte's house, anything but what was on all their minds.

Charlotte was anxious not to overstay her welcome. She turned to Margery and said, 'I have really enjoyed this visit. Thank you so much for inviting me. I hope your cough will be better soon. I'll leave you in peace now and you can get a rest.'

'I'm fine, really,' Margery protested.

'Well, I'd better go anyway while the rain's off,' said Charlotte. She got to her feet. 'You stay there and I'll get my coat.' She went out to the hall and put on her now-dry coat and hat. Alexander came out too.

'I'll walk you home,' he said.

'That's all right. Please stay with Margery.'

'No, she'll be all right,' he insisted. 'She's going to rest in the parlour.'

'All right,' she gave in. 'Thank you.' She went back into the parlour.

'Margery, thank you again. That was lovely.'

'Sorry to spoil the party.' Margery looked contrite. 'I feel so feeble doing that.'

'You're not feeble at all.' Charlotte took her hand. 'Now have a rest. I'll see you soon.'

Alexander walked in silence beside her along the foreshore. Seagulls soared above them in the breeze. The waves washed over the rocks. A few children played on the small beach with careful nursemaids in attendance, taking advantage of the dry spell to give their charges their daily dose of fresh air.

He broke the silence. 'Charlotte, I need to tell you something. I would not normally take someone whom I have known for such a short time into my confidence. However, I feel that somehow, we have become friends very quickly, and, I trust you to treat what I am going to say as very private.'

'Of course.' Charlotte looked at him. 'Alexander, what is it? How can I help you?'

'I'm very worried about Margery,' he began. 'You saw what happened at lunchtime today. This sort of thing has happened before. She is losing weight, has swings of temperature, sometimes she is very hot particularly in the afternoon and evening. When this happens she perspires a lot. And the cough is getting worse, always worse.'

Charlotte was not a doctor's grand-daughter for nothing. She recognised the trend the conversation was taking.

'Have you had the doctor?'

'Oh yes.' Alexander sighed. 'The doctor comes in and out under pretence of seeing Christina. The thing is, we have told nobody else up until now that we have a problem – nobody but Meg,' he added. Charlotte nodded, recognising a similar relationship to that which her grandmother had with Katie who knew all about what went on in Trancie House.

'And now?' Charlotte prompted gently.

'And now, Margery has asked me to tell you. She wants you to know because although we have known each other for such a very short time she values your friendship and does not want to keep this a secret from you. Margery has consumption.' His voice broke.

There was a silence as he struggled to collect himself. They stopped walking and turned to face the sea from the wall above the beach. The waves ran up the sand and sank back. The tide was nearly full, Charlotte noted automatically. It was amazing how quickly one became used to ebb and flow, wind direction and sea-going weather. Alexander also noted the full tide.

'Look at that,' he said bitterly, 'Is my wife going to go out on a tide that is ebbing too soon? That's not what I want for her, but that's what is going to happen.'

'Oh Alexander, surely there is something we can do.'

'There is nothing, nothing to stop this terrible thing. Every day I feel she is worse. She is often very hopeful herself but Dr Taylor told me that patients with consumption are often like that – they think they are going to recover. Listen to me, I'm calling her a 'patient with consumption'. She's my wife, for Heaven's sake. She has been through such a lot, she tries so hard to keep from getting too close to the children. She's so frightened they'll get it too. Today at lunchtime was just so much for her to bear. Do you think they are aware of anything?'

Charlotte thought for a moment before she spoke.

'I don't think Christina noticed anything. She is still too young. However, when you were out Magnus told me how worried he is about his mother. He senses there is something wrong but he doesn't know what. He feels he is being left out of something and I think he would like to be taken into your confidence. He is very grown-up for twelve and would cope better if he knew the truth. Another thing,' Charlotte turned to face Alexander, 'He's worried about going away to school even although he is home at the weekends. He's frightened something will happen to her. And, he wants to help, but he doesn't know what to do.'

'What do you think?'

'My own feeling is that you should tell him. He'll be very upset, but he's going to be upset anyway. Better being upset because you have told him the truth than building up a wall of resentment because you kept things hidden from him. As I said, he is very mature for his age.

'The other problem for him, is going away to school. I don't know enough yet about how this could be done and I understand he had settled well in Lerwick. But do you think he would come back to the Jarlshavn school and work with Mrs Manson for the meantime? Then he wouldn't need to go away and I think he'd be happier and more secure.' She stopped and looked at Alexander. He stood looking out to sea, his eyes far away. She waited.

At last he spoke. 'I think that would be best. But before I tell him, I must tell Margery. He could come back to school here for a while. From what the doctor was saying it won't be for that long. Less than a year.'

'Oh, Alexander.'

'Yes, we haven't got much time left. Margery doesn't appear to know this – or at least it could all be part of the pretence that she is getting better. I don't think I could tell Magnus that. But it might be better if he stayed at home – better for all of us.'

'I think that's what he would like.'

'Right,' Alexander decided. 'I'll sort that out today. Charlotte, thank you very much for listening and helping so much today. It can't take away the end result, but talking about it makes it just that little bit easier to bear.'

They started to walk up the road towards the Peerie Skule-hoose.

'If there is anything I can do to help, please say.'

'Oh, you have helped already, so much.' They reached the gate and shook hands formally.

'Thank you for walking me home.' Charlotte opened the gate and went through. He tipped his hat to her.

'My privilege.' He turned and started to walk down the road towards the harbour. Charlotte walked up her path, inserted her key in the lock hardly able to see what she was doing for the tears which now came unchecked to her eyes. Hastily she went inside and through to the parlour where she was able to cry in peace and privacy for her new friends, for herself and for the tattered hopes and dreams of a mother who had already been through so much.

Chapter 16

Charlotte's classroom was chilly and felt stale and unused. It was early on the first Tuesday of the new term. Next door, she could hear Mrs Manson clattering with the fire irons. From October the school janitor always dealt with the fires. Now, was an exception; the teachers would do it. Charlotte built her fire and felt a glow of satisfaction as the first driftwood flames took hold and crackled up the chimney.

'Are you managing?' Mrs Manson came bustling through from her room. 'Oh well done,' she exclaimed. 'I always give them a fire on their first day back. It makes the classrooms feel so much more homey.'

'Now, you'll be having three new ones.' She changed the subject as her mind leapt on to more urgent matters. 'Jeanie Thomson, Mamie Smith and Peter Goodlad.

They're all from the village. I know them all, Mamie's brother Robert is with me. She'll be fine. The others are the first in their families to come to school but they are usually all right.' She checked the new names on Charlotte's register.

'Yes, they're all there. There are a few beginning to gather in the playground already. (It was only 8.30 am) They always seem to want to get here early on the first day. Sure enough Charlotte could hear shouts and hubbub as the children entered the playground.

'Oh, and by the way, Mr Sinclair came up to see me yesterday. He spoke about Magnus. Poor boy – he's having a difficult time.'

'Yes.' Charlotte responded cautiously. She was not aware what Mrs Manson's knowledge of the Sinclair's situation was.

The senior teacher looked at her. 'You're right to be careful. But Mr Sinclair has been quite frank with me and so I know in essence about Mrs Sinclair and Mr Sinclair said you knew as well. He felt he had to tell me because he has asked that we should take Magnus back to school here instead of sending him back to Lerwick just now.'

'Have you agreed to do that?'

'Oh yes. How could I not? The boy would be so anxious away in Lerwick with his mother so ill at home. It'll be bad enough for him here but at least he'll be at home every day. No, no, to send him back to Lerwick under these circumstances just wouldn't do. So,' she continued, 'I'll take him into my class. He knows most of the children there quite well and he's great pals with Lowrie Harcus who is still with me as he was ill last year.

'Mind you, the Sinclairs have been able to keep Mrs Sinclair's illness quiet up until now, but I don't think they will for much longer. People will notice that Magnus is back to school here and he will confide in Lowrie and so on. Anyway Mrs Sinclair herself looks so ill. People are already saying how thin she is. It's better out in the open. Then everyone will rally round and help.'

'That's true,' Charlotte agreed, 'but it must be so difficult for them with the children.'

'Yes, I suppose that's why they kept it so quiet. But Magnus knows now. Anyway,' she glanced at her watch. 'Look at the time. We'd better line them up.'

They went out to the main door, Mrs Manson brandishing a large brass bell which she rang vigorously. The children immediately stopped what they were doing and formed two lines three feet apart, little ones first, the new children being bossed into place by their more knowledgeable peers.

'Right.' Mrs Manson could summon a very big voice when she tried. 'March in to your classes.' The children marched in. Charlotte followed her little ones in and found everyone a seat. Each of the three new ones she put with someone who knew the ropes. They looked very small and a bit scared.

Charlotte faced the class from behind the teacher's desk.

'My name is Miss Gordon. Good morning children.'

'Good morning, Miss Gordon.' Most of the class managed an approximation of a reply. Charlotte resolved to do an exercise later on about names, her own included.

'Now, first of all we will do the Register.' And, for the benefit of the new pupils and those who might have forgotten over the holidays, she held up the Register.

'This is the Register. It is a list of all of your names which I shall call out one by one every morning and afternoon to make sure you are here. When you hear your name being called out I want you to say, "Present, Miss Gordon". That tells me that you are here, and I shall make a mark called a tick in the book beside your name. Don't worry, you will soon become used to it. So, let us begin: Frank Adamson.'

'Present, Miss Gordon.'

'Ann Baxter.'

'Present, Miss Gordon.' And so it went on through the alphabet. Even the three new ones responded with a little help.

Charlotte put the Register away in my desk drawer and moved the class on to the Bible and the Catechism – difficult for the very little ones but the needs of all had to be taken into account. They sat quietly and listened with round eyes to the feats of the older children in the room as they struggled with the unconquerable questions about man's chief end.

As it was only the beginning of the school year the children could not be arranged in order of ability or test results as was the fashion of the time. However Charlotte

114

grouped them in their classes so that each class could have some specific attention as and when necessary. But each class had to be divided as in Jarlshavn as elsewhere at that time, boys and girls did not sit together. She managed to get them all sorted out eventually and they seemed to enjoy the moving about, which they did with much giggling and shuffling.

'Now,' Charlotte said when all was settled. 'I want you all to sit in these places every day when you come into school for the next few days. When we have a test we'll maybe change things but for the moment that is where I want you to sit. Is that clear?'

'Yes, Miss Gordon.'

The day carried on, through reading and writing and arithmetic. Lunch time came and went. Jarlshavn ran a system of soup penny dinners and Mrs Isbister who lived near the school was contracted by the Board to supply this. As at Towie, she made the soup in her own home and carried it across with the help of two of the bigger boys. Contrary to the fear that someone would suffer a scald in the transfer of hot soup from house to school nothing untoward ever seemed to happen. The children had their own bowls and spoons and washed them under the cold tap afterwards. The whole procedure of course contributed to the ubiquitous school smell which had been so noticeable to Charlotte on her first day at Towie.

During the course of a very busy first day at Jarlshavn, Charlotte had not been able to think of anything else but the job in hand. With approximately thirty children of varying ages and abilities she could not afford to let her mind wander. However, when four o'clock came she heard Mrs Manson's hand-bell going with a feeling of relief. It had been a strange day, too busy to do anything but fly past, and yet it seemed ages since morning.

She lined up her charges, little ones first, helped them into their coats, and then allowed them to go out. Some made straight for the school gate. Some, especially the very small, were greeted by mothers, anxious to hear how the day had been. One new pupil's mother came up to check that wee Jeanie had not wet her underwear as she was prone to do when overwrought (As children's underwear in the late nineteenth century remained layered and bulky, to rectify this could be quite an undertaking.) Charlotte was able to reassure her that they had managed to reach the outside dry-closets in time, three times. At last, the last child was away and Charlotte and Mrs Manson were able to lock up the school.

'Everything all right?' Mrs Manson privately thought Charlotte looked pale and tired.

'Yes, I'm fine. I think everything went all right. No real disasters.'

'No, and even the soup didn't get spilt.'

'How was Magnus?'

'Very quiet. I got him to go over some of his last term's work so that I have an idea of where he is. The teachers in Lerwick will send over their progress reports as soon as they can but it's just as well to find out where he thinks he is. He has all the books so we can work away at it. We'll just need to support him all we can.' They reached the connecting gate between playground and school house.

'Right,' Mrs Manson clicked open the gate. 'I'm away to rest my legs for half an hour. See you tomorrow.'

Charlotte went out on to the road and went down the hill. She could do with a bit of feet up herself, she thought. A few yards further down she saw a figure standing by the side of the road. It's Magnus, she thought. I wonder why he's there.

As she approached, the boy came to meet her.

'Hello, Magnus. How did you get on?'

'Fine thank you Miss Gordon.' He lifted his cap politely. 'May I carry your case?'

'Thank you.' She handed it over and they walked on together. Neither spoke. Charlotte was never one for idle chatter and she was quite happy to wait for Magnus to speak.

After a few moments he said, 'Father told me about Mother.'

'Yes,' Charlotte looked at him. His face was pale and tense. He looked as though he were trying not to cry.

'Wait a minute,' she said. 'We're nearly at 'Da Peerie Skule-hoose' and if you like, you can come in for a few minutes. It will be easier to talk there.'

'All right,' he muttered. 'Thanks.'

She felt heart-sorry for the boy whose personality had lost its previous vigour. He walked along with his head down, the epitome of one who carried an unbearable burden – as indeed he did.

'Here we are,' she said. 'Come in.'

She dispatched Edie for tea and took her visitor into the parlour. Tea came and as the door closed on Edie she attended to the tray and gave the boy a cup.

'Tell me,' she said.

'Father said you know.'

'Yes I do, but I want you to tell me what you know and then we can talk about it. You did right to wait for me. My Granpa – he's a doctor – says it's important to have someone to talk to. What did your father tell you?'

'Well, he said Mother was very ill with something called con – consumption. You remember on Sunday I told you that I was sure there was something wrong with her. Well I was right. This consumption thing is what is wrong with her. Father had a talk with Mother on Sunday evening and I thought, there they are again, not telling me. But then he came out of the parlour and called me. Christina was in bed. We went into the dining room, just the two of us and he told me. He said about the consumption. He said I should come back to school here so that I don't need to go to Lerwick during the week. I asked him if Mother would get better and he just looked very sad. I don't think he wanted to say. But I remember Lowrie Harcus's granny and she had it and she died. I don't know of anyone with it who has not died. But I don't want my mother to die.'

He sat with tears streaming down his face, shoulders shuddering with sobs. Charlotte sat quietly in her chair for a while, drinking her tea, giving him time. After a few moments, Magnus put his hand in his pocket and pulled out a dirty hanky and wiped his eyes, blew his nose and gave a huge sigh.

'Sorry. Boys shouldn't cry.'

'Don't be sorry for crying. Of course boys should cry if they need to.'

'Well I really felt I needed to.' He sighed again. 'I think my mother is going to die. I think that's why Father wants me to stay at home.'

'Well,' said Charlotte carefully. 'I know your father wants to have you at home for your mother's sake, but I think he also understands that under the circumstances it's better for *you* to be at home too, instead of worrying in Lerwick about what is going on at home. So he wants you at home for you, too.'

'Do you really think that?'

'I'm sure of it. Isn't that what you feel too?'

'Yes, but I wasn't sure if he really thought like that. I have to say I am glad I'm at home, but, but,' his voice faltered. 'It won't stop her being very ill and probably dying. I can't stop it happening.' He buried his head in a cushion in a fresh storm of crying.

'Listen Magnus,' Charlotte pushed a clean hanky into his hand. 'You maybe can't stop things happening, but you can influence the way they happen.'

Magnus looked up at her, his face dirt-streaked and tear-stained. 'What do you mean?'

'Well, what I said about boys crying when they need to is quite true. But you won't need to cry all the time. I don't think your mother would want that – she would be very unhappy and worried.'

'But I can't even think about her now without wanting to cry.'

'I know. But there is also the question of trying to make her time as happy as possible. That will take a big effort from you. I don't mean that you should pretend that it is not happening. That's called denial and it doesn't help. What I do mean, is have the strength to go on, day to day with your head up, being the loving caring son that you usually are. And you'll have the added bonus of being at home, not in Lerwick. Don't let the consumption come between you and your mother. There will come a time – or a few times – when you and your mother will be able to talk about her illness. That's fine. You'll probably feel like crying then. That's fine too.' She looked at the boy sitting twisting the hanky into a rope. 'Do you understand what I mean?'

'Yes, I think so.' He took a deep breath. 'Things can't be the same though, can they?'

'No, but you can help to keep Harbour House a happy place. And, if ever you feel you need to talk, you are welcome to come here any time.'

'Thank you, Miss Gordon.' He stood up. 'I'd better go now. Mother will be wondering where I am. May I –,' he hesitated.

'Yes?' Charlotte prompted.

'May I go and wash my face before I go out?'

'Yes of course. See, I'll show you where.'

117

Charlotte waited in the hall until Magnus returned. 'Thank you very much,' he said. 'I'll be all right now.' She smiled.

'I'm glad. I know you'll be fine. Good bye, see you tomorrow.'

She watched him go down the path and close the gate carefully. A voice behind her said, 'That poor wee laddie.'

'Edie, thanks for the tea.'

'Ach, there's little enough we can do. Dinna worry, I won't say anything. But news of Mrs Sinclair's illness is well known now. I think everyone really has known for a while but now that Magnus is back to the school here, well, that could only be for one reason.'

'It's just like home,' Charlotte commented. 'You think people don't know something but then you find that everyone is aware of what's going on.'

'Yes, but, in a wee place everybody, or nearly everybody, means well. You'll see – it really helps when people know. They all rally round. Now, where's that tea tray, I'll just clear up before I go home.'

Charlotte went into her parlour and sat down with a sigh of relief.

The next few months flew past. Charlotte's week day routine at school continued until the Christmas holidays with a break (welcome to both children and teachers) in October.

A week before the holiday, on 6 October was Charlotte's twentieth birthday. On the run up to the day Edie appeared to be very busy although Charlotte could not tell why. After Charlotte arrived at school in the morning, before the classes settled down she found Mrs Manson ushering all the older children into the younger class with the usual giggling and shuffling when something out of the ordinary was afoot. One of the older girls went to the piano and Mrs Manson said to the assembled school, 'Now children, one, two, three,' and the whole school burst into '*Happy Birthday to you*'. Then Edie herself appeared carrying a large cake she had baked with twenty candles blazing away.

'Now, Miss Gordon,' Mrs Manson instructed. 'Blow them all out.' Charlotte blew, the school clapped and the formalities were over. Edie took the cake away to cut up for the morning break and everyone returned to normal.

The school was like that. It was essentially formal and strict on the surface and conformed with the Victorian ethos of authoritarian discipline. Children were supposed to know their place, do what they were told without argument, behave themselves and work hard at their lessons. To those who transgressed there was free use of punishment including the tawse, standing in the corner with back to the class, standing out in front of the class, not getting out to play for a period of time and extra work, both schoolwork and manual like bringing in peats for the school fires, sweeping the floor. Teachers also had the authority to 'keep children in' after school either as a punishment or to finish work uncompleted during the day. These characteristics were standard in the elementary schools of the day and well into the twentieth century. Thus the teachers retained a power which, if carelessly handled, could be misused and could create a school-atmosphere of dislike, fear, inability to learn readily and eventual rejection by some children of all things remotely academic.

The Elementary School at Jarlshavn managed to maintain the discipline as laid down by the School Board and the Education Authority. And yet, probably due to the primary influence over many years of Mrs Manson's being in charge, it succeeded in fitting in lighter episodes like that of Charlotte's birthday cake while retaining the overall restraint seen to be necessary for the good running of the school. It is worth noticing that although time was taken to bring in the cake and blow out the candles, no-one had a piece until break-time.

One disciplinary item which Charlotte found difficult to use was the tawse. She had seen it used by Mr Colin Coutts and occasionally by Miss MacHardie at Towie school. However although the lectures at the Training College had included the 'Use of the Tawse and other Measures for Keeping Order in Class' as a lecture subject and all students were recommended to order one from the tawse manufacturers in Lochgelly in Fife, she disliked the whole idea so much that she had not done it.

When Charlotte arrived in Shetland *sans* tawse Mrs Manson had shaken her head and instructed her to procure one forthwith and the school would pay for it. Off went an order to Lochgelly for one leather tawse with two tongues (they were also available with three tongues, as well as in varying lengths and in various weights and thicknesses of leather). A week later, Charlotte's tawse arrived: brown, shiny and stiff. It lay folded in its box like a menacing snake ready to pounce. Charlotte, looked at it, made a face, put it into her desk drawer and pushed it to the back out of sight and hopefully, out of use.

Chapter 17

A fine late-October Saturday morning. Charlotte was determined to take advantage of the sunshine and after breakfast she abandoned the Peerie Skule-hoose and headed for the hill at the back of the village. She climbed rapidly away from the houses, above the roofs and peat-reek into the bare, treeless hillside. Above, the sky was blue, for once few clouds hung around, seagulls wheeled, landed, walked, took off and wheeled again. A few rabbits bolted for their burrows at her approach. No-one else was around. She picked up her long skirt and gave a few skips in the short rabbit and sheep-nibbled grass and laughed aloud at her own childishness. Well, I can't be Miss Gordon all the time. I'm only twenty. It was good to be away from everybody – even Edie and Mrs Manson and the Sinclairs – just for a wee while.

She reached the top of the hill and turned to look. There, reflecting the blue of the sky, was the sea, right to the far horizon. She could see for miles. Right on the edge was the Isle of Foula, with its mystical peaks, today clearly set against the line linking sky and sea. This was the first time Charlotte had been able to see Foula from this height; she had seen it from the village but on such a bright, clear day and from the hilltop, the view was dramatic, especially since she had learned that she was looking at the highest vertical cliffs in Britain.

She scanned the horizon. A few boats out there, fishing, no doubt, possibly running for home before Sunday; she was too far away to identify them. In any case she had not been in Jarlshavn long enough to differentiate between boat ownership. That took time, observation and much local learning. She found it difficult to remember that she had only been there since August. She felt so much at home and she had come to know so many people.

Not many up here today though. But – in the distance she saw a figure walking strongly uphill on the same track that she had taken. She could not make out at first who it was. The figure drew nearer, male, tall, slim, long-legged. As he drew closer, she recognised the Reverend James MacLeod.

'Hello,' he called as he approached. 'What a fine day.' They shook hands. 'What a view. It's worth the climb just to see this. Look at Foula. Have you ever seen it like that before.'

'No. Only from the village. It's spectacular.'

'Do you come out walking often.'

'I like walking but there are so many other things to do: school, preparation, the garden and so on. I would like to come up here oftener though.'

'Mind you, the nights are drawing in now,' he warned. 'Don't come up here unless you can really see your way. There is not much light in Shetland in the dead of winter. Just till mid-afternoon and then it's a long dark evening.'

'Really? Is it really like that? I had heard that but I know it's dark early at home but not as early as here.'

'Oh yes it's quite true. I could hardly believe it when I came here first a few years ago.'

'Where do you come from?' she asked.

'Perth, the Fair City.' He looked at her. 'Have you been there?'

'No,' she said. 'I haven't been anywhere beyond Aberdeenshire and Aberdeen until now.'

'I'll show you Perth one day.'

She looked at him, slightly startled.

'Oh, I'm sorry,' he said, 'I didn't mean to presume. It's just that I thought it would be nice to show you what I think is the best town in the whole of Scotland.'

'But you've left it,' she said.

'Aye, I've left it for now. I had to, to get to Edinburgh, to the University. And then I was called to Jarlshavn and so that was it.'

They walked along the path over the hill and stopped to look at the view from the other side.

'Are you happy here.'

'Oh yes, it's lovely and the folk are great. I think we get on fine on the whole. The Manse is a good house and my housekeeper Mrs Laurenson is a great cook. You'll need to come up and have a meal one day and see.'

Again she looked at him.

He clapped his hand over his mouth. 'There I go again. Sorry. I sometimes speak without thinking and I move too quickly.'

'That's all right,' Charlotte said. She smiled and her eyes laughed. 'I'd be happy to test out Mrs Laurenson's cooking some day.' They looked at each other and smiled.

'There is one thing I wanted to talk to you about though,' he said, earnestly. 'The Sinclairs. I have heard that they are in trouble. Can you tell me how Mrs Sinclair is?'

Charlotte hesitated. She did not want to gossip, and yet Mr MacLeod was asking in such a careful, professional way, it would be churlish not to say something.

'I can understand your cannyness and admire you for it,' he said. 'I just want to know in case there is anything I can do to help. You see they belong to the Congregational church and Peter Jamieson is their minister, but this is such a wee place and I heard about their trouble and just wondered if there was anything I could do for them without treading on any toes.'

'That *is* kind. They're having a bad time of it, I'm afraid. Margery is being so brave and the children – well, Christina is too young to understand, but Magnus is hurting badly under the boy's barrier that he puts up for most people. He's back at school here now. I think that's helping them all to stay together.'

'And, Mr Sinclair? How is he.'

'Well,' Charlotte hesitated again. 'He's very brave too, but... but, he looks very unhappy sometimes when he thinks no-one is looking.'

They turned and began to walk back down towards the village.

'If you think of anything I can do, please let me know.'

'Yes, I will. There are the simple things like taking down a baking of scones from Mrs Laurenson, or flowers, or asking openly when you see Mr Sinclair how Margery is. Why don't you just go to the door and ask?' Charlotte had not encountered the ethics of inter-denominational pussy-footing (tergiversation) before.

He smiled. 'I wish I could. I might have Peter Jamieson challenge me about visiting his flock though if I did that.'

'I didn't realise it was like that. But,' Charlotte looked up, 'You could help Magnus through school. You know, when you come up for your weekly session with the older class, perhaps you might find a way to help or support him in that way. No-body could object to that.'

'That's an idea. I'll think how that could be done. You've been really helpful Miss Gordon.' They were approaching the village by now.

'You're welcome. I just wish there was more any of us could do.'

'May I call on you some day,' he asked as they came to the division in the road. The Manse lay one way and the other led to the School, the School house and further down the road Da Peerie Skule-hoose before running downhill to the harbour. 'One Saturday maybe, in the morning?'

She looked at him gravely. 'Yes, thank you. Come and have some tea.'

'Well, good bye then,' he held out his hand. 'I have enjoyed our walk, and talking with you.'

She grasped the proffered hand. 'I too am glad to have had the chance to speak with you. Good bye.' As she left him to walk to her house her calm face and unhurried walk belied the sudden lift of her spirits.

Chapter 18

Magnus was finding life difficult. He was glad to be at home instead of Lerwick. But even home was hard with a very ill mother, a father who handled the situation by steadily withdrawing both mentally by becoming ever more silent in company, and physically, by working very long hours at the Harbour Office. Wee Christina was too little to help him at all. Poor wee thing he thought, she's too young to understand what it's all about.

He had more than once taken up Charlotte's offer to visit her when he needed to talk. One day after school he caught up with her as she was nearing her gate.

'Miss Gordon, good afternoon.' Ever polite, he lifted his cap.

'Hello, Magnus. How are you today?' She looked at him. He looked pale and tired. 'Are you well?'

'Well, I think I am, but, I'm just, well, fed up.'

'Would you like to come in for a while? I expect Edie has made some scones or something.' The boy brightened.

'Yes, please.'

They were going up the path when a voice said, 'Good afternoon Miss Gordon.' There at the gate stood James MacLeod.

'Good afternoon, Mr MacLeod. Do you know Magnus Sinclair? Magnus you'll know Mr MacLeod from his sessions at school.'

'Hello, Magnus.'

'Good afternoon, Sir.' They shook hands.

'We were just going to have some tea,' said Charlotte. 'Would you like some, Mr MacLeod. You'd be welcome.'

'Well, I was just coming to invite myself for a visit on Saturday morning but if you're making tea now, well, that would be most acceptable.'

'Come along then.' Charlotte ushered her visitors into the parlour. Edie as usual appeared from nowhere.

'The kettle's boiling Miss. Would you like scones with your tea.'

'Yes, please, Edie.'

Magnus slouched to a seat. He was a conflict of inward emotions. This was *his* time with Miss Gordon. What right had the minister to come and interrupt? What was he doing here anyway? Charlotte looked at him and noted the stony face. How can I help him, she thought. By getting them to talk. Edie brought in the tea tray and laid it on the table.

'Thanks Edie.'

Conversation was slow. Charlotte tried this tack and that and the boy remained stiff and formal. Eventually, the minister said, 'How's your mother, Magnus?'

Magnus jumped, flushed, then said, 'How did you know about my mother?' He turned to Charlotte. 'Did you tell him. Were you talking about her? It's not fair. It's our family business. I don't want anyone to know.'

'Magnus.' Charlotte held out a placating hand. 'We have not been gossiping about your mother. And I did not tell Mr MacLeod about her. I think you'll find he has known about her illness for a wee while.'

Magnus turned to the minister. 'Is that true? Did you know anyway? How? It was a family secret.'

James MacLeod leaned forward towards the boy.

'Magnus, this is very difficult for you. I can understand why you wanted to keep this as strictly family business but in a wee place like Jarlshavn it is impossible. Everybody knows things about everybody else and talks about everybody else. And it's not necessarily a bad thing. Once people know, when it's out in the open, they want to help.'

Magnus turned to Charlotte. 'Is that true – that they want to help?'

'Yes indeed they do. People won't be gossiping in a nasty way. They'll be working out ways of giving practical help without seeming to be taking over too much. Like taking Christina out for a walk perhaps or…'

'That's funny,' said Magnus, 'people have been taking her out sometimes when they didn't do it before, and having her to play. Is that the sort of thing that you mean?'

'Yes, that's right. It's just a wee quiet way of helping. I know you have Meg working at Harbour House but she has a lot to do and anyway it's good for Christina to be out and about.'

'All right,' conceded Magnus, 'I didn't realise that was what people were doing and it was because they want to help Mother. But,' his face registered recognition of the idea, 'Mrs Jamieson handed in scones the other day and I saw Mr Williamson digging the garden. Is that …?' He looked at Charlotte.

'Yes exactly. Everyone has their own way of giving help. They all want to do something.'

'I still feel it's very … well familyish, though.'

'Magnus,' said Mr MacLeod, 'I know this is a family thing, but how about you? Have you been able to talk to any of your friends about it even though you thought it was a secret.'

'Well, ye-es, I told Lowrie, Lowrie Harcus. His granny died of consumption last year. He's my friend. We talked about it. He, he cried when we were talking about it. He loved his granny. I – ' he hesitated, 'I cried too.'

126

'Do you think it helped you to talk to Lowrie about your mother and her illness?'
Magnus looked at Mr MacLeod and thought for a bit.

'Yes,' he said, 'yes, I think it did.'

'How do you think it helped?'

'Well, he knew. He understood because of his granny.'

'Right, Magnus, well done. Now, don't you think that you also were able to help Lowrie by letting him talk about his granny?' Magnus nodded slowly.

'And, don't you think other people are wanting to help in their own way? Even though they don't all have quite the same understanding through experience as Lowrie.'

'Yes, I suppose so.' He was looking better, less angry and defensive.

'Well,' the minister spread out his hands. 'I rest my case. Your mother's illness is not now a secret, people want to help in each and every way they can, you can see how their help works and that as far as Lowrie is concerned, you have felt better for it. Imagine how much better that makes your mother feel, too.'

'Yes, I think I understand. Thank you very much for talking like this.'

'That's what I'm here for. Now,' James MacLeod drained his tea-cup and got to his feet. 'I must get on. Thanks for the tea, Miss Gordon. Good bye Magnus, I'll see you at school.'

'Good bye Mr MacLeod. Thank you.'

At the door, Charlotte added her thanks. 'You said just the right thing.'

'I hope so. That boy needs all the support he can get just now. Now, may I call again?'

Charlotte was very aware that any calls on her, a single young woman, from a young man, even though he was the minister, required some sort of chaperonage. Since their meeting on the hill she had considered this and was determined not to put herself into a situation which could be misconstrued by anybody else. On the other hand, in her own modest way, she liked the idea of having James MacLeod to visit her. And, she thought, with a spark of rebellion, why shouldn't she have him to visit her? But nevertheless she had a position to keep up. How could she balance this? How could she achieve this while adhering to the required social niceties of the time? The answer: Edie.

'Yes, of course, you'll be very welcome,' she said. 'Come sometime after school or on a Saturday morning. Edie is around then and will make tea.' She looked at him. He met her eyes and understood perfectly. After all, he was of the time as well and came under its collective rules as well as anyone else. In his case, as a minister, the rules were probably even more firmly in place and James MacLeod appreciated this very well.

'Thank you, I'll do that. In the meantime, thank you for the tea. Goodbye.'

'Good bye.' Charlotte went back inside and into the parlour where Magnus stood looking out of the window.

'He's a nice man. I like him. I was angry to begin with but not any more.'

'Yes. I could see you were not happy. I'm glad Mr MacLeod was able to help.'

127

'I wish he was our minister.'

'Well, I'm sure Mr Jamieson is a good minister too.'

'Yes, but you can't speak to him in the same way. Oh well, I'll be able to see Mr MacLeod at school.' Magnus picked up his school bag. 'Thanks Miss Gordon. You're a real help. Come and see Mother sometime soon won't you.'

'Yes of course.' Charlotte accompanied him to the door. 'I'll be down soon.'

Chapter 19

The autumn of 1894 tore into winter with a series of howling gales, flying rain, stinging sleet and hail giving way, as the weather grew colder, to early December snow. It was cold and unpleasant to be out and about even though the snow, so near the sea, didn't lie long. The nights grew longer and the folk settled in for the long haul until the return of the sun.

Charlotte kept her promise to go down and visit Margery. Even though she was a doctor's grand-daughter and knew from what she had heard and read about the progression of the wretched disease known at the time as consumption, she had never before been in close touch with someone who actually had it. Now she visited Margery whenever she could.

She was shocked by what she saw. When Charlotte arrived in Shetland in August, Margery, although obviously unwell, was able to be up and about, take a hand with the children, and even go outside for walks. Through the following weeks she became thinner, her joints appeared to grow larger in relation to her diminishing limbs, the ever-troublesome cough became more persistent. It was accompanied by sputum, at first frothy and then as the disease progressed, blood stained. In addition Margery often had a pain in her side accompanying the cough, frequent night sweats and a swinging temperature indicated by a high, hectic flush on her cheeks which increased to the whole of her face on exertion.

At the same time Margery ate little. She didn't feel like eating and had no appetite. Meg tried all her favourite dishes. Even Christina was heard to say, 'Mama, eat, eat for Christina.' A distraught Alexander daily brought in little trifles to tempt the invalid and turned away disappointed when she could not co-operate. Dr Taylor was a frequent visitor. Although cheery at the bedside he went into repeated solemn conclaves with Alexander over how to get some nourishment into Margery and what could be done next. He considered cod liver oil to be very important, for both its fat and vitamin content and prescribed it for Margery to take after meals. She hated it but took it obediently as she could see how worried they were. In the same way Dr Taylor said she must take iron in the form of 'reduced iron' and which could be taken in soup. This was very difficult to stomach and it was doubtful whether Margery was ever able to take it in sufficient quantities to do her haemoglobin level any good.

Another fashionable restorative strategy for those with consumption was to take them somewhere with a mild climate. These included 'abroad': places like Italy, Madeira, Lisbon and the South of France; or the South of England, especially South Devon, or the Isle of Wight; and, cruising, to places like the West Indies, or even further afield like Australia and New Zealand. Dr Taylor and Alexander went through the options together. But when Alexander put the idea of a change of air and climate to Margery she was firm in her opposition.

'But,' Margery, pleaded Alexander, 'I don't want to send you away for ever, just for a change and just to help you get better.'

'Alexander, to go away from you and the children would not help me. It would make me very unhappy and homesick.'

'But I could come and visit you.'

'Alexander,' she held his hand fondly. 'That's not an option and you know it. You couldn't leave the children just like that, and anyway, you can't get away from the harbour in the middle of winter. And anyway, I'm fine, I really am. All right I have a bit of a cough, and I've lost some weight. But just you see, I'll lie low here for the winter and come the spring, I'll be out and about again as soon as the weather improves. I don't need your South of France. Shetland will do me fine.'

Nothing would move her and Alexander was forced to report failure when Dr Taylor next visited.

'Oh well,' the doctor commented. 'I suppose we knew from the beginning that she wouldn't go. But we had to try. We'll just need to keep her warm for the winter and see how things go.'

'But, can't we make her go?'

'Alexander, my friend,' the doctor laid a hand on his arm, 'what good would that do? If you forced her to go she would be angry and resentful. And that would do no good at all. In fact it would probably do the opposite. The state of mind is very important in a patient's well-being.'

'But we can't just do nothing,' Alexander's voice broke. 'She's dying in front of my eyes. She's getting thinner by the day. I can't stand by and do nothing.'

'You are not doing nothing. You are there for her. You spend time with her, talking, playing draughts and chess, reading with her, entertaining her and being a family with her and the children. We are doing all we can but that, medically, is limited. We can't force the food down her throat any more than we can force her to go abroad. She needs to have peace of mind and retain her personal dignity. And if even then it means that we lose Margery, then we'll have made her final days as happy and peaceful as we can.'

Alexander held his head in his hands.

'You're right of course. It's just that it is so difficult. This is my wife we are talking about.'

The doctor looked at him. How many times had he been in this position, of doctor, adviser, comforter and friend. And how powerless he often felt when all he could do was be there for his patient and the family and wait for what was to happen.

But, he reminded himself, that was all part of being a doctor. The mental and spiritual came along with the physical under the holistic umbrella: the caring for the whole person and, of course the family.

'Alexander,' he said, 'as far as curative medicine is concerned, I can do no more for Margery. I can give her something to help the night sweats. We can apply poultices or plasters if the pain in her chest becomes too bad. That should help a bit. But the main thing I can give her is part of what you all can give her now. That is, tender, loving care. If she gets through the winter then she'll have the spring to enjoy. But –' he shook his head, 'I really don't know if we'll get that far. So it's up to us all to help her. Give her all we can.'

'Yes,' said Alexander heavily. 'Yes, we will'.

With a brief touch on his shoulder the doctor left the room. Alexander heard the door close and voices in the hallway as he spoke briefly with Meg. The front door slammed and the doctor's gig clattered away. He sat alone for a long time trying to come to terms with his loss which he now saw as inevitable.

Margery's cheerful opposition to any abroad trip for her health was not necessarily a cover-up for the sake of Alexander, although no doubt that came into it. It would have taken a lot of trouble and arranging to take her abroad, even as far as the South of England and Margery was well aware of this. But in common with most people with consumption Margery genuinely thought that she would recover. It was only, therefore, a matter of time and patience. This was at once difficult to cope with by those who knew there was no hope, and made easier for visitors who might not be aware of the whole truth. As far as the children were concerned, Christina loved visits to Mama's room. She didn't understand why Mama did not jump around and play any more but her welcoming smile was delightful for the little girl and the reading and games they played made early happy memories for Christina.

Magnus, who turned thirteen in November found it all very difficult. It was hard to keep up what he saw as a pretence of recovery when he was with his mother. Nevertheless, his talks with Charlotte helped him to keep going and to keep up a reasonably bright front.

Charlotte herself visited as often as she could and watched her friend's physical deterioration with despair. She helped with Christina as much as her schoolwork would allow, taking her out for walks, entertaining her at Da Peerie Skule-hoose, and even sometimes putting her to bed and telling the bedtime story. She became a familiar figure flitting in and out.

One dark December day in the last week of the year when the school was on holiday, Charlotte left the house in the morning and walked briskly down the road to the harbour. Clouds hung around, a breeze was blowing offshore, a spit of rain in the air. The damp coldness of it reached the marrow of those brave enough to be outside.

Harbour House stood as always as though keeping watch over the maritime comings and goings. Charlotte knew Alexander would be in his office but Meg would let her in, the children would be there, and Margery. She had some fruit for them all, saved from a parcel she had received from Towie. Christmas was not kept in a frenetic fashion with trees, and fancy decorations and innumerable expensive presents. Indeed, in Shetland they were more likely to stick to the old calendar and celebrate Auld Yule beginning on 6th January, and (officially) culminating twenty-four days later with the excitement of Up Helly Aa. But her fruit was a special seasonal treat that the Grants in Towie received every year from some long-established grateful patients and shared with her wherever she was. Now it was her turn to share her parcel.

The house was quiet as Meg let her in.'Where is everybody?'

'Magnus is out along the beach with the boys,' Meg said, 'and Christina is in the kitchen helping me. Come and see her.'

They went through to the kitchen where Christina, covered in a very large towel was standing on a chair at the table rolling out pastry. Her tongue stuck out with her concentration. Every now and again the rolling-pin stuck to the pastry and she put her hand in the flour bag and threw more flour on it to loosen it.

'That'll be lovely pastry,' Charlotte murmured to Meg. Christina looked up and let out a squeal of delight.

'Gordon. I'se baking.'

'So I see. It looks lovely. What is it going to be?'

'I think, a pie, for Mama. But,' Christina said, 'you can have a bit.'

'Thank you very much,' said Charlotte. 'That's very kind of you.'

'Gordon, I'll play with you now if you like.' Christina made to get down from her pie-making.

'Well,' Charlotte hesitated. She did not want to turn Christina down but she really wanted to spend time with Margery. Fortunately Meg chipped in.

'No, no,' she said. 'Miss Gordon is going up to see Mama and anyway you need to finish your baking. I need your help here. And you needn't wind yourself up like that,' she said firmly as Christina made to open her mouth in protest. 'You can play with Miss Gordon another time.' Christina subsided.

'Thanks Meg. Now, Christina,' Charlotte reached into her bag. 'Look what I've got.' She pulled out the fruit and nuts. 'Now, I've got a wee baggie each for you. One for Mama, one for Dada, one for – '

'Christina,' shouted the wee girl.

'Yes, and one for Magnus and one for Meg.'

'What do you say, Christina?' said Meg.

'Fank you, Gordon.' Christina, still standing on the chair leaned over, lips pouted, to give Charlotte a very floury kiss.

'You're welcome. Watch you don't fall.' Charlotte gave her a steadying hand.

She looked at Meg. 'Would it be all right if I went up?'

'Yes, That's fine. Mrs Sinclair'll be glad to see you. She's still in bed. She is most mornings and then she gets up for a wee while in the afternoon. It must get wearisome for her, but she never complains.'

'Can I take anything up to her?'

'Well I usually try and get her to take a cup of tea around this time. You could take some up and have some yourself with her. That might help her to drink it. And have a biscuit too. Here I'll set the tray.'

'Now,' she said when all was ready. 'Here you are. You will be sure and give her this cup won't you. That's her cup and nobody else uses it.'

'Yes, I understand.' Charlotte grasped the tray. 'I'll see to it.'

The voice that answered her tap on the bedroom door was quiet. Charlotte opened the door gently and looked in.

'May I come in? I've got tea here.'

'Oh Charlotte, how good to see you. How are you? Is it very cold outside?'

'I'm fine thanks, and yes it's cold and damp and I'm not going to pretend it isn't. But more to the point, how are you?'

'Oh I'm all right.' Margery struggled into a sitting position.

'Here let me help you.' Charlotte put the tray on the table and busied herself shaking up pillows and propping them behind Margery's back. She then turned to the fire, gave it a redd-up with the poker and added another peat. The actions gave her time to blink back the tears which came to her eyes when she saw the deterioration in Margery's condition, even in a couple of days.

'There, now have some tea.' She handed the cup over.

'Thanks,' Margery took it and sat it on the bed-tray in front of her. 'You've even got the right cup.'

'Yes, Meg said this was the one.'

'Yes, all my dishes are kept separately. It's for the best. I cannot bear to think of infecting the children. Dr Taylor has been very good about telling us what to do.' She took a sip. 'But come next summer, I'll be fine and we can stop all this disinfecting. I keep telling Alexander, I just need to get through the winter and then I'll be on the go again. Won't that be wonderful?'

Charlotte held out the plate. 'Have a biscuit,' she urged, evading the question. 'Meg's orders. She says you need to eat more.'

'Oh, Meg's always on at me about eating. So is Alexander. But I'm really not very hungry.' Charlotte pushed the plate at her.

'Oh well,' she said, 'just to keep her happy.' She took a biscuit and had a tiny bite. 'She does well with the baking. You have one too. So,' changing the subject, 'what's been going on? How is school? Are you happy with everything now that your first term is over?'

'Of course I'm happy. School is really most enjoyable and Mrs Manson is so helpful. The only thing is, she made me get a tawse, you know.'

'A tawse?' Margery's eyes widened. 'Would you ever use it.'

'Well, I don't know if I could bear to use it,' said Charlotte, 'but she said I had to have it and I think she felt I was not properly equipped without it. So we sent to Lochgelly for one. The real place where they are made.'

'Does Mrs Manson use hers?'

'Only very occasionally. I don't think she has this term. I think the children are on the whole very good. I find it difficult to think of children being strapped because they can't do their tables or whatever. It just makes them more nervous.'

'Have you been able to take them out – the children I mean.'

'Yes, we've went out on a few nature walks, but we'll have to wait for the better weather and more light now. But there's plenty to do inside. It takes me all my time just keeping up with all the things we have to do in the curriculum. But my little readers are doing very well – I'm really pleased.'

Margery smiled. 'You're a born teacher. I'm sure the children are racing ahead.'

'Well,' said Charlotte modestly, 'the mothers and fathers seem quite pleased, although wee Jeanie's mother was not amused when she finally did wet herself in school just before the holidays.'

'Oh dear,' Margery giggled.

'Yes, but it's no laughing matter. I'm not surprised the child finally did it – her mother nags her so about not doing it.' Charlotte put her hand over her mouth. 'Now, I shouldn't have said that. Sorry.'

'Never mind, I won't tell. Tell me some more about what goes on. I wish I had been a teacher.'

'You've got your lovely children.'

'Yes I know,' Margery smiled. 'And I would not change them for anything. Not even,' she paused as a loud kicking and scuffling sounded at the door, 'Not even when they interrupt my conversations with my friends. Come in.'

The door-handle turned with a struggle and Christina appeared on all fours with her dress and apron tripping her at the knees.

'I'se a bear,' she announced.

'Christina,' Meg's voice floated up the stairs. 'What are you doing?' She ran up the stairs and came in at the back of her lively charge. 'Sorry, Mrs Sinclair. Come on, Christina.'

'It's all right, Meg, I know what she's like.'

'Is your pie ready?' Charlotte asked Christina.

'In the oven. Soon be cooked.'

'Come on and check it. It's your pie, you need to say when it is ready.' Meg took the 'bear' firmly by the hand and hauled her to her feet.

'Bye Mama, Bye Gordon,' she called as she went out of the door.

They looked at each other and smiled as the door clicked shut. 'She's a handful,' Margery said. 'It's difficult to remember she's not quite three yet. She does so much.'

'She'll be quite an addition to my class in a couple of years' time,' said Charlotte.

'Won't she? It will go so quickly. We must hold fast to the baby days – they're not long enough.' Margery's face saddened as she thought of those other babies and the little girl who would never grow up. 'And, now, look at me, I can do nothing for her.'

'Enjoy her visits to you, when she comes up to play in your room. I know you can't have her too near you but you could play distance reading games.'

'How do you mean?'

'Well you could, or I will if you like, make cards in big print with string on them for hanging them up. You could name everything in the room, hang a card on it and then Christina could learn to read the name of the item – like 'chair', 'bed', and so on. That would keep her mind occupied and she would be here with you without getting too noisy.'

'That's a great idea.'

'Right, that's settled,' said Charlotte. 'I'll do some cards and bring them up in a couple of days. Now, I'd better go and let you get a rest.'

'Thanks for coming.' Margery laid her head back on the pillows and closed her eyes.

'Good bye.'

Charlotte left the room and headed for the kitchen where all was warm, and smelling of baking pastry.

'I'll go now. Thanks for the tea.'

'How did you find her?' Meg turned from the range, her face flushed with the heat.

'She seems very tired now. I think she'll sleep for a wee while. She can really only cope with a short time talking.'

'Aye, but it does her good at the same time. Sets her up for the day, a visit from you does. She likes hearing what you're doing and what is going on at the school. Will you be back soon?'

'Yes, I promised to do something for her that –'Charlotte nodded her head towards Christina – 'could be done in the bedroom, not too noisy. So I'll be back with that soon.'

'That will be fine.' Meg picked up Christina. 'Say good bye to Miss Gordon now.' Christina held out her arms. 'Bye Gordon.' She hugged her fiercely.

Good bye.' Charlotte returned the hug and made for the door. 'Good bye Meg, see you soon.'

Outside, the day was as damp as before. Charlotte shivered and went back up the hill to Da Peerie Skulehoose and to her own peat fire.

Two days later Charlotte headed down to Harbour House with Christina's reading cards. Margery was awake and sitting up watching their arrangement with interest. Soon most available items in the room had a card hanging from it with its name. Christina hugged herself with excitement. Magnus looked on with the amused tolerance of an older brother. Even Alexander was there to see what was going on. Soon Christina was able to go to the article with the name card and seem to make the connection between the two. She sat on the chair, looked at the card and said solemnly, 'chair'. Everyone clapped.

'Right,' said Charlotte, 'I'll leave you to it.'

Alexander saw her out. 'Thank you so much,' he said. 'You have been so kind. It means a lot to us all.'

'I'm happy to anything to help.'

'Well, thanks anyway.'

Charlotte ran down the path and walked along the harbour. It was fine and clear that day. The wind was gentler and the sun shone. One of those memorable winter days which make folk say, 'I wouldn't mind the winter if it all could be like this'.

She wandered along, lost in thought. I wonder what Granny and Granpa are doing. Sitting cosied up by the fire I should think. I hope there's not too much snow. Granny's last letter mentioned snow and how cold it was. She could see them sitting there at Trancie House in the firelight and lighting the lamps as the daylight disappeared. She didn't hear the voice calling her to begin with.

'Miss Gordon, Miss Gordon.' At last she turned. It was James MacLeod.

'Oh, I'm sorry, I was away somewhere else. I didn't hear you. How are you?'

'Oh I'm fine.' He smiled at her. 'I thought as you are out and about, I could accompany you on your walk. I saw you from further up the road. That is,' he added hastily, 'if you wouldn't mind.'

'No, no, I wouldn't mind,' Charlotte said. 'In fact I would enjoy the company. We could walk round the harbour if you like.'

'What were you thinking about?' he asked as they walked along, 'that took up your attention so very much.'

'I was thinking of my grandparents, and wondering how they are getting on in the snow. They are getting on a bit now and West Aberdeenshire is known for its cold hard winters.'

'Is your grandfather still working – he's a doctor isn't he?'

'Yes, a country doctor, and yes he's still working. I don't know how we'll get him to stop. The folk love him and he loves them and his work.'

'You seem very close to them.'

'Oh I am. You see, I went to stay with them when I was six. They brought me up really.'

'Are the rest of your family near?'

'Yes. They live a few miles away. I have five brothers and sisters; I'm the oldest.'

'But, you went to stay with your grandparents?'

'Yes,' Charlotte said. 'It's the old story, too many children in very poor circumstances and they just couldn't cope. My grandparents volunteered to take me.'

'But was that not very hard on you? To be moved like that.'

'Well,' Charlotte considered. 'Yes – yes, it was at the beginning. I was very angry and resentful.'

'I'm sure you were. I would have been.'

'Yes, but you see they gave me a chance that I might not otherwise have had. Once I settled down, I was very happy. And I went back up the glen to see all my folks there.'

'Oh Charlotte, I mean Miss Gordon, there is so much we don't know about each other.'

'Yes,' she responded, ignoring his unorthodox slip of nomenclature, 'I suppose there is.'

'Well,' he said, 'we need to find out about each other. I want to know all about you, Charlotte, I mean Miss Gordon. Oh listen to me. I've called you Charlotte again. I always call you Charlotte in my mind. Please let me call you Charlotte. Then I'll believe there is a little hope for me.'They reached the end of the harbour wall and paused.

'Mr MacLeod, I don't know what you mean.'

'Oh, please call me James. I want us to be friends.'

'But we are friends. You've been up to the Peerie Skulehoose and borrowed my books, and had tea, and today we're walking along the harbour. Of course we're friends.'

'But I want to be more than that.'

Charlotte took a deep breath.

'Mr MacLeod, we hardly know each other. And I'm not ready or old enough to be thinking about being more than friends with anybody.' She started to walk back along the harbour. He came into step with her.

'But don't you think you could call me James, and let me call you Charlotte – just to give me a little hope? I admire you so much – all you have done and are doing.'

'Mr MacLeod, all right James,' she half smiled at his earnestness. 'I am proud to call you my friend. I'm very happy for you to call me Charlotte, for us to use first names. I never was one for this Miss Gordon business. But we cannot use them in public. And,' she added firmly, 'we are only friends, nothing more.'

'All right,' he conceded. 'For just now. But just you wait – I won't go away. I'll be there for you at any time.'

'I did not think that I'd have to point out to you that you are the minister here with a position to uphold. I also must not do anything that would make people gossip about me. Surely you see that.'

'I know, I know. It's so difficult. I've never felt like this before. I'll have to bury myself in my work.'

'Well, that's as may be. But please calm yourself and do not let us make things awkward for ourselves by unseemly behaviour.'

They continued their walk in silence to the other side of the harbour and then Charlotte turned up the hill for her house. 'I'll have to go now.'

'I should have asked earlier,' he said. 'How are they at Harbour House? Mrs Sinclair?' Charlotte looked at him.

'Well, they're coping,' she said, 'but Margery is very thin and frail. But, you know, her spirit is amazing. I left her playing reading games with Christina who is lively enough for ten people.'

'Does she get a rest from her?'

'Oh yes, Meg is grand with her. In fact,' Charlotte turned, 'here they are now, out for a walk.' The Harbour House gate clicked and Meg and Christina came out.

'Hello,' called Christina.

'Hello Christina, off for a walk?'

'Yes, with Meg.'

'Just round the harbour,' Meg took the little girl's hand. 'Come along. Good bye, Miss Gordon, Mr MacLeod.'

'Good bye.'

'And I must say good bye now, too,' said Charlotte. 'Thanks for the walk.' They shook hands in the usual formal way.

'Good bye,' he said. 'See you soon?'

'I'll be in the Kirk on Sunday morning. Good bye.' With that she turned and walked swiftly up the hill.

Chapter 20

By this time Shetland was moving into in the season known locally as 'the Yules'. The official New Year (New style) came and went, and on 6 January (although over the years that date has fluctuated) came the beginning of Shetland's own winter Yuletide festivities with the day known as Aald Yule.

The new school term also began. It was a difficult time for the teachers as the children were expected to be back in school and working hard. On the other hand, there was no escaping the feeling of excitement in the air. All the children reported having seen on Tulya's E'en (3 January), trows released from the underworld to work mischief on mankind. As protection to life and property various precautions were undertaken: very important was saining or signing the goblet before drinking, with originally the sign of Thor's hammer, later becoming the sign of the cross; crosses of straw were laid at the entrance to cornyards; hairs from beasts on the croft were plaited and hung from the byre door; and, all the houses and outhouses were smeeked with blazing peats. Special meals and food were prepared prior to and during the Yule Day and along with dancing, singing, eating and drinking and celebrating from house to house, the merry-go-round of festivities kept going until Up Helly Aa.

Small wonder then that Mrs Manson and Charlotte had uphill work trying to keep the children at work. On the other hand, it all helped the community through the darkest days of winter.

No celebrations could help the dark days which hung over the Sinclair family. Margery was slipping into a state out of which there was to be no return. Alexander became ever more upset, morose with the children, dour with anyone outside the family and falsely jocund with Margery. She in her turn persisted in saying that she would be fine when the spring came. Magnus neither knew what to do nor how to handle his mother. He leant heavily on Charlotte, visiting her every few days after school, in turns weeping, clenching fists and stamping or, sitting silently staring into the fire. At least he can be himself here, thought Charlotte. He must feel he has to put on an act with everyone at home. Unused to dealing with such situations, she had written to Granpa for advice on how to help.

'Let the boy talk to you if that's what he needs', Granpa's letter advised. 'If he cries, let him. Give him all the support you can.' Charlotte did her best.

One day Charlotte went into the Harbour House and found Meg in tears in the kitchen.

'Oh Meg, it's hard for you.' She put her arms around the older woman.

'I canna help it, Miss Gordon. We're going to lose her. These poor bairns, and poor Mr Sinclair. What are they all going to do?'

'I don't know, Meg. We'll just need to be there for them, but I know how difficult it must be for you being here all the time. You're part of the family. Is Maggie Sutherland still coming in every day.'

'Oh yes, she's a great help. She's in and out at least twice in the day making Mrs Sinclair comfortable and although she's really the howdie, she's had so much sick-nursing experience that she's a wonder. She could make anybody comfortable. And, you know the doctor was able to get special food for Mrs Sinclair?' Charlotte nodded.

'Well, Maggie persuaded her to eat it. Isn't that wonderful? Mind you they, the officials, are keeping an eye on things. They're very pernickety about keeping things disinfected. They don't let everybody who has consumption stay at home because of the infection. In a wee hoose it wouldn't have done. But here, well we're managing.'

She sighed. 'I wouldn't want her to go off to a sanatorium.' Her lips trembled. 'But that's what would happen if we didn't obey the rules. I couldn't bear it.' Her eyes filled again.

'Come on now Meg,' Charlotte said. 'You're doing a grand job. Is there anything you want me to take up to her.'

'Yes, her special beef-tea which she gets now. This is the latest the doctor has said she needs to try and take.'

Charlotte took the tray upstairs and tiptoed into Margery's room. All was quiet.

'I'm not asleep.'

'Hello, you were so quiet I thought you must be.'

'No, no, just thinking with my eyes shut.'

'Shall I go away.'

'Oh no, please stay a while.' The invalid smiled. 'What have you brought on the tray this time?'

'It's your beef tea. Meg says you must have it. Doctor's orders.'

'Oh yes, it's supposed to build me up in all sorts of directions.' Charlotte helped her to sit up and gave her the cup.

'Can you manage?'

'Yes – yes, I think so.' She took a sip and set the cup in its saucer. 'Well, I'll drink it just to keep them happy. But, Charlotte, it's not going to do any good.'

'But Margery, it will help, the doctor says…'

'The doctor says –' interrupted Margery, 'but the doctor knows this is just façade. He knows I'm not going to get better – and so do I.'

Charlotte sat by the bed and held Margery's hand. She said nothing.

'Look at us. You shouldn't be even holding my hand. I've got a horrible, horrible disease, and I can infect people with it and I'm not going to get better and I won't see my children grow up and I just feel awful about it all. I know I thought all would be well but deep down now I know I can't go on much longer.'

'Have you spoken to anyone else about this?'

'No, but sometimes I see Alexander looking into the fire and he looks so sad. I know there's no bright tomorrow for us. And the doctor never goes along with all my plans for the spring. He just says "well we'll see" and things like that. I know what he's thinking but for a long time I thought I was right, that I would get better. Now I feel myself slipping and –'she stopped talking to cough.

Charlotte took the cup and gave her a large piece of material cut ready, to cough into. The coughing went on for a long time. When the bout was over, Charlotte took the cloth with its frothy, bloody sputum, threw it in the fire and poured a little disinfectant on her hands. Margery sank back on her pillows, exhausted.

'Don't go,' she whispered. 'I'll be all right in a few minutes.'

'All right, I'm here.' Charlotte sat down on the chair and waited in silence for her friend to recover. Margery shut her eyes. She was so slight her frame made hardly a dent in the pillow, hardly a ripple on the bedcovers, hardly a movement with each shallow breath.

After about five minutes, she stirred, opened her eyes and smiled.

'Thanks,' she murmured. 'I need to talk about this.' Charlotte waited.

'I have to face up to the fact that I'm not going to get better.' She paused. 'There,' she said, 'you're not arguing.'

'Do you want me to argue?'

'No, I want you to help me face up to it. It's true isn't it? No,' she changed tack. 'That's not fair to put you in that position. I'm telling you, I have not got much longer. Charlotte, I need to talk about it.'

Charlotte met her eyes. 'All right,' she said, 'let's talk about it.' She picked up the thin hand and held it again. 'What is it you want to say, Margery?'

'I want people now to acknowledge openly what is happening to me. So that we can make the most of the time we have left in an honest way instead of being all bright in here and talking in hushed voices about me elsewhere. And yes,' as Charlotte opened her mouth to say something, 'Don't say that's not happening because I'm sure it is.'

'I wasn't going to say that. I was going to ask how you knew.'

'I'm not daft,' Margery said. 'I know it happens. So can you tell Alexander for me that I know and I want him to know that I know so that there will be no more dissembling between us. And Magnus.'

'Are you sure that is what you want?'

'Yes, I'm sure. Even if we are all upset together it will be better than this moving round each other, everyone knowing but frightened to say.'

'All right then,' said Charlotte. 'I'll speak to them today.'

'I don't know what to do about Christina. She's so wee. I don't think she would understand.'

'I think you're right. She is very young. We'll all help her on a day-to-day basis.'

'But Charlotte,' Margery said urgently. 'There's something else. Something I'm so worried about.'

'Margery, what is it? What can be troubling you so?'

'Charlotte, I'm worried about what will happen to them afterwards.' Her lips trembled. 'The children won't have a mother and Alexander won't have a wife. What can I do? I don't want to leave them like this. The children need a mother to love them and care about them and tuck them in at night.' She broke down and wept with sobs which racked the frail body until Charlotte thought it could take no more.

Chapter 21

Charlotte

It troubled me greatly to hear Margery cry like that. How long had she been waiting to let herself go as far as this? I sat and held her hand for a while until the sobbing subsided a little, supplying her with cloths to wipe her eyes and blow her nose. At last she calmed. She took a breath and looked at me.

'Sorry. I haven't done that for ages. I do apologise for putting you through that.'

'Margery, please don't worry about that. I'm more worried about you worrying about Alexander and the children. They will cope, you know. They'll be very sad and unhappy but they are strong enough to get through this.'

'But they will need help. And I won't be there to help them. But,' she said, light dawning, '*you* will be here. That's it, Charlotte, you can help them. You can mother the children, take my place.' I looked at her.

'But Margery, I can't take your place, just like that.'

'Why ever not? You're here, you love the children, they love you. It's just right. And you get on with Alexander. Oh, please think about it. If I know you'll think about it I can be happy. You might,' she smiled, 'you might even fall in love, you and Alexander, and I'll be up there giving you my blessing.'

I did not know what to say. I sat thinking how to respond.

'Charlotte,' she gave my hand a little shake. 'Charlotte, are you hearing me?'

'Yes, I am,' I said. 'You've taken the wind out of my sails. I'm not quite sure what to say.'

'Just say yes,' she urged.

'But Margery, I can't just say yes, just like that. I love the children but I could never take your place as mother. And as for falling in love with Alexander, really I have only been in Shetland for a few months and never thought of such a thing.'

'The main thing is that the children should have a mother. You could be that person. But to do it properly you need to be Alexander's wife and be in the house. Then everything will be all right. Please think about it.'

'Look Margery,' I said, 'there's too much to think about all at once. I can't give you a "yes" to what you are asking. For one thing, nobody has asked Alexander. For another, I don't love him. Oh, I like him, but liking and loving are not the same thing.

143

But I can tell you this. I do love your children and after you are gone, I will do my best to support them and give them as much love as I can. I promise. She looked at me.

'And what about Alexander?'

'I can't make any promises about Alexander. He's his own person and I can't vouch for him. But I will help him all I can, if he will let me.'

With that, she had to be content. The stressful conversation had lasted long enough. She had another bout of coughing and after I had helped her, settled her against her pillows, and tidied her bed I took my leave. She was nearly asleep but held out her hand to touch mine.

'Thank you,' she whispered. I tucked the hand under the covers and left the room with a heavy heart to find Alexander.

That visit to Margery took place on the 20th of January. The last Tuesday of the month with its Up Helly Aa excitement, came and went. The build-up of anticipation of the children in the school became increasingly intense, climaxing on the day with a school half-day. In the late afternoon most of the children went the six miles to Lerwick with their parents to see the evening procession and the burning of the Galley before going home again.

Many of the adults, if they could, stayed for the all-night partying in the halls especially prepared for the occasion. The squads of guisers moved from hall to hall to entertain with their long-rehearsed, topical, local and, sometimes very personal sketches and songs. Their special costumes, kept a dark secret until the night, were a source of long term competition and rivalry. Most people, whether guisers or other revellers including the wives and mothers who made and served food all night, kept going until the early morning before calling it a night. On Wednesday all schools and shops were closed as Shetland slept off the night before.

Charlotte found school hard to deal with at this time. She had been looking forward to being a part of the festivities. However, with the sorrow of Margery's illness hanging over her she found it difficult to join in although she did her best. Mrs Manson, knowing full well what was happening, kept a close eye on the junior class and often went through from her class room to give what support she could.

Down at Da Peerie Skulehoose Edie was a great help. For one so young she had a knowingness beyond her years. On the Tuesday of Up Helly Aa, Charlotte walked down to her house from the school at lunch time. It had crossed her mind that Edie might have forgotten that she had a half day, but there she was, greeting her at the door with a pan of lentil soup simmering on the stove.

'Oh Edie, how wonderful. Just what I'm needing. Sit down and have some with me.'

'Thank you Miss.' Edie put out bowls and spoons, plates and bread.

'How was the morning?'

'The children are so excited. I was very glad when we could let them go home. There was no keeping them today. Are you going over to Lerwick this afternoon?'

'Oh yes Miss, and my Mam, and, my Dad's in a squad. I know what he's wearing but,' she tapped the side of her nose, 'I canna tell. My Mam and I are in one of the halls doing the food. But we'll see the procession first and the burning and all the squads when they come to the halls. It should be a great night. Are you going?' Charlotte shook her head.

'No Edie, I can't. I'm going down to Harbour House to sit with Margery for a while.'

'But Miss,' Edie protested, 'this is your first year here at this time. It's special.'

'I know Edie, but you see how it is. How could I go away and enjoy myself? Never mind, I'll go next year. You can tell me which hall to go to.'

'Hmm,' Edie was still disappointed. 'I still think it's a shame. But you're really good to go and sit with her like that. That's what my Mam says and – I think so too.'

'Thanks Edie, that's nice of you. Now,' Charlotte put her spoon into her bowl. 'That was really delicious soup. You'll need to tell me the secret ingredient some day because I tell you, I can't make lentil soup like that.'

'No problem, I'll show you one day.' Edie looked gratified at the thought of teaching the teacher something. 'Would it be all right if I went now? I'll make up the time, but I would like to go with the rest of them.'

'Yes, of course, Edie. You can tell me all about it. And you're having a day off tomorrow aren't you?'

'Yes. I think I'll need it.'

'Enjoy yourself.'

February came in with a blow from the sea. The second of the month, Candlemas, was greeted traditionally with chat about the return of the sun and spring being just around the corner although the gloom-merchants spoke heavily about 'February fill-dyke' and that the winter had a long way to go.

Charlotte spent the day at school as usual. She lit a candle in the morning on her desk as a visual illustration for her Bible lesson of the day, to remind the children of Mary and Joseph carrying Jesus to the temple forty days after his birth and of Simeon's recognition of who this special baby was. But as Charlotte lit the candle she thought of Margery whose life was now ebbing fast and the family and friends who watched and waited.

Mrs Manson came through from her room.

'Magnus is not here today.'

'Oh.' Charlotte's heart dropped.

'I haven't heard anything, but if I do, I'll let you know.' But the long day passed with no news.

At half past three Charlotte showed the children out as usual and hurried down to the harbour. On her way she stopped at her Skulehoose and picked a few tiny snowdrops from their sheltered spot and bound them with a leaf spear. At the harbour folk hung about. They shook their heads sadly as she walked swiftly past. She let herself in. Nobody about.

145

Upstairs, Margery's door stood ajar. Alexander and Magnus sat with her. Meg was out for a quick walk before it was completely dark, with little Christina. Margery opened her eyes and managed a smile.

'Charlotte, I knew you would come when you could. And you've brought snowdrops. Snowdrops for Candlemas.' She stroked the tiny white petals. 'See, I haven't forgotten what day it is.' Her breathing was short, difficult, painful. Charlotte acknowledged the greetings of the others and sat down in Alexander's vacated seat and took Margery's hand.

'All right?'

'Yes, I'm all right. I'm ready now, I think. I just have to allow myself to let go now.' Talking set her off coughing again. Charlotte busied herself with the cloths. After the coughing, Margery rested. They heard sounds below as Meg and Christina came back.

'I'd like to see my wee one,' Margery whispered. Magnus got up and went out. Within minutes the room was full of Christina's happy chatter.

'Mama, I got shells, with Meg. I was out in the nearly-dark. On the beach. We could hardly see the shells but I have some. Look.' She held out two grubby sandy hands full of her different shells.

'Christina, they're lovely,' Margery whispered.

'You can have one if you like,' Christina offered generously. 'Which one would you like to keep.'

'I think,' Margery looked at them, 'this one please.' She pointed to a little pink shell with deeper rosy edges.

'That's for you then.' Christina picked it out. 'Hold out your hand.' Margery held out her hand and the little girl pressed the shell into it and curled the thin fingers over it.

'Now you will keep it for ever and ever, won't you?'

'Yes I will,' promised her mother. 'Thank you very much.'

'Christina,' Meg came forward with suspiciously wet eyes. 'Come and have your tea with me in the kitchen now. Mama's going to have a rest.'

'Why are you crying?' Christina missed little.

'My eyes are watering with the smoke. Say "Good bye" to Mama, now.'

Christina leant forwards and gave Margery a hug. Margery, ever fearful of infection looked at Meg.

'Don't worry,' whispered Meg. 'I'll change her clothes and wash her hands and face. It's all right.'

'Thank you, Meg, for everything. Good bye, my friend.'

'Good bye, you've always been good to me.'

'Good bye, Mama,' called Christina. 'I love you. I'm going to have my tea now. See you later.'

'Good bye my little one. God bless you.'

'That's funny,' they heard the voice from a distance. 'Mama God-blessed me and it isn't bed-time.'

146

Silence fell. All to be heard was the laboured breathing. The peat fire glowed in the dying light of the February day. The door opened quietly and Dr Taylor entered.

'Any change?'

'Not really,' said Alexander. 'Margery's very alert but coughs when she talks too much.'

'I'm so alert, I can hear you.' Margery opened her eyes. 'Hello, Dr Taylor. I can't speak much. Thank you for all you have done.'

He bent over the bed and counted the racing pulse, felt the fevered brow, observed the fleeting respirations.

'Are you in any pain?'

'No, not really.'

'Charlotte went over with a cool damp cloth.'

'Here, let me wipe your face.' Margery held the ministering hand.

'You're a dear good friend.'

'This,' said Charlotte, 'is my privilege.' Her voice choked.

'Don't cry,' whispered Margery. 'It will be over soon and all will be well.'

'Oh, Margery, I shall miss you.'

'I know. We've been good friends, haven't we?'

'Oh yes, such good friends.'

'Magnus?' He went and held his mother's hand. 'Magnus my first born. I am going soon.'

'Oh, Mother.' The boy wept. Margery stroked his hair. 'God bless you', she said. 'Be brave, but keep loving. Let this help you to grow in every way.' He stepped back to let his father near.

'And now, my dear Alexander. I'm heart sorry to have to leave you. Alexander was unable to speak. Then he said, 'Oh my little dear one, don't go, don't go.'

'I have to. Soon. I want to say good bye while I can. Please, help – help me do it.' He took a deep breath.

'Yes of course. My wee wife, my heart's desire, good bye and may God be with you.'

She smiled faintly and whispered, 'You too.'

A little later she took another bout of coughing. This time it lasted for longer than usual and was accompanied by a significant haemorrhage from her lungs. When it was over and Meg and Charlotte had cleaned and refreshed her, Margery lay back on her pillows once again.

'Now I can rest.' She closed her eyes.

The watchers sat and waited through the long evening. Meg put Christina to bed and Charlotte took time to read her a bedtime story. The little girl slept, unknowing of the happenings in her mother's room. Magnus kept vigil with his father. Meg, ever practical, kept the kettle boiling in the kitchen, and did her best to persuade the others to eat to keep their strength up. Charlotte sat quietly. Every now and then she got up and bathed the face and hands of the dying woman. Dr Taylor, after ascertaining that he could do no more, left in the early evening to go elsewhere.

A little later they heard Maggie Sutherland's step on the stairs. The old howdie put her head round the door and nodded in satisfaction at the peaceful scene.

'Aye, that's right, let the lassie go now,' she said. 'Time to set down the burden. I'll sit awhile with you.'

So the long evening passed and into the morning hour.

At half past one on the morning of February 3rd 1895, Margery Sinclair took her last small breath. It was all so quiet that Alexander had to listen carefully to make sure. She was gone with no murmur, so peacefully and gently that the watchers could only give thanks for such a way to die. When Maggie and Charlotte came to wash and dress her for the final journey to the Kirkyard, they found in her hand the small pink shell.

Chapter 22

The procession following the coffin with the remains of Margery Sinclair moved slowly up the hill from Jarlshavn Congregational Church to the old Kirkyard on the hill. Here were buried both families of Alexander and Margery, not least of which were their own three little ones who did not live to grow up.

The coffin bearers numbered six at any one time. Every so often the men stopped, and their burden was taken over by another group walking behind and ready to take their turn. It was considered a privilege to be invited to be a part of this ritual. There were many men from Jarlshavn and the surrounding district who knew and regarded Margery highly and who now wanted to show their last respects by bearing her coffin for part of the way. Alexander and Magnus as chief mourners, took their turn with the carrying, a hard thing for a thirteen year old boy, but he wanted to do this for his mother and Alexander.

Charlotte did not go to the Kirkyard. To do this was not the custom for women in nineteenth century Shetland. However, she was able to go to the funeral service which was in the Congregational Church at Alexander's request. This in itself was a departure from tradition which usually decreed that the service be held in the house of the person who had died. Alexander, mindful of the respect in which the whole population of Jarlshavn held Margery, had asked Mr Jamieson if the service could be in church. It was just as well as folk arrived from all over the Islands and the Church was packed. As a further mark of respect the school was closed for the day and all shops had a black-bordered sign in their windows indicating her name, the date and time of the funeral and that the shop would be closed.

Charlotte sat just behind the family. At the last minute Christina wanted to sit with her and for the sake of peace, Alexander agreed. Christina sat quietly on her lap, staring wide-eyed at what was going on. Charlotte was glad to have her there; having another to think of helped her to control her own emotions.

The service was conducted by Peter Jamieson, the Congregational minister. As a courtesy, he had invited James MacLeod to do one of the readings. Charlotte was pleased to hear his voice – almost a breath of home. Not quite West-Aberdeenshire, but a nearly-there tone for all that.

As well as seeing him in church, James had visited her as well, even after that harbour walk when he declared in such a very precipitate manner that he wanted to be more than friends with her. Although disappointed at her reaction, he took Charlotte's words about propriety to heart. He never visited her alone, but always at a time when he knew that Edie would be there. Edie for her part was discretion itself. She had been well told about discretion before getting her job as school-mistress's maid and one of her main tasks was to be careful and tactful at all times. She took her role very seriously. Not that there was anything in James MacLeod's visits to be indiscreet about. He came, with a book for Charlotte to read, or a half-dozen eggs from the Manse hens, or a bunch of flowers. They drank tea and ate scones. They were never in the fullest sense, alone. While both observed the proprieties of the day, both came to know each other well, their likes and dislikes, their families and family histories. They liked each other. It was as simple as that.

Charlotte listened to the familiar voice reading the old words: 'Let not your heart be troubled neither let it be afraid'. What was it Margery said? 'All will be well'. Very positive things.

Now Mr Jamieson was saying, 'And God shall wipe away all tears from their eyes'. She thought about this. Maybe that was for the future. For the moment, the saddest thing was for the people left behind and people were crying. But sad too, for Margery dying before her children were grown up. But, Charlotte thought, is there ever a right time? People will always be wanting to wait for children to achieve this or that. She supposed it was better to accept, but how difficult. Margery seemed to have accepted it at the end. Perhaps she just got so tired that she had to. She pulled her mind back to the present as the minister was announcing the last hymn: 'Love divine, all loves excelling'. A good one for Margery.

After the Benediction, the congregation remained standing and the main bearers stepped forward and picked up the plain oak coffin. Down the aisle, and out into the chill February air. The men present fell into line, many to take their turn at the carrying for the two miles up to the Kirkyard.

The women stayed behind, some to go to Harbour House to organise the food, tea and whisky for the wake which was planned for the men's return from the Kirkyard. Charlotte took Christina's hand and joined Meg as she left the church. Meg's eyes were red with weeping. However she pulled herself together. She now had something practical to do and she was determined not to let Mrs Sinclair down for this last gathering in her name.

For the last day or two there had been a constant coming and going at Harbour House. A wake or post-funeral gathering required much organisation and help and the people of Jarlshavn outdid themselves. Everyone involved cooked, baked, donated, lent crockery and cutlery, delivered bottles of liquid refreshment and gave of their best. All that remained to do now was to set it all out, boil water for tea and be ready to pour whisky for those who wished.

By the time Charlotte arrived with Christina, the kitchen was crowded with bustling women all endeavouring to outdo each other in spreading, cutting-up, arranging, heating, pouring, setting-out. Old rivalries showed signs of surfacing. Mamie Smith wanted her scones to be first to be out; Jean Thomson said her Victoria sponge deserved a better place; Effie Tulloch made sure her sausage rolls got the best place in the range oven; Violet Harper had brought some special brand of tea which she said had to be used. Through all the mineer worked Meg, calm now, and in control in this, her own domain, the kitchen of Harbour House. Charlotte looked in amazement. I would rather have a class of children than this any day, she thought. But they mean so well. They're just wanting to be the best.

Christina started to wail. 'Why are all these people in my kitchen?' Charlotte caught Meg's eye.

'I think I'll take Charlotte up to the wee sitting-room. You don't need me here and she's getting upset.'

'Right, once we're organised, I'll take something up to you to eat. And Magnus too. I can't imagine he'll want to speak to folk by the time he gets back. He'll have had enough for one day.'

Upstairs, the fire was lit and apart from the addition of another peat needed no attending. Charlotte sat down thankfully. Christina nestled up with her and sat still for a long time. Charlotte was just beginning to think that she had fallen asleep when the small voice said, 'Gordon, where's Mama?' Charlotte thought for a moment.

'Christina, Mama was very ill. She wasn't able to get up and play any more. She couldn't cook or go outside for a walk. She wanted to be well enough to be able to stay with you but she couldn't. So, she has gone to be with Jesus in Heaven.'

'But Jesus is in church.'

'Well, Jesus is what church is about. We go there especially to think about Him. That's why we all went to church today for Mama and remember we sang Mama's favourite hymn.'

'Yes, that was nice. For Mama.'

'Yes, for Mama.'

'I think Heaven is a nice place.' Christina wriggled off Charlotte's knee and picked up her best doll known as Beanie Two after Charlotte's much loved doll.

'See Beanie Two, Mama's gone to Heaven. Isn't that lovely for her?' Beanie Two looked at her with her doll-eyes. She turned to Charlotte.

'Beanie Two thinks so too. She told me.'

'That's good,' said Charlotte, hoping she had said the right thing. 'Now you play with her for a little while in front of the fire and we'll wait for Magnus.' Within five minutes Christina lay down on the floor and fell asleep, tired out with the unusual events intruding into her usually well-ordered day.

Magnus was soaked and cold.

'Magnus, come in. Let's get your wet things off. Is everyone back?'

'Yes. Father's down in the parlour and Meg and the others are serving food and drink. Have we got anything?'

'Meg was going to bring some up but she's probably up to her eyes. Now that you're here, I can go and get us something. Christina fell asleep a wee while ago. Will you stay with her while I do that?' He looked over at his sleeping little sister.

151

'Poor wee thing. She's just a baby.' Yes, thought Charlotte and you've just gone through an experience well beyond what your years have prepared you for. The boy looked tired, but in a funny way, grown-up, older in a way than his thirteen years.

She ran down the back stairs to the kitchen and said hello to Violet Harper and Annie Peterson who were organising yet more food for the folk in the parlour. She quickly set a tray.

'Here, Miss Gordon.' Violet Harper made a pot of tea and put it with milk and sugar on the tray. 'And mind you and the bairns have got enough to eat.'

'Thanks.' Charlotte smiled at her. 'I think that'll be enough now. I think Magnus is very hungry.'

'The poor laddie and the wee lassie. Poor motherless bairns.' Charlotte swallowed.

'Yes, it's very sad. Thanks for this.' She left the kitchen quickly before threatening tears fell. That's all I need, she thought, for me to start crying now. She carried the tray up the back stairs and into the upper sanctum.

'Here I am Magnus. Now, you must be starving.'

'I am hungry, he admitted. 'But it doesn't seem right somehow.'

'What doesn't seem right?'

'To be eating and wanting food when Mother is – is,' His lips trembled.

'Magnus, your mother would want you to eat.'

'I know,' he sighed, 'but it's still strange.'

'Come on, start on the tea and a sausage roll and see how you feel.'

He did feel better once he had started and by the time he was finished, Charlotte was glad to note that his usual healthy appetite was undiminished. Christina woke up hungry and had no scruples about not eating.

Charlotte watched the two children interact. How good Magnus was with his sister. He never seemed to lose patience with her. And yet, Charlotte felt that a thirteen year old boy required more than a three year old sister to play with. True, today was an exceptional one. But, what would happen next for Magnus. As if he read her thoughts, Magnus spoke.

'Miss Gordon, could I ask you something?'

'Yes, of course, Magnus. What is it?

'Well, I was wondering what would happen now. To me, I mean. Will I have to go back to the Institute at Lerwick right away? Or will I stay at Jarlshavn for a while?'

'I don't know. How are you getting on at Jarlshavn? Are you managing to keep up with the work the Lerwick teachers have set you?'

'Yes, I think so. Mrs Manson has been very helpful and has kept my nose to the grindstone too.' He gave a sad smile. 'This term has slipped a bit though.'

'Well, I'm not surprised at that. You've had a lot going on in your life. How do *you* feel about going back to Lerwick?'

'Well, I know I'll go back. I need to.' Charlotte nodded. 'But,' he hesitated. 'When? Do you think I could stay here for a few more months? Maybe go back then?'

'Is that what you think you need?'

'Yes, well, I feel I should be here seeing my father and Christina are all right. Break them in gently to my being away. You know.'

Charlotte knew. It would be good for the family not to have another big change too soon. On the other hand, Magnus needed to be with boys his own age and the more formal secondary education offered at Lerwick to widen his horizons and prepare him for higher education.

'When is Lowrie going to Lerwick? I know he's still at Jarlshavn but he'll surely be moving on.'

'Yes, He's stayed back a year because he was ill but he's going to Lerwick in August. If Father would agree, I think I would like to wait until then. I'll work really hard here so that I'll still be in the same class that I was before.'

'Well,' Charlotte said, 'it's not up to me but you can talk to your father about it and I'll mention it to Mrs Manson. I can't really see why not, though. It will be good for your father to have you around.'

'Thanks Miss Gordon.' They exchanged smiles and Charlotte turned her attention to Christina who by this time was eating more cake under the pretext of feeding it to Beanie Two.

'Right, Christina, I think you have probably had quite enough by now.' Charlotte loaded up the tray and put it out of reach. 'Now, how about a story.'

'Yes,' Christina, distracted, ran to fetch the book of the moment, the old friend Mr Hans Christian Andersen and his *Fairy Tales*.

Charlotte

I was glad to return to be alone in my peerie Skulehoose that evening. I had been to other funerals before in Towie and the surrounding area. But never before had I been to one where I felt so close to the person who had died and to the grieving family. That evening I stayed to put Christina to bed and sit with Magnus for a while as Alexander coped with the remaining visitors. The women in the kitchen did sterling work getting everything cleared up, while still having to prepare and give food to any late arrivals, or those who seemed like prolonging the festivities. As the evening wore on, Magnus found the sound of laughter floating up the stairs hard to take.

'How can they be laughing?' he asked. 'My mother's dead and they're having a party. Will my father be laughing too?'

'He'll be being a good host. He may not feel like laughing but this is what happens at wakes. It's all part of a process that people go through, part of a way of coping with what has happened. And after it's over, he'll be glad that he went through with it.'

Later, we heard voices in the hall, 'goodnights' being shouted, the door closing, feet and noise outside as the last of the wake walked along the harbour.

'I'll go now,' I said to Magnus. 'I'll just slip down the back stairs and say goodnight to Meg and I'll be on my way.'

'Don't you want to say goodnight to Father?'

'He'll have had enough of visitors by now,' I said. 'You say goodnight for me. I'm sure he'll want to see you. And, you'll be able to tell him Christina's fast asleep.'

Meg looked tired but there was a gleam of satisfaction in her eye as she looked at her tidy kitchen.

'How are you Meg?'

'I'm all right.' She yawned. 'Nothing that a good night's sleep won't put right. But it seemed to go well, didn't it.'

'Yes, thanks to your organising. I couldn't believe it when I looked in here when we came back from church and everybody was all over the place.'

'Delegation,' Meg said. 'Delegation and organisation, Miss Gordon. That's the way.' The gleam became a twinkle.

'In the nicest possible way, I'm sure.'

'Of course. And everyone seems happy. It's just a question of getting folk to work together instead of pulling against each other.'

'Well, Meg, you certainly seemed to manage that. Not everybody could.'

'Aye,' she said, with a sudden return to sombreness. 'But it won't bring Mrs Sinclair back. And things will never be the same again.'

I held her closely.

'I know. We're going to miss her sorely.' I wiped my eyes which were threatening to overflow.

'See here,' Meg took over the role of comforter. 'Miss Gordon, Charlotte, you've been on the go all day without a let up. You must be exhausted. Now –' Meg's panacea for all woes was food, '– you take these things that were left over and get yourself home and have a good supper before you go to bed. 'And,' she added, 'I know this is Mr Sinclair's house, but you come any time you like if you want to talk and you are always welcome in this kitchen. In fact, I need you to come, as you are the one Mrs Sinclair knew and loved the best of all her friends, and – and,' her voice broke. 'Oh, I'm going to miss her so much.'

We stood in the kitchen and held each other, comforters and comforted, and cried together. I suppose you could call it cathartic. It probably had to come and I'm sure it helped us both. When we pulled ourselves together we wiped our eyes, blew our noses, smiled at each other in a watery sort of way.

'Now,' I said, 'I really must go this time. Will you be all right?'

'Oh aye,' Meg said. 'There's nothing like a good greet for making you feel better.'

I picked up my bundle of food which she insisted I take with me and made my way back to my house. Inside all was quiet, peaceful. I was alone, it seemed for the first time for days.

'Margery,' I said, 'wherever you are, take care. Your family will be all right.'

The following Saturday Alexander called in. He had Christina by the hand.

'Alexander, Christina, how good to see you both. Come in.'

'Gordon.' Christina rushed into my arms. Alexander looked on. 'Hello, hello, 'lo,' she cried.

154

'Sorry about the noise.' Alexander came in and sat down thankfully on a chair in the parlour. 'How are you?'

'I'm well, thank you. And you? How are you, and Magnus? I can see that Christina is fine.' He smiled.

'Yes she is fine. She's a great wee girl. She helps in a way – just with her noise and zest. Mind you it can become too much of a good thing sometimes. I'm quite glad when bedtime comes. And Meg, of course is a great help. She has taken on full care of Christina while I am at work. In a way she is just doing the same as she has been with Christina for the last few months, but we have put it on an official footing now and I think it will work out all right.'

'That sounds good. And Magnus, how is he?'

'Magnus is coping. I think he'll probably be back to school on Monday. He told me he had spoken to you about waiting a few months before going back to Lerwick.'

'Yes, he seemed keen to stay here for a while.' I waited to hear what he had to say.

'Yes, well, in one breath, I really want to get him back to normal as soon as possible. And 'normal' means picking up the threads in the Institute again. But, I'm not sure…' His voice tailed off.

'Why aren't you sure, do you think?' I felt a bit embarrassed at myself asking him about his feelings so boldly but the question was out before I could stop myself. I waited to be told to mind my own business. But no.

'It's difficult,' he responded. 'What is normal now? Nothing is normal without Margery. If this is so for me, then it is likely to be so for Magnus, perhaps even more so as he is so young. Therefore, for him to go back to Lerwick just now would not be normal. In fact it would maybe make things worse for him, just at this time.'

'Have you spoken with Mrs Manson about this? She would be able to give you another side of the question.'

'Yes, I went up and saw her yesterday. She thinks he should stay here until he is ready to move again – possibly after the summer holidays. The good thing about that idea is that Lowrie Harcus will be going then too. Also, she thinks that academically, Magnus won't have a problem in catching up if he has to.'

'So,' I said, 'why are you hesitating? Surely this idea sounds all right.'

'Yes, but… Well, I feel guilty. I think Magnus wants to stay here for a while primarily to help the family and I don't want him to miss out just because of Christina and me.'

'But you would like him here for a while wouldn't you?'

'Oh yes,' he sighed. 'So much. But he mustn't spoil his life for us. We'll be all right.'

'Alexander, let him stay a while. Yes, he has this feeling of not wanting further disruption for the family at the moment, and he wants to see that you and Christina are all right. But surely these are admirable feelings. I think you should feel proud of him instead of guilty. And, at the same time, he needs time for himself to grieve for his mother in his own way before further change happens to him. Let him go when he is ready. And, as well as it being good for him, you know it will be good for you all to have him around for a while longer.'

He looked at me and for the first time a smile crossed his face.

'You and Mrs Manson, you make a persuasive team.'

'So you'll let him stay then?'

'Yes, I think you've convinced me. I'll tell him when I go back home. And, talking of home,' he said, 'I want to thank you for all your help over these last difficult weeks. I don't know what we would have done without you.'

'Alexander,' I said, emotions again coming to the fore, 'anything I did, and it was little enough, was a privilege for me.'

'Well we're very grateful. And for your help with the children around the time of the funeral. I didn't have to worry once about Christina because I knew she was safe with you. And now, thank you for your wise counsel about Magnus. Now,' changing the subject abruptly, 'we must go. Christina,' he called.

'Yes Dada.' The voice came from the kitchen where no doubt Edie was feeding her samples of the latest baking.

'Time to go home now.' The owner of the voice came running through.

'You need to learn to call me Father as Magnus does. You're going to be three next week – oh that reminds me,' he addressed me, 'Christina's birthday is on the 14th February, Wednesday. Will you come for tea after school? We're not having a party but Meg has promised to bake a cake.'

'Oh please come,' Christina begged.

'Thank you, I'd love to,' I said.

'That's settled then. Come along then Christina.'

'All right Dada – 'Christina clapped her hand over her mouth and giggled – 'Favver.'

Stern father's eyes met mine and again the fleeting smile.

'That's fine. Now, good bye Miss Gordon.' They marched together hand in hand down the path and turned along the road for the harbour. As I watched, the tiny figure turned and waved. I raised my hand in answer before turning back to the house.

Chapter 23

Towie
1895

In July 1895 Trancie House awaited its favourite daughter, or rather, grand-daughter. Andrew, newly, if reluctantly, retired, had handed over full care of his practice two months before, to his young assistant of the last two years. He watched anxiously from the window for the gig which would transport his dear Charlotte from the railway station in Alford. Jock had insisted on going for her himself, and assured him that they would make all possible speed to Towie on her arrival at Alford.

'Mind you,' he said, 'Ye nivver ken wi trains. They say ae thing an they dee anither.'

Granma bustled through.

'Is there no sign?'

'No,' he sighed. He took out his watch and shook it. 'I'm sure this has stopped.'

'No, no,' she soothed. 'It's all right. She'll be here soon. Listen, I can hear the rumble.' Sure enough, the gig came rattling up to the front door and stopped with a flourish and a scattering of gravel.

'Here they are.' They made for the door. Jock was down from his seat and handing Charlotte down like a piece of precious porcelain.

'Man lassie, it's afa fine ti see ye back far ye belang.' Charlotte stretched up and kissed him.

'Thanks, Jock, and thanks for coming to get me. It means a lot.' She turned to Granny and Granpa coming down the steps towards her, smiles all over their faces.

'Granny, Granpa, I'm back.'

They enfolded her together in a communal hug.

'Yes, yes, we can see that.' Granpa held her at arm's length. 'Let me have a look at you. A bit thinner, I'm thinking.'

'Och Andrew, don't get on at the lassie as soon as she arrives. Charlotte you look fine. Come on in.' Granny chivvied them into the house. Jock brought up the rear with Charlotte's case.

'Usual room?'

'Yes please Jock. Were the roads all right.'

'Aye, een or twa pot-holes tae gang roond but nae too bad.' He disappeared with the case and came clattering down again empty handed.

'Onythin else for the minty?'

'No thanks Jock. Thanks for your help.'

'Nae bother. See ye later, mebbe, quine.' He nodded to Charlotte.

'Aye, Jock I'll come out and have a craic with you. Thanks for getting me.'

He went away to his beloved stables and she turned to her grandparents.

'Oh it's so good to be here.' She stretched her arms and gave a twirl of happiness. 'How are things? What's going on? I want to hear it all. How does it feel to be a retired gentleman, Granpa?'

'Hmph. It's taking me all my time to keep him out of the surgery,' said Granny. 'He keeps wanting to help Leslie.'

Charlotte had met Leslie MacFarquhar, the young doctor who had arrived in Towie two years before as Granpa's assistant. A West Aberdeenshire loon from Upper Deeside, he had taken himself off to Aberdeen University to study medicine when he had passed the requisite examinations for university entry. It had not been easy, money was tight, his student life was frugal. Oatmeal and tatties supplied from home, augmented by salt herrings were traditional student fare and Leslie was glad when he passed his Finals and was able to earn a small salary as a hospital resident: at least it allowed him a more varied diet. It also set him on the road as a practising doctor.

Hospital doctoring was fine for a while. Leslie achieved the required residencies and remained in hospital to gain experience. But, especially latterly in his time in hospital, there was the nagging feeling that he was not doing what he had set out on a medical career for. He wanted to get back to the countryside, to practise amongst his folk, or at least folk not too far away from his roots. Was this possible? Would folk who knew him or knew of him and his family accept him back as a family doctor? And, were there any vacancies in the area?

It was at this point that Leslie heard that Dr Andrew Grant of Towie was looking for an assistant. Towie, he thought. Donside, over the hill from Upper Deeside, but maybe that's no bad thing. Near, but not too near. I'll get a letter away to Dr Grant.

The upshot was a trip to Towie, a very satisfactory interview with the old doctor, a tour of the practice environs and an evening glass of whisky to seal the agreement. Six weeks later Dr Leslie MacFarquhar took up his post as assistant to Dr Andrew Grant with the possible long-term view of taking over the practice.

Two years later, Leslie was well settled and Andrew, becoming a wee bit slower as his seventies wore on, gave in to Margaret's persuasive tongue and agreed at last to retire. Two months on he was still trying to get used to his new-found freedom.

'But Granpa,' said Charlotte, 'you're a free man now. Think of your garden, and the fishing, and,' she laughed, 'sitting with your feet up. And,' more soberly, 'more time with Granny.'

'I know, lassie, but it's difficult to stop when you've been at it for such a long time. I still want to know what's going on. Now, anyway,' he said, 'you're here. How are you? You'll have had a busy year I'm thinking.'

158

Charlotte sat down and told them about her first year as a teacher. Neither of her grandparents had been to Shetland and it seemed to them like a totally different world, which it was in many ways. The customs, the voices, the sea and harbour and boats, the different thinking of the children of seafarers from children of landward stock. And yet there were similarities: children's development and behaviour, the school routine, the school smell, the lunch-time soup, the eager look in childish eyes when the going home bell sounded and when holidays drew near.

Now here Charlotte was on holiday – her first time away from Shetland for nearly a year.

'You'll have made lots of friends,' Granny said. 'You mentioned some of them in your letters. It must have been very hard when Margery died. How is the family now? That wee girl, is she all right?'

'Christina, yes, she's three and a half now and a great wee girl. Meg the Sinclair's housekeeper looks after her a lot of the time. And Alexander is there in the evenings of course. Magnus is thirteen; he's taken his mother's death quite badly. Christina doesn't really understand. But Magnus really misses her acutely. He'll have to go back to the Secondary School in Lerwick in August and that will be hard. He'll have to board you see. They all do that if they go there from outside the town. I get on fine with both children. They often come up to my house and eat Edie's scones.'

Granny jumped up.

'Talking of scones, just look at the time. Come on, you go and unpack your case and I'll go and see how Katie's getting on in the kitchen.'

'I'll come through and say hello. How is she?'

'Oh getting a bit slower like the rest of us.' Granpa heaved himself to his feet and patted his kyte. 'But she can still cook like a dream.'

'I'll need to go up to the Glen tomorrow to see Mam and Dad and the bairns. They don't write much but Lizzie keeps me up to date with what's going on. But both you and Lizzie have said about Mam not being too good. Is she all right?'

'Well of course she still does far too much, in the house and outside,' Granpa said. 'She gets some headaches and she seems very tired sometimes. But slow up, she won't. The bairns are fine – not that they're bairns now. I think even Wee Alicky has left school this summer.'

'What's he going to do?'

'Oh, he's going to be fee'd to one of the farmers fairly nearby. Along with John – so he'll keep him right. He's a bit hallyrackit but he's a nice boy.'

Charlotte and Granny went up the hill to Glenbuchat the following morning. As usual, Lizzie was first out of the house on their arrival.

'Hello, teacher.' They hugged each other.

'Where's Mam, and Dad.'

'Mam's in the house and Dad's oot-by. Aye the same.'

Charlotte thought her mother was looking thinner than ever.

'Mam, do you have to work so hard?'

'Well, it's jist fit ye're used til. A canna seem to stop somewey.'

159

'Well you should take a rest.'

'Aye aye.'

Charlotte looked at Lizzie.'

'It's no use,' said Lizzie. 'Believe me, I've tried.' She appealed to Granny, unpacking the usual basket of baking. 'Even Granpa's tried hasn't he Granny?'

'Yes,' agreed Granny. 'But some folk don't listen.'

Charlotte slipped out the back door and ran out to the field where she knew her father would be working. She called to the bending figure and ran to him as he straightened up and looked in her direction. They met, hugged and laughed into each other's faces.

'Oh my Lassickie, how are you.'

'I'm fine Dad. And you? Are you fine too?'

'Fine now I see you, my wee Lassickie teacher. Thank you for all your letters. A'm nae much o a hand wi the pen or A'd have written mair nor A did.'

'Dad, Dad, it's not a problem. I enjoy writing to you and telling you and Mam what's going on. Now,' she looked him up and down. 'You look well.'

'Oh aye, I'm fine, but Mam...'

'Mam? Not so good?'

'She's afa thin. A dinna think she can be weel bit she winna let up. Jist on and on. Her faither an mither hiv baith bin on at her but she disna heed.'

Charlotte's month passed quickly. It was so good to be back. She spent time talking with Granny and Granpa, and Jock in the stable and Katie in the kitchen. She went to visit Mr Coutts, a little older and greyer, and Miss MacHardie, her early teachers and mentors. They were both anxious to hear how she was getting on and how teaching in Shetland differed from Towie.

'It's actually very much the same,' she said. 'Just the voices are different and some of the customs. The children are the same, good and not so good, and the soup at lunchtime and the happy faces at home-time and the bunches of flowers for the teacher. It's darker than here in the wintertime but lighter late in the evening in the summer. It's lovely. I'm very happy.'

'Have you used your tawse yet?' Miss MacHardie smiled as she asked. She remembered Charlotte as a pupil teacher and her aversion to the belt.

Charlotte smiled. 'No,' she admitted. 'It's hiding at the back of the table drawer.'

'I don't blame you,' Miss MacHardie said. 'But,' she warned, 'keep it as an ultimate deterrent.'

A few days before Charlotte was due to go back to Shetland on the St Clair she and Granny were sitting together in the quiet kitchen. It was a Saturday afternoon, Katie was away home for the day and Granpa was having a nap in the parlour.

'Will you be glad to go back?'

Charlotte considered. She stroked the cat on her lap. He stretched and kneaded his paws into her skirt in response.

'Yes,' she said slowly. 'Yes, I think so. I love it here. It's home, but my Peerie Skulehoose is home too now and my life and work are up there. It's wonderful to have time away and to see you both – but my place is there now. Do you see?'

'Yes, of course. And,' Granny added, 'I don't think we would want it otherwise. You've told us such a lot about it, I can just about imagine you there. You'll be glad to get back and see how the Sinclairs are getting on, too. You said Alexander is a Deacon in the Congregational Church?'

'Yes that's right. Shetland has so many different kinds of religious denominations.'

'So, do you go to the Congregational?'

'No,' Charlotte said, 'I only went for Margery's funeral. I started right on my first Sunday going to the Kirk and I go most Sundays.'

'Who's the minister?

'Oh, his name's James MacLeod. He hasn't been there long. He's all right.'

'Where's he from?'

'The Perth area.' Charlotte concentrated on the cat.

'Charlotte?' Something in Charlotte's attention to the cat made Granny look closely at her. 'Charlotte, how old is he?'

'Granny, I don't go around asking men how old they are.' Charlotte tipped the cat off her lap and looked up. 'Oh all right, he's in his early thirties.'

'And?'

'And, that's all. And, no he's not married – I'm just putting that in because I knew it would be your next question.'

'Do you like him?'

'He's all right, I suppose.'

Granny looked at her. 'But there's something going on,' she said.

'What do you mean?'

'You've gone all short-answered and no description. It's not like you.'

'He is nice,' admitted Charlotte. 'And we have had one or two walks together and he comes to the house – no not alone,' she said quickly, to pre-empt the question that would surely follow Granny's indrawn breath. 'Edie is always there in the house and we sit in the parlour and talk and exchange books. And that's all. We are both very aware of the claik that goes on in any wee place. It's not just Towie.'

'I know. But you're such a bonnie lassie, men will be after you like bees after the honey. You will be careful won't you?' Granny remembered well the trauma of twenty-one years before when Mary had been pregnant out of wedlock with Charlotte.

Charlotte went over to Granny and sat at her feet.

'Of course I'll be careful. I won't let you down. But,' she added, 'it's not easy. I do like James, but we must keep each other at arm's length. Anyway,' with a sigh, 'I don't know if I love him. I've never been in love so I don't know what it feels like.'

'You'll know.'

'And then,' Charlotte carried on. 'There's the problem of the Sinclairs.'

'Where do the Sinclairs fit into this?'

161

'Well,' said Charlotte, eyes down. 'Before Margery died she and I had a very long serious conversation. To cut a long story short, she said when she was gone the children would not have a mother and they needed a mother and she would be very happy if I would marry Alexander. Then I could be the children's mother.'

'Oh, Charlotte. Did you say you would?'

'No,' said Charlotte. 'How could I? All I promised was to do my best for the children. But it has changed things. Well, Margery's dying would change things anyway. But I've become very wary of being near Alexander without one of the children there because I can't forget what Margery said. I don't know if she said anything to him before she died.'

She put her head on Granny's lap and cried. 'It's all such a mix-up, and so difficult. Why can't I just be a teacher.'

Granny stroked the dark hair. 'Just you go on being a teacher. These other things will work themselves out, just you wait and see. Don't do anything to precipitate matters. Just wait and let things happen. You're there to do a job and I think you probably do it very well.'

'I try.' Charlotte sniffed.

'I'm sure you do. You'll know when you're in love.'

'Did you?'

'Yes, I did. And I didn't know what it was like till it happened. So just give it time and in the meantime, enjoy your job. It's a big step forward for women to be out in the world with a qualification working for a living. You're part of it.'

Chapter 24

Charlotte

I was pleased to be as Granny said 'part of it' when, a few days later I walked up the garden path of Da Peerie Skulehoose. I was so pleased to be back. It felt like coming home and I was very happy to be there. I looked around. Someone had been there. The grass was freshly cut and the flowers looked tended. The door opened and Edie stood there with arms outstretched.

'Oh Miss, I've missed you. I'm that pleased to see you back.'

'Edie.' We hugged each other. 'It's so good to be here. I'm home. And,' as I stepped over the threshold, 'you've been so busy.'

'Well, just a little bit. I wanted to make it bonny for you.'

'It's lovely. Thank you so much.'

Later, I slipped out and went away up the hill at the back. The evening sun shone on mysterious Foula. For once, the wind was away to a whisper. A pleasant evening to be out in. The sheep-grazed grass was short and pleasant to walk upon. The sheep themselves accompanied by well-grown lambs all with their distinctive 'Shetland sheep' faces walked on as I approached. I watched for a while, as they moved here and there, stopping, nibbling, moving on, standing for lambs to have a feed and then suddenly, becoming impatient with such babyish behaviour, taking a few abrupt steps away from their insistent children. On the other hand, the minute a sheep and lamb looked like being separated, such a baa-ing was set up that it seemed as though an awful event had happened. And then mother and child would be reunited and all was well and quiet again.

The sun was beginning to dip lower in the sky as I turned for home. The village lay below me, peaceful, at a distance. I could see small figures here and there: doing late work in some of the gardens; a woman going out to bring in the washing before night fell; someone bringing in the cows for a late evening milking; chimneys smoking with the smell of peat-rik in the air. I knew that there were peats used for firing in many other areas but somehow the peat-rik smell epitomised Shetland to me. Just as the 'school smell' evoked memories of school for me, so wherever I was to go in later life, the smell of peat-rik could transport me right back to Shetland.

However, the present called. Hearing someone calling children in for bed reminded me of where I was and there was much preparation to be done before term began. I pointed my steps firmly towards Da Peerie Skulehoose and went inside to my own peat fire.

The day before the Shetland schools began their winter term was always a day of turmoil and moving for any older boys who had chosen (or their parents had chosen for them) to attend the Anderson Educational Institute in Lerwick. All the boys who came from beyond an easy walking distance of Lerwick became weekly boarders in houses within the town. The plan for Magnus was to walk the six miles to Lerwick on Sunday evenings and home again on Fridays after school. However, on the first trip, Alexander took him to his boarding house in the gig to help with his luggage.

Alexander encouraged the pony into a brisk trot. It was by now the third week in August and although the days could still be summery, he was conscious of the drawing in of the evenings and wanted to get home before dark.

'Christina's not pleased at your going.'

'No Father, I suppose it's hard for her to understand.' As they left Magnus had physically had to hand sobbing, clinging Christina over to Meg. He felt guilty at leaving his little sister in this way.

'Don't worry. She's in good hands with Meg. And Charlotte's coming down tomorrow after school to play with her for a while.'

'Charlotte's been a great friend, hasn't she. It's good to have her back again from her holiday.'

'Yes. I don't think her mother is too well though. I think she worries a bit about her.'

'She seems to care about everybody,' Magnus observed.

'Yes.' His father concentrated on negotiating the pony past some evening walkers. 'Yes, she certainly is a welcome addition to Jarlshavn. Now,' changing the subject, 'how do you feel about going back to school?'

'Father, I think I'm ready to go now. I wasn't ready before, you know, when Mother died.'

'No, I know, I can see that now. We all need our own time to come to terms with these things. It's difficult, losing someone like your Mother....' He stopped and brushed his hand over his eyes.

'Father,' Magnus looked at him. 'Father?'

'Aye, lad, well fathers have feelings too and I miss her sorely. I just find it very hard to talk about.' He stopped the pony as they rounded a bend in the road. 'See that,' he continued. 'Look at that view.' The voe, widening as it approached the open sea scattered with islands, lay spread out before them. 'She loved this view. Every time we came past here she would get me to stop and look at it. She said there was nothing else like it in the world. So now, when I pass here, I stop and think about her.'

'I'll do that too. It'll help, I think.'

'You know,' the father looked at the son. 'I think it does. Now, time to go.' He clicked his tongue at the pony and they headed for the last of their journey into Lerwick and school.

But, on the way home, Alexander had time to think further about his situation. He was indeed going through a difficult time having to cope with the untimely illness and death of his wife. Grieving was a difficult area for men. At least women could cry, wipe their eyes, be more open about their mourning. It felt more normal to talk about their troubles with their friends. It seemed that men were expected to retain a stiff upper lip, not weep in public, carry on with their work as if all was well, and, not discuss their problems.

This meant that Alexander felt he had to continue with his various positions in the village without a break since Margery died. These included his daily work as Harbourmaster, very much a full-time job as well as his position as deacon of the Congregational Church. This involved, of course, attendance at church every Sunday, seeing that affairs ran properly, attention to church business, meetings of the church board and anything else churchly that came along. It also included an input into the upkeep of church property, the church itself which always seemed to be requiring repairs, the hall, which needed painting and pointing, and the manse where the Reverend Peter Jamieson and his wife Agnes lived. Alexander had to admit they did not ask for much and the manse was not in the excellent state of repair which he would have liked. However it was all a question of finance which was always difficult and added to his feelings of being burdened. As well as the church he was a leading member of the School Board. True, Mrs Manson and Charlotte were excellent at their job.

But it was just the responsibility of it all. How was a man supposed to grieve properly when he had all that to do?

And these were only the outside commitments. Regarding home and family, Alexander felt keenly his responsibilities towards his children. He almost resented the fact that Margery had died and left him with all this. Yes, that was the word. He resented having to do all this on his own. There was Magnus away now to school. Of course he had to go. It was necessary, but now he was not at home to play with Christina. Oh, he knew Magnus was too old to play all the time with Christina but it did take a bit of the burden off Alexander. Now Magnus was away and he was left holding, not quite the baby, but certainly a very lively three and a half year old. He could not rely on Meg the whole time. She was very good and willing but she was the housekeeper, not family.

Alexander sighed. What he needed was a wife. The thought came unbidden into his head and he drew in his breath sharply at the temerity of it.

But was it such a bad idea? He knew it was too soon after Margery's death to be thinking of a replacement wife on an official basis. But where was the harm in just turning the notion over in his head? After all, Margery, before she died, had anticipated that he would have problems. She had even offered him her solution: once a suitable time had elapsed, he, Alexander should marry again, and the bride she recommended for him was Charlotte.

Never one to mull for too long over an idea before taking action, Alexander managed to wait until the following Saturday morning before walking up the road to Da Peerie Skulehoose with Christina by the hand. As he expected, Charlotte was in – or rather she was in the garden dead-heading the roses and generally keeping up with the late summer gardening. Edie was in the house singing away as she worked. Her half-day lay ahead of her, the sun was shining and she was off home as soon as she was ready. Of course she loved her work with Miss Gordon. But it was good to have time off, and who knew whom she might meet when she was out walking with her girl-friends.

The gate clicked. Edie looked out and saw Mr Sinclair and Christina coming into the garden. She rushed to swing the kettle over the hottest part of the range so that it would boil the quicker.

Charlotte heard the gate click and Christina's voice as they arrived.

'Come on Favver, you're a slowcoach.'

Alexander came up the path, lifted his hat formally and held out his hand.

'Good morning, Charlotte. How are you today? Come, Christina, say "Good morning" properly to Miss Gordon.'

'Good morning, Miss Gordon.' Christine held out her hand politely. Charlotte pulled off her grubby gardening glove and shook hands with her visitors.

'It's very nice to see you,' she said. 'Shall we go in.'

'We came to see if you had recovered from your holiday and your first week back to school. I'm sorry I did not manage to see you at the beginning of the week when you came to Harbour House to see Christina but thank you for doing that. It was kind of you to spend time with a little girl.'

'But I enjoy Christina's company,' protested Charlotte. 'And, we had great fun, didn't we Christina.'

'Yes, Miss Gordon and I played in the wee sitting-room and we hid behind the sofa and said "Boo". Then we read a book and Miss Gordon showed me some words. She says I might go to school next year. When will it be next year?'

'Oh there's a wee while to go yet before we get to next year. But,' Charlotte turned to Alexander, 'Christina is doing very well. I think she'll learn to read very quickly.'

'I'm glad to hear that. You are a great help to her.'

'Not as much as I'd like to be. It would be good to see more of Christina but the school work takes up so much of my time. But I want to help as much as I can. Sometimes I feel I'm not doing enough.'

'You mustn't feel like that. I know how much you do.'

'But then I went away for a whole month.'

'Yes, well, you had your own folk to see. That's only natural. And now you're back. It's good to have you back.' He lifted his shoulders slightly and spread out his hands towards her as he looked at her. 'And, as time goes on…well, we'll see how things progress. You never know what might happen.'

How lovely she is, he thought. That beautiful dark hair and grey eyes, so different from his blue-eyed fairness. And so slim and so young.

Charlotte looked at him. What did he mean? Did Margery really speak to him too, about marriage and being the children's mother? Flustered, she got up to put another peat on the fire.

'Here, let me do that,' he took the tongs from her and lifted a peat out of the kishie. The peat landed on the embers with a shower of sparks.

'There you are,' he commented. 'Sparks to set the fire alight. Can we do that I wonder?'

Taken aback at the suddenness of his remarks, Charlotte's mind took flight. She said the first thing that came into her head. 'Where can Edie be. I was expecting tea by now.' She hurried out of the room and bumped into Edie who was coming from the kitchen with a tray of tea.

'Oh Edie, I'm sorry. Are you all right?'

'Yes Miss, fine Miss. Here's the tea Miss.'

'Thank you very much.' Charlotte took the tray and carried it into the parlour. Edie followed and opened up the gate-legged table in the window.

'Hello Christina, Mr Sinclair.'

'Hello Edie. Scones,' shrilled Christina. 'Edie's scones again.'

'I like the way she says "again",' said Charlotte shakily, trying to normalise the situation. 'Here Christina, let me help you.'

'No, no, I can manage.' The little girl spread newly made raspberry jam thickly on her scone. She held up her fingers.

'Sticky.'

'Here's your napkin. Let's wipe them.'

Alexander watched the two heads together, so different and yet so much in harmony. But something warned him that he had gone far enough in his pursuit of Charlotte for that day. Perhaps, he thought, I have sown the seed. Now let it germinate. Don't frighten her off.

Once she was alone again, Charlotte was glad to return to her gardening and turn over in her mind the events of the morning. There was certainly no doubting Alexander's meaning.

However, Charlotte did have misgivings about acquiescing with anything remotely like a romantic alliance with Alexander. Apart from anything else, it was barely seven months since Margery died. It was too soon for him to be even thinking about marrying again. Anyway, she thought, I don't know if I want this. I'm too young for him. I'm only coming up for twenty-one; he is, well he must be well into his forties. I don't love him. Granny said I would know when I loved someone. I don't think I love him. I like him and I want to help him and the children, but love, no, not in that way. And, there's no one here that I can talk to about this. What if it got out? We would be the spik of the village. She smiled to herself at her automatic use of the Scots word for gossip. No other word could describe it more accurately. Folk loved so-called irregular behaviour in others that they could discuss from every angle.

Anyway, her thoughts ran on. I'm a teacher. I've gone through a lot to get to this stage. Granny was right. I'm independent and not many women are. In my own small way I'm part of the greater emancipation of women. I know I want to get married sometime but not yet. And I want it to be right. I want to love and be loved, for me, not as a substitute for someone else.

She sighed and went to put her tools away.

Edie poked her head round the garden shed.

'That's me away Miss.'

'Oh, Edie,' Charlotte smiled at her. 'Where are you off to today?'

'Well home to see my mam first and then well, I'm going for a walk with some of my friends.'

'Well,' said Charlotte, who knew fine well what that meant, 'Have a very good day, and tomorrow. See you on Monday morning.'

'Yes Miss. Good bye Miss.' Edie ran jauntily down the path. Charlotte shut the shed door and headed for the house.

Chapter 25

On that fine Saturday morning, the Reverend James MacLeod was out and about. Saturday was usually the day for sharpening up his Sunday sermon. Sermons were funny things. Sometimes the composing of a sermon flowed as soon as he sat down to write. Occasionally he looked at his work on a Saturday and was so at odds with what he had written that he could start all over again on Saturday night. Saturdays were very necessary as a safeguard, just in case he needed to make serious adjustments to his preaching of the Word.

Once one Sunday's worth was over he could breathe a sigh of relief and hope that it had gone down reasonably well with his listeners. Occasionally at the church door amid the hand shaking and Good mornings someone would come up to him and say, 'who was that you were getting at the day?' or even, indignantly, 'why did you point your finger at me so obviously?' and sometimes, from someone who thought himself particularly knowledgeable, 'well I ken who that was all about.' And then with a tap on the nose, 'but I won't say a word.' Which probably meant he was away to spik amongst his friends and was probably barking up the wrong tree altogether. James often wondered if sermons were really worth the bother. And then someone would approach him and say, 'thank you, that was just right,' and he knew then that they were worth the hours of head scratching and book referencing. Sometimes he had even heard on his rounds that folk had been discussing through the week what he had said. Now *there* was a thing.

Anyway James was breaking with his Saturday morning self-imposed tradition by being out down the harbour on Saturday morning. He had been down to see old Mr Bertie Inkster who had fallen down some stone steps leading down a vennel and landed heavily on the path below. As well as breaking a leg he had bumped his head quite severely and was currently confined to bed. Dr Taylor was keeping a close eye on him as the old man seemed sometimes a little confused and forgetful and tried to get up when he was clearly not yet able. His wife Elsie, herself not a youngster, was exhausted keeping up with Bertie's demands and questions about why he was like this and why he could not go out.

The village was rallying round and Bertie had a constant stream of visitors, partly for his own sake for he was a popular old man and was often to be seen regaling his companions in the public house with extravagant stories of long ago days at sail. Whether these stories were all strictly true is another matter. Bertie loved telling them and his listeners loved egging him on to yet another tale of life on the high seas. Now his listeners came to him for the time being.

But Saturday morning was quieter. Saturdays had a different feel about them somehow. Perhaps the men were sleeping off the excesses of Friday night; perhaps they were visiting their own grand-children; or, they could be out having a wee sail round the harbour if the wind was in the right direction. Who knows? Whatever the reason, the harbour was quiet as the minister walked past to the house where Bertie lay in the box-bed in the kitchen of his home within the sound of wind and wave.

He was delighted with his visitor. Not everyone got the minister to visit. Elsie rushed off for the best chair available, tea in the best cup and saucer (the wedding china) and a rock bun from a batch of baking handed in just an hour ago from her best friend Ellen Hunter (who in her spare time was a hennie or henwife and sold the best eggs in the village as her hens wandered far and wide). With a sigh of relief, knowing Bertie would be safe from any unauthorized wandering for the next half hour, Elsie slipped out for a break and a blether with her friends up the street.

James's visit with old Bertie went well. He hardly needed to talk at all. The old man sat against a mound of pillows and cushions in his box-bed covered over with old bedding. This was totally eclipsed by a hand-wrought patchwork quilt which had taken Elsie many years to make and was her pride and joy. How glad she was that she had taken the time to spread it over Bertie that morning. So, covered in quilt, and holding his cup with a shaky hand the old man told James what had happened, how this sort of thing had never happened before, no not even in fifty years of sea-going, rope ladders and rigging and steep companionways. He couldn't understand it.

Neither could he quite understand who was visiting him. He had forgotten that Elsie had told him that his visitor was the minister. He just thought what a nice young man to take time to come and see him. With his loss of short-term memory brought about by his fall he could not remember that he had been in the Kirk only the previous Sunday let alone who the nice young man was. No matter, he was happy with his visit and James stayed with him until Elsie returned from her half hour away.

'Oh, thank you Minister,' she came bustling through the door. 'I'm sure Bertie has enjoyed your visit.'

'Aye, and so have I. Bertie's been telling me about some of his days at sea.'

'Aye he would do that all right. How did you find him?' She nodded to her man on the bed. 'Do you not think he's a bit raivelt – in his mind, you know.'

'A wee bit forgetful,' James conceded. 'But, that should come back as he recovers. What does Dr Taylor say?'

'Aye he says the same thing. I hope it's quick. He's much easier to be with when he can remember what's happening.'

'James smiled at her. 'I'm sure that's so. I'll come back another time, if I may.'

'Oh aye, Minister, my kettle's aye on the boil.'

James leant over the bed and took old Bertie's hand. 'Good bye Mr Inkster. See you again. I've enjoyed my visit with you. God bless you.'

'Eh, eh?' The old man, by now dropping off into a dwam, roused himself. 'Oh aye. See you again sometime.' His eyes closed as he settled himself for a snooze under his pretty quilt.

Walking along the harbour, James saw two figures in the distance. One was small, energetic, jumping from place to place, jerking at the hand which held hers firmly. The other taller but not over-tall, straight-backed, peak-capped as a concession to the fact that it was Saturday: Alexander Sinclair and Christina returning from visiting Charlotte. The two men approached each other.

'Mr MacLeod, good morning. How are you?' Alexander was affable, holding out his hand and smiling.

'I'm fine thanks. How are you? And you too Christina?'

'I'm fine too. We've been for a walk, up the hill to Miss Gordon's house. I like Miss Gordon. She's helping me to read.'

'Shush, Christina. Mr MacLeod won't be wanting to hear all that.' Alexander tried to tone down any mention of his visit to Charlotte. But James responded to Charlotte.

'Indeed, I'm very interested. Helping you to read is she?'

'Yes, and she says I will be a good reader.'

'That's excellent.'

'And we had Edie's scones,' went on the wee clype.

'Christina, we must go now. Come along.' Alexander took her by the hand and turned to James.

'Good to see you Mr MacLeod. Perhaps we'll see you again.'

'I hope so.' James, surprised at the interview was so summarily cut short, nevertheless smiled at Christina, who was still trying to tell him about her morning.

'And,' she said, 'raspberry jam, from this year's raspberries. It was delicious. I got my hands sticky and Miss Gordon said…'

'Christina, come. Good bye Mr MacLeod.' They were on their way.

'Good bye.' James's answer was lost as Alexander hustled his stubborn daughter off.

Hmm. Something going on there. The poor wee thing, she wasn't doing any harm. There's a thought. Perhaps I'll take a walk up past Da Peerie Skulehoose myself and say hello in passing. His heart appeared to miss a beat as he thought of this delightful prospect and he turned his direction up the hill.

Five minutes later James stood leaning on Charlotte's garden wall looking admiringly into the tidy garden. He was just about to open the gate when she came round the side of the house from the shed. She looked up and saw him.

'Hello, I mean, good morning.'

'Good morning Charlotte,' he said, 'I was just admiring your garden.'

'Thank you. I've just been trying to tidy up the roses and bits and pieces.' She wondered what he was doing out and about on a Saturday morning. As if he could read

171

her thoughts he said, 'I've just been down to see old Mr Inkster. He fell and hurt himself so I ran in to see him.'

'Oh dear,' she said, 'Is he all right. I hope he's not badly hurt.'

'Well his leg is broken so that will take a wee while. But he also bumped his head quite badly and is a wee bit confused. He'll be fine in a few days I hope.'

'Poor Mr Inkster. It's good for me to know these things about folk sometimes. His grandchildren are in my class and it helps if I know what might be worrying them.'

'I met Mr Sinclair and Christina at the harbour. Christina said they had been to see you.' He glowered. He suddenly felt incredibly jealous.

'Oh yes.' Charlotte looked at him. 'They came to see if my holiday had gone well.'

Fine excuse thought James. Out loud he said, 'And did it?'

'Yes, thank you. It was very enjoyable.'

'How are your folk?'

'Well my grandparents seem to be fine. My Grandfather has just at last retired and Granny's having a hard time keeping him away from the surgery. The new doctor needs a clear run at things but Granpa is loath to let him.' She told James about Leslie MacFarquhar and his path to Towie.

'It must be hard to give up when you've been doing something like that for years. But this Leslie sounds like a good doctor.'

'Oh I think he is, or he will be – if he's allowed to be.'

'I'm sure your grandfather will appreciate the benefits of retirement in time. And your parents? How are they?'

'Well my mother is not too good. Nothing to put your finger on but just too much work, which she could slow up with if she would, and she's losing weight too. Granpa and Granny have both been on at her.' Charlotte looked worried.

'I'm sorry to hear that. I hope you hear better news soon.' He took a deep breath.

'Now, I wanted to ask you, would you come up to the Manse for lunch one Saturday.'

Her face lit up. 'Oh yes I'd like that. But, would it be all right?'

'Yes, of course. Mrs Laurenson will be there, she will cook for us. Which Saturday will we have?'

She smiled. 'I don't mind. You choose. You're the one who has to preach the next day. I thought Saturday was sermon day.'

'Ach, surely I can have some Saturday time off. Let's make it a week today at 12 noon.'

'Thank you very much.'

'I'll look forward to it.' James straightened up from Charlotte's garden wall. 'Well, I'd better be off and get this week's effort checked over. Good bye. See you in Kirk tomorrow.' And, with the air of a man who has just achieved something pretty worthwhile, he was off down the hill again.

Charlotte

I wanted to watch James going down the hill but I did not dare. I was too aware that someone passing might notice me watching and put two and two together that did not make anything correct. Or, that James himself might turn round and see me watching. It would be just too awful to be caught looking like that. I turned round, went back up the path, in the door and shut it firmly.

I went through the mechanics of post-gardening hand washing, all the time trying to control the excitement in my mind. James MacLeod has invited me to lunch. The though ran through my head like a train on the track. I went into the parlour and sat on the edge of my favourite chair. He must like me before he has invited me to lunch. He wouldn't have invited me if he didn't like me. Then the calming bit of me was saying, 'Stop it Charlotte, it's only lunch. What's a lunch after all?'

But unmarried men don't invite unmarried women for lunch if they are not interested. So that means he must be interested. What will I do? I have no one to talk to. No Granny here to advise me. But listen, what did she say? As I thought about it, I could hear her voice say, 'Don't do anything to precipitate matters. Just wait and let things happen.' The sound of her voice in my head calmed me and I sat at the table and marked some of the children's books. But all the time as I checked their addition and subtraction and writing, my head was saying, 'Lunch, lunch, what will I wear? How on earth will I do my hair?'

Chapter 26

Mrs Laurenson was up to her eyes in the Manse kitchen. Not that she minded being busy. She loved cooking and all that went with it. But this time. Well, she did not know what had got into the young minister this past week. He wouldn't leave her in peace to get on with her work at all. In and out of the kitchen. He was usually so relaxed about food. Agreed with what she suggested he should eat, was easily satisfied and did not complain. What more could a cook-housekeeper ask for? But this week had been different. All because young Miss Gordon was coming to Saturday lunch.

Now it was Saturday morning and she was in the kitchen coping with the roast chicken he had asked for and he was in the study writing a sermon. Or, she thought, should be writing a sermon but he had been through to check things with her at least six times – things that no cook preparing a lunch would forget like, had she salted the tatties? She would be sure and use the best tablecloth wouldn't she? And was she sure the cream for the special Apple Charlotte pudding (in honour of the guest) was fresh? If she didn't feel she knew him very well by now and was very fond of him, she would have been insulted. As it was she gave him a piece of cake and a cup of tea and scolded him back to his study. She shut the oven door firmly and gave the gravy another stir. All seemed to be right. Now all that was wanting was the guest of honour.

Nice lassie, Mrs Laurenson thought. She seems to have settled down in Shetland right well. Mind you she comes from near Aberdeen, not like one of those from the deep south. But even so, any sooth-moother takes a while to get used to Shetland ways and the Shetlanders take time to accept anyone from the south.

But Miss Gordon had done pretty well. Mrs Laurenson was no gossip – working in the Manse precluded any form of claik from that direction and on the whole it was not in her nature to tittle-tattle too much about other folk. However, she did listen to her grandchildren's reports about the new teacher when she arrived a year ago. All, on the whole had been good. She was kind and helpful, had gone out of her way to help the Sinclairs in their trouble, went to the Kirk on a Sunday and was friendly all round.

There had been some doubt at first when it ran round the village that she had arrived without a tawse – what like a teacher was this without a tawse? However, that problem had been resolved when the village drums had sounded that Mrs Manson had taken her in hand and sent for a tawse from Lochgelly. This had arrived post-haste to the parents' joy and the children's sorrow, only to be put into a drawer and never seen since. Mrs Laurenson knew this for a fact. Her grand-daughter Gertie who was in Charlotte's class had told her. Mind you, she had also told her that the children were very well behaved with Miss Gordon, on the whole that is. You could never get everybody to behave all of the time. But she did seem to have a knack with children. There was never any trouble getting them to go to school as there had been with that last teacher – what was her name again? Mrs Laurenson thought a minute. Oh yes, Mrs Auld. She was a right bissom, the tawse was aye out and in use and the children were scared out of their wits. No wonder the mothers had a job getting them up to the school in the morning. Changed days now though. The children went running up the road like little lambs.

A bell rang. Mrs Laurenson looked up at the bell-board and noted that it was the bell under which was the letter 'F' indicating that the noise was emanating from the front door bell. She was very proud of her bell system. Without the letters under the bells, one could go off and the person destined to answer might have no idea from whence the sound had come. Mrs Laurenson was justifiably proud of her system: other bells were indicated by 'P' – parlour, S – study, W – withdrawing-room, 'D' – dining-room, 'B' – back door and 'B1, B2, B3, and B4, each indicating bedrooms in order of size and position. There was even one indicating 'Ba' – bathroom, for indicating a need to wash someone's back? she wondered. There were other rooms in the Manse which was, as was customary, a large establishment, but they were bell-less as befitted their lowlier status. Of course, all these bells were seldom used with one bachelor living there. However, Mrs Laurenson thought, the system was in place and she felt that by instigating this and a few other helpful wee changes, she had placed a managerial hand on the running of the Manse that would not easily be turned around.

On hearing the bell and noting its source, Mrs Laurenson whipped off her large white all-enveloping cooking apron to reveal a smaller one underneath deemed appropriate for answering the front door. Not a tiny wee frilly one like some of the lassies wanted to wear – but nevertheless more genteel than a great big cooking apron. She made her way past the so-called servants' door. She never called it by that name, which she thought should be used only when a house contained a large retinue of servants. She did not think a housekeeper came under category of 'servant'. Friend, mentor, advisor, helper, perhaps, depending upon whose housekeeper you were, and the age, sex and marital status of your employer. Certainly Mrs Laurenson felt almost motherly towards Mr MacLeod and did not hesitate to offer advice if she thought it necessary.

The outer front door was open and through the pretty stained glass of the inner door Mrs Laurenson could see the expected visitor standing there. She opened the door just as James MacLeod opened his study door on hearing her footsteps.

'Miss Gordon.' She smiled at the young teacher. 'We were expecting you. Come in.'

'Thank you.' Charlotte smiled at her, her smile widening as she saw James bringing up the rear.

Charlotte

It took me all my time to ring the Manse doorbell on what was quite a formal occasion. After all, this was the first time James and I would have sat down to a meal at table together. True James had visited me at Da Peerie Skulehoose on an informal basis and we had met and walked together on the hills and at the harbour. But this felt different. I spent some time dithering about what I should wear – not that I had that much to choose from. In the end I chose a dark green dress of fine wool which Granny and Katie had helped me make before I went to Shetland. It fitted me well, the skirt was just on the ankle which kept it from trailing in the mud and was set off by a hand-made ecru lace collar sent in a surprise parcel by Granny. With this I wore my best boots polished to a high shine by Edie who was determined that I would not let her down. I also spent some time on my hair. I did not want it to be too formal and school-mistressy. On the other hand having my hair down completely left me looking like the schoolgirls I purported to teach. In the event, I put it up but not too tightly and left some ringletty bits of hair 'escaping' from the bun. I hoped it did not give too untidy an effect – that would be the opposite of what I wanted.

I could hear the bell jangling away in the back of the house. Within moments Mrs Laurenson was opening the door and rushing along behind her came James.

'Come in, come in,' he said. Mrs Laurenson smiled and held the door wide and I entered. James led me into the parlour, a comfortable room, not overpowering, with comfortable if shabby armchairs and where a fire burned brightly in the grate.

'Sit down,' he said. We sat. He leapt up and started fiddling with the fire.

'How are you this week? Have the children been good? Did you manage to get them out for their nature walk? Did the rain hold off for you?'

'I'm fine thanks James, and, yes to all your other questions.'

'I'm sorry,' he said. He turned from the fire and looked at me. 'I'm just a bit well, nervous. Do you realise this is the first time you've been over my door?'

'Yes, but James that's all right. And I have so looked forward to today.' I rose from my seat and strolled towards the window more to assuage his nervousness than anything else. 'How's your garden getting on.'

'Oh it's grand,' he said enthusiastically. 'But huge. Old Bob comes in often, far more than he's paid for really to keep it going – it's a real labour of love for him. I just tinker at the edges – but I enjoy it. It gets me out and doing something completely different. And you know what they say about being "nearer to God's heart in a garden".'

'"Than anywhere else on earth".' I finished the quote for him. 'Yes, there's probably a lot of truth in that.'

Suddenly a loud gong sounded. I jumped. James laid his hand on my arm.

'Sorry about that. We never usually use the gong – left by the last incumbent. I think Mrs Laurenson is trying to impress you. That's lunch ready I expect.'

In the hall Mrs Laurenson was hanging up the drumstick beside the rather important looking brass gong.

'Noisy thing,' she commented, 'but it needs an airing every now and again. The last minister used it all the time. And, to make it even more important, they called it a "tam-tam".' She sniffed. 'Showing off that their folks had been to India.'

Lunch was perfect. Mrs Laurenson served us our roast chicken then discreetly retired to the kitchen. The specially chosen Apple Charlotte with cream was left on the sideboard for us to help ourselves. James and I sat at one end of the rather large dining table and as the meal went on I could feel us both relaxing and enjoying each other's company.

'That was delicious,' I said. 'I must see Mrs Laurenson to thank her.'

'You'll see her later. Let's go out now while it's still fine and we can have a walk in the garden and I will show you what old Bob has done to it.'

Outside it was an early autumn day, still and quiet for once, awaiting the equinoxial gales. Leaves just turning to autumnal colours, trembled as they maintained a hold on shrubby branches. Charlotte shrugged her wrap around her shoulders against the slight nip in the air and they walked side by side down the steps and along the path. Apple and pear trees hung with fruit. A beautiful Victoria plum was thoughtfully espaliered across a high wall, branches growing out equally on either side. Carefully tended late summer flowers lined the path.

'Bob really is a wonder. I could never have done all this. Here's his vegetable garden.' Vegetables of many descriptions waited in line to be harvested. A graip stood stuck into the ground at the end of a half-dug row of tatties.

'Now I know where the vegetables at my back door come from.'

'Well,' James said, 'some of them. But I think other people drop things in too. But Charlotte, I didn't take you out here to talk of vegetables. I want to talk about us.'

'About us?'

'Yes, I cannot wait any longer. I know we talked about this a while ago and I really have tried to hold my peace and be patient.'

'James, James,' Charlotte held out a restraining hand. 'You're going too quickly. Please don't say anything. Let's just carry on as we are.'

'But Charlotte, I love you, I want you to be my wife.' There, he had said it. He stopped and faced her. She looked at him with those dark grey eyes, so deep, often so full of happiness. Now, the face was undecided, unsmiling, unsure of her next step.

'Oh Charlotte, don't look like that. Don't you see? It's perfect. I love you and, well, I hope you love me and here we are – both here and happy to be here. I never knew I could feel like this.'

178

'But James, we spoke about this before and I told you I did not feel ready or old enough to be thinking about being more than friends with anybody. James, I need time to be myself. I like you so much, but if you go on like this we won't be able to see each other at all because it will be too uncomfortable. Please James. Can't you see? I was so – well, so excited and happy about coming to lunch but I don't know if I'm ready to go into anything deeper than friendship.'

'But you might?' He grasped at the straw.

'Well, I can't promise anything, but …'

'Are you interested at all?'

'Of course I am.' And as he gave a cry of delight she buried her face in her hands.

'Now look what you've made me say.'

'But you do hold out some hope for me then?' His anxious finger ran round the inside of his starched linen dog-collar.

She looked at him. How fond she had grown of this man in the year she had known him. She watched him on a Sunday as he came into the Kirk, she listened to his strong confident voice, she shook hands with him with everyone else when the Kirk skailed, she welcomed him as a visitor in her home and accompanied him on walks. She heard the folk of the village speak of him as a respected man of the cloth giving him a deference usually reserved for older men. And she glowed with a secret pride when she heard folk speak of him in this way. When she was alone, she thought of him, recalled him to mind, and liked what she saw.

The only person she had been able to confide in was Granny. Granny said that she should not do anything precipitate. But what was she to do here? Events had taken on a life of their own. She still carried the burden of what Margery had said to her about Alexander and the children. She was sure that Alexander was going to say something sooner or later. But that shouldn't change this. This was separate. James was – special.

'Charlotte? Come and sit down, you've gone quite pale.'

'I'm all right.' But she allowed herself to be led to a garden bench against a sheltering wall.

'Now,' he said. 'I didn't mean to upset you. But I do love you so much. Don't you think you could love me too?'

'Oh, James,' she laughed shakily. 'It wouldn't be difficult.'

'Try turning that negative around and see what you have.'

She looked up. 'Yes,' she said, 'It would be easy to love you.'

'Oh Charlotte, Charlotte.' He picked up her hand and held it between his two warm ones. She did not pull away, enjoying the feeling of warmth and security and comfort. Surely this could not be wrong.

Slowly he drew her nearer to him. He moved his right arm until it was lightly resting on her shoulders and from there he pulled her gently towards him. With a little sigh of contentment she responded almost involuntarily.

Then she remembered. She remembered her life as a teacher – achieved by such hard work and contributions by so many people as well as herself. She remembered her own role in the emancipation of women. It sounded so pompous when she put it

179

like that but would she be letting the side down if she got married so young? It was still unusual for professional women to continue with their careers after marriage especially when pregnancy, in those days of poor contraception, usually followed quickly on the nuptials. So, if she agreed to James's proposal, she would have to stop work. She couldn't see any way round it, especially as a Manse wife. On the other hand, perhaps if she got married and had James's children, then she could go back to work as a teacher when they were older. Then she wouldn't feel so bad about wasting her training. Mind you, she thought, no training is ever wasted but nevertheless it would be a shame to cut a promising career in teaching so very short. Or, perhaps James would be prepared to wait a year or two before they got married to let her fulfil what she felt she had to do.

She moved under his arm.

'James?'

'Yes, yes, please say you will. I love you so much. We'll be so happy. I will make you happy.' He tried to hold her more closely again.

'James,' she wriggled free. 'Listen, James. I have to say this. I have never been in love before. I really don't know what to expect, or what to feel. If this is love then it's a very nice feeling.' He moved towards her. 'No, wait a minute. You need to hear what I need to say. You see, James, I have gone through a lot to get to be a trained teacher. This is not just for me. It's for everyone who have helped me, and given up so much for me, and, and I know this sounds really grandiose but I feel, and I know Granny feels, that women are just coming out of centuries of darkness and being downtrodden and in my own way I feel a part of it, and that although I do want to get married so much, I need to do a bit of giving back professionally for my training, and, well, to pass some of my thoughts and feelings on, in however small a way. And then, for my sake too, I haven't even got my Parchment from the Scotch Education Board yet. I won't till next year.' She stopped and looked at him.

'So what are you saying?'

'Well, I'm saying that I would like to wait a while, to think about and get used to the idea of marriage and carry on teaching for now.'

'But you're making me wait a very long time. We have a lovely house here all ready. I'm past thirty and I love you so much. I want to get married now.' He reached for her again. Again she fended him off.

'James this is too new to me. I need time. And space. I'm not ready.'

He sighed deeply.

'Charlotte. Given all that you have said, will you consider marrying me when you are ready?'

'Are you prepared to wait for me?'

'I'll wait for ever if I have to.'

'Oh, James.' Charlotte leaned towards him and this time it was she who took his hand. The two heads came together and their very private first kiss sealed the love of the moment, regardless of the breakers ahead.

Later they returned to the house, walking apart, not even hand in hand as one might have expected. Charlotte was adamant that no whisper of their love should get out in the village.

'But I want to tell everybody.' James was exasperated.

'Look James, we've been able to see each other for the last while quite happily without arousing any claik, at least as far as I know. Can't we go on for a while longer, please?'

'Mrs Laurenson is bound to jalouse.'

'And you know as well as I do that Mrs Laurenson is as close as anything when it comes to Manse business. And Edie is just as good. It's more than their jobs are worth to go talking out and about.'

'Hmm.' James was not easily convinced. He wanted to tell the world, or at least his world how happy he was.

'Come on James, don't be grumpy. Think about how happy we are inside and let's keep our secret as our own for a while.'

'Oh, all right,' he said. 'But it's very difficult.'

Mrs Laurenson did jalouse that something was afoot when she saw the two figures walking back to the house – albeit they were three feet apart. Maybe it was that apartness that made her look thoughtfully at them. However she said nothing, keeping her own counsel. After all, she always said there was a time to be silent and, she thought, this was one of them. Her air of confidentiality was demonstrated by her discreet knock on the parlour door before she entered with their tea.

'Thank you very much Mrs Laurenson.' Charlotte got up to help with the tray. 'And thank you for the lovely lunch. I ate so much I shouldn't be having tea.'

'You're very welcome Miss Gordon. Any time. Did you enjoy your walk?'

'Yes, indeed. We've been admiring old Bob's fruit and vegetables. They should be in a show.'

'Oh, Bob's won prizes in his time.'

'Has he?' James said. 'I didn't know that.'

'Oh aye. Long ago. He stopped competing, oh, about ten years ago. Now he says he does it for love. Right,' she said, looking at James. 'I think that'll be me away now then, Minister if that's all right with you. Everything is laid out for you for the morn. Your clean collar with extra starch and preaching-bands are on top of your dressing-table. Good bye, Miss Gordon. See you again, I hope.'

'I hope so. And thank you again.'

'Thanks very much, Mrs Laurenson.' James got to his feet as she left.

'I should be going too,' Charlotte said. 'I *have* enjoyed today.'

'So have I, and now I have my own prize – Bob's not the only one.'

'James, I'm not a vegetable.'

'No, you are a little ripe plum, just ready to fall into my arms.' He laughed at her scandalised expression and said hastily, 'Have a cup of tea first. Then I'll walk you down the road.'

'All right,' she responded, 'but,' primly, 'no silly comments outside or anywhere or I'll be going nowhere with you.'

'Oh all right.' James poured the tea. 'Have a piece of cake.' And contradicting the sharp words and strict rules, they looked in each other's eyes and smiled.

Charlotte

That Saturday lunch marked a turning point in the way James and I regarded each other. It was inevitable, I suppose. While before, we had been good friends, happy in each other's company and see each other on an informal basis, now, although the situation was concealed from anyone else, circumstances had changed. We now had an understanding, however unceremoniously it was made and however far in the future we intended to fulfil it.

I thought about this that evening when all was quiet and I had time to sit and mull over the events of the day. One part of me felt very excited. I wanted to tell someone especially Granny and Granpa. But I wanted to tell them to their faces and I could not do that then. And they had to be the first I told. Like James, I really wanted the world to know how happy I felt. But something was holding me back, making me keep quiet, damping down the excitement. I knew this did not suit James but when I looked at the 'something' in the peace of my parlour that evening, I thought I knew what the problem was.

My conversation with Margery before she died was one thing, with her pressure upon me to be a mother to her children, and a wife to her husband. In addition, were Alexander's strange comments to me the previous week.

All that I said to James about wanting to teach, paying back some of what I had been given, getting my Parchment, emancipation of women was quite true. Even if I had not had that conversation with Margery I would have felt the same way about teaching and my desire to continue in the profession, at least for a while before marrying. However, then, there would have been no need to keep even an informal engagement a secret. But with this burden of the Sinclairs I felt I did not know what to do and as long as I felt like that, we should keep quiet about it. At the same time I had an uncomfortable feeling that by not telling him about the Sinclairs, I had not been completely open with James.

So, my engagement day, if I can call it that, ended, not on a high note full of plans but on a lower, more discordant tone which took the edge off my gladness.

Chapter 27

February 1896 saw Christina's fourth birthday. As usual they marked the day with, not a party as such, but with what was known as a 'tea'. In this case, this comprised sandwiches – egg, cucumber, and salmon in brown bread (Christina loved those); scones; pancakes with jam and butter; homemade shortbread; and, the pièce-de-résistance, the birthday cake. This was one of Meg's concoctions. In truth, it was only an ordinary Victoria sponge cake. However, Meg was adept at cake decoration and very fond of Christina. The ensuing confection was the result of hours of work the evening before the birthday when Christina was asleep. White icing, lavishly decorated with pink icing roses and writing, along with four pink candles ready to be lit.

The tea was not a huge affair. A few guests were invited for four o'clock. As the birthday this year landed on a Friday, Magnus en route from school in Lerwick would be late to the gathering but Meg had promised to leave him some food and especially the cake. He had been most particular about that. After all why should he miss out from all that special food especially as he had been away working at Latin, Maths, Science, English, Geography and the rest all week? It wouldn't do at all. So the fast-growing, ever-hungry fourteen year old had paid a special visitation to Meg in her kitchen the previous Sunday before he set off on his six mile walk to his lodgings (or 'digs' as the boys liked to call them).

'Meg, Meg, are you there?'

'Yes, here I am.' Meg came bustling through from the pantry, wiping her hands on a cloth.

'Hello Magnus. Is that you away again?'

'Yes Meg, but you know Friday is Christina's tea, for her birthday?'

'Yes. Oh dear,' said Meg, with a smile in her eye, 'you'll miss it. You'll miss all that nice food, and the cake. What a pity.'

'Meg, Stop teasing me.'

'I'm not teasing,' said Meg. 'I'm just saying what a pity it is that you will miss the food.'

'Meg,' he wheedled. 'You wouldn't do that to me would you?'

'Do what?'

'Eat all the food.'

'Ah,' said his tormentor, 'you mean you want me to keep some back?'

'Meg, would you? Please.' She burst out laughing.

'Of course, you dafty. I wouldn't leave you out. Believe me, you'll have more than enough to eat.'

'Thanks Meg. You're the best.' He leaned over (he did not even have to reach up now, he had grown so much in the last year) and kissed her rosy cheek. 'I'd better go. Lerwick calls. Bye. See you on Friday.' He swung his bag on his back and left via the back door.

Meg smiled, thinking, what a difference in that boy in the last few months. He's so much happier. She hummed a tune as she returned to her Sunday evening chores. In theory, she had the whole of Sunday off. Most weeks she came back from her day off early to check that all was well for Monday morning. This involved making sure that Mr Sinclair's clothes were laid out, that his breakfast was laid, that there were enough eggs in the basket, and that the oatmeal for the porridge was soaking in its own special pan. In addition she had to set the bread ready for further kneading and proving in the morning. It's funny, she mused, as she organised her world in the kitchen before going up to see if Christina was ready for bed. Sunday is supposed to be a day of rest, but there are still things to be done and somebody has to do them. That's the way it is.

That was another thing that Meg liked to do herself. She liked to be the person who put Christina to bed. The only other person she was happy to see taking over this rather special job was Miss Gordon and certainly Meg acknowledged that Miss Gordon did it very well. When you were putting a small child to bed things were better done in a certain order to which the child became accustomed. If someone came in and changed the routine, then, well, total disruption could ensue. Yes, children were creatures of habit and it was better for all concerned that routines were adhered to.

Meg remembered some nights when Mr Sinclair had been left with the putting Christina to bed job and it just had not worked at all. To begin with he had not put her pig in her bed and her bed was therefore cold. Then the ritual was done in the wrong order. Whoever heard of washing before you took your clothes off? He missed out the teeth-cleaning altogether; and when it came to the story, well, to speed things up he missed bits out which Christina knew should be there and the young lady was not amused. Mr Sinclair had come thundering downstairs for Meg and grumbling that girls were just far more difficult than boys, he didn't remember all this fuss with Magnus and furthermore probably Meg was spoiling her.

Meg had been cross with him that night. She was the one who had to go upstairs to Christina and pick up the pieces, calm her down, read the story properly including the important bits, and cuddle her down with her favourite toy lamb. Really, if she had been a drinking woman, she would have taken to alcohol that night. As it was she returned to her kitchen and made herself a cup of strong tea and read her well-worn copy of *The People's Friend* for a while to calm herself.

She quite enjoyed her magazine. It would have been good to be the first person to read it – but as it was, it was passed around the village and she usually received it about sixth hand. Then she had to take it to the next in line. There were quite a few magazines circulating at any one time and woe betide you if you kept it longer than was agreed before passing it on. No matter, she had it to herself that night and she made the most of it. And when Mr Sinclair put his head round the kitchen door she was ready to make peace with him and share her pot of tea.

Christina was getting on, though, she thought, as she went to get her for bed that February Sunday evening. No longer a baby, she was independent, spoke very well, was learning to read under the watchful eye of 'her' Miss Gordon who appeared two or three times a week to play and work with her and take her out for a walk if it was fine. Meg was always glad to see Charlotte appear. She liked her for her own sake – they were good, trusting friends – but time that Christina spent with Charlotte was much-appreciated time that Meg had to herself.

She had noticed, however, that Mr Sinclair had taken to being around when Charlotte was there. Maybe not when she arrived, but he seemed to be home from work early on those days. He liked to go up to the back sitting-room where they kept their books and sit in on the reading. Meg wondered about this. Why was he so keen to do this? And anyway she had a suspicion that the reading lessons proceeded more smoothly without him, but who was she to say? But sometimes when she passed she could hear his voice interrupting and Miss Gordon saying, 'Sshh. Go on Christina'.

Meg opened the parlour door.

'Bed-time Christina.'

Christina, who was on the whole a very biddable child, jumped to her feet. 'Coming, Meg. Can we have this story tonight please?' She waved the latest book at her.

'Yes, indeed. Come on now, your milk is ready and your pig is in your bed. Say good night to your Father.'

'Good night, Father.' She went over and held up her face for a good night kiss.

'Good night my daughter,' he responded. 'Sleep well. God keep you safe.'

All was quiet. Alexander could hear in the distance sounds of his little Christina going to bed under Meg's guidance. He frowned slightly. Why couldn't he get it right? It shouldn't be that difficult. And yet every time he tried to do something which should in his eyes be reasonably easy, like putting Christina to bed, or giving her food, he made chaos of it. He sighed. Perhaps it was because Margery had sheltered him from those tasks for such a long time. And then Meg was so good with her too. So that sheltered him as well.

The last two weeks had been difficult. The first anniversary of Margery's death was on the third of February. Not an easy day. In the morning he took the gig up to the Kirkyard two miles out of the village and visited the grave holding Christina by the hand and walking carefully over the snow lying there. Someone had been there before him. There was a tiny bunch of snowdrops lying at the head of the grave. He laid his offering of a few branches of forsythia which had just come out in the shelter of his greenhouse, beside them. Meg had helped Christina find three early crocuses under a tree that morning. She stepped forward and laid them there.

'Do you think Mama will like them Father?'

'I'm sure she will.' His voice choked.

'Why are you crying? Is it because of Mama?'

He held her hand tightly. 'Yes.'

'Do you miss her?'

'Yes, I do.'

'Poor Father. You can come here and visit her any time. But,'the little voice trembled, 'I miss her too. I wish she could be here, really, really here.'

'I know,' he said. 'I wish that too, but she can't be. We just have to learn to live without her.'

'I know,' Christina held his hand tightly, 'we can be brave together.'

'All right,' he said, 'we'll do that.'

Hand in hand, they walked back to the gig, where the patient pony was snuffling into his empty nosebag and made their way back to Harbour House.

Then, a few days later there had been the first anniversary of the funeral. Alexander could not believe that so many people would remember the date and that one year before they had been at Margery's funeral and wake. He went to work as usual and his office door was hardly closed all day with people going in and out. He felt very proud in a way that Margery was remembered so kindly. At the same time he was exhausted by mid-afternoon and glad to hand over to his deputy and walk home along the harbour wall.

As he entered he could voices from upstairs in the sitting-room – Charlotte and Christina. He took off his coat, hung it up and calling to Meg as he went that he was home, he ran upstairs. The two readers looked up as he entered the room.

'Hello Father.' Christina jumped to her feet and ran to him. 'Miss Gordon is doing reading with me. Listen.' She held the book and read slowly, '"The cow jumped over the moon". What do you think Father? I can read it myself.'

'That's very good indeed.' He looked at Charlotte.

'You're doing a good job.'

'Well, I have a good pupil. She'll be well on before she starts school.'

'When can I start school?' pleaded Christina. Alexander looked at Charlotte.

'Well, how old are you?'

Christina drew a big breath. 'Nearly four. Four on the fourteenth of Feb'uary.'

'Well,' said Charlotte. 'What about thinking about starting in August when you will be just about four and a half? I'm sure Mrs Manson will allow that. We've had some quite wee ones before and they've been fine.'

'Oh goodie,' shrieked Christina. 'I must go and tell Meg.' She shot out of the room and they could hear her feet clattering on the stairs.

They looked at each other.

'Well, that was a successful thing to say. Are you sure?'

'Yes, she'll be fine. She's so keen.'

And so am I he thought. Aloud he said, 'Thank you for putting the snowdrops on Margery's grave.'

'I wanted to,' she said simply. 'The beginning of February will always mean Margery to me.'

'But,' he said, 'we must also think to the future.' She looked at him.

'I really think,' he continued, 'that we should try to get to know each other better. I have been watching over the last year how you have come regularly to play and work with Christina and take her out for walks. Also the care you have shown to Magnus. I want you to know how much I appreciate it.'

'But Alexander, they're lovely children. Anything I have done I have found to be a pleasure.'

'Yes, I know, but now the time has come to look further than the children. We must look at each other too. No, don't stop me,' he said as Charlotte was about to interrupt. 'A year has gone past now since Margery died. I could not say anything before, not outright anyway, but I have watched you with my children, seen how good you are with them, noted how much they care for you and feel you would make the ideal mother for them. A widower should not consider re-marriage until after a year but the year is up now and I can speak. Charlotte, would you consider marrying me and coming to live here at Harbour House as my wife.'

There was a long pause. Charlotte sat, head bowed, hands clenching and unclenching in her lap. What could she say? Alexander knew nothing about her very unofficial arrangement with James MacLeod. He had said nothing about loving her. He just wanted a mother for the children. She looked at him.

'Alexander, I thank you for your proposal. I want you to know I consider it a great honour to be asked to marry you. However, I feel that marriage is out of the question.'

'But why?'

'Well, I am very young, only twenty-one and there is a big age-gap between us.'

'But that doesn't matter.'

'Well, it might not matter so much if we were in love.'

'In love,' he interrupted. 'What does being in love mean? Silly phrase.'

'Or,' she said, struggling to keep calm, 'if we loved each other. But you see, Alexander we don't, do we. Oh, we like and respect each other, but I don't love you, not in that way, and you don't love me, do you?'

'Well, we could get to love each other.'

'Could we? I don't know that it's as easy as that. And how about promising to love and to cherish? I don't think we could do that easily, do you?'

'But Margery wanted this so much.'

'I know that Margery wanted this, and now I see that she spoke to you about it as well. And I know I promised to do the best I could for the children. But I did not promise to marry you even though she was very clear that this was what she wanted.'

'But what am I going to do?' He sat slumped in his chair, the picture of despondency. 'I was so sure you would say yes.'

'Well, I'm sorry. I've done nothing to make you feel like that.' Charlotte felt quite irritated at being so taken for granted. She continued, 'I think we should just go on as we are. I'll carry on helping Christina, and seeing Magnus when I can. And I'm delighted and honoured to be your friend. But anything more than that is not an option.'

'Now,' she firmly changed the subject. 'I must be off. I have some marking to do this evening. Are you all ready for the birthday tea on Friday?'

'Yes, Meg has organised it all. I feel like a useless appendage.' He rose to his feet as Charlotte put on her coat and made for the door.

'Oh, Alexander, you know that's not true.' Her eyes softened as she looked at his depressed attitude. 'This is a difficult time, I know. But this too will pass and you will feel better.'

'But I'll still be alone.'

'And who knows, you may meet someone who can make you happy again. I hope so. Now I must go. I'll see myself out the back way.'

So, it was with a sombre heart that Charlotte slipped out through the kitchen, saying goodbye to Meg and Christina (who was excitedly extolling the virtues of going to school in August) on her way.

Da Peerie Skulehoose on that dim February evening did nothing to cheer her up either. She was back later than she expected and the ever-cheerful Edie had gone home leaving the key under its usual stone. When she let herself in Charlotte found that because she was late, her fire had all but gone out and required extensive re-building and puffing and blowing to get it going again.

Charlotte

What else could I have done or said? I sat by my fire that evening and thought over the events of the day. I suppose in my heart of hearts I knew that a discussion like that was inevitable. But I did not think that Alexander would broach the subject of marriage so openly so soon. It was only just a year since Margery's death. But it seemed to be the custom for widowed people to give it a year and then before you knew it they were engaged and then married again. I felt ill at ease about all features of my part in this.

The most important aspect for me was James and the fact that I had not taken him into my confidence on the subject of Alexander. I felt guilty about this and still did not know how to handle it. Should I tell him or not? Since the day of my first lunch at the Manse away back in September we had continued to see each other on a very informal basis as before, although my visits to the Manse increased. Of course all was within the eye and ear of Mrs Laurenson whose discretion James trusted absolutely. And, as before, Edie was there when James came to Da Peerie Skulehoose.

When I thought about it at all, I considered the mores of the day to be singularly stifling. All we were doing was visiting each other's houses, lending books, talking and discussing what we saw as topical subjects, going for walks in places where other people went. And yet no whiff of scandal (and for scandal, read love, romance, an innocent kiss) was allowed to reach the outside. I sometimes wondered how folk managed to fall in love or come to love each other under such close scrutiny. However, James and I managed to love each other even within the constraints of our controlled careful relationship and I counted the days between our meetings. But I did miss not being able to tell someone or be open about the whole thing and I also felt James was becoming more anxious about this as the weeks passed. I was also quite surprised that people did not jalouse (as we put it), that we were seeing each other regularly. And yet, on the other hand, I suppose I was seeing Alexander as frequently if not more often, through my contact with Christina. Were Alexander and Christina then a sort of unintentional smoke-screen for my times with James? I couldn't tell. What I did know was that I did not want to be duplicitous with James and I felt that by not telling him what was afoot and all about Margery's dying wish, that that was what was happening.

In no way did I feel that I was being duplicitous with Alexander regarding my relationship with James. In effect, it was none of Alexander's business what I did and with whom I spent my time. The whole problem was now complicated by Alexander's proposal and I felt angry at his taking it for granted that I would say 'yes'. I also felt angry that Margery had put me into this position. She had not only spoken to me about the future with Alexander but also with Alexander himself.

And then there were Magnus and Christina. Magnus was getting on well and happy at school. He still came to me for talks and used me as a sounding-board when he had a problem and I helped as much as I could. Nevertheless, he was becoming much more independent. Christina was a different matter. She had a long way to go, was very little-girly, and I could see would become more reliant on me as a female figure as time went on. We were great friends and as I had promised, I felt I should be there for her as much as I could. Could I still be there for her if I were married to James and living up at the Manse? I did not see why not. But perhaps Alexander might not agree.

Christina's birthday arrived. I spent the day in school as usual and in the afternoon after school, as soon as I could, I went down to Harbour House to help Meg. Everything was ready. I think she just required some moral support and help when it came to handing round cups and plates.

All seemed to go well until after tea. Christina was very excited but reasonably well-behaved. I handed over my birthday present when I arrived – the inevitable book. With her current passion for the printed word, I knew that a new book would go down well and so it proved. Leafing through the pages kept her quiet for the last few minutes before her other guests arrived.

Two little girls, Rebecca Peterson and Ann Thomson and their mothers came on the dot of four o'clock. It was Ann's Granny who had made the Victoria sponge for Margery's wake and indeed, who usually took the prizes for this at inter-island baking competitions. Rebecca and Ann handed over presents to Christina and the two mothers sat and made conversation with Alexander. He, in his turn looked distinctly uncomfortable and looked relieved when Johnny Tulloch (grandson of Effie Tulloch: sausage rolls for the wake) appeared with both his parents. Mrs Tulloch immediately engaged the other two mothers in conversation and Mr Tulloch and Alexander got down to business about the local bowling club.

If I had not been so occupied (and anyway it would have been very rude of me) I would like to have had time to watch the three groups of participants as they interacted

189

with each other. The four children, three girls and one boy sat in a corner and played with Christina's new acquisitions. They were simple enough: as well as the book I had given, her father had given her a brooch of Margery's which she was wearing on her frock with great pride. He also gave her a skipping rope which I could see was going to be my duty to teach her to use. Meg gave her a work-bag for her sewing which she was just beginning to attempt. The Tullochs gave her a pair of hand knitted Fair Isle mittens; the Thomsons a ball which the children were rolling from one to the other and the Petersons ceremoniously handed over some hand-made doll's house furniture.

Alexander and Mr Tulloch (whose name appeared to be John) were engaged in deep discussion about bowling club politics and the three mothers had their heads together about some local scandal when Meg came in with the teapot. By this time I had finished laying plates of food on the table and was able to go and tell the children to come and sit down.

Tea went well. The sandwiches were praised especially the brown bread and salmon. The baking was well up to Meg's usual standard and she smiled politely as the three mothers tested and then extolled the lightness of her scones. And the cake: Alexander brought it in fully lit, the company clapped and Christina shrieked with joy. (Somehow she needed to learn to stop shrieking). It not only looked good but it also tasted first class, and I could see Ann's mother mentally filing comments to report to her mother-in-law just in case Meg should suddenly take it into her head to enter the inter-island cake-making competition. The whole tea was a success. And Magnus's share was not forgotten; Meg made sure of that.

After tea, the children were allowed to get down from the table to play. They left the room quite amicably and we could hear them in the hall where there was more room, rolling the ball from one to the other, giggling and chattering, playing snakes with the skipping rope.

We heard a scream of rage and then a bump and then another yell. The door burst open and they all flew in headed by Christina who ran straight to her father, clung on to him, pointed to Ann and shouted, 'She said I don't have a Mama. I want to have a Mama. You need to get me a Mama.' Tears streamed down her face. Alexander appeared at a loss. Meg, thinking to defuse the situation went over to her.

'Come on Christina, let's go to the kitchen and talk this over.'

'No, no, no.'

'Christina,' Alexander found his voice. 'Stop that shouting at once.' The noise stopped. But in place was the heartbroken cry, 'but I don't have a Mama like other boys and girls.' She left his side and came round to where I sat. She put her hand on my knee and looked up into my face.

'Please, will you be my Mama?' I now in my turn did not know what to say. I could feel my face turning hot and pink under the scrutiny of the other adults.

'I will be very good if you will be my Mama,' she said. 'We could read together and you would be there just for me. And you could live here with us and not have to keep going back to your Peerie Skulehoose.' I thought, the plans of the daughter are exactly the same as the plans of the father.

190

I looked, firstly at the three mothers who, to my distressed eyes anyway, seemed to be suddenly gathered together in a dynamic group with speculative messages speeding from eye to eye. I had to get away before this situation deteriorated further but first I had to see that Christina was all right. I looked at Meg who immediately and very firmly took control.

'Come on now, Christina, you've had a lovely birthday tea. Let's go through now and I'll help you wash your face and cool down.' She came over to us, took her by the wrist and dragged her away from the table. I rose from my seat, addressed Alexander and said, 'Excuse me please. I must go now. Thank you for tea.' In the distance I could hear Christina wailing, 'I want Miss Gordon to be my Mama.' The rest of the company looked at each other in confusion. This was beyond their social ken and they did not know quite what to do or say next. I picked up my gloves and coat and left.

Alexander was left, to his discomfiture, with the remains of the party. Although socially gauche, he was an intelligent man and realised that he could not just leave things as they were without making some attempt to rectify the situation. There he was with three small children struck speechless and clingy, three mothers, and one father with whom he would much rather have continued his dissection of the bowling club board. However, he had to do his hostly duty.

'Here,' he hurried to the chiffonnier. 'Let us have some cordial to finish off with.' His hands shook a little as he searched among the bottles.

'Can I help you, Mr Sinclair?' Mrs Peterson was by his side. 'Here do let me take the glasses. I can imagine how difficult it must be for you without Margery. No wonder Christina wants another Mama.' She gave a little laugh. 'Don't worry about it at all. She's a lovely little girl.'

'Thank you,' Alexander said as graciously as he could. Really, he thought, I could have done without this. What a performance. And in front of these women too. There'll be repercussions from this I'll wager. He gritted his teeth and poured cordial into the glasses which Mrs Peterson laid out.

'Do have some. Yes, Meg makes it. She's a wonder. Now,' to move away from any topic where women might be seen as indispensible, 'would the children like some sweets?'

The little ones crowded round, all strife forgotten until the next time. The adults politely sipped their cordial.

The following day Charlotte decided to spend the day at home. Edie had for once, a whole Saturday off. Charlotte had nothing planned for the day and was glad of it. She felt depressed and tired after the events of the birthday party and spent the morning in her parlour, trying to write to her grandparents to update them on the latest events. A difficult letter to write she thought and one which was not coming readily. I'm really too tired to write this. She sat down at the fire with her book.

191

A sharp rap at the door. Who can that be, she wondered. I'm not expecting anybody. The rap came again as she got there. James Sinclair stood there, arm upraised for his third knock.

'James,' she said. 'I wasn't expecting you. Come in.' He did not smile, but followed her through to the parlour.

'What is it?' she said. 'Is there a problem?'

'I've just been down to the harbour.'

'Oh, is it Mr Inkster? Is he all right?'

'Yes, yes,' James brushed aside her questions, 'But...'

'Yes,' she prompted, 'what is it?'

'I have just heard that you are going to marry Alexander Sinclair. I was under the impression that you were going to marry me – when you found the time. So, how did this happen? Is it true?'

Chapter 28

Charlotte stood there looking at him. She was wearing an old cardigan for extra warmth over her morning dress. She pulled it together in front of her as she automatically and defensively crossed her arms. The colour had drained from her face and she appeared tired and dispirited. If James had not been so angry he might have felt sorry for her. As it was he was so annoyed that he regarded the figure standing in front of him and waited with increasing impatience for an answer.

'Well,' he said, 'is it true.'

'James, I'm appalled. This is not true. Where did you hear it? What happened?'

'I was in visiting Mr Inkster again. Mrs Inkster is friends with Mrs Thomson who was also in visiting. They were all agog with the latest gossip coming from Harbour House.'

'What?'

'Yes. The story goes that Mrs Thomson's daughter-in-law was at Harbour House with Ann at Christina's birthday yesterday and there was a scene after tea. The story going around is that you and Mr Sinclair are to be married. There's great excitement about it. It's gone round the village like wildfire. Perhaps you will be able to inform me when the happy day is to be.'

'James, sit down please.' Suddenly Charlotte felt as though her legs were not willing to hold her up and she sat down in her chair. He reluctantly sat down opposite her.

'There is no wedding date or 'happy day' as you call it. Let's be quite clear about this: I am not engaged to Alexander Sinclair.'

'So, what happened, to make this claik go around? You're the spik of the village, Charlotte, after all your fine words about discretion and propriety.'

'But James I haven't done anything wrong.'

'Well, tell me what happened yesterday. Something must have come about to spark this off.'

As clearly as she could, Charlotte started to tell James about the happenings of the previous day. She heard him mutter 'wee vratch' when she reported on Christina's temper tantrum and ordering Alexander to get her a Mama.

'No James, she's not really a wee vratch. She's a wee girl who's mother has died and she's noticing that other children have mothers and she doesn't have one. It's quite

193

understandable that she should be upset. The problem is that she has shown her distress so publicly.'

'So what did happen?'

'Well, Alexander told her pretty sharply to be quiet. So she came round to my side of the table and put direct pressure on me to be her Mama and if I did, she would be very good and so on and so forth.'

'So what did you say?'

'I didn't know what to say. I was very embarrassed. It was in front of all these folk. I just wanted to get away. So when Meg came to take over Christina, I made my excuses and left and went home.'

'You mean without denying anything?'

'There was nothing to deny. And,' she added with a return of spirit, 'I can tell you this – the word "marriage" was never mentioned. That's a figment of someone's imagination'.

'So what did Alexander, I mean Mr Sinclair do then?'

'I don't know. I left.'

'Well, as far as *I* can gather he got out the cordial and gave them all a drink, probably as a sweetener, before they went home. I bet these women couldn't wait to talk about it. They will be thinking that Christina's let a cat out of the bag and will be making the most of it.'

Again Charlotte was at a loss for words.

'Anyway,' he said abruptly, '*do* you want to marry Mr Sinclair?'

'James, no.'

'Well what is it?' he said. 'What is it that is making you look so white and unhappy and as though you haven't slept for a week?' He looked up, light dawning in his eyes.

'Does *he* want to marry *you*, is that it?'

'James, I – I ...'

'That's it,' he said. 'That's it. I knew there must be something. What have you not told me?'

'James, James, just give me a minute.' He leapt to his feet and paced to the window and back.

'James?' She had to say something.

'Go on.'

'Could you sit down please?' He sat across the fire from her.

'Last year,' Charlotte began, 'when Margery was very ill we got to know each other very well...'

'I know that,' he interrupted.

'James, if you interrupt you make it very difficult for me.'

'All right.' He put up his hands in a placating way. 'Go on.'

'Well, we had many long talks and not long before she died she spoke to me about her worries about the children and Alexander.'

So, Charlotte told him the whole story, not forgetting that she had not promised to marry Alexander, that Alexander had made a few hints a few months previously and

194

had proposed marriage quite recently and that she had refused on the grounds that they did not love each other.

'Now you can see,' Charlotte finished, 'why I was so embarrassed yesterday when Christina came out with what she did. I didn't know where to put myself.'

'But why didn't you tell me all this before?'

'I don't know. I just felt I couldn't. I didn't mean to be deceitful to you, James, truly I didn't. I've felt very uncomfortable about this. I just didn't know what to do about it. And now it's all blown up in my face.'

He was on his feet again, walking up and down.

'What are you going to do about it?'

'What can I do? I can't go near Harbour House. That would just make matters worse.'

'But you have to scotch the rumour that you're going to marry him,' he insisted.

'But,' she said, 'I haven't even heard the rumour yet – only from you.'

'What do you mean, only from me?'

'Well, what I mean is, you're reporting to me what is going on. I think I need to wait and see what happens. I'm really unhappy about it all.'

'Look here Charlotte, if you do nothing I'll be thinking that there is something in this after all. That you do want to marry this man twice your age. That you've fallen for his charms and all that he can offer you, instead of being the wife of an impecunious country minister.'

That hurt.

'James. That's not true.'

'It feels pretty true to me. How can I compete with a man of property like Alexander Sinclair. Prove that it's not true. Go on, tell them all that you're not going to marry him. Tell them about us.'

'If you go on like this there will be no 'us'.'

'Well, that will suit me just fine.' He looked at her defiantly.

'All right, James.' Charlotte got to her feet. 'If you feel like that, will you just go, please.' She went to the door and held it open. He marched through without meeting her eyes and she did not escort him to the front door. It banged behind him and she heard the sound of his feet growing fainter as he walked away.

Charlotte

The next to arrive was Edie. She also had heard the news. I was horrified that a piece of tittle-tattle could wing its way around a place so quickly. Granny and Katie and Mam had all warned me about gossip. Indeed I knew the theory and of course had used it in my reasoning with James when I wanted to keep our informal engagement very private. But knowing the theory of gossip or claik, was nothing to being the object of its practice with all the speed and excited dissemination of its perpetrators.

'Are you all right, Miss?' Edie took one look at my face and went to put the kettle on. 'Have you had anything to eat?'

'No.' I suddenly realised that it was well after lunch time.

'Miss,' Edie's voice was tentative. She set a cup of tea down in front of me.

'Thank you Edie.'

'Miss.'

'Yes, Edie?' She took a deep breath.

'Are you going to marry Mr Sinclair?'

'Where did you hear that?'

'It's all over the village.'

I looked at her and couldn't stop the tears from running down my cheeks.

'Oh Miss, don't cry. I'm sure marriage, even to… I mean, I'm sure it's not so bad.'

'Edie,' I almost shouted. 'It's not like that. I'm not engaged to Mr Sinclair. It's all a mistake.'

'Oh,' she said, 'well that's what everyone is saying.'

'Then everyone is wrong.'

There was a silence. I wondered what was coming next. Then she said, 'I thought there must be something funny about it. After all he's twice your age, and he hardly ever comes here not like Mr MacLeod, popping in and out. Now *he's* nice I always think. So good looking and that dog-collar he wears; it really sets him off. Not that I ever speak about his coming here. You know that Miss,' she said earnestly. 'You know I don't talk about what happens here. Why, I would get the sack and,' she smiled, 'you know who would have to sack me? Well it would be Mr Sinclair and the Board, wouldn't it? That would never do.' She smiled mischievously. I had to smile back.

'That's better, Miss. I don't like to see you cry. Now what are you having for tea today? I'll see to it for you,' ignoring my feeble protests. 'I can see you are in no fit state to get it yourself.'

'I heard about the birthday tea at Harbour House,' she carried on. 'It must have been some carry-on. Mind you,' she went on confidentially, 'I'm glad you're not engaged to Mr Sinclair. He's too old for you and even though he does have rather nice blue eyes, his hair is very thin on top and he's very fixed in his ways – so my Mam says anyway. But it is a pity about Christina though. She could have done with a Mama.'

Who hasn't heard about it? I thought. I was slightly taken aback at how much Edie knew and at myself for sitting listening to her. A part of me felt I should have stopped her sooner. On the other hand, I reasoned, Edie has now had it straight from me that I am not engaged to Alexander Sinclair. That will surely go round the village as quickly as the other story. And, I'm pretty sure that she won't mention James.

And then, finally, Alexander himself arrived.

It was beginning to get dark and Edie had gone home after she had peeled my potatoes and prepared my supper and made me promise that I would eat it when I was ready. I did not feel like eating but realised the necessity of it.

Alexander entered formally when I opened the door to his knock. He shook hands and, leaving his coat and hat in the hall, followed me into the parlour.

'Can I get you anything? A cup of tea, perhaps, or something stronger?'

'No thank you.' His tone was, formal, distant, as if he did not know quite how to deal with the situation.

'I have come up to, well, firstly apologise for Christina's behaviour yesterday. She is a little madam and is very much in my black books today.'

'Poor Christina.'

'Poor Christina, nothing. I really wanted to give her a good smacking for her undisciplined behaviour of yesterday but Meg persuaded me that it would do no good and probably make things worse. In the end, I took the easy way out and let Meg deal with her. But before that, Meg took her to the kitchen and I tried to cool the situation down by offering the guests some of Meg's cordial. That woman Peterson – she and her friends just couldn't wait to get away and spread the word. You could see it by their sneaky glances at each other. Anyway after I got rid of them Meg put Christina to bed. She did a great job but Christina has to understand that tempers like that will not be tolerated. Now,' he added, 'will you please accept my apology?'

'Very well,' Charlotte said, 'I accept your apology for the moment on her behalf. But don't you think you need to talk to her about this? After all she is four. She will sit and listen if you are prepared to be patient and reach out to her.'

'The whole thing would be resolved if you would just agree to marry me. Now the whole village thinks this is going to happen. Why don't we make it real?'

'I will not make it real. If you remember, the word 'marriage' was never mentioned yesterday evening. All right, Christina made the implication, but Alexander, she's a little girl. It took the tale-bearers to spin yesterday's hullabaloo into a situation where we are getting married. So apart from anything else, I'm not going to get married just because the gossips say so.'

'And the 'anything else'?'

'The fact is, as I have said before, we don't love each other. When, or if, I ever get married, I want to love the man I marry.'

'Romantic rubbish.'

'How dare you. Didn't you love Margery?'

'Yes, but that was different. We were young with no responsibilities, our whole world revolved around each other and I suppose we were romantic. But now I am older, with children and I have to think of them.'

'But what about me? I am young. I need to have the chance, if I can, to love, to be in love.' It was hard to comprehend how he could be so solipsistic, so centred on himself and his situation and not make any effort to understand mine.

'But just think what you stand to gain,' he said. 'You will move out of this little but-and-ben – he looked disparagingly around my parlour of which I was so proud, with my books, and sewing and writing things – and move to Harbour House where you will want for nothing. You will be able to stop working at the school. You can give all that up. My wife is not going out as a teacher. You can have an extra servant if you like. Maybe Edie will come and work at Harbour House for us. That would be good. And then, when the babies come along, as they will, we will employ a nursemaid to look after them.' He looked at me complacently.

'So how about it? We can have the banns proclaimed very soon if you like.'

At that, I could feel myself bursting with highly inappropriate, difficult to restrain, hysterical laughter – the kind of hilarity which if not brought under control, quickly turns to tears. Banns would have to be proclaimed in the Kirk. The thought of the incongruity and irony of poor James with whom I was in love and who said he loved me (setting aside the fact that we had quarrelled) proclaiming the Banns for the marriage of Alexander and me did not bear consideration.

At the same time, I was astounded at the arrogance which assumed that I would be happy to marry for such gains as leaving my Peerie Skulehoose, no teaching, extra servants and someone to look after any babies of the marriage for me. I took a deep breath and turned slightly away to give myself time to control my features. Alexander looked at me sharply.

'Are you all right.'

'Yes, thank you. But Alexander, I cannot marry you. I have no desire for the improvements you offer me in exchange for marriage. In fact I don't consider them to be improvements – I am very happy as I am thank you.'

I kept the tone as polite as I could. I had no desire to quarrel with Alexander. I had no desire to quarrel with anyone and was sorry that James and I had fallen out. But some things happened despite best efforts, and I was still very angry with James for what he had said. But I also did not want to fall out with Alexander because of Magnus and Christina. I had, it must be admitted, come to care for them both deeply and I really was trying to keep my promise to Margery to look out for their welfare in whatever way I could. If I quarrelled with their father, then that could make things very difficult. On the other hand, I had to keep firm about this idea of marriage.

As if he could read my thoughts, he brought further pressure to bear.

'Charlotte, think of the children. I know this last episode has been unfortunate, but couldn't you think of their well-being and put all that happened yesterday aside for their sakes? You know you love them. Couldn't you consider being a mother to them? After all, if you don't marry me now, after all the publicity, they will think you don't love them, that you don't care. They will feel very rejected.'

This, I thought, is moral blackmail. I was about to react indignantly but thought better of it. What was the use of another row? I would only alienate him further and then I would never be allowed near the children. Also, and I had to think of this: Alexander as a prominent member of the School Board was my employer. I liked my job very much and did not want to lose it.

'Alexander, I will carry on helping and supporting the children as well as I can. There has never been any question of that. I'm sure Magnus at any rate will understand and if Christina is not quite old enough to see that I cannot marry you just to be her mother, then she will come to appreciate this in time. Now can we leave it at that please? I'm very tired today.'

'Well,' he grumbled, 'I really can't understand how you can't see the sense in my arrangements. However,' he added, picking up his hat, 'have it your own way for the moment. Let us be friends at least.' He held out his hand.

'Of course.' I responded to his overture and we shook hands.

'Now I must go back to my little girl.'

'Isn't Magnus there today? I thought he was coming home for the tea yesterday.'

'He did come yesterday but he went back to Lerwick this morning as they are having a sports competition today and it won't be over till now, really.' He looked at his fob-watch which as usual sat in his waistcoat pocket attached to its gold chain suspended across his front. 'Yes, they'll be finished by now. So he wanted to stay for rest of the weekend. He would have stayed in Lerwick last night but he wanted to see Christina on her birthday.'

'He's a good brother to her.'

'Yes, but of course by the time he got home for his specially saved birthday tea, Christina was in no fit state to be a nice little sister. She was very much in her own personally created dismal mood.'

'Did you tell him what it was about?'

'Oh, we just told him that Christina had become overtired at her birthday tea and had a tantrum. I told Meg not to give him any details. Now, I must go. Good bye, Charlotte.'

He clicked his heels and bowed as he left. His politeness did nothing to take away from the feeling of unease with which I was now left.

Chapter 29

Magnus was having a growth spurt. He couldn't believe that his clothes, bought for him for his return to the Anderson Educational Institute in August 1895 should now in early 1896 be feeling so tight and short. Could they have shrunk, he thought? But they have not been wet, not like washing anyway, and any of his clothes which were washed were designed for that.

He didn't think they had shrunk. It must be me, he thought. It's great, I'm as tall as Father now, not that he's very tall but at this rate I am going to be quite a reasonable size. He and his friend Lowrie Harcus, with whom he shared digs in Lerwick and walked back and forth from Lerwick to Jarlshavn at weekends spent many hours measuring each other, height, weight, biceps and triceps and so on. They read books and instructions on muscle development, breathing exercises, heart-lung efficiency. They played football, ran, walked, went out into the Lerwick hinterland and selected boulders of differing sizes to practise putting the shot which they heard was great for developing all the muscles but particularly arms and shoulders.

Some of the other boys joined in but Magnus and Lowrie threw themselves into the quest for physical fitness with a passion grounded in the Day School Code which appeared in 1895 as Physical Drill. Until then many adults considered that the informal exercise taken daily during the breaks in lessons was enough for any child. However the Keep-Fit movement of the 1890s stressed the importance of physical fitness and Physical Drill took this forward. It was only to be a few years before the Scotch Education Department urged the need for controlled physical exercise. This was as a result of the shocking evidence of medical examinations of military recruits to fight in the Boer War.

Magnus and Lowrie and their friends were therefore ahead of their time in their quest for physical fitness. The benefits showed, not only in their growth, but also in the air of wellbeing which they conveyed, and probably in the amount they ate. Their landlady Mrs Blance often threatened to increase her charges as she said they were eating her out of house and home. The boys only laughed. They knew she was delighted to see them consume such mounds of her home cooking.

Their academic work did not suffer either. Both boys worked hard on their various subjects and seemed to be able to keep up with the rest despite the time spent in physical activities. Indeed, when Alexander spoke to him about it, Magnus assured him that he was probably doing well because of the extra-curricular exercises and all the fresh air. Certainly, after six months in Lerwick, Magnus was happier and healthier.

On the Friday of Christina's birthday tea, Magnus headed out of Lerwick for Jarlshavn. For once, Lowrie was not with him. If truth were told, Magnus would have liked to have stayed in Lerwick that evening as well. The following day was scheduled for an all-day sports meeting. As they didn't have many of those, particularly in the winter, he would have liked to have stayed and done a bit of gentle preparation in readiness for the following day before having an early night. As it was, when he suggested this, Christina was not amused.

'But then I won't see you on my birthday.'

'But I'll see you the next weekend. And the weekend before.'

'But not on the day. I want to see you on the day.'

Magnus had given in. Lowrie said he gave in too much to her.

'You're probably right,' said Magnus. 'But I feel she needs me somehow. Especially now that Mother's gone.'

'Yes, but she'll never learn, if you keep doing everything that she wants.'

'Well, this time, I'll do it, and then we'll see. Maybe I should try being firmer with her.'

'Yes, you should.'

However, by the time Magnus reached home, as he had expected, the birthday tea was long past. Also, as expected, Meg had saved his share for him in the kitchen. What he had not expected was Harbour House's atmosphere of silence and gloom. As soon as he opened the door he felt it. He looked around the empty kitchen.

'Meg,' he called. 'Meg, are you there?' No answer.

He went through to the hall. Sounds from above. Meg was up there with Christina. That's funny, he thought. She was going to wait up for my arrival. He bounded up the stairs, two at a time.

'Hello, where's my birthday girl?'

Meg came out of Christina's room.

'She's in her bed.'

'What's the matter? Is she well? Has she been sick? I bet she ate too much.'

'No, no, nothing like that.'

'Well...?'

'Well,' Meg hesitated, 'she had her birthday tea with her visitors and then she threw a tantrum. Your father's not pleased.'

'But what was the tantrum about? Did she fight with the children.'

'Well, there was a small altercation,' said Meg carefully. 'We didn't hear the whole thing as they were in the hall playing ball.'

'And?'

'Well that's it really. Christina came into the dining room in a rage and the birthday was well... rather tarnished to say the least.'

'Where was Charlotte, I mean Miss Gordon?'

202

'Oh she was here but she went home soon after. I took Christina away to the kitchen to quieten her down and your Father gave the parents some cordial before they left.'

'Sounds like a jolly party. Can I go in and say "Happy birthday?" '

'You can try.'

Magnus opened the door. Christina lay on her back staring at the ceiling. Her face was tear-stained.

'Boo,' he said.

'Go away. I don't like anybody.'

'But I've come home especially to see you on your birthday. See,' he coaxed, 'I've brought you something.' He took a small parcel out of his pocket.

'Come on. Have a look.' He held it out. She turned away.

'Christina, I spent my pocket money on this for you.' She turned towards him. He could see that she was very near to tears.

'See, sit up, and open it.'

She sat up, leaning on her elbow. He held out the parcel again. This time she took it and with a sigh, as if to say, 'well I'll just do this to humour him' she started to undo the wrapping. Inside was a string of red beads. Bought in Lerwick, this had taken a significant amount of pocket money and Magnus felt she should have shown some enthusiasm. Instead, she put it on her bedside table and lay down again.

'Thank you Magnus.' She resumed her scrutiny of the ceiling.

'Come on Christina, what's the matter?'

'I have had a tantrum and Father is very cross.'

'Well, can't you speak to me?'

'No, I don't want to speak to anybody.'

'Oh, well.' Magnus knew when he was beaten. 'Good night then. Want a hug?'

'No thank you.' The chin quivered but the small voice remained firm.

Magnus went down to the kitchen where Meg was laying out his tea. His father stood warming his hands at the range.

'Hello, Father. I hear you're cross with Christina.'

'Yes, and I don't want to talk about it. How are you, Magnus?'

And that was that. Magnus could get nothing out of anyone. Even Meg was not her usual self and after he had eaten, she went out for the evening to visit her sister who lived in the village.

The next day he was up and about early to get back to Lerwick in time for the sports meeting which began at ten. Ah well, he thought, as he jogged along the side of the road. At least I'm getting warmed up for the day. But that's all really strange. I wonder what the tantrum was about.

The Saturday sports-meeting was a success. Magnus met up with Lowrie at his digs and they went up to the field and did a few bends and stretches and little bursts of running to limber up before the competitions began. They both did well, competing with each other to beat the field in most events for their age-group. The landladies, including Mrs Blance appeared at lunch-time to dish out mugs of soup.

'I'll have your dinner ready later boys. You better not fill up too much just now when you are in the middle of your running.'

The afternoon was all but over when a boy by name of Alfred Twatt came over to Magnus. He came from Jarlshavn but was not a particular friend of Magnus. For a start, he was older than Magnus, had been in school in Lerwick for three or four years, was one of the seniors and generally did not consort with the younger lads whom he considered were beneath his dignity. In addition his interests lay in directions other than those of Magnus: he was not a fitness enthusiast. So, it was with surprise that Magnus heard Alfred calling his name. It was not like Alfred to single him out; neither was it usual for Alfred to be at a sports meeting.

'Magnus, hi, Magnus. I have something to tell you.' Magnus turned.

'Hello, Alfred.'

'I heard something in Jarlshavn this morning. Something that will interest you.'

'Oh yes?' Magnus busied himself tying his laces.

'Yes, it's about your father, and that wee teacher in Jarlshavn. You know, Charlotte Gordon.' Magnus looked up.

'What about them?'

'I heard in the village that they are going to be married. That your father can't wait. And that Charlotte, I mean, of course, *Miss Gordon*, is just as keen to get him hooked. So what do you think of that?' Magnus, stood up.

'It's not true,' he said.

'Oh yes it is. Didn't you know then? Were you kept out of the big grown ups' secrets? Poor didums.'

'It's not true, I'm telling you.'

Alfred was enjoying himself now.

'I hear they can't wait to get at each other. Your pal Miss Gordon is on to a good thing there. I mean that's the only reason she could want to marry an old man like your father. She stands to gain quite a bit. Ah well, glad I could pass on the news to you…'

He got no further. Magnus, goaded into action ran at him. Lowrie, tried to hold him back.

'Magnus, don't. Leave him. He's not worth it. He'll be making it up.'

Alfred turned on him. 'Making it up? Not likely. It all came out at that lump's wee sister's birthday yesterday. It's all over the village. Everyone's hooting at the very idea of that wee lassie and old Alec together… Ouch, you wee blighter.' He staggered back clutching his lower jaw. Magnus surveyed his right knuckles. What am I doing? he thought. I don't want to fight. But I won't have Charlotte's name being dragged in the mud like this. My father can look after himself, but Charlotte, I won't have it.

Alfred leapt forward.

'All right laddie, if you're looking for a fight you've got one coming.'

He put his fists up and skipped about on his toes.

'Come on then, come on. Don't tell me you're scared.'

Magnus, shrugged off his jacket, raised his fists and moved forward.

'Magnus don't do it,' shouted Lowrie.

'I must,' said Magnus.

The fight began in earnest in the midst of a growing crowd of yelling schoolboys, self-generating as more spectators following the noise with glee, arrived from across the field. There was nothing like a good scrap and although fighting was against school rules, the teachers had gone home. The field was clear.

It was Magnus's reach that finally let him down. He was fit for his age and very fast. Alfred, however, was older, probably more practised in the guile of schoolboy fighting, and although not as physically fit as Magnus, was at least six inches taller, with the corresponding extra arm length with which to get past Magnus's defence. Magnus benefited from the additional adrenaline born of rage at Alfred's insulting comments. This did him well for the first few minutes of bare knuckle boxing, feinting, ducking and swerving. But try as he could, he could not move in past the long arms of his adversary. Alfred, on the other hand, after being taken aback by the surprise first punch to his jaw, proved himself to be more than a match for the younger Magnus. He used his long reach to the full, keeping Magnus back while at the same time landing jabbing punches to his body, calculated to tire Magnus while Alfred enjoyed the feeling of goading the younger boy into keeping the fight going.

But it could not go on too long. In a calculated manoeuvre, Alfred mentally lined Magnus up and delivered a swift right hook to the side of his face. Magnus's feet left the ground and he landed heavily. He lay, winded, as Alfred casually dusted off his hands and, escorted by his followers, walked away.

'Magnus, Magnus.' It was Lowrie by his side. 'Open your eyes.' Magnus heard the voice from afar off.

'Come on. Let me know you're all right.'

He carefully opened his right eye. His left was completely closed. His breath came in short gasps but he could feel that settling down.

'Give me a minute,' he croaked. Then he realised the fight was over. He struggled to sit up.

'Where's the swine? Let me get at him.'

'You're not going near him. Anyway he's gone. He's not worth it Magnus. You've had the fight. Now let's get you home. What Mrs Blance is going to say when she sees your face, I don't know.' Magnus touched his cheek gingerly.

'How can I hide this?'

'You can't.' Lowrie was organising help to get Magnus on to his feet. 'You'll need to rest up for a day or two. Mrs Blance will know what to do. Here's your jacket Magnus. Come on boys – one, two, three, up.' They pulled Magnus to his feet. He stood swaying in the chilly early evening air.

'Let's go.' Lowrie took one side. 'Come on, George, take his other arm.' George Hay (another of Mrs Blance's boarders) scurried to offer a shoulder.

It was a sorry party which arrived back at Mrs Blance's a while later. She took one look at Magnus.

'Bed,' she said. 'No, I don't want to hear yet what happened. It's quite obvious he's been fighting. Now let's get him sorted. Upstairs.' Lowrie and George helped him off with his outer clothing and put him into bed. They could see that he was badly bruised on his body but the worst injury was to his face where Alfred's last punch had landed.

'You've got a right shiner there,' remarked George.

'Aye,' Lowrie agreed, 'it's quite impressive. It minds me on the one I had a year or two back when I fell off the shed roof. D'you remember Magnus?'

'Yes,' muttered Magnus, 'but it doesn't make me feel any better.'

'Right boys,' Mrs Blance came in with a bowl of warm water laced with something smelling strongly of disinfectant, some old soft cloths, and a bandage. 'Let's have a look.' She scrutinised the injury and bathed the shut eye gently.

'Was he knocked out at all?'

'I don't think so,' Lowrie had been reasonably close to Magnus all the time and had watched as his friend went down. 'He was winded for a bit but I think he was conscious all the time.'

'Well, a day in bed tomorrow anyway,' instructed Mrs Blance. 'Now, any other sore places?'

'I ache all over.' Magnus sighed. She pulled up his shirt.

'Goodness me, who did this to you? What like a fight have you been in?'

'A one sided one,' said George.

'Who started it?'

'Well, I did,' Magnus admitted.

'You started the fight?' Mrs Blance could hardly believe it. Lowrie leapt to Magnus's defence.

'Only because that horrible Alfred Twatt goaded him into it. It wasn't Magnus's fault. He only gave Alfred what he deserved.'

'Hmm. But you came off worst?'

'Aye,' said Magnus. 'His arms were too long.'

'Ach,' said George. 'Arms like a gorilla and a brain to match. Anyway, he's bigger than you altogether. Mind you,' he added admiringly, 'You're a lot faster than him. You just need to grow a wee bit more and you'll beat him fair and square.'

'I don't want any more fighting coming out of my house,' warned Mrs Blance. 'Now boys, go away and leave Magnus to rest. Magnus, I'm going to bring you up a nice cup of tea and then we'll see what has to be done next.'

Sunday came and went. Magnus spent the day in bed supposed to be relaxing but in reality his brain was racing over the previous day's events and what had sparked the fight off.

Alfred Twatt said his father and Charlotte were going to be married. He had made the most of the news but even without Alfred's snide comments it was the thought of his father's marrying Charlotte that was so upsetting. He admitted to himself that Alfred's words had goaded him into striking the first blow. They had never been particular friends. Even though there was a seniority gap, the two boys' activities were also at variance. Alfred spent much time standing around with his friends and in a sense, looking for trouble. The shopkeepers did not trust him; he was suspected of a quick shoplift here and there; the boat-owners were reluctant to let him anywhere near their vessels in case he damaged them – and this in a time and place when boys were positively encouraged to take an interest in all things maritime. He was also a bully. Magnus had heard of Alfred's taunting of younger boys before and both he and Lowrie tended to give him a wide berth. Now it seemed that Alfred had picked up this bit of gossip and deliberately used it to wind Magnus up.

So, Magnus thought, the fight is done, he beat me, now I have to face the consequences of starting the fight. Consequences like being reported to the headmaster tomorrow as I surely will be, and then facing Father at the weekend. But that should be the end of it but it isn't. The cause of the fight is still ongoing: Alfred said Father is going to marry Charlotte.

It's disgusting, he thought. My father, that old man, and Charlotte. How could he marry her. It shouldn't be allowed. I don't want it to happen. How can I stop it? I'll go and speak to Charlotte myself. But she thinks I'm just a little boy – she won't listen to me. She has been so kind to me. I could talk to her, as I never could to Father or even Mother. Now things will be totally changed. I'll never be able to speak to her again. He thought with horror, she'll come and stay with us but she'll sleep with Father. She'll be my step-mother. I can't bear it.

His thoughts moved on. And what about Mother? Doesn't he miss her at all? And Charlotte – she was Mother's friend. Apart from anything else, doesn't she know what she's doing?

But, his reasonable side argued, it's quite natural for Father to want to be married again. This was the first time he had really thought about this since his mother had died a year ago. So what was the problem? He thought about this for a while. In theory there was no problem about his father's taking another wife. After all he was probably lonely, it was quite legal, and after a year's mourning, not unusual. Many men in the same situation as his father went about getting married as quickly as was respectable after the death of a wife. After all, a new wife provided a housekeeper, bedfellow (Magnus shuddered) company in the evenings and a mother for any children of the first marriage. The new wife would get a good home and all the trappings and status of marriage. A practical arrangement.

Magnus thought it would be good for Christina to have a mother. But what about himself? His father would probably say he would benefit from a mother too. He was not so sure. But if it were to be any woman that his father took up with just to meet a practical arrangement then from Magnus's point of view, he could be out of it for most of the time. At school all week, and then at the weekends, well he could spend more time in Lerwick as he grew older, and then in a few years' time he would be grown-up and able to decide for himself where he wanted to be.

But, his mind raced on, Charlotte? Charlotte as mother: to me? What a terrible idea. But why not? Because she's far too young for Father, he countered himself. She's half his age, she's a beautiful young girl, she's only seven years older than me, I hate him for wanting to marry her. She's mine.

He caught his breath and gasped at the strength of his own feelings. He sat up in bed and put his hands over his face. That's it, he said to himself. That's the problem. I don't want Father to have her because I love her myself.

Magnus had a restless night during which he tossed and turned and coped with impossible dreams in which he and Charlotte were on the St Clair together and trying to get away from his father pursuing them on the starboard side of the deck and Alfred Twatt chasing them on the other. There was a raging storm going through the Roost and the St Clair was about to capsize and spill the young lovers (and everyone else on board) into the sea when he woke up with a jump and realised it was at last morning.

He insisted on going to school – black eye and all. Mrs Blance wanted him to stay at home.

'No, no. There's no escaping. I might as well get it over with.'

'But you're not fit.'

'Well I can go back to bed when I get home. Thanks Mrs Blance, but I really have to go. Come on you lot.' Lowrie and George lined up alongside him.

'We'll stand by him Mrs B,' they assured the worried landlady. 'See you later.'

Two prefects awaited him at the school gate.

'You're to go straight to the head,' said John Simpson.

'Can we trust you to go alone?' asked Adam Moar.

'Yes,' said Magnus. 'How did he hear?'

'Oh, word gets about. I think you were seen by two locals who clyped to one of the teachers who informed Mr Robson.'

'Will we come too?' Lowrie was concerned that Magnus should get a fair hearing.

'No, it's all right, thanks, I don't think he'll be interested in anything but the fact that we were fighting.'

Alfred was waiting by the headmaster's door.

'Lovely shiner,' he mocked as Magnus approached.

'You're not so pretty yourself,' responded Magnus. Indeed, although Alfred did not have a black eye, the side of his chin, where Magnus had landed his first punch, was black and blue.

The door opened.

'Come in boys.' They followed the head in.

'I do not like having to be faced with this at any time let alone first thing on a Monday morning. What do you think I felt to be told after church yesterday about your appalling behaviour?' Magnus straightened.

'I'm very sorry, Sir. It won't happen again.'

'I should think not. And what about you, Twatt?'

'I'm sorry,' muttered Alfred, 'But he started it.'

'I don't want to hear.' The head went into his drawer and took out his well-worn leather tawse.

'Right, six each.'

Magnus had never had the belt before. It was not a pleasant experience. The headmaster was a strong man and used his three-tongued tawse to good effect. Mind you, he always gave it straight-on which meant that the leather hit the palm fair and square. Magnus had heard of some teachers who had perfected a way of giving the tawse incorporating a motion which meant that as the tawse hit the palm of the hand, somehow it curled around the hand and swung up and around the victim's wrist. This made the punishment at least doubly painful and had even been known to raise blisters rather than the usual red stinging palms.

'Back to your classes,' the head ordered when it was over. 'I don't want to have to do this again.'

'Yes Sir. No, Sir.' The boys left.

I will not cry in front of Alfred. I will not. Magnus could feel the tears at the back of his eyes. His hands stung. He longed to comfort them by sheltering them in his oxters or blowing on them but he kept them by his side while Alfred was there.

'See what you get for picking a fight.' Alfred was needling away. 'Go on, go on, you're crying, I can see you are. Just a few wee belts. Who's a mammy's baby then. Oh I forgot, dearie, you're going to get a new mammy. Isn't that what all this is about?' Magnus kept walking, head up.

The headmaster's door opened.

'Twatt,' thundered Mr Robson. 'I can see why *you're* not a prefect. Go to your class. You too, Sinclair.'

At the end of that long week Magnus walked through the gate of Harbour House. The gate creaked as he shut it. He walked slowly up the path round the side of the house to the back door. As usual, Meg was in the kitchen.

'Aye, Magnus. How are you, then?' She examined his face critically.

'That's been some punch.' He could now open his eye and the swelling was going down, but the bruising round about was extensive and changing colour daily.

'You heard, then.'

'Well we heard there had been a fight. That Alfred Twatt is spreading it about that you attacked him but he soon put you in order. What was it all about?'

Magnus looked at her. 'Just a fight.'

'Well,' Meg realised that that was as much as she was going to get. 'Your father wants to see you. I think you had better go through to the parlour. He's not best pleased. I'm surprised he didn't go through to Lerwick.' She turned to her cooking. 'Go on and get it over with.'

'All right.' Magnus took off his outdoor things, dumped his bag on the floor and knocking carefully on the parlour door went in at the abrupt 'come in'.

'Good evening Father, that's me back.'

'Well,' Alexander, brushed aside any preliminaries. 'What's this I have been hearing, boy?'

'I don't know Father, what have you been hearing?'

'Don't be insolent. Let me look at you. What a mess you're in. How dare you spend your time fighting when I have worked myself to the bone to give you a good education and see you all right and this is all the thanks I get. As soon as I turn my

209

back you get into fights and show yourself to be no better than the rest. I won't have it, I tell you. I was black affronted to hear that you were brawling like any common lout on a Saturday night. And then had to be practically carried home and put to bed. And cleaned up by your landlady. How dare you behave like this.'

'Father, that's not fair. I don't 'get into fights' as you call it. This is the first fight I have been in.' Magnus was furious at the injustice and tone of his father's remarks.

'How do I know that? This is probably the first one I have heard about. And with the likes of Alfred Twatt. How could you so demean yourself? He's a thief and a vandal.'

'He's also a boy at the school to which you have seen fit to send me.'

'Don't answer me back. What was the fight about anyway?'

'Nothing, just a fight,' muttered Magnus.

'You don't fight for nothing. Come on, what were you fighting about?'

Magnus thought swiftly. He had had a very difficult week trying to think how to handle his problem, his newly-found knowledge about himself that he thought he loved Charlotte. There was also his distaste for what he still understood to be his father's and Charlotte's pending marriage. Of course, for him the two problems were inextricably linked. For some reason, his father had not seen fit to tell him about any association with Charlotte and its link with Christina's birthday party. (And anyway Magnus did not know that Charlotte had refused Alexander's proposal.) All he knew was what Alfred Twatt had reported the previous Saturday in his immature inaccurate schoolboy gibes.

Magnus also could not mention that he thought that he loved Charlotte. He would be an object of ridicule to his father who would not miss the opportunity to put down any such notion. At the same time he felt it would be better, if he could manage, not to mention the fact that any marriage between Charlotte and his father was anathema to him and that hearing this news had indeed (plus Alfred's glee and goading) been the cause of the fight.

'Well,' Alexander had waited long enough. 'Tell me. What were you fighting about?'

Magnus straightened his shoulders. In his effort not to tell, he swung the other way into sullen rudeness.

'Never you mind,' he said. 'Leave me alone and let me get on with it.' He turned as if to leave. His father grabbed him by the shoulder and swung him back. Magnus winced as Alexander's hand fell on a still tender bruise.

'How dare you. You will not leave this room until I give you permission. Now,' he persisted. 'You *will* tell me. If you don't I'll beat it out of you.'

Magnus looked at him. 'Yes, and add to the bruises I already have. Right, I'll tell you what the fight was about. I was fighting because of you.'

'Because of me?' Alexander looked at him. 'What do you mean because of me?'

'It's all because of you and the fact that you're going to marry Charlotte. Alfred Twatt heard in the village and told me on Saturday after the sports-meeting. He also told me about the carry-on here at Christina's birthday tea. I think you could have had the decency to tell me on Friday night so that I wouldn't hear all the gossip second or third hand about what is going on in my own home.' His voice rose along with his temper.

'Anyway, now I do know, I can tell you straight that I think it's quite disgusting. Here you are, practically an old man and that young lassie. You've been currying favour with her right from the start. You're twice her age, she could have the pick of any man in the country and she gets pressurised into marrying a widower with two children. And you, if it's just a woman you want, or a mother for Christina then I'm sure the women more your age are queuing up. You should leave Charlotte out of it. I tell you, you're too old for her.' He paused for breath.

'Have you quite finished?' His father's voice was icy. 'Right,' as Magnus made no response, 'let me tell *you* something. What I do, or whom I marry, *if*, repeat *if*, I ever marry again, is my business and mine alone. Nothing to do with you or anyone else. Understood?'

And as Magnus did not respond, he shouted, 'Do I make myself clear?'

'Yes, Father. Quite clear.'

'Get out. Now. I believe Meg has your supper ready.'

In the kitchen, Magnus sat down at the table and put his head in his hands. Meg, waiting to give him the meal so carefully prepared and kept warm for him went over and sat by him. Neither spoke for a few moments. Then, Meg said, 'Are you going to tell me now what the fight was about?'

So Magnus told her. Not about what he felt about Charlotte, but about what Alfred Twatt had said, what the gossips were saying, how it had originated at the birthday tea, what he felt about that, and what he felt about the people who had spread the story.

'How can people do that?' he wondered. 'Here they are invited into a private party, something goes wrong or not according to plan and instead of keeping it private they spread it all around and create havoc.'

'Yes,' agreed Meg, 'and embellish it as well.'

'What do you mean?'

'Well, gossiping doesn't just repeat exactly what happened. That would be bad enough and probably a betrayal of trust especially as in this case it was a private occasion with only a few people present. But what makes it worse is the fact that often gossips are not content to leave it there. They have to exaggerate the story and therefore, in their eyes, make it a better story.'

'So, did that happen in this case?'

'Yes. At Christina's birthday tea, the word 'marriage' was never mentioned. That was the gossips embellishing the story.'

'But, Christina said…'

'I know what Christina said and I know that what she said implied marriage. But the fact remains that marriage was never mentioned. Believe me, I was there.

'I'll tell you something else. And,' she smiled, 'just in case you think I'm repeating gossip, I'm not. Edie came in the other day. She said that Charlotte had told her quite firmly that she was not planning to marry your father. She also said that Charlotte was

211

in quite a state about the whole thing. So yesterday I left Christina playing for a wee while next door and went up to Da Peerie Skulehoose after school to see Charlotte.'

'How was she.'

'She was a bit quiet but you know we are great friends – we have been ever since your mother was so ill – and she soon relaxed. Anyway, once we got around to it, she made it very clear, just as Edie said, that she has no thoughts of marrying your father. Of course she knows about the gossip and as far as I can see, she is carrying on at school as normal, not talking about it but has made her position clear, to Edie, which counters the village gossips and to me as a friend. And I am sure she would want me to reassure you too.'

Magnus thought about this for a moment. 'Yes,' he did not sound sure. 'But are you certain?'

'About what?'

'About Father and Charlotte?'

'Look Magnus, I'm as sure as I can be. You know as much as I do now.'

'I can't help feeling there'll be more yet. We've had such a row.'

'I know. I heard you both shouting. But come on, Magnus, come and have your supper. You must be starving. Then you can think about how to make your peace with your father.'

But Magnus knew that whatever happened now, words had been said which could not be unsaid and the relationship between him and his father would never be quite the same again. And, now he carried the additional burden which he could not tell to anyone that even as a fourteen year-old schoolboy, he cared very deeply for Charlotte Gordon.

Chapter 30

However difficult her life at that time was, Charlotte maintained a show of dignity and calmness in the face of the folk in the village. She even made herself go to church, outwardly joining in with the hymns and prayers, shake hands with the robed figure at the door and make small conversation as she left. It was easier at school. She was popular with the parents, loved by the children in her class and felt, in school at least that she could relax her guard and be her old self. She felt she owed Mrs Manson an explanation of a kind. After all they worked very closely together and had become good friends.

One day, during the week after Christina's traumatic birthday tea Mrs Manson and Charlotte were sipping their mid-morning tea while keeping an eye on the children playing happily in the late February sun. They were sitting chatting when Mrs Manson said, 'Charlotte, do you feel you have a problem of any kind?' Charlotte looked at her.

'In what way?'

'Well, they're talking in the village. Now, I don't want to listen to gossip, but when it involves someone of whom I have grown very fond and who is a member of my staff, which puts two sides to it, then I feel a little worried. I also think that you are up here with no-one of your own as it were, to talk to. If you feel the need to talk then I would be very willing to listen and,' she smiled, 'it would go no further.'

Charlotte sat and thought for a few moments. It would be so good to talk this over. Mrs Manson had been such a strength to her in this her first teaching post and had even wiped Charlottes eyes when she, devastated by having to use her tawse for the first time, had gone to the tiny cupboard-like room they euphemistically called 'the staffroom' to have a cry at her anger at herself for having used it. Mrs Manson found her sniffing in the old horsehair armchair.

'What is it?'

'I've failed. I've used it. I wanted never to have to use it and now I have.'

'Used what?'

'That... tawse.' Charlotte could hardly utter the word.

'Oh, that.' Ina Manson nearly laughed but straightened her face when she realised how seriously Charlotte was taking this failure of self-resolve.

'Now, Charlotte,' she said firmly, 'it had to come sometime. Who did you use it on?'

'Charlie Tait.' Charlotte sniffed and groped for her handkerchief.

'Well, I have no doubt he deserved it. Now come on, back to your class. They'll be sitting like mice as they've never seen this spectacle before.'

So the two teachers had grown very close. Charlotte felt she could offload at least some of the story. Indeed it was probably only fair that she did. As Charlotte's supervisor, Mrs Manson had to face the folk too and it was just as well for her to have an idea of what it was all about.

'It all goes back to before Margery Sinclair died,' Charlotte began. She finished her story at the happenings of the previous Saturday when she had told Edie that she was not going to marry Alexander.

'That fits with both stories I've heard in the village,' Mrs Manson said. 'First I heard one, then a day or two later it was contradicted by the one coming from Edie.'

'I can't understand why they bother,' said Charlotte. 'It's only me.'

'Ah yes, but you know the old Scottish thing about people in a parish looking up to the dominie, the doctor and the minister. Well, while they traditionally look up to these folk, they also like to find something wrong with them as well. So, if they can find anything to claik about these three then they'll do it. And, here, even though we're only women,' she sniffed, 'we're the equivalent to the dominie. Add to that the fact that the other person in the story is the harbour master and no wonder the pot wants to boil over.'

'Yes, my grandfather used to say that sort of thing too. He was the doctor.'

'Oh well, there you are.' Mrs Manson said, satisfied her point was made. 'Now, what are you going to do about this?'

'I don't see that there is anything I *can* do. I've said I'm not going to marry Alexander. I think I'll just have to wait and let it blow over.'

'Perhaps that might be best. At least, don't do anything in a hurry.'

Charlotte felt better after confiding in Ina Manson, but the problem did not go away. She constantly bumped into Alexander. As a member of the school board, he attended all its meetings. In addition, he often seemed to be in school checking that this or that was working properly or that the teachers had everything they required. And, Charlotte did not want to lose touch with Christina. She had kept faithfully her promise to Margery and she saw no reason for stopping their activities. They both enjoyed the contact and she believed Christina benefited from it. On the other hand, under the present circumstances Charlotte didn't want to fuel the gossip fires by being seen too much at Harbour House.

Meg knew well what was going on. She suggested that instead of Charlotte going to Christina, Christina should go to Charlotte at Da Peerie Skulehoose. They came to the agreement that Meg would wave Christina on her way to Charlotte's two or three times per week. To be allowed to walk up the road by herself was a big step forward. She had never done this before and Meg worked hard for Alexander's permission. However, he finally gave in and she now went up the road by herself and Meg collected her a couple of hours later. In time, they all promised her, as the evenings

214

grew lighter, she could to come home by herself as well. Charlotte's problem was set aside from that point of view at least.

Charlotte was spared the problem of meeting Alexander in church as Alexander went to the Congregational church. However Charlotte found that when she went to the local shops on a Saturday morning, Alexander seemed to be around. He didn't have to be, as Meg usually did the Harbour House shopping. The first time it happened Charlotte thought nothing of it. She smiled, said good morning and got on with what she was doing. But after a few of these coincidences, she began to see a pattern in the behaviour. Then he began offering to carry her basket home for her.

'No thank you Alexander,' she responded on one such occasion. 'I'll carry it myself, but,' softening, 'thank you for offering.' She walked away swiftly along the harbour and up the brae to her house.

The next time, she walked off again, only to find him by her side.

'Please allow me to walk with you.'

'Alexander, don't you see, I don't want this. Please go away.'

'But I want to walk with you. I want to carry your shopping.'

'No thank you. See, here's Mrs Peterson. Charlotte didn't want to be seen arguing with him. 'Good morning Mrs Peterson, How's Rebecca?' Rebecca had been off school with a bad attack of the chicken-pox which was currently cutting a swathe through the school.

'Oh she's much better thank you Miss Gordon. She'll soon be back to school. The spots are drying up now. Dr Taylor says to give her another week and she'll be fine.'

'I'm glad to hear it.'

Mrs Peterson looked at Alexander.

'And Christina, has she had it?'

'No not yet, but the school children seem to have been badly hit with it.'

'Yes indeed.' Mrs Peterson looked at them slyly. 'And you both, are you well?'

'Yes thank you, I am very well.' Charlotte hastened to squash any sense of being part of a couple. 'And now I must go. Good bye, Mrs Peterson, Mr Sinclair.' She hurried off.

Edie was sweeping the steps of Da Peerie Skulehoose as she came up the path with her basket.

'Hello, Miss, did you get everything?'

'Yes, I think so. But, Edie,' she hesitated.

'Yes Miss?' Edie brushed the dust into her shovel and made to put it in the rubbish pail.

'I think, if it's all right with you for the time being, we'll make a shopping list and you can go down and get it please.'

Edie looked at her. 'Well if that's what you want Miss. But why? I thought you liked to go and get your bits and pieces.'

'Yes I do but, well, just do it will you please?' Charlotte marched into the house, dumped her basket on the table and took off her outdoor things. Edie said nothing but began to put the shopping away.

215

'Edie, I'm sorry, I shouldn't have jumped at you. I just think it's better for the moment to do it this way.'

'That's all right Miss. I don't mind.'

But Charlotte could not avoid Alexander for ever. She had not forgotten her promise to Christina about starting school after the summer holidays and Christina reminded her frequently. She even, Meg told Charlotte, had a calendar with the weeks marked off till she started. She'd pestered Meg to help her work out how to do this.

It was the custom for children who were about to start school to be registered with the teacher sometime during the previous term. One day in early June, Charlotte was tidying up for the day and she heard feet coming towards her classroom. It was Alexander.

'Good afternoon,' she said. 'I'm just about to finish for the day.' He bowed formally and took off his hat.

'Yes, I'm sorry to be late. I have just walked up from the harbour to register Christina for school. You may remember we talked about this some time ago and agreed that August would be a suitable time even though she is slightly young.'

'Indeed I do remember, and she has made great strides with her reading work she has been doing with me. But,' Charlotte said, to avoid spending time with him, 'don't you want to register her with Mrs Manson as head teacher.'

'No no, that will be all right. I'm sure you register other children too.' This was so true that Charlotte could do nothing but comply with his request and get out the big blue Register with the page ready marked with a few new children's names.

'Right,' she said, 'now I need her full name, address, date of birth, and therefore age at starting school, parents' names, father's occupation and names of any siblings who are at or have been at school here.'

Once the formalities were over, Charlotte carefully blotted the page and closed the Register.

'So, we'll expect her in August. I'll look forward to welcoming her to the class. But I hope she will continue to come and see me sometimes as usual.'

'Thank you Charlotte. Now,' Alexander lowered his voice. 'There is something else. Charlotte, I haven't forgotten your help, your care, how lovely you are. I have not seen you for a few weeks but you are as beautiful as ever. Please, please will you be my wife. I will do anything to make you happy.'

'Alexander, we have talked about this before.' Charlotte rose from her chair at the desk. The tone of her voice changed. She was no longer welcoming a parent but fending off an unwelcome advance.

'Now please go away and leave me in peace. The answer is no. I thank you for asking but I do not want to marry you. Now please go.'

He picked up his hat from the table and turned.

'I am deeply grieved by your attitude. Now I must live the rest of my ...'

At that moment the sound of brisk feet made them both look up. Mrs Manson came bustling in.

'Is everything all right, Miss Gordon? Ah Mr Sinclair, good afternoon. How are you? And Christina and Magnus? Are they well?'

Alexander caught at a disadvantage recovered quickly.

'Good afternoon, Mrs Manson. Yes indeed they are well thank you. I am just up registering Christina for starting school next term.' He looked around with approval. I think she will like it very much.'

'I'm sure she will. Miss Gordon here is a very good teacher. Now,' she added, 'we are just about to lock up for the day.'

'Yes of course.' Alexander took the hint. 'Well good bye, Mrs Manson, Miss Gordon. Thank you for your help. I look forward to seeing you again.'

On his departure Mrs Manson turned to Charlotte.

'Are you all right?'

'Yes, thank you. And thank you for coming through.'

'I saw Mr Sinclair coming into the playground so I knew he was there. I did not listen to your conversation. Neither did I want to interrupt until I heard the tone of your voice change. If you are sure that you are all right, let's lock up and go home.'

Chapter 31

Charlotte

That last brush with Alexander was in early June. By the end of the month I was ready for the holidays. Even the children seemed tired and jaded. Shetland was at its summertime best with long days of daylight and fingers of sunshine stretching through the sky from the north even in the early hours of the morning. But I was ready for a change of scene and people and, some personal breathing space. Ten days after midsummer I once again boarded the St Clair bound for Aberdeen and found my cabin for the overnight trip south.

Aberdeen harbour in the morning: the noise of seagulls screaming after fish guts; the smell of fish in the air; the sight of fishing boats moving here and there some propelled by huge coloured lugsails, some nearer shore by oars; the shouts of fishwives selling their wares with heavy baskets on their hips; the more formal fish merchants, and of course the fishmarket; a few cats weaving here and there to see what they could pick up; some human scroungers wanting a fry; a few groups of retired fishermen with pipes in their mouths discussing how much better it was in their day; and, ships' chandlers selling everything you could possibly want for a boat or its sailors.

I felt really refreshed that morning as the St Clair steamed her way carefully to her berth in the busy harbour. Perhaps it was because I had slept well, The ship had neither rolled nor tossed with little wind and the water calm. Perhaps also my mood had lifted because now I was away from all the stress of the last few months. I watched the busy scene as we approached. Then a rattle of chains, an extra loud rumble of engines and the St Clair docked.

A few hours later the Aberdeen – Alford train came to the end of the line. A few folk waited in the afternoon sunshine on the platform at Alford. I was expecting Jock to be outside the station looking after the gig. This was our usual routine, set up during my College days. Jock came to meet me in the gig but remained outside the station until the train arrived as he did not like to leave the horse by himself too long. When I got off the train and the guard had dumped my luggage for me on the platform, I would go through to the outside of the station, find Jock and he would come and help me with my bags.

Today, as the train drew to a halt and I opened the carriage door, to my surprise, I saw Granny standing there, still straight-backed despite her seventy-three years. She saw me and held up her hand in greeting before I jumped off the train and ran to her arms outstretched. She held me closely.

'Granny, how lovely to see you.' And, when she did not say anything, but just held me more closely, I said, 'Granny, Granny, what's wrong? Is it... is it, Granpa?'

'No, no, child, it's not your Granpa. It's your mother.'

'Mam? What's happened? Has there been an accident?'

'Charlotte,' Granny spoke carefully but her voice shook. 'Charlotte, your Mam is dead.'

'Dead? How can she be? She's not old.'

'No, I know but she wasn't well, either.'

Bad news travels fast in small rural communities and the Guard, who knew us all had already taken my luggage off the train and was trundling it in his big wooden trolley through the station hall to the other side where Jock waited for us with the gig. I stood with Granny on the now nearly empty station platform and tried to take it in. Mam was dead. But how? Granny led me to a bench. 'Let's sit here for a minute.' We sat down and I turned to her.

'What happened? It must have been very sudden.'

'Yes, it was.' Granny swallowed and then gathered herself to tell me what she knew.

'She took an apoplectic seizure two days ago. Your father found her when he came in for his fly-cup in the afternoon and sent the loon straight for us and of course for Leslie. It was better that he should attend her rather than your Granpa.'

'How was she?'

'Well, she was conscious but she couldn't speak and she was paralysed down the right side. There must have been considerable brain damage.'

'Oh, poor Mam.'

Granny sighed and I was very conscious that it was not only my mother who was dead but also it was Granny and Granpa's daughter. That, for them, was equally hard to bear.

'Yes, poor Mary. She didn't deserve this. Well, we got her to bed, and for a wee while we thought things were looking better. She knew what we were saying and indicated what she wanted with her good hand. We wanted to get in touch with you but knew that any news we got to Shetland would be too late to make any difference for you as we knew you were leaving by boat yesterday evening. And yesterday evening she took a turn for the worse. Leslie was very good. He stayed with her for a long time. And Annie was there too. She is such a strength. So she just gradually became unconscious and drifted away.'

She bent her head and her shoulders shook.

'My daughter, your mother. Gone before her time.'

I cried. There at the station in the Alford summer sunshine, I cried for the mother who had borne me with such gladness, who had eventually been unable to cope with six babies arriving at too great a speed, and who had given me into the care of my grandparents to give me a chance. We sat on the bench together until the storm passed. No one came near. The train started for Aberdeen at some point, trailing skirts of steam which hung around before dispersing. The stationmaster sat discreetly in his office. We knew Jock would wait patiently until we were ready.

'Come,' Granny said, 'we should go home now. We mustn't keep Jock waiting any longer. And, I'm sure you will want to go up to the Milton.'

Jock waited with the horse. He was good at waiting. He had been Granpa's horseman for many years and had waited outside many a house for bairns to be born, folk to be treated, the dying to depart. He got down from his seat as we approached.

'Man, lassie, a'm afa sorry aboot yer mam.'

'Jock,' I hugged him. 'Thanks for coming,' I whispered, 'and for waiting for us so well.' We got up into the back of the gig, he clicked his tongue at the horse and we set off for Towie.

On most of my home journeys, I usually settled myself down at Towie and headed for the Milton on the day after to re-acquaint myself with my family there and my much loved fields and hills and wild pastures. Not this time. I felt I needed to get there as soon as I could to see Mam, to hug Dad, and to support if I could, my brothers and sisters. Jock seemed to understand perfectly what I needed to do.

'Ye'll be needin ti gang ti the Milton ee noo?'

'Jock, would that be all right?'

'Ay, ay. Nae bother.'

'Granny, is that all right with you?'

'Yes, child, just come in first and say hello to Granpa, and then off you go. I think Katie will have a cup of tea ready. It would do you good if you would stop for ten minutes to have it.'

'All right thank you.' I knew this made sense. I also wanted to see Granpa.

He looked old and tired. Mam had been his youngest child and he loved her dearly. Now he was very conscious that the usual order of parents going before the children had been upset. I felt guilty about leaving them so soon after my arrival. But he would have none of it.

'Ay lassie, you go on. Yes, Mary was my daughter, but she was your mother. You go and pay your respects. That's only right and proper. Jock will wait and bring you back later and then we can talk.'

Charlotte returned to Towie with Jock from the Milton later that evening. It had been a distressing evening. The family, gathered at the farm cottage seemed to be in a state of disorganisation and shock. When they arrived Jock said, 'Noo, Charlotte, jist ye tak yer time. There's nae hurry. A hae a piece wi me fur ma tea – Katie made shair o that. A'll awa roon tae the stable an hae a craic wi the ither lads.'

'Thanks, Jock.' Charlotte put out her hand to touch the old man's arm in gratitude. Ever since she had known him he had been there, supportive, patient and kind.

She slipped quietly in the back door. The kitchen was in a complete mineer. Unwashed dishes lay about from the last scratch meal; the hen's pail sat in the middle of the floor; a stray hen clucked in a forlorn fashion under the table; dirty washing lay in bundles awaiting attention. Lizzie sat staring into the range which was out. Charlotte stopped and looked around.

'Lizzie. Lizzie?' She went up to her sister and touched her shoulder gently. Lizzie jumped.

'Charlotte. A didna hear ye come in. A wis that far awa. Oh it's afa fine ti see ye.' Her eyes filled with tears. 'Fit are we gaan ti dee? Mam's gone.'

'I know.' Charlotte held her. 'I know.' The two young women cried and held each other close.

'She wisna weel.' Lizzie sniffed. 'She's had headaches for ages. She wouldn't stop. You saw what she was like last time you were hame. I kept tellin her but she wouldna listen ti me. I wish I had been stronger with her.'

'I know. But Lizzie, you did all you could. You couldn't tie her to a chair, now could you?'

'No,' wailed Lizzie, 'but if she had only listened, she wid be here noo.'

'Where is Mam? Where do you have her lying?'

'In the ben room. Mirren came and washed her and dressed her. She made her afa bonny. Mirren's the howdie noo – Annie's getting afa aald' she added in answer to Charlotte's enquiring look. 'Mind you, Annie wis wi her fan she deed. She wis afa upset. Greetin, she wis.'

'She would be upset,' said Charlotte. 'She was very fond of Mam and she brought all of us into the world. I'll need to go up and see her.'

'Onywey,' continued Lizzie, 'then Tam the jiner, came up and he's awa noo makkin a coffin. He'll be back the morn. A suppose ye'll be wintin ti see her.'

'Yes,' said Charlotte, 'I want to do that. But where's Dad?'

'Ach, he's awa oot ti the field aa by himsel. He's nae spikkin ti onybiddy.'

'Well, I'll see him in a whilie. What about the rest.' Lizzie shrugged vaguely. 'Willie's oot by, they're aa aroon somewey.'

In contrast to the state of the kitchen, the ben room had an air of quietness. All was tidy. The antimacassars on the old leather armchairs were white and fresh. A few flowers stood in a vase on the table. The fire was cleaned out and set ready to light. The body of thirty-nine year old Mary Gordon, daughter of Andrew and Margaret Grant of Towie, wife of John Gordon and mother to six children, lay on the bed.

Charlotte approached calmly and looked at her mother. Far from the harassed dispirited woman of the previous year, the woman she now looked at had an air of tranquillity. The stressed lines were gone, the soft brown hair carefully brushed, the eyes closed as though Mary had just dropped off to sleep for a while. Charlotte touched her mother's forehead gently, bent down and kissed the folded hands.

'You're right, Lizzie, she does look afa bonny.'

A little later, Charlotte went out to find her father. He was as Lizzie said, in the field. He did not speak as she approached, but held out his arms to her in a silent embrace. They stood there in the evening sunlight saying little, letting the happenings of the last two days wash over them.

'I miss her,' he at last confessed. 'Even already, I miss her. Fit am A gaan ti dee wi'oot her?'

'Dad,' Charlotte hesitated. What could she say. What could anyone say. She couldn't trot out all the clichés about it taking time, and Mam was in a better place and at rest now. Lines like that were said when folk felt they had to say something but didn't know what. She didn't know what to say to comfort her Dad. He probably didn't know what to say to help her.

As if he could read her mind he spoke, 'We canna say onything ti help, Lassickie. A'm jist that glad ye're here. That is help eneuch.' At that she cried again, but this time it was her father's arms which held her. And in the holding, each gave comfort to the other.

Charlotte returned to Towie for the night. Willie, John and Wee Alicky made up beds in the stables. Lizzie and Jean took over the box-bed in the kitchen of the cottage. Their father said he would spend the night watching with Mary – he felt it was something he could do for her. And, indeed it was a fulfilment of an old Scottish tradition where a family member or close friend would sit up to watch the night through with someone who had died.

The lights were still on in Trancie House as the gig rolled up to the door.

'Come away in.' Granny was there almost before they stopped. 'You too Jock. You must have a dram after your late travelling. Now, how are things, up at the Milton?'

The following day Granny and Charlotte took the gig back up to the Milton. They also took a load of baking. Scones, cakes, pancakes, sausage rolls and other comestibles suitable for serving to the folk who would come and go to the Milton over the next few days to pay their respects to the family and to Mary's memory. They were also prepared to help and encourage Lizzie into cleaning and tidying. The cottage wasn't large. Once they all got down to it wouldn't take long.

Granpa stayed behind that day. Someone had to be at Trancie House to greet any visitors who might come there to offer condolences to the Grants on the loss of their daughter.

'I feel bad about leaving you alone, Granpa.' Charlotte joined him in the parlour before she left for the Milton.

'Ach, lassie, I'll be fine. I know you have to go, and I know Margaret has to go as well. It's one of those things you must do. And I will stay here and then I'll come up in the evening for, for...' he swallowed, 'the kisting.' He put his hand over his eyes.

'Oh Granpa, I'm so, so sorry.'

'Aye, I'm sorry too – but it has happened and we must live with the fact that she is gone from us. Now my dear, get on your way. I hear the gig at the door.' Charlotte kissed him gently and went away.

'Ready?' Granny was on the box, reins in hand. Katie and Hilda the new, very young maid were loading the baking in at the back.

223

'Yes, I was just saying good bye to Granpa. Is he all right, do you think?'

'He's as right as he can be for the moment. It's a bad time for us all. What we really want to do is go and hide and grieve by ourselves. But we can't do that just yet. There is so much to do and so many people will be wanting to see us over the next few days that there is no time to give real space to our innermost feelings. That can come later. I'm sorry too to leave him today but we must help Lizzie. Andrew will be all right at home with Katie to help him when people come to visit, as they surely will. Jock has arranged to borrow another gig and will take him up later on.'

The day passed in a flurry of cleaning, washing and tidying inside and raking sweeping and mowing outside. Charlotte's father, silent and sad, kept away from the busy group, occupied with his own thoughts. Charlotte took some soup to him at lunchtime.

'Dad, it's lunchtime. Have some soup.'

'I'm not hungry.'

'Come on Dad, you must eat. Look, I made it myself.' She poured out a bowl for him. Reluctantly he sat down and took the bowl and a spoon from her. She observed another figure walking over.

'I'll keep him company.' Charlotte looked up. A young man was approaching from the direction of the barn. She had not met him before. He spoke again.

'I'm Gavin Leith,' he offered. 'I've been here for a wee while noo. I'll bide with yer faither for company.'

'Would you like some soup? I brought some extra in case it was needed.'

'Thanks.' Gavin Leith sat down beside Dad and accepted a bowl from Charlotte.

'Now, John, foo are ye deein the day?'

Charlotte slipped away seeing her father was in what seemed to be capable hands.

Later on, at around half past four, Tam Forbes the joiner arrived with Mary's coffin in the back of his cart.

The family were all gathered. Kisting of a body was an important rite performed by a privileged few close friends and family members. Granpa arrived in the late afternoon with Jock. To Charlotte's pleasure she saw that Katie, her grandparents' old and valued housekeeper and friend was with them, squeezed into the back of the gig. The rest of the family from the Milton were there: John the father, changed and into a white shirt and hard collar for the occasion, leading his children, Charlotte, Lizzie, Willie, Jean, John, and Wee Alicky. They stood around him in a supportive group. Granny and Granpa held hands to help each other, sustained behind by Jock and Katie. The Glenbuchat minister, the Reverend Donald Forbes was there, as a family friend, but also in his professional capacity as he was to say a prayer at the kisting. At the last minute Leslie MacFarquhar the young doctor and the two howdies, Annie and Mirren who had been so close to Mary came to complete the group.

Tam the joiner brought in the coffin he had just finished making and stood back respectfully as, with tender hands, John and his sons lifted Mary into it. The women folk arranged her hair again, settled her hands, placed a cover over her. Charlotte placed some flowers from the garden by her side. The minister said a prayer and the private family ceremonial was over.

Compared to the peaceful, special privacy of the kistin, the next few days were public, with folk coming and going, from far and near to pay their respects. Charlotte spent her days up at the Milton, baking and cooking, greeting and talking to visitors and escorting them into the best room for the ritual viewing of the coffined body of her mother. She, Lizzie and Jean served the visitors with endless cups of tea and innumerable scones, pancakes and other delicacies.

This was the social side of having a death in the family. Other people had to be catered for. These old customs of paying respects on the one hand and offering hospitality on the other had to be maintained. There was no time to think in depth about what they were doing or why. They just got on with it, ably supported by supplies of food from Trancie House and other neighbours who came in with their offerings. For those few days in the run-up to the funeral Charlotte only returned to Trancie House in the late evening to sit with Granny and Granpa for a while before going to bed.

The family group also received other help. John's grieve discussed his bereavement with the owner of the Milton of Glenbuchat. They agreed that John should have compassionate leave for two weeks. This he was reluctant to accept. After all, he argued, he was out in the fields every day anyway. Why stop him from doing this?

'We dinna want to stop you, John. We just want to make life a wee bit easier for you for a wik or twa.'

'But man A'm oot by onywey. A jist wint ti be left alane.'

'Ay, ay, aa richt. Bit tak it easy onywey.'

So at least John was supported in his outside work by his superiors and of course his boys were around for the time being and they were not ones to stay inside. But they did come back and forth with firewood, kindling, peat and any heavy burdens they took on to spare the women.

Another person who helped noticeably was the young man whom Charlotte had not met before, Gavin Leith. He had come via a farm on Deeside a few months back and quickly settled into the ways of the Milton. He was a good worker, lived in the bothy and often ate in the farm kitchen. When a death occurred on a farm, although the essential work of the farm like feeding animals and milking had to carry on, for the few days between the death and the funeral other work slowed up a bit as if in respect for the bereaved family. Thus Gavin Leith had time on his hands which he put to good use. He always seemed to be around, fetching and carrying, offering to run errands.

By the day before the funeral, all was ready. All their clothes were laid out and cleaned, brushed and pressed. Donald Forbes the minister had been along a few times as well as for the kisting, to make arrangements for the funeral and the burial in Glenbuchat Kirkyard. In the late afternoon Charlotte went outside. It had been a busy day of visitors and she was standing leaning on the big five-barred gate looking out over the hills, enjoying for a moment a little respite from the cares and worries. She saw Gavin Leith coming from the peat-stack with a basket of peats on his back for the kitchen range which had to be kept going in all weathers. He came up to the gate, dropped his basket and stood beside her.

'Grand weather.'

'Yes,' agreed Charlotte, privately wishing he would go away and leave her in peace.

'I meant to say this earlier, Miss Gordon, but didn't get the chance – I'm very sorry about your mother. She was a very nice lady. Always very good to me.'

'Thank you Gavin. I'm glad to hear that. It helps a bit to hear good things said.' She paused, 'Don't worry about calling me Miss Gordon. I'm Charlotte to everyone around here.'

'That's fine then, Charlotte. It's a bonny view. Do you miss it when you are away?'

'I suppose I do, in a way. But it's lovely where I am – in Shetland. But here is where I was born.'

'Would you come back?'

'I'm not sure.' She hesitated. 'A lot depends on what happens now.'

'You mean now your mother's gone?'

'Yes. We can't really talk of arrangements until after the funeral. And which reminds me, I'd better get back and help Lizzie. Thanks for all your help Gavin.'

'My pleasure,' he said, heaving the peats back on to his back and heading for the house.

On the day, Charlotte and her grandparents arrived early. Just before twelve Tam the joiner came to do the final screwing down of the coffin-lid before the funeral.

Charlotte

Then it was over. It was very strange how such a huge thing in our lives like burying our mother should be over in such a short time. The minister, the Reverend Donald Forbes came to the house first where we had a funeral service in the ben room where Mam lay. Then Dad and the boys and the farmer and the grieve shouldered the coffin up and carried her out of the house and away to the Kirkyard for the committal. I really wanted to go too – but women did not do this. It was the same at Margery's funeral in Shetland. Women did not get the chance to be a part of such an important final ceremony. One day I hoped things will change as they are slowly changing for women at work.

However, as it was, we women stayed behind to prepare for the men coming back for the wake. Once the whisky was flowing everyone cheered up and when the men had been served with what they needed, we left them with the bottles and drifted away, wandering through to the kitchen, outside into the fine evening chatting in small groups until gradually the wake began to disperse.

I was reminded of the other wake of which I had been a part, Margery's. I could hear Magnus's hurt indignant voice saying, 'How can they be laughing? My mother's dead and they're having a party. Will my father be laughing too?' I felt I understood exactly now what he had been feeling on that evening. It seemed very hard to be having a party when my mother was lying up in the Kirkyard, and yet it was our way of coping with the moment.

There had to be a family meeting of course. Dad asked us all to make a point of being together at the Milton two days after the funeral before Jean, John and Wee Alicky returned to their jobs. Lizzie and Willie stayed at home anyway. We all sat around the kitchen table at the Milton, Dad and the six of us.

'Richt aabiddy, we need ti work oot fit we're gaan ti dee noo.'

'Fit div ye mean Dad?' Wee Alicky had no idea about running a house or being a farm wife with eggs, hens, cows and butter-making as well as housework, washing, ironing, cooking, baking and all the rest of it.

'Weel, there's aa the things a wife needs ti dee. And there's nae wife noo. Noo, Charlotte,' he turned to me. 'Ye're the aalest. Ye've been awa fae hame lang eneuch. Since ye were a wee quinie really. Fit aboot it? Fit aboot comin hame and keepin hoose ti me.'

I held my breath for a moment to make myself take this suggestion slowly. I didn't know what to say. After all that had happened to me as a child, being sent away so young, the anger and resentment I had felt at the time, not forgetting the complete change and acceptance of new customs and habits – even to the extent of replacing my Scots language which I had spoken as a little child with the more acceptable English. Then came the dawning of the knowledge of what I could do and the encouragement to pick up this knowledge and use it; my work and training to be a teacher; my parents' gladness for me when I succeeded. Was all this to go because my father needed a housekeeper? It was not that I did not love my father and my brothers and sisters. But why me because I was the oldest child? And, because I had been away from home for a long time. Whose fault was that at the beginning? And yet, wasn't it my duty to do my best for my family. I took a deep breath.

'I don't know. I'm not sure. You see, I have a teaching contract.'

'Ach, you can easily get oot o that.' Dad patted my hand. 'Nae bother. I ken someone doon the road who wanted ti get oot o her job and she jist telt them she wisna comin back and nae argy bargy.'

'And what did her employers say to that?'

'They were furious, bit there wis nocht they could dee aboot it.'

'Well, I can't do that. I would have to work out an agreed notice. And anyway, I can't just make up my mind like this. I have other things to take into consideration.'

'Like fit?' My father kept the pressure up. 'Come on Lassickie, ye ken A need ye here.'

That was almost my undoing – he probably knew that to use the old name which he kept only for me would get under my skin. I unconsciously bit my lip until the pain of it made me realise what I was doing.

'I'm not going to decide anything today. Now, I hear Jock with the gig. He said he would come up for me. I'll see you tomorrow.'

I squeezed Dad's hand as I passed him, to show daughterly affection, that I was not wilfully leaving him, that I cared about what happened. But I had a lot to think about.

Jock was silent too as we made our way down the glen. He probably felt my mood. Certainly, after handing over the traditional granny's sooker we sat in companionable silence as I contemplated what I was to do.

Chapter 32

In the busy days after the funeral Charlotte continued to go up and down to the Milton to help Lizzie. Jean, John and Wee Alicky went back to their own jobs. Willie and Charlotte's father tried to get back to normal on the farm. Even though John Gordon was supposed to be having something like compassionate leave, he kept going and Willie stuck to his duties too.

Charlotte still did not know what to do about her father's request that she should stay at the Milton and be his housekeeper. She and Lizzie talked about it as they tidied out Mam's closet.

'Fit are ye gaan ti dee?' Lizzie folded clothes and thrust them into the bag which Charlotte held out.

'I don't know.' Charlotte looked at her. 'I really feel Dad doesn't have the right to expect me, or any of us for that matter, to be his housekeeper. What do you think?'

'Well I dinna wint tae dee it. A've been at aa'biddy's beck an call since A wis fifteen. A steyed on ti help Mam, she wis that thrang. Bit Charlotte, A'm really wintin tie gang in fur nursin at Aiberdeen, like Auntie Jessie. She's deen afa weel an she's awa up in the nursin warld noo.' Jessie was one of Mam's older sisters.

Lizzie went on. 'A wis spikkin wi Auntie Jessie the ither day. She wis tellin me fit ti dae ti get in. A'd really lik ti hae a go at it.'

'Have you told Dad?'

'Na, na. He'd throw a fit. If ee dinna agree ti be his hoosekeeper, he'll be efter me. Fit wy shid it ay be the wimmen that disna get tae dee fit they wint?'

Charlotte agreed. Later she went outside and breathed the fresh air. Lizzie's predicament did not help her undecided feelings. Why did it have to be like this? Her father could surely manage to employ someone to do the 'woman's work' around the farm. He had been at the Milton all his working life, was now at the level of horseman, an important person on a farm, with pay which, while not overly generous, was still reasonable by the day's standards. He had never had to pay for female employment before and Charlotte knew well that her mother had for many years scraped by on very little. Latterly though, things had been easier. Fewer mouths to feed as the family left home, housekeeping only for Mam and pocket money for Lizzie: surely he must have some money saved away.

Again her thoughts were interrupted by the presence of Gavin Leith.

'Charlotte,' he walked over to her. ' Foo are ye the day?'

'I'm well, thank you. And you?'

'Oh, A'm fine. Workin awa. Your faither's keepin goin'.'

'Yes, I think it's his way of coping with things. Anyway the work has to be done.'

'Charlotte, A wis winrin,' Gavin hesitated. Charlotte looked at him. What was the matter with him she thought.

'Yes?'

'Fit are ye aa gaan ti dee noo?'

'What do you mean?'

'Weel, ye ken, noo at yir mither's awa. Fa's gaan ti dee the wimmen's wark?'

'Well, I don't really know. We have not decided this yet. It's a family decision.'

'Ay, ay, A ken, bit A winnert if A could help in ony wey?'

'Oh? What did you have in mind?'

'Weel,' Gavin put out his hand and lightly touched her arm. ' A winnert if ee wid mairry me. It wid be afa fine – an afa honour, ye ken.' Charlotte stepped back.

'But Gavin, I don't know you.'

'A ken at, bit at disna maitter. We'll get to ken each ither. Div ye nae see, it's jist richt. We could get mairrit an move in here and your faither wid hae his hoosekeeper and A wid hae a wife and ee wid hae a man. An shairly ee're wintin at. Efter aa in anither year or twa ye'll be on the skelve. We canna hae at noo, can we?'

He stepped towards her again. 'An ee're afa bonny. Much bonnier lookin an Lizzie. Ach, she's aa richt, bit she canny haud a canle ti ee.'

Charlotte, speechless, stepped back again to avoid the outstretched arm which threatened to come around her shoulders.

'Mr Leith, I do not want to marry you, not even to help my father out, nor to avoid the shelf as you so delicately put it. Now please let me pass.' She picked up her skirts and hurried round to the kitchen door. She marched in and slammed the door shut.

Lizzie was there at the range stirring the soup-pot.

'Fit's the maitter. Ye've fairly got yir birss up.'

'That man.'

'Fit man?'

'Och, you know, Gavin Leith.' Lizzie stopped stirring, spoon held still, above the pan.

'Fit's he been sayin?'

'He's just asked me to marry him. Says it'll suit everybody. We're to move in here, if you please, and apart from all the other benefits, I'll have a husband – so it will spare me a lifetime on the shelf. Lizzie, why are you laughing?'

Lizzie was indeed shaking with laughter. Charlotte, exasperated at getting nothing out of her to begin with, went up to her and gave her a shake.

'Lizzie, leave the soup and tell me what's so funny.'

'A canna help it.' Lizzie put the soup to the back of the range and composed her face. 'The bauld Gavin asked me the very same question just two days ago? A wee bittie ower croose, A'm thinkin.'

'What? I don't believe it. He couldn't be that presumptuous to ask us both.'

230

'Oh ay he cud, an he did.' Lizzie was contemptuous. 'If ye're askin me, Gavin Leith is only interested in Gavin Leith an his easedom an naebiddy else. A think he's efter Dad's savins at he's bin pittin awa. An o coorse, it wid be a gweed wey ti get oot o the bothy. Nae fun bein in a bothy if ye can get a fine warm bed in a hoose and wi a wife forby.'

The cheek of the man. Charlotte found it difficult to believe that this was her third proposal of marriage in a year, and the second in which the man did not seem to think that love was necessary.

'Right, Lizzie.' She sat down at the table. 'We need to think about this. We're agreed that Dad needs a housekeeper.'

'Aye.'

'Dad has asked me to do it but I haven't decided yet. You want to go and do nursing and if that's what you feel, you should go and do it. In the meantime, Gavin Leith has proposed marriage to us both and been rejected by both of us. We think he wants to get himself into the house and ingratiate himself with Dad with the long term view of getting his hands on some of Dad's savings. Either way the one of us who marries him would have to be the housekeeper as well as Gavin's wife.'

'But we've baith said no ti him.'

'Yes, but he's very friendly with Dad. Just wait, the pressure will be on that way.'

When work stopped for the day John appeared around the corner of the house with Willie and coming behind, with an air of a man who knows what he wants, walked Gavin Leith.

'Ay quines, fir hiv ee bin up tae the day?' John appeared to be much more at ease with life in general.

'Just the usual, Dad.' Charlotte set the places at the table.

'Gavin'sbidin fur his denner.'

'That's fine.' Charlotte set another place. Lizzie brought the stew and doughballs and tatties over and started to serve up. Silence fell as the men attacked their food. It was a long day out in the fields although they did stop for fly-cups and a longer mid-day break. But in the summer the days tended to be longer especially if the weather was fine. Anything to get the work done and make up for the short dark days of winter. Sometimes they were out in the moonlight if there were outstanding tasks to be completed. No wonder they were hungry.

'Ah.' John pushed his chair back. 'That's better. Fa ivver made that maks it jist lik Mam eesed ti dee.' Lizzie made a mock bow.

'Noo,' said John, 'Gavin here his been giein me the benefit o his advice.'

'Fit aboot, Dad?'

'Weel, A've askit Charlotte here ti be ma hoosekeeper an yir thinkin aboot it, Charlotte, are ye nae?'

'You have asked me,' Charlotte responded, 'but I haven't given you my decision yet.'

231

'Ay, ay, bit Gavin here his come up wi somethin. He'll mairry ye, an ye'll hae a man an aa. We winted ye tae come up in the wardle. Noo ye've deen it. Ye've proved ye can dae it. Noo ye can come back hame an settle doon as Gavin's wife and oor hoosekeeper. Fit cud be better?'

'Well for a start,' Charlotte said, 'you could ask how I feel about it.'

'Ach lassie, feelins dinna come intil this. It's sense, ats aa.'

'An onywey,' Lizzie cut in, 'Gavin's nae carin fa he gets, he askit me an aa ti mairry him. A wid watch him, Dad. He's takkin a len o ye.'

'Fit's is?' Dad turned to Gavin. 'Ee askit Lizzie an aa?'

'Ay, weel,' Gavin defended, 'as ye said yersel, it maks sense, fur een o them ti get mairret an hoosekeep.'

'Jist a meenit,' Lizzie was on her feet. 'A can dee the hoosekeepin as weel as onybiddy bit A'm nae gaan ti be parcelled up an handed ower ti Gavin Leith or onybiddy else like a coo at the mart. Onywey Dad, A hiv helpit Mam since A left the squeel. Ye hinna askit me yet ti be the hoosekeeper bit A ken ye will if Charlotte disna dee it. A'm tellin ye noo, A'm nae gaan ti dee it. A'm gaan awa inti Aiberdeen ti be a nurse.'

She sat down, glowering.

'My, my, anither een wintin ti gang up in the wardle. An fa's gaan ti pey fur this expedition? Nae me, A'm tellin ye.'

'It's aa richt, Dad, Auntie Jessie telt me aboot the nursin an said if A winted ti dee it she wid gie me a haund.'

'Jessie, A micht a kent it.' Dad slapped his hand on his thigh. 'Ay tryin ti interfere.'

'She's not interfering,' Charlotte said. 'She's just got Lizzie's interests at heart. And I would like to say this: you keep going on about 'going up in the world'. But please remember, when you and Mam agreed to send me to Granny and Granpa when I was six, I had no choice in the matter. But what happened then and since, changed me. It was bound to. Right from the start, I had to learn to be different because of the living with Granny and Granpa, the language, teaching, college and so on. I enjoy doing what I do. But even so, I look back and think about what I have left. It's like having a foot in both worlds, almost like – like dividing yourself in two.' She stopped, suddenly unable to carry on.

Dad softened and held out his hand to her. 'Ach, Lassickie. Fit did we dee ti ye?'

'Nothing bad, Dad.' Charlotte said. 'But you need to accept that what happened made a difference.'

'And div ye nae think ee cud come an be ma hoosekeeper.'

'I haven't decided that yet.'

'An ye micht re-consider aboot being ma wife.' Gavin leant over towards her. 'The offer is still open. We cud be afa fine in here thegither.'

Charlotte looked at him. Was there no end to this man's arrogance?

'I think I'd better get myself away down the road,' she said without giving him an answer. 'Granny and Granpa will be waiting for me and Jock will be waiting to stable the horse. He won't let anyone else do it.'

Trancie House lay quiet in the evening light. Charlotte guided the gig round to the stable where Jock sat polishing away at the leather harnesses.

'Ay, ay, quine.'

'Hello Jock. Thanks for waiting. I'm sorry to be so late.'

'Na, na, ye're nae late. A'm here onywey.' He took the reins from her, unharnessed the horse and led him into the stable.

'Thanks Jock. See you tomorrow.'

'Ay well, gweed nicht.' He started to rub the horse down.

Charlotte walked over to the house.

'I'm home,' she called.

'Oh there you are.' Granny stood in the kitchen. 'Tea?'

'Yes please.' Charlotte went over and hugged her grandmother.

'How are things then?'

'Mmm, well, I really need to talk to you and Granpa about this.'

'Come on through, and you won't need to tell it all twice.'

In the parlour, the fire was lit, despite the mild evening.

'Oh I do like a fire.' Charlotte went over and gave Granpa a hug as well.

'Isn't it funny. We don't really need it just now but, I suppose it's more psychological than anything else.' Granpa sat in his usual chair next to the fire. 'Sit yourself down and tell us how the Milton is today.'

'It's bonny,' said Charlotte accepting a cup of tea from Granny. 'The Milton's bonny, and bright, and argumentative and, hard.'

'Charlotte,' Granny put her hand out, 'what's going on? What do you mean?'

'Well,' Charlotte took her time, sipping her tea. 'This has been going on for a day or two.'

'What has?' Granpa asked.

'To be quite blunt, now that Mam is gone, Dad is left without a housekeeper. Dad has asked me to be his housekeeper. My desires and needs don't come into it. To cap it all, Gavin Leith – I don't know if you know him – do you?'

'Aye,' said Granpa. 'Is he the one who started at the Milton say, less than a year ago.'

'Yes.'

'Oh aye, a brash young man.'

Charlotte laughed. 'Well you'll be pleased to hear that the "brash young man" has asked me to marry him. That would suit everybody. Dad would have a housekeeper, Gavin would have a wife and I'd have a husband and I won't be left on the shelf.'

'Is that what he said?' Granny was incredulous.

233

'Yes, and not only that, he asked Lizzie to marry him two days before he asked me. Lizzie has warned Dad he's trying to take advantage of him. Needless to say we have both said no.'

'I should think so too. And your Dad is conniving with all this?' asked Granpa.

'Well, he seems to be.'

'So what have you decided – about being housekeeper.'

'Well, Lizzie has made herself very clear. She has helped Mam since she left school. She had a word with Auntie Jessie at Mam's funeral and she says she wants to go and try and do her nursing training in Aberdeen. Auntie Jessie says she will help her.'

'That's grand.' Granpa sounded very pleased at this news. 'But,' he added, 'what about you? What have you decided.'

'I haven't given a final answer yet,' admitted Charlotte. 'Dad has made out that I should go back and housekeep, that I've been away from home long enough and I've proved I can make my way up the world. Now I should go back. But it's not as easy as that. He just doesn't seem to understand. He seems to think I can just drop everything and do it. And I love the Milton and Donside. It's my real original birthing place and I feel guilty at even thinking about not agreeing to be Dad's housekeeper. But, my life has changed. It began to change when I was a little girl of six when they agreed to send me to you, and it has moved on from there. And, even if I wanted to do it, there is a little matter of contracts and working notice to the School Board. And, besides,' she stopped –

'Besides?' prompted Granny.

'Well, as well as my work,' said Charlotte, 'there are all the other things now in my life. We haven't really had time this summer to talk properly as things have been so upset, but I need to tell you about what has happened with James and the Sinclairs.'

They sat there for a long time as Charlotte poured out the story of the happenings of the past year. Granny's face lightened as she heard of James's proposal made and accepted with such love and then fell as she heard of the proposal from Alexander and Christina's part in the story. And then the subsequent falling out between Charlotte and James.

'Oh my dear, I'm so sorry. I wish we could have helped you.'

'I know, but it's good to be able to tell you both now. You can see I have some thinking to do.'

'Yes, but the first thing is, do you want to be your father's housekeeper.'

'No,' admitted Charlotte. 'Although I do feel guilty about it.'

'Right,' said Granny, 'listen to me. Your Dad, I know he feels very sad just now because Mary's gone – believe me,' she sighed, 'we all do. But your father is not old, he'll get over this and I'm pretty sure he'll be married again before the year is out.'

'Do you think so?'

'I don't think so; I know so. I've seen it happen so many times. Widowers are fair game. Just you wait.'

Charlotte's worried brow cleared a little. 'What do you think Granpa?'

'I agree with Margaret, my dear. We've both been around too long not to be very aware of human nature. I would think there is a queue forming right now to see who can get there first as soon as he looks like being ready.'

'If you don't want to do this, Charlotte, you don't need to, and neither does Lizzie. I think she's quite right to do her training. I'll tell you what. I'll come up in a day or two and put him right about a thing or two. It's about time I went up and said hello to Lizzie and Willie. How is Willie anyway? What about him being the housekeeper?' She laughed. 'That would never do. Or your father could get Gavin Leith to do the job. That would take him down a peg.'

So, it was a happier Charlotte who went to bed that night. True, she had not sorted all of her problems but this new one looked as though resolution was in sight.

Breakfast brought bad news. For once the occupants of Trancie House were late and were still sitting at the table finishing their toast as the postie came walking up the drive. Charlotte went to the door to meet him.

'Good Morning. Fine day again.' Jimmy the postie handed over the letters. 'A few the day.'

'Thanks Jimmy.' Charlotte took the bundle and went back to the dining room.

'Oh,' she noticed as she was handing them to Granny. 'There's one for me, from Shetland.' She recognised the writing. 'It's Alexander.' She ripped the letter open with suddenly anxious hands. The letter was brief.

> Harbour House,
> Jarlshavn,
> Shetland.
> 26 July, 1896

Dear Charlotte,

I am writing to let you know that Christina is very ill with whooping cough. She has been asking very much for you. Please come as soon as you are able. I fear she may die as she is very weak.
In haste.
Yours affly.,
Alexander Sinclair.

'Oh Granny, Granpa.' Charlotte's voice shook. She handed over the letter. 'I'll have to go. Christina needs me. I'd better go and pack.'

'Now Charlotte,' Granpa's calm voice slowed her. 'Let's think this through. Yes, I know you must go, but wait a minute. When is the boat?'

'Oh, dear, there's not one today. It's tomorrow.'

'Well, you could go on that one. That gives you a day to organise yourself.'

'I won't be able to book. But I know some people just turn up at the boat. If I can't get a berth, I can go steerage.'

'You'll be very tired.'

'I know but there's nothing I can do about it. I must go on the first boat there is. Oh, poor little Christina. I wonder how she is.'

'Look,' said Granpa, 'I know whooping cough is bad, but Christina is well fed and very healthy. She'll probably come out of it all right. She's a strong wee thing, by all accounts. Now, in the meantime, because you can't go today, you can go up to the Milton and say your good byes and explain why you are going. Then come back and get your things organised.'

'And don't worry about your father,' said Granny. 'I'll go up tomorrow and talk to him.'

Charlotte arrived at the Milton just about mid-day. She clattered into the courtyard with the gig and gave the horse his nosebag before going in the kitchen door. Her father was in for his customary soup and bread. He was by himself; Willie and Gavin were away to the market.

'I winnert far ee'd got til.' Lizzie was doling out the soup at the range. She looked up. 'Charlotte, fit's the maitter? Ye're afa sair-made lookin.'

'I have to go,' Charlotte burst the words out without any preliminaries.

'Fit?' Lizzie looked at her. 'Fit's gaan on?'

'I have to go. I've had a letter from Shetland, this morning, from Alexander Sinclair. Christina's very ill, with the whooping cough. She needs me. So I'm going up on the boat tomorrow.'

'Fa's Christina?' her father asked.

'She's Alexander's wee girl. She's four. I told you about her, Dad – her Mother died last year. Now she's very ill and asking for me. I need to go to her.'

'Oh aye, I min noo.' He spooned his soup. 'Bit fit's she ti ee? Fit wey div *ee* hiv ti gang.'

'But she needs me. She might die. I must help her.'

'But we need ye here. And we're yir blood relatives. Neen o these ither fowk. Let them get on wi their ain lives. Ee bide here.'

'Dad, I can't do that. I must go.'

'Aye Dad,' Lizzie nodded. 'A think Charlotte shid gang. If the wee quinie is that bad, an greetin fur her, you hiv ti gang.'

'Bit A'm needin ye fur a hoosekeeper here.'

236

'Weel, ye'll jist hae ti need, an be deen wi't.' Lizzie's voice was sharp. 'I nivver heard the like o sic selfishness.'

'Why, ye cheeky bissim.' He turned to Charlotte. 'Weel Charlotte, A'm afa disappinted in ye gaan awa tae help ither fowk fan A'm needin ye here. Fooivver, A canna dee onythin aboot it. A'll jist be aa alane here an growe aal a masel. Na, na, A winna hae nae mair soup. It's gaan wersh on me.' He walked out without saying any more. He did not meet Charlotte's eyes. She stepped after him, 'Father … '

'Leave him,' said Lizzie. 'He's been spilt. Aa his mairrit life he did this tae Mam an she gied in time efter time. Noo, Charlotte. Ee gang noo. Dinna worry aboot us.'

'Granny's coming up tomorrow.'

'That'll be fine. Maybe she can talk some sense into him.' And, Lizzie took a letter out of her pocket. 'I wrote Auntie Jessie last night. Will ye pit it in the post fur me.'

'Of course,' Charlotte's eyes lit up. 'You're really going to do it?'

'Of course. A've been waitin fur this fur a lang time. Noo, min an write ti me an tell me foo the quinie is. Awa ye gang.' The sisters hugged.

'Thanks Lizzie,' Charlottes eyes were moist.

'Aye aye,' Lizzie said, 'we mak a fair team. Noo, get on. Yer horse is waitin.'

There was one last obstacle before she got away. She was just turning the Trancie House horse and gig out of the Milton courtyard when the cart drew up with Willie and Gavin up top.

'Far are ee aff til?' Willie was fond of his big sister and liked to hear about her doings. Charlotte explained what was going on.

'Ach, peer wee quinie,' he was beginning when Gavin cut in, 'Fit div ee mean ye're awa tae Shetland. Ye're gaan tae be here are ye nae? Ye canna jist gang awa lik at. And if ye're gaan ti be Mrs Gavin Leith ye need ti ask my permeesion afore ye gang gallivantin aff ti the ends o the earth.'

'But,' Charlotte responded, 'I am not going to be Mrs Gavin Leith. I told you that Gavin. It's you who can't take no for an answer.'

'Bit,' Gavin stamped his foot on the step of the cart with such a dunt that the mare whinnied in front. 'This is nae gweed eneuch. A'm needin a wife an yer faither's needin a hoosekeeper.'

'Well it won't be me. Now Willie,' Charlotte got down from the gig and turned her attention to her brother who by this time had run around to the mare's head and was whispering soothing words into her ear. 'Is she all right.'

'Ay, ay, she'll be fine. She jist got a fricht when that stupid gomeril carried on lik aat. Noo Charlotte, ee tak tent, min. A'm aye here fur ye. Nivver min fit Dad says – we'll manage fine.' He towered above her as he put his arm round her. 'See ye're ma wee sister noo.' She reached up and kissed his cheek.

'I'll be in touch.' Her eyes filled. 'Sorry, I can't help it, it's so difficult.'

'Gavin,' Willie, called, 'tak the mare roon please.' He walked Charlotte back to where her gig awaited, the horse patiently pulling up soorocks by the roadside. 'Noo, Charlotte, Dad's pit an afa lot o birse on ye lately. A jist wint ye ti ken A think he's nae bin fair ti ye. Let it aa wash ower yir heid. Get on an dee fit ye need ti dee. We'll

237

be fine, an as fur at feel –' he indicated the departing back of Gavin Leith '– if he disna sort himsel oot, he'll nae be here after the next feein. He's afa sweir ti wark unless he thinks onybiddy's watchin. Ye widna wint ti mairry him.'

'Thanks Willie,' Charlotte sat up in her seat. 'I needed that. Take care.' She raised her hand in farewell as she clicked to the horse and made her way down the road to Towie, away from Glenbuchat. It felt very final.

There was nobody to meet Charlotte two days later as the St Clair moved slowly into her berth in Lerwick harbour. There were the usual groups of summer holiday makers making for their guesthouses, a few business men suited and bowler-hatted, nobody whom she knew. She went down the gangway and picked up her baggage from the pile just unloaded on to the quay.

The customary morning carriage for Jarlshavn awaited just beyond the harbour. The coachman did his best to fit in his morning six mile journey from Lerwick to Jarlshavn with the arrival of the St Clair on the days she was scheduled to dock. On days when she was very late or stormbound then the carriage could not wait for ever. Today however the boat was on time and the carriage was there.

'Hello, Miss Gordon.' The coachman was a Jarlshavn man and knew most of the folk. 'That you home again. Here, let me lift that up.'

'Thanks.' Charlotte accepted the offer gratefully.

'And, don't worry, I'll drop you off at your gate. We can't have you struggling up the road from the harbour with your bags.'

'Thank you very much.' She got into the carriage and sat back with her eyes closed. Poor lassie, the coachman thought, she seems tired.

Charlotte *was* tired. She had not been able to get a berth on the boat and had spent an uncomfortable night sitting up in women's steerage. Now all she wanted to do was get to bed. However she knew that that objective was a way off.

First she had to go to Harbour House and see Christina. As soon as she returned to Da Peerie Skulehoose and deposited her bags in the little hall, she came out again, locked her door and made her way to the harbour.

Magnus answered her knock. 'Charlotte! It's great to see you. When did you arrive? Oh we've needed you. Christina is so ill.'

'Magnus, can I come in?'

'Yes of course.' He remembered his manners and ushered her in. He felt suddenly bashful in her presence but covered by calling, 'Father, see who's here.' Alexander came out of the parlour. 'What a noise, boy, don't forget we have an invalid in the house – oh,' he stopped. 'Charlotte, how are you. Did you get my letter.'

'Yes,' she replied simply. 'That's why I'm here.'

'Christina,' he said, 'she's crying for you. Meg's at her wit's end. Will you come up.'

Charlotte could hear the persistent coughing as she went up to Christina's room. She heard Meg's voice saying, 'that's a good girl. Now have a rest,' as the coughing eased. She put her head round the door. Meg looked up and smiled. 'Christina,' she said, 'Look who's here.' The little arms, grown so very thin so quickly, came up out of their coverings and reached forward. Charlotte went over and held the little girl closely. Christina snuggled into her as she sat on the bed beside her.

'My little mama, she's here now,' was all she said before her eyes drooped and her head relaxed against Charlotte's arm.

Alexander looked on approvingly. 'She'll do now.'

From that day Christina began to improve. The whooping cough hung around for a while, as it does, but her will to fight it came back. She grew stronger as she began to eat and was able to eat more without coughing and vomiting. For the first few days after her return Charlotte stayed at Harbour House and she and Meg were able to spell each other in the sickroom. A week later the invalid was able to make her first wobbly steps downstairs. The great fear that history would repeat itself with another childhood death from whooping cough was gone from Harbour House.

Chapter 33

Charlotte heard her door knocker bang. She was, metaphorically at least, counting her pencils before the new school term began. As she went over lesson plans, and checked books, wrote out a new register, she thought about how to rearrange her classroom and way of practice, to put a new slant on all things academic for the primary ones to threes. She sighed and got up to answer the door. She really did need to get this done. What with one thing and another she was all behind with her preparations. She opened the door to Alexander who stood there, alone, hat in hand.

'Alexander, is everything all right. Christina…?'

'It's all right. She's fine. I've left her with Meg for a while. She really is better. And it's thanks to you. That's what I've come to say.'

'But come in. Come and sit down.' She led the way into the parlour. He looked round.

'Sorry about the mess. I'm getting ready for school. We begin again next week.' She laughed. 'But of course you know that. What do you want to do about Christina?'

'Well, in the first place we can never thank you enough for coming when you did. She might not have recovered otherwise. She didn't seem to have the will without you. So, we're forever in your debt.'

'Alexander, I'm sure I did very little. My Granpa said she's such a strong child that it was likely that she'd recover. But,' she added hastily, 'I don't want to belittle how ill she was. I'm sure she was indeed a very sick child.'

'Yes, and now she is better, thanks to you,' he insisted. 'I have discussed this with Dr Taylor and he agrees. So thank you.' Charlotte saw no use in arguing further.

'I'm glad she's better. Now,' to turn the subject, 'what do you think about school. She's not infectious now; the question is, is she able?'

'Well, we all think she should go. She has been so looking forward to it that she'd probably have a relapse if we said no. Are you happy to have her?'

'Yes, we'll just take it slowly and see how she goes.'

'Right that's settled then. Meg can take her up on Tuesday morning when you start. Now, there was another thing – I wanted to say how sorry I was about your mother. I didn't get a proper chance earlier.'

'Thank you Alexander. Yes, it was sad. She was very young.'

'Did you not want to stay at home and help your father?'

'He wanted me to,' Charlotte admitted, 'but it wouldn't have done. My place is here.'

'Well, I'm glad about that and delighted to see you back.' Alexander got to his feet. 'I'll be on my way. I hope all goes well on Tuesday. Christina can't wait.'

Alexander walked down towards the harbour with a light heart. His Christina was better, and his (or he looked upon her as his) Charlotte was speaking to him normally. Maybe if he took things carefully she would yet agree to marry him. But canny, canny, now, he warned himself. Don't frighten her away.

Charlotte returned to her preparations. That was good of him to come up, she thought. It was true, when she was looking after Christina, there was no chance for conversation. The traumatic events of her summer holidays: her mother's death, all the coming and going of the kisting, the funeral and, receiving and talking to folk had somehow gone into the background. You just coped with the crisis of the moment and moved on. She had moved on to where she was most needed in response to Alexander's letter. Now that crisis was acknowledged and over too.

Charlotte sat down. Her mother. When had she had time to think about her mother? Not since the day at Alford station when Grannie told her the news. After that she had been too busy, too busy to grieve for the woman who had given her life. I should have thought about her before, she thought. Poor mother, overworked in life and even in the busy-ness of her death we were so thrang that we didn't take time to take stock. She sat on the sofa in her parlour and let the tears slide down her cheeks.

Magnus was out for a walk. He was meeting Lowrie up the hill but first he walked round the harbour and then made his way up the road which led to the hill behind the village. He breathed deeply as he climbed. A voice called, 'Halloo.' He looked up and saw Lowrie waiting further up.

'Come on slow coach. You're out of training.'

'I know. I meant to do so much in the holidays, but somehow I didn't.'

'How's Christina?'

'Much better, thanks. Thanks to Charlotte. Everyone's saying that day was the turnaround. That day she arrived.'

'How's your father?' Lowrie knew about the row between father and son.

'Well, we're talking. But not a lot. I think when Christina was so ill he found he had to talk to me – but it's not the same.'

'Well,' Lowrie said. 'You'll be back to school soon. I'm quite looking forward to it. Come on, race you to the top of the hill.'

They ran, together at first then Lowrie pulling away as the gradient steepened. They collapsed at the top, panting.

'I need this,' Magnus admitted. 'Fresh air and exercise. The house is so stuffy when there's illness about.'

'You'll soon get going again.'

Magnus sat silent and breathed deeply.

'How are your bruises?' Lowrie asked. 'I've hardly seen you since the famous fight.'

'They've gone now. My ribs still twinge a bit but I think I'm fine.'

'What did you go off the deep end like that for anyway?'

'Well,' said Magnus. He picked at the grass beside him. He hesitated and then burst out, 'I'm not so bothered about that Alfred Twatt mocking my father. He can look after himself. But I couldn't stand the way he attacked Charlotte. I just saw red. And I really can't stand the idea of my father and her being married. I'm glad she isn't going to marry Father. I couldn't bear it if she were my mother.'

'It sounds as though you have a notion of her yourself.' Lowrie was nearer the mark than he knew. Magnus could feel his face going red.

'No, what a thing to say. That's rubbish.'

'Come on, you've gone all red.'

'No I haven't.'

'Yes you have. Magnus, do you really like her?'

'Of course, I like her. Don't you like her.'

'Yes, but you know what I mean. In that way.'

'In what way?'

'Come on Magnus, you look as if you are in love with Charlotte.'

'What a stupid suggestion.' Magnus got up and walked off with what he thought was dignity.

'Wait, wait.' Lowrie ran after him. 'Sorry Magnus, I didn't mean to tease you.'

'Well, just don't that's all. I am not in love with Charlotte.' Lowrie gave him a long look.

'All right,' he said. 'You are not in love with Charlotte.'

'Anyway,' Magnus said, 'even if I were, and I'm not, remember, but even *if*, then there's not such an age difference – she's only twenty-two not quite, and I'm almost fifteen. It's only seven years. It's not that much.'

'No,' Lowrie said, 'and that age gap in a way gets less and less as the years go on. What you need,' he advised, with all the wisdom of one who had already reached his fifteenth birthday a few months before, 'is to get back to school and concentrate your mind. Whatever happens in the future, you have to get on, get your exams and get a career. Try and think forwards. Come on now, race you down the hill.'

James MacLeod threw down his pen in frustration. It really is too bad, he thought restlessly, to expect ministers to churn out so many thousands of words of sermons every week, or think up enough to fill whatever time was available without repeating yourself all the time. I wish my barrel of past sermons were fuller so that I could dig into it for inspiration – at the moment all I'm getting is perspiration.

He got to his feet and picked up his jacket.

'Mrs Laurenson,' he called, 'I'm going out. I think I need a breath of fresh air.'
She came to the door drying her hands on a towel.

'Right you are, Minister. See you later.'

He marched out of his gate and along the road. Unthinkingly his feet walked in the direction of Da Peerie Skulehoose. Well, it can't do any harm, he thought. Just see if she's in. After all I'm her minister and her mother has died. He stopped at her gate. Go on you fool, he chided himself, as he hesitated.

Charlotte heard the knocker go again. Who was it this time?

'Charlotte, hello, I thought I'd come and see how you are. I'm truly sorry to hear about your mother. That must have been such a shock for you. Charlotte, are you all right? Charlotte, you've been crying. What can I do to help you?' He stepped forward and held her arms.

'Come in,' she said. 'I'm sorry, I'm just feeling sorry for myself. I was thinking about my mother and realising that I had not taken time to think properly about her since she died. We've all been so busy.' The tears fell again.

'Come,' he said, 'come here.' He pulled out a large white handkerchief, beautifully laundered by Mrs Laurenson with *JM* embroidered in blue in the corner and handed it over. He guided her into her parlour.

'Mercy, you've been busy.' She blew her nose and looked up.

'Getting ready for school. It's come round very quickly.'

'I'm not surprised. You haven't had much of a holiday. How were things at Glenbuchat?'

'Not easy.'

'Do you want to tell me about it?'

'Yes, perhaps I could. Would you – like some tea.' She felt a little bit hesitant in the offering as she suddenly remembered that the last time he had visited she had ordered him from the house.

'Yes, please,' he answered promptly. 'And especially if you have one of Edie's scones.'

'I think we might manage that. She's not here just now; she's got some time off as she did so much to help when I came back first. If you wait here, I'll go and get some.' She went away. James wandered round the parlour looking at the things laid out in order for school.

'Now,' he said when the tea was poured. 'Tell me about your time away. Not what you had planned, I think.'

'Is anything ever what you have planned? This certainly wasn't. I was looking forward so much to my break and to seeing them all again. I got to Alford on the train and there was Granny on the platform. She never comes to the train. It's a sort of routine that we have developed. So I knew then that something had happened. I thought at first it was Granpa. But it was Mam.'

Out came the whole story. James's reaction changed from sympathy at the sadness of the occasion, to anger and frustration and the usual twinge of jealousy as he heard about the push to get Charlotte to be her father's housekeeper and Gavin Leith's wife.

'The arrogance of it.'

'Yes, I know, but it would have been handy for them.'

'Och, come on Charlotte, what about you?'

'Oh, my feelings don't matter.'

'They matter to me. Charlotte, I'm very sorry for my behaviour the last time I was here. I was very rude, and jealous and I behaved abominably.'

'I was a bit sharp myself.'

'All these months when we have not been together – I've missed you so much. It must have been very difficult to keep coming to the Kirk and listening to me when we had had words like that. And being polite to me in school. And now you've had to go through all this at Glenbuchat. I'm sorry.'

'James, it's all right. I'm sorry too.'

They both felt better having cleared the air and mended the differences between them. James asked further about the Gordon family and was very interested to hear about Lizzie's nursing plans.

'What will you're father do?'

'Well, Granny went up to speak to him the day after I left. He was very angry with us for not agreeing to do what he wanted. He was most unhappy that I came back to Shetland after I got Alexander's letter about Christina's illness. But, James what else could I have done?'

'Nothing,' he said. 'But I can see how your father might have been a bit upset.'

'A bit upset. He and Gavin Leith were not amused at all. But both Lizzie and Willie were really supportive. And Granny and Granpa, of course.'

'And she went up to sort him out.'

'Oh yes, she went up. She told me about it in a letter. She told him he was a selfish man who had been given in to all his life by Mam, and his daughters were perfectly entitled to decide what they wanted to do. And she also asked him how long did he think he would bide single. She thinks the band of hope will be queuing up as soon as he crooks his little finger. He's only in his forties.'

'So that should be him sorted?'

'Well, I hope so. I don't like 'not speaking' to him. I have written to him but so far no reply.'

'Give it time, he'll probably come round. And, for what it's worth, I think your Granny's right. A fine upstanding man like that won't be left alone for long. Now,' he said, 'I have a bit of news for you. Want to hear it?'

'Oh James,' she cried, 'I'm sorry, I've been going on and on about my own problems and never asked how you were getting on. Of course I want to hear your news. What's been happening?'

'Well,' he said. 'A long time ago, well at least a couple of months, June I think it was, I had a letter from St Fillans in Perthshire, saying that the Kirk there is vacant and that they were looking for a new minister and were considering calling me to the Kirk.'

'But how did they know about you?'

'Well, I come from not that far from there, and within the Presbytery, everyone knows everyone else and I was an assistant minister in Perth and someone mentioned my name and so it goes round.'

'So what happened then?'

'I wrote back and expressed an interest and asked for all the details of the parish. It really is a lovely place, Charlotte, and right on Loch Earn. And the folk seem so nice. It seems a very lively Kirk. They took up references immediately I showed that I was interested and the Vacancy Committee have had a meeting and they want me to preach as Sole Nominee in September. So,' he added, 'now you'll have to make a decision. A few months ago you agreed to be my wife. I know we've had our differences but now I'm asking you again, but this time, please will you come to St Fillans with me as my wife. If all goes to plan we would be going in, say, November.'

'But James, what about my teaching? My job here with the children? We've discussed this before and I thought you understood.'

'But don't you understand that this is a Call? It's very important and serious.'

'And is my job and vocation not important and serious?'

'Yes, but...'

'Yes, but. Yes but.... You men are all the same. You all think of your own needs and aspirations first. Anything a woman wants is well down the line. James, I thought better of you. You just said a wee while ago that my feelings mattered. And yet, here you go organising your life and apparently including me and you didn't take my feelings into consideration. You say you want me to go with you but this is two months on from when you knew first and you didn't even have the decency to write me a letter and tell me what was happening or what you were doing. You just took it for granted that one apology from you for your silly behaviour in February and I would come running after you like a puppy. So you went ahead with your plans.'

'Charlotte,' James pleaded, 'Please come with me. I love you and I need you so much. I'm sorry if I took you for granted.'

'And I am needed here. Sorry James, I won't be used like this.'

'In that case, I'd better go.' He picked up his hat and let himself out. No door-slamming this time. Just the quiet click of the door behind a man who felt he was walking out into a life by himself. I will never love anyone else, he thought soberly as he walked home to the Manse. But I have to go now.

Back in Da Peerie Skulehoose Charlotte gazed at what she was holding in her hands. It was a white handkerchief with the initials *JM* worked in the corner.

Chapter 34

The October school holiday was known as the tattie holidays. This was a week out of the school term given by School Boards for children to help gather the tattie harvest. It was a back-breaking job enough but one which boys and girls of a wide age-range did. Some because they lived and worked on farms and it was part of their family income; some from other homes who went 'to the tatties' because it supplemented their pocket money and probably the family income as well. Most mothers took a share of tattie money for the housekeeping. In the days before official authorisation of tattie holidays many farm folk kept their children off school at this time to assist with getting the tatties out of the ground and under cover before the frost came and ruined them. School Boards found they were fighting a losing battle in trying to force children to attend and gave in more or less gracefully to the pressure and made the week official. As that term in Scottish schools lasts from August to December more than the children were glad of the break.

Charlotte certainly was glad of the break. On the first Monday of the holiday she luxuriated in the unheard of excesses of a long lie in bed, hair washing, a late and leisurely bath with bath salts and her wet hair piled up on top of her head and tea (brought by the ever faithful Edie) in her parlour in her dressing gown. To behave with such decadence felt slightly sinful to Charlotte (whoever heard of having a long lie on a Monday morning) and it was with a guilty start that she heard the door. She turned to run for the stairs but met Edie who had been dusting the hall entering the parlour with Christina by the hand.

'Hello Christina.' Charlotte was glad at least that her guest was neither male nor hyper-critical. On the whole, anything she did found favour in Christina's eyes, and, especially since she had started school. So if Charlotte found her on a Monday morning in her dressing-gown and with wet hair, then that, in Charlotte's eyes would be perfectly acceptable.

'Good *morning*, Miss Gordon.' Christina gave the greeting the school slant which she had picked up on day one. 'I have a note for you from Father. I know what it says,' she added. 'Please come.'

'Oh, thank you. Wait a minute until I read it.' She read aloud for Christina's benefit:

'Dear Charlotte,

It would give Christina and myself much pleasure if you could come to lunch on Wednesday at 12 mid-day.

Yours sincerely,

Alexander Sinclair.'

'Why, that would be delightful. Thank you for bringing the note. I suppose you would like to take a note back.'

'Yes please.' Christina at nearly five years old was business like, on a mission. She felt her importance keenly.

'Right, could you please go with Edie for five minutes until I get dressed and then I'll be with you.'

Five minutes later they were cosily together in the parlour. Charlotte had let her hair down to dry and it was hanging in long curls down her back. Christina looked at it admiringly.

'I like your hair like that. Why don't you always wear it like that?'

'Because it would get in the way. And it would get all chalky with the dust at school.'

'I wish mine would grow as long as yours.'

'Well it will, just give it time. Now, 'Charlotte picked up the letter. 'Lunch on Wednesday. Let's get a letter written for you to take back. What do I need to write a letter.'

'I know, I know. You need paper, and a pen, and ink.'

'That's right.' They went over to Charlotte's table at the window and sat together. 'Now I'll show you. First you take the clean paper out.' She took a piece of blue paper out of the stationery box and laid it on her blotting writing base. 'Always make sure you have a clean place to put it. It would never do to send anyone a dirty letter.'

'Father got a sticky one once,' Christina commented. 'He went and washed his hands.'

'Well, exactly. Now,' continued Charlotte, 'you get your pen from the pen tray and then you have to check the nib to see that there are no hairs or bits of fluff on it.' They checked. 'What do you think would happen if your nib had fluff on it?'

'Emm, I know, it would get inky and the writing would be traily.'

'That's right. Now, another thing you have to do, is to look at the nib and make sure that the two bits at the top of the nib are not crossed. If they are, your writing would really be like a hen's scratching on the paper.' Christina thought this was very funny. She did a hen-toed walk across the room.

'So what else do we need?'

The little girl came back and stood beside her at the table.

248

'Ink.'

'Yes, so I have my ink in a little inkwell here. Now be very careful. If ink gets spilt it's very difficult to clean up.'

'Oh, like that mark on the school floor.'

'Exactly. I remember that day. Mrs Manson and I tried everything to get that mark off. Now, we're ready. We have paper, a clean place to do the writing in, a good pen and ink in the inkwell. So, we'll write the letter.' She wrote in her copperplate handwriting:

> Da Peerie Skulehoose,
> Jarlshavn.
> Monday morning

Dear Alexander,

I should like to thank you and Christina for the invitation to lunch on Wednesday at 12 mid-day. I have much pleasure in accepting.

Yours sincerely,
> Charlotte Gordon.

She blotted the letter and read it aloud to Christina. 'Do you think that's all right?'

'Yes. Why has it got my name in it?'

'Because you are in the first letter inviting me to come. See,' she picked up the letter. 'It says "and Christina". So I should include you in my answer.'

'Oh I see. That's nice. Shall I take it back to father now.'

'Yes please. And thank you for being the post-lady.'

Charlotte

We were a threesome for lunch. Magnus did not appear as he was out at the tatties with Lowrie.

'He comes in at tea time all dirty,' said Christina. 'But he gets money for it. He told me. At the end of the week. The man – called the grieve he said – counts up the days they have been and gives them money. Father, when can I go to the tatties and get money too?'

'Oh you'll have to be a good bit older,' said Alexander. 'I'm not really sure about girls going out to the tatties at all. It's not girl's work.'

'But Father, lots of the girls have gone. And that's what the holiday is for.'

'Yes I know, but anyway,' he added, 'you're not even five yet. Just enjoy your holiday.'

'Oh, I might as well. I'll go and play with my dolls. Please may I get down from the table.'

'Yes certainly.' She slipped off her chair and left the room.

We sat in silence for a few moments. I nibbled a piece of cheese and oatcake. I could hear distant sounds of Meg in the kitchen.

'How's the school term going?' Alexander had not been up to school so much this term. I had a feeling that Meg had advised him to keep away and let Christina settle down by herself.

'It's been fine,' I said. 'It was good to get back and into a routine again. But on the other hand, this holiday comes just at the right time. I'm just enjoying this week drawing breath. Christina has settled in well.'

'I'm glad. She's very small compared to some of the others.'

'Well, she is the youngest in the school. But she's coping very well. The bigger girls in the class have taken her under their wing.'

'So I noticed. I hear that they have taken to escorting Meg and Christina home in the afternoon. It's not a problem,' he added hastily. 'They're all coming the same way anyway.'

He changed the subject. 'I also hear that you're about to lose your minister. He's off to Perthshire. Did you know?'

'Yes I did know. It was announced in the Kirk on Sunday. He leaves very soon I believe.'

'Hmm, pity. Nice man and, a good minister from what I hear. We could do with folk like him staying. Now the Kirk will have to go through all the palaver of a vacancy.'

'Well,' I said, 'he's accepted the Call now, and handed in his notice here so we'll just have to get on with it.'

I couldn't believe I was being so calm about it. Since James's last visit to me, I had felt very bad about his treatment of me, about my treatment of him, whether or not I should just have given in to him, or would he give in to me (in which case I would have felt very guilty. What a destructive emotion guilt is). Now, as far as I was concerned, James had made his decision. It did not include me as my feelings were not taken into account. It hurt very badly and probably this is why I had worked so particularly hard that first half of the term before the tattie holidays to keep my mind off the hurting part. And, probably why I was so tired and so glad to have the break from school.

Alexander looked out at the afternoon sunshine.

'What about you and me taking Christina round the harbour? For a wee walk before the light goes.'

I looked at him. I'm sure he knew I was worried about further gossip.

'Just a walk,' he said. 'Half an hour. Christina too.'

I mentally chided myself for my hesitance and smiled.

'All right. I'll get her.'

It was fine outside. Not that warm but still sunny, seagulls calling, the usual harbour busy-ness. Christina skipped ahead. The men called 'Good afternoon' or 'Fine day' as we passed.

'Can we go up the hill a bit, Father?'

'Just a wee bit.' We rounded the corner and started up the hill. Christina ran up and down the path.

'Come on, higher, higher.'

Eventually we called a halt, laughing and breathless. 'Come on, home now,' ordered Alexander. 'I don't know about you but I've had enough.'

As Christina ran ahead he said, 'See now, that wasn't so bad, was it?'

'No,' I admitted. Indeed I had enjoyed the afternoon. Uncomplicated and simple; why couldn't life be like that?

Three weeks later, James MacLeod left the Kirk in Jarlshavn to respond to his Call from the Kirk Congregation of St Fillans in Perthshire. The Kirk was full for his final service. Charlotte sat in her usual place and tried to concentrate. When James came in he looked pale but resolute. A wee bit like putting his hand to the plough and not looking back.

Edie said later, 'He was very pale, did you not think, Miss.'

'Yes, I suppose he was, Edie. He was maybe tired.'

'Yes that'll be it, with all the packing. Mrs Laurenson says there were a lot of crates. I heard that the movers, Shore Porters from Aberdeen, are sending a horse-lorry tomorrow to take the stuff to the boat. They'll meet the boat in Aberdeen and take it to St Fillans.'

James had stood at the Kirk door and said 'Good bye' individually to each of the congregation. When it was Charlotte's turn, she met his eyes and said, 'Good bye, Mr Macleod, I wish you well in your new Kirk.'

'Thank you, Miss Gordon.' He inclined his head very slightly, gave her a long careful look, shook her hand firmly, and the parting was over. It was difficult to believe it had happened so quickly. Edie's voice broke into her thoughts.

'Such a nice man. I'm sorry he's gone. You know, Miss, I always thought he liked you. He kept coming and bringing things. And you and he seemed to get on so well.'

'Yes, we did get on well,' said Charlotte. 'But, I like to get on well with everyone if I can.'

'Yes, I know,' said Edie, 'but you know what I mean.'

Charlotte did know, but she was not disposed to go down that road with Edie. She turned the conversation to safer topics.

'How's your mother these days?' Edie's mother had recently been 'under the doctor' for various unmentionable ailments. Because Charlotte came from a medical household, Edie had long since decided that she was herself practically as good as a doctor and confided in her if allowed, on all her family's aches and pains. In vain had Charlotte told her to desist from reporting her family's health details. Edie said, 'But Miss, it's all right telling you, you know all about it.' So for Charlotte to divert Edie by asking after her mother was slightly risky. However, this time the confidence was a going-about fact. Edie's mother had slipped and fallen – not down the Vennel steps as did Mr Inkster some time before, but a little closer to home, when she was throwing out the rubbish.

'Well, do you know, the doctor came last week. He looked at her ankle and said she could probably walk on it soon. It seems a bit quick. What do you think?'

'Well, if the doctor said that, then I've no doubt he'll be right.' Charlotte always made a point of agreeing with what Dr Taylor said. If she had disagreed, it would have gone right round the village.

'I just hope she takes care,' Edie sounded anxious. We don't want the 'artheritis' to set in.

'Did the doctor suggest it might?'

'No, but, well…'

'Well, if the doctor says she can walk on it then that should be fine. She just needs to take care and not over do things.'

'Right, well, I'll tell her you said that.' Edie went away satisfied. Thus, Charlotte was able to avoid any further discussion with Edie about the Reverend James MacLeod. But not talking about him did not stop her thinking about him.

Chapter 35

Alexander Sinclair walked up the road from the harbour towards Da Peerie Skulehoose. It had been a wild December week but today, Saturday morning, you might have thought if you didn't know better, that bad weather was an unknown thing in Shetland. The wind had dropped, the sun shone, the air was relatively mild.

Just the day for the examination of a project, Alexander thought.

Alexander was a man with a mission. He had been thinking about his self-imposed assignment for some time now and with the sale of a field on the outskirts of Jarlshavn most satisfactorily completed only a few days before, he felt he was on track to getting his plans underway. But he wanted to be able to discuss his ideas with a sympathetic listener. Christina was too young to contribute and Magnus – well Magnus and Alexander had not been truly right with each other since Magnus had spoken his mind to him at the time of his fight with Alfred Twatt. Alexander felt unable to confide in him at this point. It was a pity because Magnus was an intelligent young man but was, in Alexander's eyes at least, going through a particularly awkward stage in his development. This was demonstrated by surliness and lack of communication towards his father (although Alexander often heard sounds of chatter and laughter emanating from the kitchen as Magnus regaled Meg with stories of school and what he and Lowrie had been doing). They did not exactly have rows but there was a barrier there and Alexander had no idea how to breach it. He sighed. He would have given a lot to have been going on his undertaking with his son by his side.

He reached the gate of Da Peerie Skulehoose. This, over the last few weeks had become more familiar territory to him again as he cautiously worked his way to regain favour with Charlotte. He had thought carefully about his previous handling of Charlotte and felt he had come to see that her opinions and beliefs must be taken into account if he were to make real, long-lasting and deep peace with her. So here he was at this stage at least, able to go to her house openly and ask her to walk with him.

The gate clicked behind him. The door opened as he approached.

'Alexander, hello. What brings you here this fine day?' Alexander took off his Saturday cap and bowed slightly before shaking her hand. He found it very difficult to get rid of the formal manners with which he had grown up and now he felt at the age of forty-four, he was too old to change.

'Charlotte, are you well?'

253

'Yes, I'm fine thanks. Are you out for a walk?' She nodded towards his stick.

'Yes, yes, you could say that. I wondered if you would have time to walk with me? It's such a beautiful day after last week's atrocious weather. The fishing boats were stormbound for half the week.'

'Is everyone all right?' Charlotte still found it difficult to imagine fishermen going out in what to her were sometimes very big seas.

'Yes, they're all fine. Some of the boats were a bit late as they ran for shelter up the coast but they're all accounted for now. Now, will you walk?'

'Yes all right. Just wait till I get my things. Edie,' she called, 'I'm going out.'

They set off up the road together.

'No Christina today?'

'No I've left her with Meg. They're baking.'

'And Magnus, is he here or in Lerwick this weekend.'

'He's at home doing some schoolwork. I expect he and Lowrie will go out later. They're very keen on this keep fit that they do.'

'Well, at least it's good for them and keeps them out of mischief.' They turned a corner and continued on to the very edge of the village.

'Alexander, where are we heading?'

'I want to show you something. Something I've been thinking about for a long time.' Charlotte, intrigued, followed as the road became a track suitable for farm carts but not much else.

At last he stopped. 'There,' he declared, sweeping out his hand. Charlotte looked.

'But Alexander, it's a field.'

'Yes,' he said rather grandly. 'It's a field. I have just bought it.'

'You've *bought* it? But why?'

'Charlotte, this is a two part project. I want to build a house.'

'But you've got a house. Harbour House is lovely.'

'Yes but Harbour House belongs to the harbour authorities. I don't own it. The day will come when I stop being harbourmaster and then we will have to leave Harbour House. So, you see, I must think ahead.'

'I see,' she nodded slowly. 'I never knew that it wasn't yours. I don't suppose I ever gave it a thought.'

'No,' he agreed, 'we've been there so long that everyone thinks of it as ours, but it isn't. So, hence the buying of this field. I'm going to build a house on it.'

Charlotte looked around appreciatively. 'It's a lovely site. What views you'll have, all round.' She started to walk over the grass. 'Just imagine, we're walking where one day there will be a house. It's a funny feeling.' She stopped. 'But Alexander, you said you had a two-part project. What's the second part?'

'I'm coming to that. Have you ever thought that Shetland lacks anything? Something that you perhaps are very used to?'

'You mean Shetland all over?'

'Yes, what's missing?'

254

'Well the first thing that I noticed was – but you'll think this is silly,' she hesitated, not wanting to offend the Shetlander by finding fault with his country.

'No, go on.' He looked at her eagerly.

'The first thing I noticed was that there are hardly any trees. I'm so used to trees that I missed them to begin with.'

'Exactly.' He was delighted with her perspicacity. 'You've hit the nail on the head.'

'Have I?'

'Yes, that's what I want to do here. Grow some trees. What do you think?'

'It's a wonderful idea. But would they grow. After all there must be some reason why there are no, or virtually no trees in Shetland.'

'Ah, but, there used to be. A thousand or so years ago there were trees on Shetland. We know because of the old sagas and of course because we have tangible evidence in the peat banks.'

'Of course, the peats.'

'There's no peat like a Shetland peat.' He repeated the often stated view. 'It's probably true. Anyway, peat aside, there are now hardly any trees in Shetland, and those that are here are only behind sheltered structures and once they get above the shelter they lean forwards with the wind and don't get any taller. I would like to have a try at growing some trees in this field as part of the garden to the house. I remember visiting in your part of Scotland – not as far west as Upper Donside but certainly Aberdeenshire. What took me was the amount and size of the trees. I don't think we will manage anything like as big but I would like to try.'

'What kind would you grow?'

'We'd need to do some research into what would do best, something that could withstand the wind and the salt air and of course we would have to think of how to keep out the rabbits. Look at them.' Rabbits which had dashed for their burrows on their approach were now, emboldened by the fact that the walkers were now at a standstill, beginning to reappear.

'Wire netting, for a start. Dad has it tightly all round the bits where he doesn't want rabbits. It's a big job.'

'So, what do you think of my project?'

'It's a surprise certainly. And considering what you say about Harbour House, a very sensible idea. And I like the idea of the trees. When are you hoping to start?'

'I would like to think, in the spring. I've been to see an architect in Lerwick, talked over my ideas and he's drawing up some plans for the house for me. The first drafts should be ready next week. Would you like to have a look at them when they come?'

Yes, I would, thank you. It sounds very exciting. I've never seen architect's plans before.

Right, I'll let you know when they come and we can spread them out in the dining-room.

'Do the children know?'

'Not yet, but I'll tell them now before they hear elsewhere.'

'How will they take it, do you think.'

'Not sure. Christina will be all girly and excited. I think once she gets used to the idea she'll be fine. As for Magnus, his face clouded, well Magnus is at school so much, I shouldn't think he'll care one way or another.'

'Alexander, of course he'll care. What's the problem?'

'Ach, he's just being a bit difficult just now. I think it's his age. He won't communicate with me. All I get is the bare minimum.'

'How long has he been like this?'

'A good while. Do you remember he got into a fight at school?'

'Yes, I do. But Alexander that was ages ago.'

'Yes I know. But we had words when he came home and well, we had a time of not speaking at all, and then things improved slightly. When Christina was so ill, we had to talk to each other, we were both so worried. It's funny isn't it,' he mused, 'how some good can come out of such a bad time.'

'So, you are speaking to each other now?'

'Yes, but, it's not the same. I wish it could be. We were building up quite a good rapport.'

'He's such a nice boy, Alexander. Keep trying. Perhaps he'll be really interested in this house and trees project if you let him.'

'Would you help us then? He turned to look at her. 'He admires you very much. I think you could get him to participate if you are in on it.'

'Do you think so? He hasn't been up for a while. I was thinking he had maybe grown away from the primary teacher.'

'No, I think he's just fed up with father.'

They walked back to the old gate. Alexander closed it with a proprietary air. He smiled.

'I'm beginning to feel this is going to happen now. Thanks for coming today. You've been a great help.'

They walked back into the village together.

Chapter 36

1897

'What do you think we should call the house?' Alexander was walking carefully round the skeleton of the inside of the new house, pausing from room to room to check workmanship, admire the view from windowless openings, look up the hole where the stairs were going to be, to the upper rooms beyond. Charlotte and Christina were coming behind more warily, anxious not to catch their skirts on a stray nail nor pick up too much wood dust on their clothes.

'I don't know. Have you any ideas?'

'Something to do with trees? After all the trees are a big part of the project.'

Charlotte considered. 'What kind of trees have you thought of.'

'Well, mixed deciduous mostly – sycamores, rowans, birches, a lot of birches because they are such bonny trees, whitebeam and …'

'What about something to do with birches? I know. At home we call birches "birks".'

'Yes, it's the same here.'

'And a place that has a lot of birks is a 'birken'. What about calling the house Birkenshaw – a small wood of birch trees? I like that.'

'Birkenshaw, Birkenshaw,' he tried it out. 'That's quite good. I don't know if it sounds typically Shetland but I don't know if that matters. I think I like it.'

Alexander was also pleased that it was Charlotte who had come up with a name for the house. It was yet another aspect pulling her into the project. There had been many visits to the 'field' over the months since the first walk and discussion of the undertaking which lay ahead. Since then, the architect's plans had been examined, discussed, re-designed in many aspects and generally turned upside down in order to satisfy everyone.

Charlotte had joined in with growing enthusiasm made greater by the fact that Alexander seemed to listen to and accept her ideas. One evening they had been poring over the papers in the dining room of Harbour House. Her mind went back to her first day at Trancie House when she and Granpa had examined the bathroom with such interest and fun, the H and C on the taps, the pride with which he had shown her the separate water closet and, when he pulled the chain, the three gallons of water coming down with such abundance.

The original plans for the new house contained no such watercloset. Instead, outside the house plan, albeit not that far away, was included a plan for an 1897 version of 'the wee hoosie' with a dry-closet. A modern strong draft-proof version indeed, but still to all intents and purposes, a wee hoosie with a dry closet to which one had to repair when the need arose. She took a deep breath and plunged into the discussion.

'I see the dry-closet is in another wee hoosie.'

'Yes, but,' Alexander said, 'a really good one, with no draughts and a good locking door.'

'But,' she said, a little tentatively, 'you'll still have to go outside.'

'But that's what everybody does.'

'Well,' she persisted, 'most people do. But Alexander, we're nearly into the twentieth century. You've always been one for thinking ahead. Look at the way you've upgraded the harbour with modern machinery and helped the fishermen get modern up-to-date equipment for their boats.' This was true. Alexander had spent many years working on the harbour and the authorities to make it as safe as possible a place to work in and, for those who worked out of it on the high seas.

'So, what are you saying?'

'Well, I think you could be a wee bit more modern than an outside wee hoosie.'

'You mean have an *inside* wee hoosie? Say, in the hall?'

'Alexander, you know I don't mean in the hall.' She couldn't believe she was having this conversation. With a man.

Christina was listening with her eyes popping. No one ever *talked* about the wee hoosie. You just went and used it and hoped nobody saw you. It was that private. At some point Meg cleaned it but when, how or why was not discussed.

'Well, how or where do you think we should modernise to?' Alexander liked to think he was an up-to-the-minute man and his activities at the harbour bore this out but in matters of bodily excretory function, he was blinkered. It was distasteful but necessary and that was that. Comfort did not come into the equation. All should be functional and clean and that was it.

Charlotte had never seen a water-closet such as existed in Trancie House, in Shetland. But that was no reason why this new house should not have one. It might even be the first house in Shetland to acquire such a luxury. She looked again at the plans.

'Where are you putting the bathroom? Oh yes, I see it. So, it's upstairs. Why don't you put a water-closet upstairs beside it.'

'A water-closet? But no one here's got a water-closet.'

'All the more reason why you should have one. Set a new trend. Modern thinking. And I'm sure the idea will catch on. More work for the locals as everyone in Jarlshavn changes over to waterclosets. Think of the headlines in *The Shetland Times*.' She was laughing now as she expanded on the idea. Magnus whose input into the discussions had grown markedly over the weeks with Charlotte's encouragement, had withdrawn in teenage embarrassment at the first mention of wee hoosies. He now joined in.

'Yes, I could take a note to school telling them of the wonders of it. I could write an essay on it.'

'Me too, me too.' Christina had no idea what they were talking about but was not to be outdone.

'Stop, stop.' Alexander called the meeting to order. 'Charlotte,' he demanded, 'how do you know so much about water-closets?'

'Trancie House,' she said.

'You never said.'

'Well, we don't exactly talk about it, do we?'

'Right, we can talk about it now. I'm a bit worried about having that sort of thing in the house. Do you think it's clean?'

'Granpa is a doctor,' she reminded him. 'I don't think he would have anything not clean in the house.'

'I suppose not. So, what happens?'

'Three gallons of water every time you pull the chain.' She went on to tell them about her first visit to the 'offices' at Trancie House which had turned out to be very forward thinking for their day. 'And that was a while ago,' she concluded. 'I'm sure things will have updated since then.'

'It's certainly worth thinking about.' Alexander conceded.

By summer the house was well on its way. As soon as the frost was out of the ground in the spring, the team of builders made a start. It was going to be a big house – by Jarlshavn standards. Charlotte liked its firm traditional lines. She and Meg had long discussions about the kitchen, because as Meg was to make the move to the new house with the family, she wanted to have a say in how the kitchen should be designed. She was delighted to be having the latest in modern kitchen ranges, a 'Wilson' no less, as recommended in *Mrs Beeton's Book on Household Management*. Upstairs, although the adults could not access the area because the stairs were not yet there, were four big bedrooms and a little one over the front hall and, the rudiments of the bathroom and, now, the water-closet. Magnus went up the ladder to have a look.

'Mercy.' He had never seen the like. 'Does it work yet?'

'Magnus, don't you dare. It's not plumbed in yet.'

'All right, all right, I'm only teasing. You'll be able to charge people to come and see.'

Alexander and Charlotte wandered outside.

'You know, he's so much better,' Alexander remarked.

'Yes, I know. It's been lovely to watch him come round to you again, and,' she added, 'you welcoming him and helping him.'

'It's been a difficult time. But I think working on this project has helped all of us come together. What about you,' he asked. 'Have you felt a part of the plans? I've certainly enjoyed having your commitment and advice but how have you felt about it?'

'I have enjoyed this thoroughly,' she said. 'I had never seen an architect's plan before and you learn an awful lot from listening to the professional discussion and then the way they can change the plan – they make it look so easy, but I'm sure it takes a lot of learning and experience.'

'Well anything professional does. But Charlotte, I also meant how have you felt about being with our family again?' They walked along in a silence that was almost tangible.

'Charlotte?'

'I have been very happy to be able to work with you all in such a way. I have felt very welcome.'

'You say 'all', Charlotte. Does that mean me, too?'

'Alexander, of course I've been happy to work on this with you. I don't think I could have done it otherwise.'

They were well away from the house by this time. Charlotte could see Christina trying to make acquaintance with a caddy lamb. It had spent the first few weeks of its life being bottle-fed in the farm kitchen. Now it was out into the field next door and it was desperate for some of the human company it was used to and from which it had suddenly been deprived. Charlotte pointed. 'Look at Christina.'

'She'd have it home if she got half a chance. Charlotte,' he returned to the subject.

'Yes?' She was still watching Christina.

'Charlotte, you say you've been happy working with us on this project, and I have to say you've been a great help and encouragement. But, what about making it permanent? Charlotte, I know I'm older than you, I know I said the wrong things before and spoilt it all, but... but, we go so well together. Charlotte, I love you for you, not for anything else. I know that now. Please, will you do me the great honour of becoming my wife?'

Chapter 37

Charlotte

With hindsight, I suppose I should have seen it coming. That first visit to the field on top of quite a few exchanges back and forth between the two households had broken down many barriers. I felt much more at ease and comfortable in Alexander's company. But he in turn seemed to be gentler, less ready to take me for granted, more ready to listen to my opinions. And while before he only seemed to want to marry me so that he could have a mother for the children, now, he had declared he loved me, for myself.

The question was, did I love him – enough to marry him? I certainly cared deeply about him. Here we were in summer 1897, two and a half years after Margery's death. A lot had happened and each of us had changed. I felt more mature, with the years, the happenings, with my mother's death, my relationship with James and what had happened there, the ups and downs of my time with Alexander since he was widowed. Margery's death had affected us all. Looking back, I could see that she had placed a huge burden on me which weighed heavily for a time.

That burden was not there now. I felt I had done and was doing what I could for Magnus and Christina. I had worked hard to include Magnus in his father's dual house and trees project, Christina I saw at school and often on other occasions. She had improved tremendously over the year, no longer the spoilt little girl crying for the moon. That is not to say she did not have her moments. But the moments were becoming further apart and perhaps the new more tolerant patient Alexander was becoming better at handling them. So the vicious circle was broken.

At the same time the conversation with Margery had not gone away. But the more mature me was more able to handle it. And therefore, marriage to Alexander would be if and because I wanted to, or rather because we both wanted it, rather than by the demand of someone no longer in the immediate picture. It was quite a relief to think this out and accept the freedom the raising of the burden afforded me.

I had to admit to myself, that I really enjoyed our meetings, discussions, plans about the house and garden and trees. I actively looked forward to our times together. Was this love? I don't know. What I did know was that I felt comfortable when I was with Alexander now, that there had been a big leap forward in our relationship and understanding of each other.

I should have seen it coming but was still taken aback that day. I hesitated, looked at him, my hands in front of my face. I could feel myself reddening, my pulse quickening, my breathing raised. It was so quiet, seagulls cried, sheep and their lambs called for each other, Christina's voice came and went on the breeze as she played with the caddy lamb. Still I could not speak.

'Charlotte. Make me the happiest man alive, and the most fortunate. Marry me. Marry me and we'll live here at Birkenshaw, our house which you named.'

We stopped and faced each other. Very carefully, tentatively almost, he put his arms out and drew me to him. Very slowly, I moved towards him. Still I could not make the final leap. I quite unconsciously put my arms up between us as a barrier even though his were, by this time, enfolding me.

'Charlotte,' he whispered, 'my little dove, come to me, I love you.'

He was so sincere, I could feel myself surrendering the suspicions I had felt, the anger at his early arrogance, the doubts I had experienced about his earlier motives. Now, I thought, you can believe he really wants to marry you. I let my elbows relax, my arms dropped first to my sides and, as we moved closer, I allowed them to creep around his waist as he held me to him.

How long we stood like that I do not know – probably only for a few moments. Time stood still. I could feel his breathing, regular and safe, hear the deep lub-dub of his heart, smell the clean smell of him, touch his warm woollen jacket.

'Charlotte,' his hand came up and gently turned my face to look at him. 'Will you? Marry me?'

'Yes,' I said. 'Yes, I will.' With a deep sigh of happiness his embrace became firmer, more confident and there in the bare field of Birkenshaw with the half-built house behind us, the closeness of that enfolding paved the way for our first tentative but sweet and memorable kiss.

The reverie was broken by the sound of Christina's return from her sojourn with the caddy lamb.

'Father, Father, here I am,' she called, with the confidence of one who thinks that the world revolves around her and her alone. The two grown-ups who had been thinking that the world was theirs, reluctantly pulled apart, looked at each other ruefully and laughed.

'Come on Christina, race you to the house.' Charlotte picked up her skirt and made for the front door.

'I'm catching you,' she shouted, and Charlotte slowed up to let her pass as they approached the house. Alexander followed more slowly.

'Magnus, are you there?' Christina ran in and drummed her heels on the wooden boards, enjoying the echoey sound she made in the empty house.

'Yes, I'm up here. Hang on, I'm coming down.' He clambered down the ladder. 'You get a great view from my bedroom. Can I have the walls any colour I like?'

'I don't see why not,' Alexander said. 'What did you have in mind?'

'I don't know. Black maybe.' Charlotte and Alexander looked at each other and burst out laughing.

'What's so funny?'

'Nothing,' Charlotte said, still giggling, 'but it's just, well, so, *dark.'*

'Anyway, plenty time to think about it. Time for home now.' Alexander was ready to lock up.

They were all together in the wee upstairs sitting room when Alexander made his announcement. They both felt that this time, all should be in the open. There should be no misunderstandings and no secrets.

'Hmm,' he began, 'I, that is we, have something to tell you both. Today, I asked Charlotte if she would be my wife, and to my great delight and happiness, she said yes.' There was a silence.

'What does that mean? 'Christina said, perplexed at the long sentence.

'Your father has asked me to marry him and I said yes.'

Christina gave a shriek of joy. 'You mean you will be my Mama? Oh Miss Gordon, I'm so happy.'

Alexander's and Charlotte's eyes met as if to say, 'no trouble there then'.

Magnus was quiet. Charlotte looked at him.

'Magnus?'

'I thought you were outside for a very long time,' he said. 'Now I know why.' He took a deep breath. 'Well, I hope you'll both be very happy.' He turned to Charlotte, 'but I can't call you Mother.'

'Magnus,' Alexander moved towards him, 'you….'

'That's all right, Alexander. I don't mind at all. After all I'm not Magnus's mother, am I? And he's too old to pretend. Magnus, why don't you call me Charlotte – I know you do sometimes anyway – and treat me as a friend. Do you think you could manage that?'

Magnus's mind was in a turmoil. Here he was in the situation which he had hoped had passed. The thought of his father's marrying Charlotte before had caused him great anxiety. Now he had to deal with the real thing. He could not show how he felt about her. And he could not afford to fight with his father. He would surely be the loser. He straightened his shoulders and eyed the two who regarded him not a little anxiously.

'I mean it,' he assured them, 'I hope you'll be very happy. And of course we'll be friends Charlotte. Haven't we always been?' He stepped forward and gave her a hug before turning to his father, hand outstretched.

'Father, I wish you every happiness with Charlotte.'

The formality of the occasion was interrupted by Christina. She could not understand why all were not jumping for joy like her and she watched the previous few minutes with puzzlement. Now she hugged them all about the legs, and said, 'let's go and tell Meg.' She rushed off. Her elders looked at each other, smiled, shrugged and followed. This was as good a way of broadcasting news as any.

263

So it proved. Once Meg knew the information was accurate and could be made public no time was lost before the whole of Jarlshavn was aware of the momentous news emanating from Harbour House. True, Meg just needed to tell one person. Then the snowball rolled expanding with each revolution. Fortunately Charlotte made it up to Da Peerie Skulehoose before someone took it upon themselves to inform Edie.

'Edie, don't go just yet. I have something I need to tell you.'

'Yes, Miss?' Edie looked at her.

'Edie, I was up at Mr Sinclair's new house today with him and Magnus and Christina. It's coming on very well. It's going to be a lovely house.'

'Yes, Miss. So I hear. I haven't been up myself for a while.' Edie busied herself buttoning her coat.

As she reached for her hat, Charlotte said, 'Edie, I'm going to marry Mr Sinclair.' Edie stopped, hands and hat halfway up.

'Miss? Marry Mr Sinclair?'

'Yes, Edie. I wanted you to be one of the first to know, and,' Charlotte said firmly, 'I wanted you to hear it from me.'

'Oh, Miss, well, I hope you'll be very happy.' Then, very suddenly, Edie said, 'Oh, Miss, are you sure?' Her eyes were wet as she said, 'I really want you to be happy, but I want you to be sure you are doing the right thing.'

'Edie.' Charlotte gave her a hug. 'How good of you to say that. But rest assured, all is well. Mr Sinclair and I've had time to think about this and we're looking forward to being married. Now,' she sniffed, 'look at me, you'll have me crying too. And look at your hat – I've bashed it.' She pushed out the offending dimple in the crown of the hat and handed it to its owner.

'Ach, never mind about that,' Edie rammed her hat-pin through the hat as she stuck it on her head. 'It's an old one. Well,' she said, going back to the matter in hand. 'We have a wedding to arrange. Any idea when?'

'No idea. This is all very new – we haven't had time to make any plans.'

'How are the children?'

'They're both fine. Christina is jumping about and shrieking.'

'She would,' commented Edie drily.

'And, Magnus is fine too. No problem.'

'That's fine. Well, I hope you'll be very happy. Is this a secret.'

'No, I'm glad to tell you, no secrets. I can't stand them.'

Chapter 38

The school year began once again.

'What are you going to do about the school?' Mrs Manson and Charlotte were sharing a cup of tea before they shut up the school on the first day of term.

'I'm not sure yet,' Charlotte responded. 'I like my work so much, I'd really like to stay on for a while. Would that be all right do you think?'

'All right by me. But what about Mr Sinclair? Won't he want you to stay at home?'

'We-ll, before, you know,' Charlotte looked at Mrs Manson, who nodded in understanding, 'before, he was adamant that I should stop work. But now, well I think he might agree to my staying on – for a whilie at least. You know, until, until…' her voice petered out.

'Until you are going to have a baby?' Mrs Manson did not believe in mincing her words.

'Well, yes, I suppose that's what I mean.'

'Right, well I have no problem with your being here as Mrs Sinclair. In fact it'll suit me fine. I was not looking forward to losing you. We work fine together and anyway the thought of having to get used to someone new leaves me quite unenthusiastic.'

'Alexander, I'd like to discuss something with you.' Charlotte and Alexander were in the parlour of Harbour House, discussing paper and paint and curtain materials for the new house. Preparations for a spring wedding ran alongside a decided effort to have Birkenshaw ready for occupancy so that the bridal couple could take up residence immediately they were married. The house was wind and watertight but they realised that anything special they ordered would need to be shipped to Lerwick from the south.

'What's that?' Alexander was leafing through a book of specimen fabrics. 'Look, what do you think of this one?' He held out a sample.

'Yes, it's very nice; we could put it on our short list. What's the number?' Charlotte noted the sample number on her list. 'But Alexander, stop a minute and listen. I need to talk to you.'

'I thought we were talking.'

'Yes, but something important.'

'Isn't this important.' He gazed at her fondly. 'Isn't this and our lives together the most important thing we could be talking about?'

'Yes, Alexander, and what I have to say is all part of it. Alexander, I want to carry on teaching for a while after we are married.'

'What?'

'Just for a time.'

'No. I want my wife to be at home.'

'But what about what your wife might want? Oh, Alexander, just for a whilie. I like my work at the school so much, and I would see that it wouldn't upset your home life. And, I could walk home with Christina.'

'But other men's wives don't work, that is unless they can't keep them. No, no, Charlotte. It's out of the question. People will say I can't keep you.'

'And some might say, "well done" for allowing women to move forwards and not waste education and training by not using them after marriage. Oh Alexander, I've worked so hard to be a teacher. I don't want to stop until I have to.'

'Well, he said, 'I don't know. I see what you're saying but, it's so unusual – for women who don't need to, I mean.'

'Well you could say, don't need to in a money sense, but what about needing to, in another sense?'

'What do you mean?'

'Well, I think I need to go on teaching for a while, not because of the money although that's always welcome, but because of, well, a whole range of different reasons, for me and my self-esteem if you like, for women and their advancement as a whole, for the school – I happen to think I'm quite a good teacher – and therefore the good I can do there for a while longer.'

'What about if you start a baby?'

'Well then, the picture changes and we can change with it.'

'Hmm. Well, I don't know,' he hesitated. Charlotte sensed he was weakening. She went over and sat beside him and put her hand on his arm.

'This is really important to me, Alexander. I'm a good teacher. Don't take it away from me before I need to. Please?'

'Ach, seeing you put it like that, well all right. But if it all gets too much for you then you stop. All right?'

'Thank you, my dear.' Charlotte cupped his doubtful face between her hands and kissed him. 'Now, what sample was it you liked so much?'

The Candlemas school term ended just before Easter. For two weeks the school was to be on holiday. The children were in a turmoil of excitement. Not only did they have two weeks off, but their Miss Gordon was going to be married and they were all invited to the wedding. Most of the children had never been to a wedding before. Those who had, spent a lot of time informing those who hadn't, about wedding ceremonies, rings, flowers and the like. Christina, who had not been to a wedding

266

before was nevertheless the centre of attention as it was her father who was marrying Miss Gordon. Her cup of happiness was full.

Charlotte was preparing to move out of Da Peerie Skulehoose to Birkenshaw. The idea was that she, with Edie's help would pack most of her boxes during the days before the wedding. Alexander engaged Doddie Isbister, local joiner and husband of Mrs Isbister who made the school soup on a daily basis, to take them up to Birkenshaw on his cart. Two days into the holiday, they were nearly ready.

'I can't have gathered so much stuff.' Charlotte carried yet another box downstairs and dumped it in the hall.

'Oh yes you could. I've been watching you.' Edie came out of the parlour with a picture in her arms. 'Do you want this in a box, or could we wrap it in a blanket. It's not for long.'

'Yes That'll do fine thanks. Are we nearly there do you think?'

'Aye, I think so. And just in time too. It's eleven o'clock and I can see Doddie and his cart coming up the road.'

'Mercy, so he is. Oh Edie, everything's going.' Charlotte looked round her house where she had been so happy. 'It's a new chapter.'

'Yes, Miss, and a happy one too, I'm sure. Now Miss, Is all this to go? Here's Doddie now.'

'Yes, everything here is to go. I have a wee bit more upstairs. Nothing heavy. I'll take a couple of light bags over later today.'

The cart clattered to a halt outside.

'Morning Mr Isbister.' Doddie climbed down, went round to the back of the cart and lowered the tailgate.

'Morning Miss Gordon. Fine day for it.'

'Would you like some tea before you start?'

'Well, now, that would be very acceptable, thank you.' He stepped over the threshold. 'My, you have a few boxes there.'

'Yes we were just saying that. It's amazing how much you gather.'

'Tea.' Edie appeared with her tray.

Charlotte looked around her bedroom. Not much left, she thought. Her wedding dress covered in a dust sheet, hung on the wardrobe. She lifted up the sheet and smiled. No one else except Edie and Mrs Manson had seen her dress. Edie, because she was not only Charlotte's housemaid, but she had also become a dear friend, and Mrs Manson because she had almost taken on a motherly role towards Charlotte. Certainly she had been Charlotte's mentor since the younger woman's arrival in Jarlshavn. Now Charlotte had asked Ina Manson to be there for her as she was married: to stand up for her. This meant that Ina had an important role escorting Charlotte to church, standing with her during the marriage service and signing the register afterwards. She had been delighted to be asked.

'Charlotte, what a compliment to pay me.' They were sitting in the schoolhouse after school one day just after the turn of the year. 'But, don't you want your father to escort you?'

'I'm afraid none of my family can come.' Charlotte said. 'I would have liked especially Granny and Granpa to come but it's a long way for them. And my father, well, what Granny foretold has come true. He didn't need to employ a housekeeper very long. He got married again last summer and he's too busy with his new wife to come all this way. It's a long way – I must remember that. But it would have been nice. Never mind. I would be really happy if you would be with me and stand up for me, as they say.'

Charlotte smiled to herself, folded the dustsheet around the dress again and went over to her last small boxes to be packed. She set aside all she would need for the next day or two then sorted the other things into the box. At the back of the top drawer of the dressing table she came upon some small pieces including a small soft bundle wrapped in tissue paper: a whitewhite cotton handkerchief with *JM* in blue in the corner.

She held the handkerchief in her hands a few moments, biting her lip, thinking, remembering. Then, she folded it, wrapped it up in its tissue again and, placed it in the box.

She ran downstairs to Edie and smiled. 'That's everything ready now.'

Glossary

A: I
an: than (eg, much bonnier lookin an Lizzie)
aa richt   : all right
aabiddy: everybody
aalest: oldest; eldest
aat: that
abeen: above
ae: one
afa: awful; also used to mean awfully as in 'he's awfully small': 'he's afa smaa'
argy bargy: argument
ava: at all
ay,aye: yes
aye: always
aye aye: hello; a greeting
baith: both
banterin: joking; teasing
bauld: bold
beets: boots
ben room: innermost room
bide: stay
birled: twirled
birse: pressure
birr: force; energy; passion
birss: fit of bad temper; get yir birss up – to get angry
bissom, besom, beesom: broom; brush; term of reproach for woman
blaa: blow (wind)
blether: chatter; talk; talk nonsense
bli'; blithe: good (weather); pleased, happy
bothy: cottage where farm servants were lodged and cooked their own food
bothy loons: young men who lived in farm's bothy
braddies: meat pie; (similar to bridie)
breenge: rush forward impetuously; batter; bang
caip: cap
canle: candle

269

cannyness: carefulness; gentleness
cheery bye: good bye
claes: clothes
claik: gossip; tittle-tattle
cloot: cloth
clype: tell tales (v); someone who tells tales (n)
coorse: coarse; very rough
cooried: cuddled (in); cowered; crouched
craic: chat (Come an hae a craic)
cried: called
croose: confident
da peerie skülehoose: the little schoolhouse (Shetland)
darg: day's work
dee, deein: do, doing
dee: die
dee: you (Shetland)
dinna fash yersel: don't get too excited/anxious
dochter: daughter
dominie: head-teacher (usually male)
dunt: bump
dwam: dream
easdom: comfort
ee: you
ee noo: *lit* the now: now
een: eyes
een: one
eesed: used
eneuch: enough
fa: who
fair awa wi masel: very happy with myself
fairm: farm
fairm-toun : farm house and surrounding buildings and land
falsers: false teeth
fee, fee'd: engage a farm-hand; (fee'd: past tense); fee: a farm-hand's wage;
feein: hiring
feel: fool
fit: what
fly-cup: a sly cup of tea but usually taken ritually
foo: how
foo: full
fooivver: however
forby: as well

forrit: furrit: forward(s)
fowk: folk
fricht: fright
fyachie: insipid; sickly
gaan, gyaan: going
giein, gied: giving; gave
girdle: circular iron plate with bow handle for making oatcakes, scones etc.
glaur: mud; dirt
glowering: scowling
gomeril: fool; blockhead
gorblin: very young, unfledged baby bird
graip: large fork used in farming; term often now used for garden fork
granny's sooker: round white peppermint sweetie; sometimes known as pandrop (see below); said to last the time that a minister should take to say his or her sermon.
greet: cry, weep
greetin: crying
grieve: farm overseer
gweed: good
gweed nicht: good night
haein ye on: having you on; joking
haet: hot
hale: whole
hallyrackit: boisterous
harling: roughcast (covering of house)
henwife: woman in charge of poultry; hennie: familiar name for henwife
hine: far
hinna: haven't
hirplin: limping
hiv: have
hodden doon: down hearted; overcome
hooer: whore
howdie: midwife (originally without formal training); at howdie haste: at high speed
hud awa: command to horse
ither: other
jalouse: guess; suspect; imagine
jean: attractive young woman
jiner: joiner;carpenter
kin: kind
kirkyard: churchyard
kishie: basket for peats
kist: chest; coffin; (*vt*) to put in a coffin

271

kisting: the coffining; the occasion when a body is placed in the coffin
kittlins: kittens
kyte; kite: stomach; belly
larn: learn; (sometimes used as: that'll larn ye: that will teach you.)
lassikie; lassockie: young girl
limmer: woman of loose morals
loon: lad; boy
lüft: wind; air
mair: more
mairrit: married
manna: mustn't
mart: market
masel: myself
midden: dunghill; rubbish-heap
min: remember
mineer; minneer: great noise; fuss; sometimes used as 'mess' as in 'fit a mineer'
meaning 'what a mess/state'
minty: minute (diminutive)
mony: many
naither: neither
neen: none;
neuk: corner; nook
naethin: nothing
onybiddy: anybody
onywey: anyway
oom: atmosphere (to do with smell)
oot-by: out in the fields; out and a little way off; adj:out of the way; distant
ower: over
oxter: armpit
pandrop: peppermint sweetie; see Granny's sooker (above)
peat-rik: peak reek; smoke coming from a peat fire
peenies: aprons
peer: poor
peerie: small
pey: pay
piece: portable snack (often taken to school)
pig: stone hot-water bottle
pinkie: smallest finger
pu'in your leg: pulling your leg
quinie: quine: girl
raivelt: mentally confused; tangled
redd-up: poke (fire); make burn brightly; tidy

reek; rik: smoke (as in peet-rik)
richt: right
roost: tidal race between two pieces of land.
    In this case the Roost is the stormy stretch of water between Fair Isle and
    Sumburgh Head.
saining: cleaning
sair-made: worried; anxious; hard-pressed
semmit: vest
shair: sure
shoogle: shaky
skailed: dispersed (as in school pupils); spilt
skelve: shelf
smeeked: smoked; 'smeekin the hoose' entailed carrying a burning peat throughout the
    house to let the smoke into every nook and cranny.
sooth-moother: In Shetland, someone from south of Shetland
soorocks: sorrel
spik: speak; (*n*)subject of gossip or talk; speech, conversation
spilt: spoilt
squeel: school
steadin: steading, farmstead
stour, stoury: dust, dusty
stracht: straight
sweir: unwilling
tackety: boots/shoes with studs/hobnails in the soles; eg tackety beets
tak; takken: take; taken
tak tent: take care
taken a len o ye: *lit* taking a loan of you: making use of; taking advantage of
tattie: potato
tawse: leather strap for punishing child eg in school
thegither: together
thrang: busy, overworked
toorie: topknot (on bonnet), (like a pom-pom)
troo: trust; believe
trow: troll
vennel: alley; narrow lane
voe: inlet of sea
vratch: wretch
wardle: world
weel deen: well done
wersh: tasteless
wid: would
wid: wood

wifie: woman
wik: week
winnert: wondered
winrin: wondering
wy: way

Note: Some of the glossary meanings are from Kynoch D, 1996, *A Doric dictionary*, Aberdeen, Scottish Cultural Press.